To save his family—and the free world—Red Harmon is back in the line of fire . . .

A sinister enemy is stalking elite military operator Red Harmon and his loved ones. Turning the hunter into his prey, Red uncovers a plot that spans nations and draws him into the remote snow-covered ravines of North Korea. His objective: penetrate the darkest prisons of this mysterious nation to restore national security—and save all he holds dear.

Caught in the danger . . .

Red's not the only one who's been living with secrets. His wife Lori is a lot more than the typical suburban soccer mom she appears to be, and she's stumbled onto something massive. The future of world peace depends on them—and on an enemy soldier with a powerful personal agenda. If Red's mission fails, the balance of superpowers may never recover . . .

G000041871

# Books by David McCaleb

Recall

**Published by Kensington Publishing Corporation**

# Reload

*A Red Ops Thriller*

## David McCaleb

**LYRICAL UNDERGROUND**
Kensington Publishing Corp.
www.kensingtonbooks.com

First Electronic Edition:
eISBN-13: 978-1-60183-864-3
eISBN-10: 1-60183-864-6

First Print Edition:
ISBN-13: 978-1-60183-865-0
ISBN-10: 1-60183-865-4

Printed in the United States of America

*Dedicated to the hundreds of thousands of men, women, and children who, this day, suffer in North Korean gulags.*

# Acknowledgments

As always, my debt of thanks is enormous and spread among so many who contributed to this work. Thank you to my family for putting up with my hyperfocused fits of writing where I disappear mentally, though my body may still be seen. To my bride, Dorie, for allowing me the time and freedom to write. This gig will pay the bills one day...maybe. To Abby and Jesse for being my biggest fans, listening to my first drafts, and providing that innocent, divergent thinking I so desperately crave.

Thank you to my author's workshop: Ken Sutton, Frances Williams, Mark Nuckols, and all others, for your brutally honest feedback. I need it in great amounts. Thank you to Lenore Hart and David Poyer for sacrificing the time to lead us, for your willingness to share your wisdom, and for plying your red pen.

To my agent, Anne Hawkins, for setting me on track about how a sequel is properly executed. To my editors, Michaela Hamilton, James Abbate, and April LeHoullier for your plethora of contributions and support. To Alexandra Nicolajsen, Michelle Forde, Lauren Jernigan, and the entire Kensington marketing team, for your designs, posts, tweets, interviews, memes, and endless efforts that push these books to the top.

I am always indebted to the entire thriller community. Thank you for your support, openness, and willingness to help. You guys know how to have fun. For Marc Cameron and George Easter for your encouragement and blurbs. To International Thriller Writers for your constant support of all your members, myself included.

To my readers, you guys rock! Thank you for reading and giving me the inspiration to write. Many of you, unknowingly, make it into these pages in one form or another. If you enjoyed *Reload* half as much as I did writing it, the book's success is assured. The next in the series is even more exciting. We've included the opening chapter for you. I would love to hear from you! Your comments keep authors motivated. Connect with me on my Web site (DavidMcCaleb.com), Facebook (McCalebBooks), or Twitter (@McCalebBooks).

Many apologies if I have left anyone out. All errors, as always, are my own.

# Praise for the first Red Ops thriller

*Recall*

"David McCaleb has a real winner here. Recall is a smart and well-plotted thriller, a fantastic read that I could not put down. Red Harmon is a guy I'd want on my side."

—**Marc Cameron**, *New York Times* best-selling author of *Brute Force*

"If you're looking for suspense, nonstop action, and a hero you can root for, The Red Ops series will clean your X ring."

—**David Poyer**, *USA Today* best-selling author of *Tipping Point* and *Onslaught*

"One of those wild rides where you strap in tight and leave your disbelief behind. Just my type of action thriller. I read it in a blur."

—*Deadly Pleasures* **magazine**

# Chapter 1 – Wiffle Ball

*New Kent County, Virginia*

Tony "Red" Harmon scratched his coarse copper beard, gazing at unrepaired holes from automatic weapon fire that had stitched a neat line in the beige siding beneath his neighbor's second-story window. Several inches shy of six feet, he gripped the top rail of a cedar privacy fence and hoisted himself up, stretching his neck to see over. Sunlight glinted from the cracked glass in a first-story window, busted by the same shooter.

"What ya lookin' for, Dad?" Jackson, his five-year-old, called from behind him. "Mom says it's not nice to stare."

Red's forearms burned as his grip grew weary. He dropped to the ground. Was he getting out of shape? No. He was tired of the constant burden of an unknown enemy gunning for his family. The wet team had attacked them in their suburban home three weeks ago. Neighboring houses had received collateral damage. That night, the facade of safety had been shot to hell as bullets flew through their middle-class neighborhood by the mag-full. The rounds had been 5.56 millimeter copper with a hardened tungsten steel core, tipped with a coating of polytetrafluoroethylene. *Cop killers,* as the media called them, rendering most Kevlar vests useless. *Armor piercing,* in Red's vernacular. One projectile from the attackers' initial salvo had even passed through three walls and shattered picture glass in his four-year-old Nick's room while the child slept.

Red turned from the fence and stepped onto the pitcher's mound, now nothing more than a bare spot of dirt where a dog had peed and burned the grass. He flipped a Wiffle Ball from his palm to the back of his hand. "Batter up!" he called with a glance to Nick.

His boy knelt in the batter's box and tied mismatched black and purple laces. No matter. He'd be tripping over them again in minutes. But the kid just had to have real sneakers, no Velcro. He switched to the other foot, fingers gripping the 550 paracord. Red could almost read his son's mind as he made the loop. *Around the tree and through the—*

Red jerked his neck at a flash of movement off to the side. A different neighbor snapped shut white-lined curtains with a blue-scalloped hem, tugging the edges so they sealed tight. Couldn't blame them. A couple of rounds had hit their home as well. Probably thought Red was a Mafioso. He scratched the back of his fist, irritated.

He stepped off the mound while Nick finished with his laces, and gazed around. It was Sunday, and quiet as a Mexican town when the drug lords passed through. Maybe he shouldn't have brought his family back here after all, not even for this quick visit. He should be more protective. But he'd promised the kids a last good-bye to their home, because that's what this house had been for the last six years. He'd been jerked all over creation when he was Nick's age, whenever his father had been assigned a new station.

Not Red. He was going to give his kids the stability he'd never enjoyed. At a minimum, the family would have a proper farewell.

Penny, his nine-year-old, tossed her head to clear stray blond strands from her eyes. "Here's another!" she called and wound up. She threw a second Wiffle Ball in his direction, this time necessitating a jog outside third base. He stifled a contented laugh as he stooped and picked it up. She had been all ballet and Barbie dolls for years, but now her arm was a .50 cal. Get some accuracy and college was paid for.

"It's getting late, kids. We need to go."

Her shoulders slumped. "Daddy...we just got here. You *promised.*"

*You promised.* His princess's trump card. To her credit, it usually worked. "I promised you could say good-bye, not play a ball game. One more pitch."

Nick stood over a yellow Frisbee, home plate, his thick orange plastic bat slung atop his shoulder like a hobo's bundle. This would be quick. Jackson, one year Nick's elder, eyed his younger brother warily, then squatted as catcher.

Red's arm drew back in a slow arc, giving his boy plenty of forewarning. Nick pounded the disc with the bat like Bamm-Bamm from the Flintstones, closed his eyes, and swung. A hollow *tunk* and the ball flew between first and second. He stood motionless.

Penny slapped his calf. "Run, dork!"

Nick hesitated, then turned toward third base. Jackson shoved him toward first. The boy looked down at his feet as if expecting them to decide, then started pumping in a half trot, flinging the bat back toward

Penny. The ball smashed into a holly hedge against the privacy fence and dropped out of sight behind the prickly green shrub.

Nice hit. Best ever for the little man. Red raised his arms and shouted, "Touchdown! We're done. Inside." *Wrong sport, but who cares.*

"But what about my ball?" whined Nick.

"I'll get you another."

"But it won't be a home run ball!"

Red stomped over to the bushes. Dandelions rubbed his cheek as he searched under the branches on hands and knees. Dandelions that wouldn't die no matter what chemical he sprayed. Dandelions he no longer cared about, now that the wet team's welcome had pushed *new identity* to the top of the family's to-do list.

A chill needled his spine as he recalled the helplessness of that night. Not even playing with his kids could save him from the memories. Even now a heat burned his chest, a familiar sensation as if he was being watched. He forced it from his thoughts.

"I can't see it," he said. "It's not under here."

"There it is!" Nick exclaimed, kneeling beside him. He pointed toward the back of the holly row, near the bottom of the fence.

Red followed the line of Nick's index finger, hand still scented with citrus from the orange his wife, Lori, had peeled for him on the ride over. The fruit was the two boys' favorite treat. "Come on. Not even Br'er Rabbit could wriggle in there."

Penny's nose wrinkled. "Who's Briar Rabbit?"

Red gasped. "You mean I never...we've never... Oh, forget it." He couldn't believe he'd never read Br'er Rabbit to the kids. He lay on his belly and stretched an arm under the hedge. Stiff twigs pushed up his sleeve and leaf barbs clawed at his wrist. His hand was still a couple feet short. Muttering curses, he ducked again and low-crawled underneath, breathing in damp, partially decayed leaves. Why was it that simple tasks required such effort? A brown wolf spider sprinted out just below his forehead. He closed his eyes and shoved in a few inches, the sharp leaves now scoring his neck. His fingers landed upon the plastic orb. He hooked two into the holes and squirmed out backward.

The ball caught on a branch and popped off. He shoved a hand back in after it and hit something else—cold and hard like metal. A beer can from a summer barbecue? No, heavier. The ratchet he'd lost a couple years ago? *How'd it get way out here?*

He wrapped his fingers around the thing and it fell into his palm, like the familiar tool it was. No ratchet.

\* \* \* \*

Red sat in the back seat of a supercharged white Chevy Suburban, courtesy of the CIA. He straightened his back so as to not appear too much shorter than Lori, who sat next to him. A red plaid wool jacket rested across his lap.

She glanced in his direction, and a corner of her mouth seemed to curl upward. Resting her hand on his knee, she gave it a squeeze. "Thanks for letting us come back. Even though it was a short visit, it meant a lot to the kids."

Red's heart began to hammer. In their decade of marriage the couple had developed an unspoken code, and the knee squeeze was the mother of all good signals. Tonight would be an especially good night.

Her lips drew flat again and she stared out the window. Shit. Was she still mad? She'd been brooding over a week and he'd not been able to figure out why. Had he misread the knee squeeze?

A stoplight turned green and the force-fed engine gulped air, singing a muffled high note. The crew-cut driver, the family's constant minder since the attack, rolled a shoulder back as if his holster was chafing. Steering with one hand, he weaved between cars like he was dodging potholes. He pressed a phone to an ear with the other, speaking in hushed tones.

The truck weighed almost twice what it had coming off the assembly line, heavy now with bulletproof glass and armor plates hidden inside the body panels. The first day in this vehicle Nick had managed to empty a juice box onto his leather seat, while Penny had dropped her bubble gum on the carpet. Bulletproof.

The driver's attention diverted elsewhere, Red lifted the nearest corner of the jacket toward Lori.

"What is it?" she asked, glancing down. A blond lock fell from behind her ear and twisted till it almost poked her eye.

He turned to look at the back seat. All three kids were strapped in, heads down, each thumbing some small electronic gadget. The driver was still mumbling into the phone. "A pistol," Red whispered.

She rolled her eyes. "Of course. I meant, where'd you get it?"

"Under the hedge out back."

She held a breath. "What type?"

"Holly."

The tendons between her jaw and temple stretched tight. She was gorgeous when angry. Sometimes it even—

"Not in the mood, damn it."

He whispered, "German, P08 Luger. Stamped 1941 on the barrel." Her one visible eye was rimmed in red, with dark flesh puffy beneath it.

"Wasn't trying to piss you off."

"Just comes naturally." She leaned back but kept her voice low. "We'll talk about it later. Not in front of the kids."

Jackson made *boom-boom-boom* noises behind them, imitating gunshots. Lori flinched when he yelled, "Got 'em!" A little touchy, even for her. The two young boys hadn't desensitized her to sudden noises yet. *Wait till they turn sixteen,* Red thought. Having endured a childhood in the company of two raucous older brothers, he would need more than kids' games to rattle him.

He inched closer to Lori. "It needs to get to your guys." By that he meant the CIA, Lori's employer. She held down a chair somewhere in a big building with lots of other chairs that seemed to fill the intelligence bureaucracy. Her job was to investigate...stuff about money. She didn't talk much about it, thank goodness. Sure, the government needed financial analysts to combat terrorist funding, but he'd prefer eating glass to sitting behind a desk. And since she'd been a target in the attack, the CIA had been the agency to investigate.

Lori frowned. "You should've left it under the hedge and called forensics. FBI Evidence Response Team Unit was the one we used to process the scene." She glanced up at the distracted driver.

The *scene?* It had been their home. "They missed it the first time. Haven't turned up anything for three weeks. No one is getting it. The more time passes, the longer whoever took a shot at us has for a second chance. I'm tired of waiting. We've got to get this to someone who knows what to do with it."

Her nostrils flared and she shoved a hand beneath the weapon. "See this scar?" She tapped an indentation at the bottom of the grip. "This was shot out of the guy's hand. The round hit here."

"A *guy.* How do you know it was a man?"

"Right-handed, at that." Her tongue pressed the corner of her mouth. She wasn't kidding.

"Seriously, how you figure? They teach you that in money school?"

She tucked the stray blond bangs behind her ear. The dull redness seemed to fade and a glow of interest lit her eyes. She rubbed her fingers over the retracted toggle. "The slide is locked open. He emptied the entire clip. More concerned with quantity than quality." An accusatory glance. "A guy thing, obviously."

"You're straying from the subject."

Lori held the handle toward him, displaying a brown crust across the butt. "Also, it hit near the bottom, yet the round drew blood. It's stained into the wood. So the shooter had big mitts. Again, probably male."

"But why right-handed?"

"Look at the scar. The round hit and ricocheted that way. If he'd been left-handed, the projectile would've hit him square in the chest. Then you'd have found a body instead of just the gun."

Red squinted. "How do you know all this?"

She glanced at the kids. "Not now, dear."

To hell with that. Ever since the attack, it'd seemed this woman he'd married was morphing into someone else. She hadn't retreated into herself, but instead had slowly, as if unwittingly, disclosed traits that were aggressive. As if discovering the real Lori were obscured by fog. A shadow still indecipherable. But moving toward him nonetheless.

His chest warmed again. Was she the threat he felt? Even so, the scent of Extatic drew his nose closer to her neck and he left a kiss there.

"Gotta do something with it," he whispered. "Your folks may have asked FBI for help, but CIA was the cleanup crew for this mess. Get it to someone who will know what the hell it means. Your side deals with it."

She leaned close. "They won't care. They've already closed the file, reassigned personnel. In their minds, taking us off the grid will fix all this. They'll run forensics on it, then stick it in an evidence warehouse. The weapon won't be traceable. They never are."

"Then what?"

She looked him in the eye and her shoulders drooped. "You do it."

What? That made no sense. Red was a military operator, not an investigator. His special ops background was mottled, spanning two different military branches, including a stint in Force Recon, the US Marines special operations. But now he drew an Air Force paycheck and was commander of a unit called the Det: Detachment 5 of Special Operations Command. Calling the Det a unit was misleading. It was a motley crew. A fusion cell on steroids. A battlefield where the cooperative members shared intelligence, assets, and efforts for the common good. These co-ops consisted of three-letter agencies, the Department of Defense, and sometimes select foreign governments. No single co-op *owned* the Det. That was the nature of a fusion cell. But its physical headquarters were located inside a huge aircraft hangar on Langley Air Force Base. And upon the recent death of his predecessor, Red had been appointed commander of this ghost organization. It was a thin line to walk. But one directive was clear. The Det never operated autonomously.

Red slipped the weapon back under the coat. "The Det can't do that."

"You guys have access to the same intel, maybe even more. The National Security Agency is a co-op. You get info faster than we ever could. Just tell them you need it for mission planning."

"We're operational. That's part of the deal with the co-ops. Someone else figures out who owns this thing. We just, you know—kill 'em."

"Just?" she snorted. "What if the owner of that pistol is on our side?"

"Above my pay grade, dear. We're the gorillas. Someone else plays detective. Give me an investigation and I'll screw it up. Hell, I wouldn't even know where to start. We don't have a clue who's after us or even if they're still trying. With my occupation, the list of enemies could be long. Or maybe they're after you or the other bean counters."

The Suburban slowed at a stoplight, pausing next to a green Honda Odyssey. Paint peeled on the hood. A woman with gray-streaked hair gripped the steering wheel, yawning. A bald man's cheek pushed against the passenger window, his breath fogging it in rhythm, eyes closed. Two car seats with snoozing toddlers were belted in back.

"That'll be us in few days," she said. "New identity. No more escort. Be nice to get back to normal."

"Hmm," he muttered. In whose world was this normal? Being an operator felt natural as an alpha wolf leading a pack, marking territory, sniffing out rivals, hunting mule deer. But when the op's over, you're supposed to be safe. Obscured by the Det. "You think this guy is a danger to us? Or the kids?"

Lori crossed her arms. "Someone's after at least one of us. Or who we work for. Reinserting us on the grid will only delay them discovering us again. Maybe not even much."

"So I'd better figure it out."

She lifted her hands. "Red, it's only one piece of a puzzle! One in a box on a shelf in a warehouse full of a million others. The only way it'll get opened again is if something actionable comes up. That's not gonna happen, not with the agency spread as thin as it is. *This* is our new reality, even in a new home. We've got to accept it."

"But if something actionable turned up?"

"Then maybe the powers that be would let you gorillas out of the cage." Her slender fingers brushed his cheek, pulling his face to hers. "Honey, look. This may be something we just can't fix. You've got to be OK with that. Once information is out, it's like a virus. It spreads fast. Secrecy is our only ally. We may even need to hop the grid again sometime."

Like hell. Red pulled the jacket close to his belly and leaned in to her ear. "But intel is stored. Maybe on a computer, or on paper. Or just in someone's head. I've *fixed* all that stuff before. Sniff out the trail, back to the source, then kill it." He winked. "I'll take it. Our kids may have a normal childhood yet."

She gaped. "What're you saying?"

"I'm going to bend the rules. I know a bloodhound."

# Chapter 2 - Jordan Leman

*New Kent County, Virginia*

Jordan Leman slowed a Ford E-350 van with Worton's Commercial Painting scrolled on its side, a logo of a brush arcing a wide pastel rainbow ending in a pot of gold. He'd switched the plates late last night with a similar one parked beside a heating-and-cooling contractor's storefront. The tags being registered to someone two counties away shouldn't get him pulled over in case a cop happened to run them. The important fact was they wouldn't be flagged as stolen, and this van was. He never kept the same plates for more than a week, or the same van for more than two. One of the problems with being deep undercover—he wasn't provided a car. Equipment was limited too. It was Mossad's equivalent of dropping you in a jungle with a pocketknife to kill rattlesnakes and live off the land.

He turned a corner and spied his destination: a culvert. Not the best choice to hide electronic equipment, but he'd weatherproofed the black plastic device with silicone caulk. This drain was as close as he'd been able to get that explosive night three weeks ago. At the time, he'd pretended to be just another neighbor walking over to see what all the police lights were about. "No sir. I didn't see anything," he'd said, shrugging. "Just heard fireworks. Then some sirens."

"And where do you live?" the chubby-necked officer had asked, his pale skin seeming to glow in the dark. The man had glanced at Leman with suspicion, having already marched toward him with a purposeful step, past two olive-skinned observers. Indians, most likely. Probably owned a hotel chain. Even they faded into the muddy suburban background better than dark-skinned Leman. But he'd dressed in fitted, clean blue jeans and a turtleneck, both suburban staples, which accentuated his tall, athletic build. He appeared to belong. But having passed middle age several years ago, he might have been the reason for the officer's too-obvious profiling. Mossad had trained Leman to profile as well, and he'd used it to his advantage many times, so he'd given the policeman the benefit of doubt.

"Three blocks down, on Havenwood Road." Leman lied, of course. "You want my address?" He'd walked to the scene down that street and had noted the house numbers for such an inquiry.

The cop had lowered his pad and pen without taking a note. He'd said, "Thank you," and walked into the yard across from a bullet-riddled cruiser. He'd stopped and pointed at the home's front door. "Any of you people live here?" he'd yelled to the crowd.

Leman had exhaled a tense breath as a bushy-eyebrowed man with the moon glinting on a bald spot raised a hand and shuffled over. Leman had pretended to tie his shoe then and, with his good hand, had stuck the tiny video camera into the culvert, clamping the magnet firmly to the cast-iron frame.

But now the snow had melted and, damn, a clean-swept curb meant a street sweeper had made at least one pass down it. Probably broke the camera if the rotating brush swung into it. Not long ago, hopefully, so he'd still have some good footage.

He opened a laptop and used the passenger seat as a work desk. His network manager located the device and synced. Lithium batteries still at forty-four percent after three weeks. Not bad. The device worked over standard Wi-Fi, largely ignored by the CIA, as the neighborhood was full of it. Impatient Americans had probably already fixed the problem and moved on, at least in their minds—till the cancer came back. They knew the enemy, but refused to acknowledge his mentality, the rules of his game. Much like the redcoats marching rank and file into the Battle of the Monongahela. The CIA, like George Washington, had reformed their tactics. Even Leman had to agree. But their infernal impatience...

An inquiry last week to Mossad's cyber division revealed Harmon's county records, which were housed on a not-so-secure server, had been sterilized, along with bank accounts, drivers' licenses, passports, even kids' birth certificates. Today Red's family had never lived here, or even in this county. The CIA, like the hare, was off to a good start. *But now is when they'll take a nap. Now is when a tortoise could sneak by and win the race.*

He rubbed his eyes with a palm. Their infernal impatience.

Ten minutes and thirty gigabytes of video later, Leman started the motor and drove to a McDonald's. He parked and sipped a chocolate shake while the file ran through motion detection software, cutting any portions with little movement. The video feed showed FedEx had dropped a package on the front porch. The real estate agent who stopped by each evening walked around the home, picked up the package, and drove away. Leman stopped the video when a white Suburban pulled up and parked in front of the home. A crew-cut, thick-necked driver stepped out and fiddled with a button on his blazer. Red and his wife got out of the back, then herded the kids inside.

"Unexpected," Leman said to himself. "And sloppy." The cup gurgled as he sucked the last bit of sticky sweetness from the bottom through the straw. He clicked fast-forward. The family returned to the Suburban after only twenty minutes according to the time stamp. The vehicle drove away; then the video jumped to a street sweeper turning the corner, its huge round brushes spinning menacingly toward the camera. The picture shuddered. It dropped abruptly and the next few seconds of video were of the bottom of the culvert. The image jumped forward once more, to a grease-slicked rat nibbling on one corner of the lens.

Leman gazed at the roof. The Harmon family must've come for a final visit. Three weeks coincided with what he'd seen before from the CIA. The home would no longer be under surveillance. He'd make his move tonight.

* * * *

The cast-iron grate pushed cold through Leman's jacket and into his chest the second he lay upon it. The video of the nibbling rat had shown the grate as a near background, so the camera couldn't have fallen far. He stuck a forearm down the culvert's short mouth, but his fingers didn't reach the bottom.

A door opened on the house across the street. Light arced across trees behind the home. Someone in the backyard.

He shoved his fingers down farther and wriggled closer to the opening, but his shoulder still couldn't fit through. The same one he'd dislocated at thirteen, playing soccer outside Jerusalem, in Palestine, though he'd called the sport *football* then. The family had immigrated to the US the following year and, once he had learned to cover his accent, everyone who saw his dark skin assumed he was American. The shoulder sometimes popped out when he slept on his side. He relaxed the arm, angled his back down toward the opening, and pushed. The ball slipped from the socket, but not all the way. Leman sank a little lower. His neck brushed the curb.

If someone spied him and asked questions, he'd have to be a painter, working nights because the current job was a remodel of an office and they didn't want him there during business hours. He'd have to be off on his lunch break and...what would explain why he had his arm down a culvert? Dropped his cell phone. That's what he'd tell them.

His fingers hit a gooey moistness and groped the culvert bottom, blind. Nothing. With his free hand he grasped a mini-Maglite and pushed the slim head through one of the holes in the grate, then snapped it on and off, like a camera flash. Still nothing. Must be farther down than he could see. A draft rose from below, heavy with the vegetable funk of rotting leaves.

*Maybe I can just leave the video recorder,* he thought. His eyes rolled back as he concentrated. The hole was probably cleaned by the city once in five years, maybe ten. The camera would more likely be washed away in the next heavy rain. Chances were less than one in a thousand it would be discovered, much less get into the hands of anyone who could access the recording. Then again, the case was waterproof. A hacker could bypass the data corruption feature and connect some dots. Though not many. Like seeing two stars of the constellation Orion. Still, standard operating procedure required retrieval of all field equipment.

He forced his arm farther down and the pain in his shoulder shot through his back into his spine. His fingers scraped a hard surface but clumsily pushed it away. Another flash of the beam illuminated a twig. Gripping it, he saw that it was a two-foot branch. He waved it in a sweeping arc. Its tip struck something, and he swept the object toward him. He flashed the light once more and exhaled in relief, his breath vibrating a dusty spiderweb. He grasped the camera and pulled his shoulder from the vise grip.

Securing it in the van, he hurried across the road to the Harmon front yard. The gate latch was stiff but yielded. The same gate he'd used for cover the night of the attack, trailing the South African wet team Mossad had broken protocol to brief him about. "Protect the asset at all costs," they'd said. "The CIA ignored our warning. You have no backup." He'd engaged the attackers, and one of their rounds had glanced off the butt of his pistol, tearing a chunk of pinky-finger flesh with it. The bullet had knocked Leman's weapon to the ground. He'd suppressed a yelp when the ricochet had smacked his Kevlar vest square in the chest, its tungsten steel core pricking his sternum. If the round hadn't hit his pistol first, it would've slid through the ballistic material like a hot needle.

He counted cedar fence posts. At the seventh he dropped to his knees, thrusting a meter-long pole taped with neodymium magnets beneath the holly hedge, wanding it back and forth. He'd thought about using it back at the culvert to help retrieve the camera, but decided against it in case the magnets could damage the electronics. Retrieving the camera had been for security purposes. Retrieving the Luger was for sentiment. The weapon was untraceable, lifted from a dead German lieutenant in 1943 by his grandfather. Used in anger by his father only twice, he'd claimed. Once in the winter of '52 on a Russian family who'd been acquitted of war crimes. Well, Leman wasn't going to be the son who lost the family heirloom.

The pole tapped the fence, and he wanded it through the undergrowth again, working his way out from under the hedge. He counted posts once more and moved two meters farther down the row. The pole slapped something hollow, like plastic. A Wiffle Ball rolled out from under the prickly holly leaves into the yard.

Leman's eyes flashed back like a dreamer's as he recalled the video he'd reviewed in the McDonald's parking lot. Right—one of the Harmon kids, getting in the Suburban. Dragging a huge plastic bat.

Leman's forehead rested atop a clump of thistle. "Shit," he muttered. He'd lost the Luger.

# Chapter 3 – Weakness

Red turned the Ford Explorer off Racemon Road, down a gravel drive toward riding stables. "This the right one?"

"Think so." Lori's eyes flashed across green wheat fields, betraying doubt. "Only been here once."

The washboard surface vibrated the steering wheel, numbing Red's hands. He slowed and the ride smoothed out, like a boat finding calm water. Nice to be the one driving the family again. No escort. Lori's leg bounced. What was it with girls and horses, the attraction to them? The huge animals ate more than a Ranger platoon and cost twice as much to outfit.

The family's new home had brought an unexpected but welcome calm. Warm wall colors, secluded, even enough acreage to board a horse of their own one day. "Maybe," they'd already told Penny. She'd attempted a guilt trip, playing up the trauma of having to change schools in the middle of the year, missing friends, so close to Christmas. "You'll get over it," Lori had told her. "Maybe we'll think about leasing one come summer. Let's see how your grades go."

But they hadn't moved that far from their old home. Lori needed to be within driving distance of DC, and Red to Langley. It was nothing as thorough as witness protection. Kind of like a CIA-abbreviated version of it. But they'd crossed into a new world out of suburbia and into the country. And near enough to a marina that every time they passed a vessel with a for sale sign Red took notice.

Lori had shaken her head. "They're for sale for a reason. You know what they say. A boat is just a hole in the water into which you throw money."

"Horses are much more practical," he'd countered. She'd given him that smirk that said *I'll get you back,* which she had. And it was awesome.

He stared across the bowing heads of winter wheat toward the barn of Stillwater Stables. The drive to it from their new home had been almost an hour. Everything was farther away in the country. Could distance buy concealment? Maybe Lori had been right. *Secrecy is our only ally.* He hadn't spoken with his bloodhound yet, Detective Matt Carter. Red was still working up the nerve to talk to his friend. Carter wanted nothing to do with the Det ever since its prior commander had almost gotten him killed. But he would have called him by now, Red reassured himself, if it weren't for moving out, moving in, registering kids for school, and the many other fatiguing tasks that made him sink into bed at night with a resigned sigh, thinking, *Maybe it'll happen tomorrow.*

Red squinted toward the edge of a hardwood forest. "That a fawn over there?" It looked more like a large dog or wolf by its gait, but he couldn't see the tail. There weren't any wolves left around here.

"Just a deer, dear," she said with a grin.

Red rolled his eyes and squeezed his left elbow to his side, feeling the hard outline of the 9mm Sig Sauer beneath his jacket. Fawn or wolf, even here there could be threats. Peace could turn ugly in a second. He'd taken many kills inside other borders, even in peaceful countryside just like this. Maybe he was just being paranoid. Maybe no one was still gunning for them.

The animal turned and bolted into the woods between tall trunks in a startled sprint. A flash of gray shot from the wheat field in pursuit, too quick to identify. Dry leaves stirred by the commotion twisted in a gust. He needed to get Carter working on who was chasing them.

Penny grabbed the back of Lori's headrest and jumped in her seat. "Are you gonna ride with us, Daddy?"

"Not this time. Just you and Mommy."

"But all the horses are nice. It'd be fun. None of them are like Grenada." Grenada, Penny's old riding school teacher's horse, had been gentle as a swallow feeding her young. But she'd rear and snort whenever Red got close. Penny hopped some more. "Why didn't she like you?"

He laughed. "I think Grenada had dominance issues. I'm alpha. She didn't like it."

"Or she thought you were a predator," Lori said, staring at the void where the fawn had disappeared.

Red glanced at the back seat in the rearview. "What kind of ice cream you guys want?"

"Chocolate!" came the shout from the far back. Red rubbed an eyebrow. Anything but chocolate. Nick needed a power-washing every time he had it.

The tires slid on slick mud as the Explorer broke to a stop and the ABS vibrated the pedal through the sole of Red's boot. They stepped onto soft ground with a *squish.*

"I wanna pet the horsies first," Jackson said.

Electric-stranded rope stretched from a wood-fenced riding ring around a long pasture dotted with thistle. It clicked every few seconds, the sound louder near the poles where the line was worn. Penny reached toward a rope gate, then jerked back at another *click.*

"Grab it by the yellow handle," Lori said. "It won't zap you there."

The boys picked long strands of grass from the edge of a ditch and waved the clumps like flags high over their knit caps. Several horses and a pony lifted their curious heads and ambled over, hoping for a more appetizing treat. One was brown with a white-spotted rump. Another was darker, almost black. The aged pony had silver eyelashes and stepped with a limp.

Red stretched Nick's palm out straight. "Hold your hand flat so they don't bite your fingers off." Nick shrieked and threw the grass on the dirt, then hid behind Red's legs. "No, no. It's OK. As long as you keep them flat, he won't bite." Red picked up the fallen grass and showed him how. The soft lips moved as dexterously as fingers and vacuumed up the snack. Then the horse jerked his head upward as if to say, "That's it?"

Nick laughed and pointed from behind Red's hip. "He's smiling!"

The brown-and-white stallion pawed the ground, flashing thick carved legs. He whinnied, but didn't come near the fence.

"What's wrong with that one?" Jackson asked.

The horse's chest bunched, its tense veins bulging through thick winter fur. A sense of heat came from the animal's aura, the same way Red had felt back on their visit to their old home. "He doesn't trust us yet. Let's watch Penny ride before we get ice cream."

Lori led her daughter astride a huge black horse from a stable sided in bare, rough-sawn planks. Thick mane, tail almost dragging the ground. Tall as a Budweiser horse, but not as wide. "Isn't that one too big for her?"

Lori walked aside, lead line in one hand and in the other, a long skinny whip with a string at the tip. "It's a Friesian. Gentle as a baby." She pointed the lash at Penny. "She rode it all by herself last time. We're just going to lunge her a bit. Get her warmed up."

The long mane shimmered like waves against a beach as Lori lifted the whip and the horse rose to a trot.

"You sure?" Red asked. "Looks like the Marine Corps version of My Little Pony."

Lori turned slowly in place as the horse trotted in a circle around her, Penny grinning, bouncing in the saddle.

Red lifted Nick into a car seat, but the buckle balked. Red unsnapped it and tried again. This time it latched with a metallic click as smooth as his Sig. Jackson climbed into his own car seat and pulled the shoulder harness down. Short fingers fiddled with the buckle.

Red touched his thumb to the other palm. "Take the male end and shove it into the open slot there."

Jackson looked down at the buckle quizzically. "How's it a boy, Daddy?"

"Watch this!" Penny called in an undulating voice, the horse still trotting in a disciplined circle. Red walked back to the riding rink and leaned on the top rail. Something prickled his skin, and he jerked his hand up. But this fence was wooden, not electric. He turned his wrist over and pulled a long splinter from his palm, the sharp end tipped in blood.

Lori yelled, "Halt! Halt!" Red glanced up. The long whip was falling from her hand. Her arms stretched out toward the still-jogging animal. Penny's saddle had slipped sideways and she was clinging to the horse's mane. It continued toward a white pole laid atop two cinderblocks. The horse hopped over the low jump and Penny lost her grip. She landed on her side in soft sawdust, but one leg struck the pole with a familiar *crack*.

"Shit." Red vaulted over the fence. Lori was already kneeling at Penny's side, cradling her head, holding a hand below her chin so she couldn't look down at her injured leg. Red unzipped the paddock boot, the one Penny had been so proud of when she came home last week after shopping with Lori. He gently pushed up her jeans. The shin was straight but one side of her calf angled unnaturally, already darkened with a bruise.

"I'm OK, Mommy," Penny said, trying to sit up.

Red met Lori's eyes and shook his head.

"Just lie here for a couple minutes," she said, "till Daddy has a chance to look."

Red pulled over a cinderblock and used it to elevate the leg above her heart, then jogged toward the truck. He stopped in the middle of the pasture and turned around. He could drive it through the gate and they could go... where? He stumbled over a thistle. Shit. The stable owner had run to town. No instructors to ask directions. Where was the hospital around here? He grabbed his phone.

"911. What's your emergency?"

"I need an ambulance. My daughter broke her leg."

"Where are you?"

He closed his eyes and poked his forehead. What was the address of the damned stables? What was the name of this place? "I...I don't know," he answered. A white tail flitted across the field of wheat as another startled deer leapt into the woods. "This phone's got GPS, right?"

\* \* \* \*

A short, black-haired Hispanic doctor at Rappahannock General Hospital waddled with her hands on her hips, cradling her back. Maybe she was pregnant, but Red had learned never to ask. She pushed through swinging double doors that slapped closed behind her. Lori broke into sobs. Red stroked her hair. He noticed a gray strand for the first time, mixed in and twisted deep among the others, tangled around a blade of grass from the pasture.

"I'm so sorry," she said, in tears.

Red held her, rubbing her back. "She's OK. Doctor said it was a clean break. The fibula. Kids heal quick. Maybe four weeks in a cast. It's not your fault."

"Not my *fault*?" She pulled back and walked to a row of green vinyl seats, then fell into one. She patted her chest. "*I* tacked up the horse. *I* told her, 'Watch how Mommy does it. Make sure it's tight.' Now she won't ever trust me again." She bit a knuckle. "Neither will you."

Red sat and pulled her close again. "You're right.... If you think about it that way, it *is* your fault. But accidents happen. We all make mistakes. She'll forgive you. And so do I. Remember, we've got two boys, so this won't be our last trip here. It'll be my turn to screw up next."

"I can't take any more of this crap. I just want life to be normal again. New house. School orientation. I don't even know where the damn grocery store is." Her voice cracked. "And you—you're calling in a medevac chopper to the 911 operator. Shit, Tony, what were you thinking? Next you gonna call in an airstrike?"

"I just got turned around for a sec. You know, panicked. It's different when it's your kids. Thought I smelled jet fuel, then..." He smiled. "They must've thought I was crazy."

She laughed and grabbed a tissue, wiping moisture from her lip. "Not the only one."

Not the only one? How had he missed that? Was she really doubting his sanity? Ever since the attack, something as simple as finding a repair shop for an oil change seemed to weigh on her. He had to admit, while he was wrapped up in his own work, she'd been going through much of the transition solo. Not the way a team should operate. No doubt she'd project some blame onto him. And the nagging stress of wondering if they were still being hunted...

He held her hand. Soft, warm, no calluses in the palm. "You did good, feeding me directions from the dispatcher. You got us here. Now we've got four weeks. We'll get through this, you and me, together. Then things will be back to normal...at least our version of it." He put an arm around her shoulders. But she tensed, much like the stallion back at the stable.

He stood to give her space. He walked to the other side of the waiting room and around a corner, slipped a hand inside his pocket, and grabbed his cell phone. With one hand he punched Carter's number. With the other he squeezed the hard, reassuring bulk of the weapon under his jacket.

# Chapter 4 – Carter

Sitting atop the hood of a Ford Ranger parked near Courthouse Circle, Red shoved hands under his blue Levis. Engine heat warmed his pants, but each breath stung his nose, bringing the crisp scent of spruce. The hem of his green L.L.Bean rag wool sweater had crept up his back and the cold air chilled his skin. He yanked it down. Craning his head backward, a red-bricked spire loomed overhead like a stout church steeple silhouetted against the noonday sun. New Kent County Courthouse, 1909 streaked down the side in whitewashed letters below a blue slate roof. He pulled up the collar of his sweater.

A white-bearded man with a blaze-orange cap and tobacco juice stains on the corners of his mouth limped below the spire toward the front doors. He stopped short, patted his hips, then returned to his blue Chevy pickup with a Ducks Unlimited license plate. He removed a pistol from his belt, shoved it under the bench seat, then limped back toward the courthouse without locking the truck.

A white wood-plank door below the spire opened and a young boy stepped out, long straight hair pulled to one side, denim jacket open, his black T-shirt depicting a gaunt rock star screaming into a microphone. He flipped his hair and ran fingers through thin locks as he walked. Having opened the door for the boy, a red-cheeked man followed. That man's hair was a salt-and-pepper crew cut.

Red pulled out his hands and rubbed them. *My kids ever look like that,* he thought, *my hair would be gray, too.*

The panel started to swing back, but bumped into Detective Matt Carter as he stepped out, shoulders nearly as wide as the doorframe. His first strides from the courthouse seemed to reflect a limp, but it was as if the detective realized he was displaying a malady and pinned back his shoulders. Red smiled at the sight of him. It would only take a few fingers to count the number of men he considered *friends*, but Carter would be the first on the list.

The arms of Carter's shiny silver suit framed his shoulders perfectly, body tailored to his narrow midsection. Even Red could see the designer threads had been custom fit. Considering his friend's taste in style, maybe even handmade. Bumps dappled the leather of his slender black briefcase. *Ostrich skin? Really? What the hell's wrong with good ol' cowhide?*

The detective walked toward a white Chevy Malibu, next to which Red had parked his pickup. He hopped off the hood.

Carter stopped on the sidewalk and squinted in his direction. No smile or change in expression. "Haven't seen you in a while."

Red tried for a cheery tone. "Been a couple of weeks."

"Not long enough."

*Well, that didn't work.* "You're not returning my calls."

Carter shoved a hand in the pocket of pressed slacks, fingers moving as if playing a bugle. The Malibu's lights flashed, and he opened the door. "You blame me?"

Red's predecessor, killed only weeks earlier, had coerced Carter into cooperating with the Det on a recent operation. Ever since, the detective had kept his distance, even from Red.

He tapped the vehicle's tire with a leather boot. "Sorry about what happened. The colonel didn't do you right."

Carter placed a foot on the floorboard. "That what you came to tell me?"

Red sighed and pointed at the briefcase. "No. Came to tell you how much I like your pocketbook. Get that from Walmart?"

One of Carter's eyes narrowed—his deer-in-the-headlights look when caught off guard. Then a slight smile. "Screw you." He slipped into the driver's seat and shut the door. The Malibu's engine fired and the car inched back. Red tapped on the glass. Carter let out a sigh, then slid the gearshift forward and dropped the passenger window. "You're here to ask a favor. I can see it in the way you're not meeting my eye. Am I right?"

Red gazed at a row of tall pines and lifted his chin.

"You already owe me. Big-time. I did my duty."

"Can we just talk? Won't take long, I promise."

"Red, I just *talked* with your predecessor and next thing you know I've got ghosts from my past calling me from every branch of the government, telling me I had no choice but to cooperate with the man. You're in his shoes now. I'm sure you can appreciate my suspicions of our assumed friendship."

"The colonel ran things one way. I do it a little different. No arm-twisting. I promise."

Carter slipped the gear into reverse. "I'm headed to the diner for lunch, if you absolutely have to. Join me and we can talk. But I gotta be back in an hour."

"Maybe somewhere more private?"

"With you? Not a chance."

Red opened the door and slipped onto a stiff vinyl seat.

"What? Can't you drive your truck?"

Red's belly was warm from the heat inside the car. He unbuttoned his vest. "No. I just want to make sure you're not trying to stand me up."

\* \* \* \*

The diner was packed and balmy. The two stood just inside the door. Two patrons rose and squeezed by, scented of Old Spice and jalapeños, opening bar seats at the end near a gas heater blowing across the tight room. Carter and Red quickly filled the void. Men with slick black hair and dark business suits sat shoulder to shoulder with camouflage jackets and John Deere caps. Cheesesteaks and onion rings and fried okra filled the sticky air. You needed a shower just after getting a seat. The fan whirred loudly, mixed with the hum of an ice maker, masking their words. Carter ordered a clam fritter sandwich and coleslaw, having to yell. Red, a chicken salad cold plate.

Red leaned close. "Someone's after us. Me. Or maybe Lori."

Carter snorted as he took a draw of ice tea. "You think? What clued you in? The wet team?"

"We're not convinced it won't happen again. Someone else may be waiting for us."

Carter's cup splashed condensation onto Red's hand as he tapped it on the counter. "Welcome to life as an operative."

The cool beads rolled off Red's skin. "I'm an operator, not an operative. We're not spies. I shouldn't have to worry about my family."

"Get to the point."

"I need someone to figure out who's after us. Where the intel came from. If we can get it pinned, I can eliminate the threat."

Carter folded a sweet potato fry into his mouth. "What do you need me for?"

"You're a detective. I need someone to lead the investigation."

Carter squared to the bar. His shoulders brushed Red's, pushing him against the whirling heat machine. "Not my jurisdiction. Got a gag order bigger than Texas. Every time someone asks about the attack at your home, I refer them to the CIA."

"You'd have full access to any intel I can get my hands on."

"Get Lori's employer on it. That's what they're supposed to do, isn't it? The CIA protects their own."

The waitress at the far end of the bar wiped the counter, then straightened, almost as tall as Lori. She stuffed a ticket into her apron and disappeared through the kitchen door. Red started to speak, but the heater's blower was so loud Carter leaned to hear. "She's not convinced they're taking it seriously."

"Your problem. Not mine. The company is supposed to be fixing you guys up." Carter tapped brown Formica with a thick middle finger. "You're not even supposed to be here, I'll bet. In this area, I mean. Too close to your old home." He turned his head, peering through grease-fogged windows toward the parking lot. "If someone's after you, that could be a threat to me. To *my* family."

Red set his fork back down, only one bite taken from the chicken salad. "Hadn't thought about that."

"That's 'cause you're not a spook...or a detective."

"Exactly! Which is why I need you. I've seen your file, Carter. Navy intel? FBI special investigations? What the hell you doing in New Kent County? Enjoying an early retirement?"

"Early retirement. Semiretirement, actually. And it's going to stay that way."

No way was Carter happy investigating vandalism and drug peddlers. "I already cleared it with your boss."

"Sheriff Jenson?"

"Yeah. Says you've been worthless, moping around last couple weeks. Said he never saw you happier than those couple days you were working with us."

Carter grunted. "Don't confuse happiness with stress. I am not working for the Det again...ever."

"What would it take?"

Carter removed the top bun of his sandwich and shook blood-red ketchup onto it. He took a bite and chewed slowly. "More than you want to give."

"Name it."

Carter leaned in. The scent of some designer cologne mixed with tomatoes. "You know the Senate hearings on FBI's handling of that terrorist cell up in New York?"

"Think so. That investigation they just announced? Some terrorists were killed after being apprehended upstate. Happened five years ago."

Carter took another bite. His eyes focused on the distance. "They've given it a name. Marble Hill Madmen. The terrorists were in Marble Hill. We were the madmen. Came right before I left the bureau. After they'd caught those guys in New York City, I was called to the action center. Intel said an imminent threat existed. I was told to use whatever means necessary to extract the info. It was a tactical interrogation—perishable information. If we got it a day too late, it would be another 9/11." Carter turned to Red again. "That's what they thought, at least. What's the greater good? If we had to kill a couple terror suspects to save a thousand Americans, that's a no-brainer. I was in Marble Hill one day only. I want my name out of that report."

"Hasn't it been subpoenaed?"

"Not the one I'm in. But once the hearings start, they'll know more of what to ask for. It'll be required eventually."

Red rubbed his eyes. "I don't know, Carter. We just use intel. We don't manipulate it."

"Yeah, you don't do anything outside your jurisdiction. And you're not here trying to hire me with government funds for personal reasons. I don't want the report manipulated. I want it gone, lost, stolen, burned, whatever."

"If they find out what I did, I'd be..." Red sighed. "What'd you do?"

Carter chewed slowly, then swallowed hard. "I got the information."

"And..."

"Two died from injuries, but the other two talked. Only problem is they weren't anywhere near as far along as intel thought. Those guys couldn't have put together a dirty bomb even if they were standing in the middle of Radford, Virginia."

What the hell? If Red did nothing, his family lived in fear. If he started his own investigation with Carter, he'd be breaking a hundred military regulations and misappropriating funds. Now he was considering using his connections to deliberately destroy evidence that related to a US Senate hearing case. Even worse, he knew exactly who would know where the evidence was stored and how to erase it. But if caught, his kids would grow up while he rotted in a jail cell. This was madness. How far was he willing to go? "Shit, Carter. This could be my ass."

The detective's eyebrows lifted and he coughed into a napkin. "Don't go out of your way or anything. It's not like you owe me."

"Carter, it's just—"

"Oh, and my rate's two fifty an hour."

"Two fifty!"

"An hour. I got a mortgage that I want out from under before I retire...again."

Red pushed his plate away. The CIA had advised Higher there was no actionable threat against his family. Higher was the name given to the Joint Chiefs of Staff, the same organization that had spoken the Det into existence almost a decade earlier. All Det taskings were cleared through them. He was uncertain exactly who was included in the term "Higher," but all communication flowed through the vice chair.

The tall waitress came back through the kitchen doors and lifted his plate, then wiped down the counter again, cloth scented with a disinfectant. Maybe it wasn't such a bad thing. He'd have something on Carter, and Carter would have something on him. Both would have motivation to toe the line. That was only fair, wasn't it? Red breathed deep and held out his hand. "OK. I'll do it. Deal."

They shook. Carter's grip was a vise. His smile seemed to glisten with menace. The same one Red had seen while witnessing Carter during an interrogation. The detective wiped his mouth and stood, then pulled out a phone and tapped it. "I'm on the clock as of now. You're coming with me."

"Now? I gotta get back to the Det. Why don't you just call when you need something?"

"Because we're going to interrogate our first suspect."

"Who?"

Carter's words were stone. "Your wife."

# Chapter 5 – Letting Go

*North Korea*

As the Kozlik topped the hill's crest, a bitter western breeze clawed through the passenger window. Staff Sergeant Ko Chung Ho peered across the edge of the glass, which was rolled up to his nose. A short valley of calf-deep snow lay below, its smooth surface covering jagged rocks, pine stumps, and green sheets of moss, musty and moist in warmer months. The Yalu River, the homeland's northern border with China, lay frozen only a half kilometer away. His cheek stung with the welcome cold, but Ko shivered instead at a whiff of spruce and the memory of decaying pine needles falling down his shirt, sticking to his sweaty belly.

He smiled. Funny how smells evoke past emotions, associations, even events forgotten. How many years ago had that exercise been—eight? It wasn't this same valley, but one like it, maybe fifty klicks south, and then a sweltering 33 degrees centigrade. His infantry corps had been running small-unit maneuvers. The drillmaster had them low-crawling up a bluff, shaded by spruce, a thick bed of undisturbed needles prickling his forearms.

"Stay low!" the drillmaster had yelled, rapping the back of Ko's helmet with a heel, driving it into the earth, its rim gouging through a woven blanket of dried needles. Black dirt lay beneath, and a centipede wriggled near his nose. "Stick your head up and a faggoted *boseul-achi* will drill one through your skull."

Even while maneuvering in the northernmost part of the homeland, soldiers set their teeth perpetually against the south.

Ko inhaled frozen winter air and squinted at a bright, waxing gibbous moon, then back to the valley where tops of evergreen perforated the smooth white cover of snow like miniature darkened guard towers across the valley.

The nose of the Kozlik dipped and the engine spun higher. He tapped the driver's shoulder. "Slow down. Ruts are underneath." The washouts were still unrepaired from last spring's thaw, or maybe the year before that. "Hit one hard enough and you'll break the axle."

The corporal bobbed his head. "Yes, *Sangsa*."

Ko lifted his chin at the mention of his rank. He turned back to the window and concentrated once again on the frozen landscape. "Snow's only two days old. Look for tracks. They try to cross in valleys like this."

When the driver's side wheel dropped hard, Ko gripped the dash in anticipation. A second later his side sank, and for a blink he lifted in his seat before the wheels slammed the bottom of a hidden rut. The engine strained, throttle open to pull the jeep through. Spinning tires threw white handfuls of snow streaked in deep brown by the windows. They settled behind the truck like the foaming wake churned by his father's fish boat. The jeep settled and resumed downhill.

"Better, but less gas. Don't spin the wheels. If we'd been going uphill, we'd be stuck now."

"Yes, *Sangsa*."

The corporal was progressing well, even Ko had to admit, despite the driver oversleeping his first morning and backing a jeep into a pine tree as thick as any the earth could produce. The man had even claimed he'd not seen it. How the hell could you miss a trunk that big?

Ko suppressed a snicker. He'd been just as naive on his first assignment. In the week since the accident, his disgust had ebbed. The corporal's eagerness to please had sprouted respect through frozen ground.

These rotations to border patrol were all too often now, done to reduce corruption—or so Ko was told—and the possibility of refugee brokers forging relationships with his guards. It seemed every time he trained a new one, they were rotated out. This corporal would be gone in a few months.

The Kozlik leveled. Ko looked up at towering green-and-white guard towers—spruce rampant against a speckled night sky. Maybe one of the stars was his father, watching restfully from the afterlife. He'd be proud of Ko now, wouldn't he? A *sangsa*, a staff sergeant in the world's fiercest army.

Yes, the fiercest, though his sister had implied differently. Ko bit his lip. He'd put her in her place, though, and she never mentioned again what the drunken news officer babbled in her bed.

Ko taped the dash.

"*Sangsa?*" The brakes grated as the jeep stopped.

"Got to pee." When Ko opened the door, the snow was to the jamb. He planted his soles atop the frozen crust, which for a second appeared to support him, but then it splintered with a *crrrch* and he sunk to his knees. Ice crystals were shoved deep into the back of his boots as he pulled his legs from the frozen holes, lifting his knees high, trudging to create new ones a half meter ahead. Once he'd lost his shoe as a kid in a similar trap, the rubber sole having been held fast by sucking mud as he pushed his father's boat from soft grass flats. Abeoji's back had arched, straining against the heavy load, veins bulging from his wiry forearms. Ko had added his own strength and the vessel launched into shallow waters.

Now, Ko pushed only himself across a flat of white snow. He stepped behind the nearest spruce, head slapping a low branch weighed by frozen crystals that dropped down the back of his jacket. He unbuttoned his fly, searching frantically in the merciless cold for the purpose of this brief reprieve. He stabbed at his member with gloved fingers, but couldn't grasp it with their bulk. At last he stuck a finger into his mouth and bit down on leather, yanking off the glove. Open to the air, his fingertips were instantly numbed.

He heaved a sigh and pitched his head back as the hot piss melted a neat yellow hole in the snow crust. A short plume of steam rose from it, disappearing at eye level. The Yalu River murmured a hushed melody somewhere beyond the trees, its percussion the occasional *crack* of breaking ice. He stared at a bare rock a few paces away, then turned toward the headlights and started to button his fly. His eyes adjusted to the dark. He could see the buttons now, working them slowly with one gloved hand. One free.

The last one stubbornly resisted.

Ko frowned. Why didn't the one gray rock have snow on it? Keeping his head low, he pretended to fumble again with his fly, lifting only his eyes. In a single motion he unsnapped his holster and raised a TT-30 toward the rock. Two limbs grew from its side. Slowly a man stood, arms raised.

Ko cocked the weapon. He had just opened his mouth to speak when more limbs grew from a snow mound a few meters away. Another figure stood, arms up in surrender. Maybe a woman, by her height. Ko squinted around. Several other mounds were scattered in the open patch among the trees. He smiled broadly. The last time he had turned in a defector he'd been rewarded with university for his daughter. There were at least six here. He might even be able to—

A baby cried a birdlike wail, and one of the figures stooped. He swung his pistol at the commotion and his trigger finger, never able to feel cold due to severed nerves from an old wound, sensed only pressure against the metal. But he held his fire. The person rose slowly again, one arm raised, another cradling a bundled blanket emanating a muffled cry. Ko discerned the gaunt face of a woman. Despite the dark and their layered winter rags, their thin frames and sunken faces demonstrated the extent of their malnourishment.

Ko turned toward the jeep, pistol still aimed at the defectors. A frozen exhaust cloud covered the rear half, thicker than even the morning fog in spring that had always hung low over the water near Ka-Do where his father had taught him to use a trotline.

"How do you know where to go?" a young Ko had asked.

"I follow the compass," Abeoji said, pointing at a plastic-domed instrument bolted to the gunwale. "When the fog lifts, you'll see we're close."

It was the peak of winter now, and most peasants were already half-starved in the homeland. He couldn't truly blame them for this disloyalty. They were just trying to feed themselves and their children. Ko had briefly considered defecting himself, back when his daughter's injured hand started to turn gangrenous and he could obtain no aid for her. And now surely the corporal had not heard the cry of the baby above the jeep's rumbling engine.

If he let these ragtag defectors go, they'd have to make it across the homeland's fence. Only two meters high, of course. A broker had probably already cut a way through. But there's another, higher fence along China's side. If they don't die of exposure, they'll have to hide for weeks from the Chinese authorities as they creep painfully toward Thailand. The women will be targeted for the sex trade. Even worse in Thailand. But he'd heard rumors the Thai government is known to arrange transport to Seoul for refugees that make it into their borders.

Ko had never told his daughter the truth about why she could suddenly attend university. Looking at these bony faces now, his belly soured. If he turned them in, they'd die in a labor camp. If he let them go, there was a small chance they'd live. And he wouldn't have to lie to his daughter again.

He rubbed the trigger back and forth with his deadened finger. Always numb from the cut that had saved his daughter's life.

He uncocked the weapon.

"I see nothing but rocks," he said. Then turned and trudged back to the waiting jeep, pulling on a stiff leather glove, eyes lifted to the sky.

# Chapter 6 – Realignment

*September 1952, Fanchang, China*

One of Zhāng Dàwe's eyes opened to a slit against the glare of morning sun, then closed again. His sleep-heavy mind wondered why it was already light. Must be dreaming. He rolled to the opposite shoulder and sighed. The welcome scent of fresh hay pressed from the mattress eased him back to sleep, despite a full bladder screaming for relief.

Through the window came muffled *thuds*. His brothers were stacking bags of rice in the barn. Faintly, his mind recognized this, though harvest had not yet begun. Maybe a land renter was delivering grain for payment. He cracked an eye again. It *was* bright, the brilliance of morning. Why hadn't anyone woken him? Papa would whip him sore. Fear tightened his belly. He jumped to calloused bare feet, stepping over cool, clean straw as he ran past his brothers' empty cots out of the bedroom. He bounded through a deserted kitchen, the small black woodstove still radiating warmth. The thick, weathered, outside door was already propped open.

"I'm sorry. So sorry!" he pleaded, blinded by a sun risen to a height that meant he'd overslept by at least an hour. Another bag of rice thudded onto a stack, but the sounds seemed to come from the front of the ancient pine storehouse. A cow lowed nearby. Blinking, still blinded, Zhāng held up a flat-bladed hand to shade his eyes. A group of dirty renters were gathered in a circle in front of the barn. His uncle stood among them. What was that snake doing here? Father had said quite plainly what he'd do if he ever showed up again.

Zhāng shouldered past dirt-caked thighs, pushing toward the middle. He jostled through an opening. In the center of the throng stood two men, younger than Tabor, Zhāng's eldest brother. Both wore green uniforms the shade of a rice field ripe for harvest. One hefted a long rifle aloft and shouted at the crowd. The other kept his weapon slung over a shoulder.

"Who else has grievance with this man?" the first demanded. "Who else has been wronged?" He pointed down toward...*Papa!* Zhāng's father was on his knees, bowing his face to the dust at the feet of the crowd, as if at the temple.

Zhāng rushed toward him but was jerked to a halt so hard his feet left the ground. Someone had snatched him back inside the line of people. Strong fingers clamped over his lips and squeezed. "Don't, little bug."

The voice was Tabor's. His eyes shone with wetness and fear. The same eyes that only last week were red with rage as he'd chased a lone Tibetan wolf away from the chicken coop, waving only a hand sickle. Even as it had loped away, the wolf seemed to laugh at him, trotting with a bloodied muzzle, carrying the carcass of their bird. "Go back inside."

"No!" Zhāng wriggled down, but his brother's grip was fast. Only seven years old, Zhāng possessed the will, but not the strength to resist. "Let me go."

"Obey, little bug! Or I'll beat you myself." The words sounded harsh, but his brother's expression betrayed his lack of sincerity. "Papa said not to interfere," he pleaded.

Zhāng caught the flash of a green pant leg. One of the uniformed men kicked Papa in the ribs. Another sack of rice thudded down.

"This struggle meeting is for all of you! Have no more fear of this man. He can oppress you no longer. Surely someone else has grievance."

Uncle Snake stepped from the circle. The viper who had inherited twice as much land as Papa, Zhāng had been told, and yet the sloth couldn't manage it. The year Zhāng had been born, Papa had borrowed much from the Chans, a greedy family tearing as briars against their own, in order to buy Uncle's land and keep it in the family. Seven long years they'd struggled to pay off that loan, with even Zhāng having given the strength of his own young back, to keep the Chans from calling the debt and claiming the land.

His uncle raised a fist to the sky. "This man stole my land for himself! He forced me to sell against my will. He oppresses renters and molests their daughters. I have seen it with my own eyes. He is no brother of mine!"

A low *oohhh* rose from some in the crowd, angry cries from others, as if they were onlookers at a bloody cockfight. Uncle Snake spat on Papa's neck and slapped his ears.

"Again!" the young soldier shouted, waving the rifle over his head, turning and glaring at the crowd. "You have struggled against this man. Fulfill your destiny now. Justice! He must pay, and you must learn to overcome. You are no longer weak and powerless."

Uncle Snake spit and kicked Papa more, each blow as deep and muffled as a ten-kilo bag of rice dropping to the floor, the gusts of breath being forced out of his father's chest. Dust rose from the earth with each flashing strike, settling onto his back and neck. How could the snake lie so flagrantly in front of Tabor? Papa was a just and fair owner, even delaying the collection of rent payments from farmers whose crops suffered. Why weren't Zhāng's brothers shielding Papa? It must be they feared the soldiers. Yes, *they* were protecting the serpent. These men were even more wicked than he.

Tabor lifted Zhāng again and started carrying him toward the house.

"Stay!" a soldier shouted after them.

Tabor turned slowly, returning to his spot on the inside edge of the circle. A woman stepped forward into the opening this time. Old, dark with deep wrinkles and rice-paper skin from years laboring in the sun. Who was she? Zhāng had never seen her till now. Glaring around at the jeering crowd, he didn't recognize half of them. They weren't neighbors. The soldiers must have brought them.

* * * *

Papa lay on the wooden kitchen floor as Tabor wrung a bloodied rag into a bowl and gently blotted crusted scabs and dust from his cheeks. The stove lay cold, forgotten. Their breath frosted in the cool air.

The crowd had left only after the sun was directly overhead. Many people had come forward, shouting dishonors upon Papa's back. Never had Zhāng heard such blatant lies. And every time the crowd had calmed, the soldiers yelled and shouted till the frenzy was rekindled. All the time, Papa hadn't said a word in his defense, but merely bowed humbly before the false accusations.

Now, Zhāng tried to give him a hug, but Mama pulled him back and scolded him. "Not now! You'll hurt him." She'd torn their only bedsheet and wrapped it so tight around Papa's chest and belly he'd objected, "I can barely breathe." She held back sobs, biting a finger, then stood and walked to the window where the woven grass shade was rolled up, and faced the trampled yard before the barn.

"We knew this day might come," Papa said hoarsely, tousling Zhāng's stubby hair with feeble, thin fingers. "The communists are no longer underground. Their lies find a home with people too ignorant to know better. We mustn't cherish hatred against the renters."

Tabor's face grew red. He gritted his teeth. "I know he is your brother, Papa. But please, let me—"

Their father lifted a quivering hand. "It will make no difference, son. One who fights evil with hatred becomes a *you hun ye gui*, a demon, as well." He tried to sit up, but grimaced and fell back. Zhāng reached for his hand but Tabor pushed him aside and lifted Papa to sit upright.

Glancing at all seven siblings, Papa said, "We've spoken of this many times. And heard of the struggle meetings from Wuhu and other towns. Landowners have been imprisoned, beaten, and maimed. I'm thankful I wasn't sent to a labor camp. The communists will incite more of these mobs against us. I am certain of it. We survived this one, and will continue to do so."

"Perhaps." Tabor glanced at Mama. "But what of our land?"

Papa hung his head, then lifted it again. His chin stuck out farther than usual. "The land is no longer ours. It belongs to *them* now. The renters. We will find a way. Remember the drought three summers ago? We survived a year then, on less."

Tabor stood and walked to the window, gripping the rag so tightly it left a trail of dirty pink water. More pooled at his feet.

"I know your thoughts, son. Promise you will not seek vengeance. The family needs you now. If you do something foolish, we will all suffer. Promise me." Zhāng was amazed. He'd never heard such graven pleadings from his father, who'd always ruled his home with firm words and a leather strap.

More water splashed into the puddle before Tabor's shoulders finally drooped. "All right. I promise."

Zhāng stared at Tabor now. He was facing the window, back toward the family. Why had he given in so easily? Surely Papa *wanted* him to strike back, despite the soft words. Their land had been stolen! The earth upon which even little Zhāng had labored many long summers, seemingly half his life. Whenever any of the brothers had teased him, Papa had set them right. Strength, but with justice, was the law of their family. It was the same law by which he'd governed his land. And now the fields almost ripe with rice were no longer their own. Even Uncle Snake would reap Zhāng's labors. Everyone but the family who'd done the work.

Tabor might have promised, Zhāng thought, but he hadn't. The family law had been branded into him by belt and open palm. Justice must be upheld regardless of circumstance. That was what made it justice. Very well, then. He would wait, just as he crouched among the cabbages with the small bow Papa had crafted for him. It was the job of the youngest to wait for greedy rabbits to wander back through the rows, in order to protect the crops. Many times he had effortlessly drawn the string next to his cheek and loosed an arrow, straight to the mark, piercing an animal's soft pelt. Uncle would pay, along with the soldiers. They would all scream like skewered rabbits before he was finished with them. Zhāng was patient.

# Chapter 7 – First Suspect

Red stared at the Glock 19 in Lori's hands. It fired and lurched up, toward the indoor pistol range's low concrete ceiling, bumping her arm like a piston. Her legs were spread shoulder width apart, one ahead of the other, her weight on the balls of her feet as she leaned forward slightly. Dominant arm almost straight out. Overall, a nice Weaver stance. Pretty good for an accountant. Guess the CIA makes even their analysts practice every once in a while. Funny seeing a woman fire a weapon in a pencil skirt and two-inch heels. Curiously, the pistol seemed fitting, snug as the dress cradling her ass.

He stood in a hallway behind the range, separated by inch-thick glass. A glance to Carter, next to him, just to make sure his eyes were on the target and not elsewhere.

The alley had only two narrow stalls, and maximum target distance looked to be fifty feet. Buried deep in the basement of Merkel Research in Fairfax, Virginia. Some sort of political think tank, whatever the hell that was supposed to be. Red had visited Lori here only twice before. Merkel was a cover, a company owned by a venture capital firm, buried beneath a network of other corporations, investors, and filings. All to camouflage a CIA branch operation.

Lori was tall, blond, gorgeous. How had he married so far above himself? He was short, pale, with a flaming red beard and skin that freckled in the summer. Her father was a three-term state senator who had previously worked his way up to a deputy directorate position in the CIA, and before that even played pro ball for the Colts out of college. Red's father was an aged, crippled Vietnam vet with PTSD who only now seemed to be getting it under control as his body was failing. Her entire family was a bunch of A-type high achievers, her mother even a concert pianist. She found terrorists just by looking at bank accounts. And now it seemed she could handle a pistol as well. The only negative was that Lori's relationship with her parents always seemed oddly distant and strained.

A hushed *pop* sounded through the glass with each muzzle flash.

"There she is," said the escort, hair slicked back like a Geeks on Wheels intern. A round, flesh-colored Band-Aid stuck to his forehead. He smelled of plastic. "Need anything else?"

The intern smiled, but didn't move. Red glanced to the door. "We'll take it from here."

"I'm not supposed to leave anyone with—"

"She's my wife. We're not going anywhere, son. You've got our weapons, and she's armed. Plus you've got cameras on us." The boy rocked on his heels, then turned and trotted toward a stairwell.

*Pop, pop.* Lori paused when the heavy door closed with a bass resonance like far-off thunder, looking over her shoulder. An awkward wave to Red, then she finished the magazine. The walls pressed in. The air was stale, cramped.

Carter stood stiffly, as if at parade rest. "Those last five shots were off. Till then, she was keeping a four-inch group."

Why did Carter need to question Lori? She'd already said she didn't have any idea who might be after them. Waste of time. "I still don't understand why this can't wait."

Carter's reply was a sneer, but his deep-set eyes were soft. "It'll just be some questions. If it were a real interrogation, you wouldn't be along. You're only here to encourage her to open up. This'll tell us if I need to dig deeper. Detective work is methodical, boring." His eyes brightened. "We need to start at the top and nail down unknowns." *Pop.* "She's a big one."

The range door squeaked open and Lori emerged with a scent of spent gunpowder. Hair pulled into a ponytail, she swung her head in a *follow me.* She led them through a narrow door into a hallway with a workbench on the side, a four-inch vise bolted to it along with a drill press. Pliers, screwdrivers, and other hand tools hung on the wall. A miniature gunsmith nook. She placed the Glock, slide locked, on an oil-stained brown T-shirt. She cracked another door and peered in, then swung her head again, motioning for Red and Carter to follow.

This room was even smaller, no windows, with one row of shelves holding a few boxes of ammo. Buckets of spent brass were stacked in the corner. When the door came to, she leaned against the far wall with crossed arms. "How'd you get in, Tony?"

Red flashed a federal marshal star from his pocket. "Got a drawer full of these things from other agencies. But your employer has access to my file. Did you know CIA doesn't issue creds?"

"I need to ask some questions," Carter interrupted.

Lori kept her eyes locked onto Red. "Carter your bloodhound?"

He dipped his head.

She gave a scoffing smile to the detective. "I've been expecting this. Just thought Tony and I could talk it through first."

What the hell did that mean? What were they supposed to talk through? Carter gave a dismissive wave. "We need to—"

Red gripped Carter's elbow and pulled him back a step. "You don't need to be in her face. Give her some room."

Carter jerked his arm free, keeping his gaze on Lori. "Start us from the top."

Red interrupted, "But the wet team wasn't after her."

Carter squared up to Red. "We had a deal. I've been on the clock an hour and you're already slowing my investigation. Shut up and listen."

A metal shelf protruded from the wall behind Carter's skull. A quick smack would be all it took to drop the man. "I'm not leaving her with you. I've seen you work an interrogation."

"Tony, it's OK. Let's just get this over."

"Good," Carter said, tugging on the hem of his coat. "We're in agreement. Start with what you do here."

"I can't tell that. You've got to go through channels."

Carter turned to the door, fists clenched. "What the hell is the matter with you two? You want to figure out who's trying to kill you or not?"

The detective had a point. Red reached for Lori's hand, but she pulled away. What the hell was that about? "Carter may be right. This is about our family. The kids. Their safety."

She stuck out her chin. "They're safe. I've made sure of it."

"Like Penny and the horse?" No good. He didn't mean for that to slip out. No sex tonight.

Her stare iced his spine. "That's low, Tony."

"I didn't mean it like that. Just an example. We can't be overconfident." She shifted her feet uneasily. "Look, this sorry-ass ammo closet isn't bugged. Carter's off the record. Plus, he's got no dog in this fight. You know he'll get the job done. We can't wait around till we're hit again."

She gazed up, eyes glistening. Was she really that upset about Carter suspecting her? Her mouth opened several times, but nothing came out. Her tongue finally slid across her tightened lips. "OK... For the kids." She bumped her shoulder against Red's, almost playfully. "And for us." She eyed Carter. "Quick and dirty?"

He lifted his chin, as if peering down his nose to her.

"The CIA recruited me at graduation. Approached me in Harvard Yard. A blond lady with a program in one hand, her card in the other. Said Dad had told her I might be interested in a job. I had already nailed one at the UN as a translator, a starter position. Even so, we met later for coffee and that's how I found out who she was with. I kept my UN job, but drew a check from CIA as well. Not a bad deal. Eventually did some fieldwork out of London. About that time is when I met Tony. Dropped out of fieldwork. Started a family. Been an analyst ever since."

Not exactly how Red understood it, but not far off.

Carter raised an eyebrow. "You were shooting a four-inch group."

"Like I said, did a little fieldwork."

What did she mean by *fieldwork*? Red cocked his head. "You saying you were some sort of spy?"

Carter held up a hand to Red's face, gaze locked on Lori. "And now?"

Lori tightened her arms across her chest. "Financial intelligence. Terrorism funding tops the list, but we deal with all economic espionage. Anything that threatens the financial standing of the US."

"Anything that would make personal enemies?"

Red almost laughed. How would a government financial analyst do that?

She grunted. "Of course we've made enemies. We screw up terrorists' bank accounts. But they don't know how or who. Merkel Research is a well-respected firm. It's a real think tank with real contracts. A good cover. Plus, I'm smart as hell and fit the role."

"Humble, too," Red added.

"Shut up." Harsh, even for Lori.

Carter pressed. "Any leaks? Moles?"

Lori's eyes pleaded at Red. What was she hiding? "We need to know," he said.

"Sharing something like that could mean my life. If it got out I mentioned it, it's treason."

Red pointed at Carter. "We really gotta go here?"

He lowered his voice. "Yeah, we do."

Red drew a deep breath. Story of their life, as of late. Either way, they were damned. He leaned on the wall next to his wife. "I'd prefer this path. The one with Carter. At least then we'll have some control. If we don't do anything, we're acting like prey. A good offense is the best defense."

Lori rocked across the back of her shoulders. Confidence seemed to build into a soft smile. "Control would be nice.... Yeah, we've had a leak. Had it for years. Sensitive financial information. At first, just a trickle. We thought it might have been coincidence, or maybe just good intelligence gathering on behalf of China. But it built until we knew we had a problem. It came to a head recently when a source in China got their hands on a bundle of hundred-dollar bills—the new ones that are supposed to be counterfeit-proof." She rubbed her thumb and forefinger, as if feeling paper. "They were good. Best we've ever seen. That wasn't the worst of it. What really scared us was the source."

Red passed his tongue over a chapped bottom lip. "Where?"

Lori glanced at Carter. "Treason. You got it?"

Another nod. The man seemed to have gone mute.

"North Korea. That's where my efforts have been concentrated over the last year. I've been getting close, too. Another few weeks and I should have our mole. No one in CIA knows about my investigation...well, except a couple. Obvious reasons. When investigating a mole, you involve as few people as possible."

Carter shoved hands in pockets and stepped toward the door. His eyes flashed back and forth, as if reading an invisible text. His shoulder knocked over a short stack of fifty-round boxes of 9mm ammo. He put one back atop the other and paused. "That doesn't get us closer to your attackers. Last I heard, the only suspected backers were Iran and Israel. Any contact with Israeli intelligence, Mossad?"

"I've got contact with them all the time," she said. "We're not worried about them funding terrorists, though some consider Mossad a terror organization in its own right. Our relationship is primarily information sharing. We've got the technological sophistication to track funding flows that Mossad doesn't. They sometimes provide the insiders, the human interface, in places we can't. Overall, it's rather one sided in their favor, but it's worth it to us."

Carter's eyes drew to a narrow slit. "You've got a leak. Sure, you might have one giving intel to China, but the one we're after is with Mossad."

"I just told you we don't suspect—"

Carter counted on fingers. "One: The only leads the CIA managed to gather regarding your attackers were Iran and Israel, Mossad. Two: You work with Mossad in your job, sharing intel and assets." He wriggled his fingers. "That's all I need. One connection can be coincidence. But any detective will tell you two is damning. I'm not saying they ordered the wet team, but there's your leak."

This was good. One talk and they already knew the guilty party. But, who in Mossad? Red couldn't just target the entire organization. "Lori says the CIA has a leak spilling fintel to China. You're saying they've got one with Mossad. Could they be connected?"

Carter shrugged. "Maybe. Methodical, remember? I'll see where the facts take me."

But any successful op needed to maintain momentum. An investigation couldn't be too much different. They were on the move and needed to gain focus. He squeezed his hand into a fist and rubbed his knuckles. "Who you need to question next? I can put out a request to—"

Carter's hand fell upon his shoulder, his thumb as thick as a big toe. "Your knife stays in the sheath for the moment. Lori continues her investigation. We handle Mossad with tact. If we're figuring this out now, they've known it a long time. They've got their own investigation going."

But Red had worked with Mossad before. They were a co-op sometimes. "Why wouldn't they tell us?"

Carter smirked. "Would you tell them? This is Mossad. They do what's in their own best interests. Be realistic."

"What, then?"

Carter turned to Lori. "Old-boy network. Unofficial. Below the radar. I'd like to use the resources at the Det but, just like Lori said, when you don't know where the leak is, you involve as few people as possible. Can't tip off any mole."

Red was still confused. "What do you mean *old-boy network*? How?"

Carter's eyes widened. "Don't be such an idiot. We bluff. Use an unofficial channel to tell Mossad that the CIA has evidence." He pointed to Lori. "*Financial evidence*, that implicates them in the attack. Then tell them we want an explanation or else it will get released through official channels. Don't give them more than an hour to respond. If guilty, they'll object, but explain. If not, we haven't lost anything."

"But Mossad denied involvement earlier. Why would they change now just because we use an unofficial channel?"

Carter opened the door. "Don't have many friends, do you? Relationship. Trust. None of that exists in official channels. But we get the right two old boys together, and we'll make progress. You know who I'm talking about, Lori?"

Lori studied to the floor. Why was she hanging her head? "Yeah," she said. "But I don't think Dad will agree to it."

# Chapter 8 – Market Beating

*Pyongyang, North Korea*

Ko Chung Ho's fingers interlocked with his daughter's as they ambled through the Tongil farmers' market. Eun Hee, now fifteen, still allowed him that pleasure. He'd taken leave early in the afternoon, not bothering to change out of uniform, and they'd caught a bus into the city.

The market was strewn with patrons milling about like green draftees in the marshaling area on the first day of training. The display cart rows were bent like crooked twigs. Conscripts walked slouched and erect, long haired and shaved bald, the rich ones still plump. The aisles stretched before them at irritating angles. Couldn't they just make a straight line? Vendor stands stood sparse, displaying remnants of bok choy and tatsoi and pak choi, shades of green from light to dark, highlighted only by an occasional orange pumpkin, all that remained this late in the season. The structure's coal-hard concrete floor and high steel roof barely contained the sprawl, like a packed warehouse. But even in winter, the farmers smelled of sweat. Echoes of children's laughter mingled with chatter and a baby's cry.

Eun Hee squeezed his hand. "Thanks for taking me, Abeoji. Want some cucumbers?"

Ko lifted an arm and pointed toward an orange awning against the far wall. "Down that way. But they've been gone, weeks ago."

She smiled and tilted her head playfully. "I'll still try. Maybe someone brought in leftovers." She skipped off, though Ko knew she didn't do that anymore. Only in his imagination. Past the ugly-goose stage of adolescence, she now displayed her mother's DNA in full bloom; her body curved such that even grown men turned their heads as she passed. She swung a blue plastic milk carton by a handle of white rope. The other hand only a rounded nub.

Ko opened his palm and, with his thumb, felt the scar that crossed it. He looked up, as if worried someone could discover his secret.

Six years earlier Eun Hee had cut her hand on a wooden stake in their own vegetable garden. Harmless, they'd thought, but it had grown inflamed and puffy and wept yellow fluid. Red lines had webbed up her wrist.

The nurse, Ko's friend from elementary school, had pulled him into a separate room. "We have no medicine. The sanctions, you know." She'd winced. "Her arm, it will have to come off."

The next day, Ko had held a match to a blade and, crouching behind a jeep in the motor pool, sliced his own hand, careful to not go too deep. The results of the first pass hadn't been convincing, so with a shaking blade he'd done another. The final cut had looked jagged enough to be accidental. He'd smeared dirt over it and told the medic he'd cut it catching a shovel as it fell. They'd stitched his flesh and given him some pills, which he'd slipped to his nurse friend. She'd said it had saved Eun Hee's arm, but in the end, not her hand.

The nub had healed well, and through the years she'd learned to compensate. Now the blue basket swung so carefree no one seemed to notice the absence of her other hand.

He pushed a thumb against a pumpkin's skin. It sank only a bit. He thumped it and it rang a wonderful hollow note. "I'll take this one." He held up the orange fruit to the gaunt man behind the stall, who seemed to awaken from a stupor.

Ko strode toward the orange canopy and spied his daughter, her back to him. A man in a green army uniform stood next to her, squeezing oranges. Couldn't tell what rank from this far off, but he was young. It was well past noon; many soldiers stopped at the market before heading home. The man's head turned. So, he was talking with Eun Hee. Ko frowned and stepped faster.

As he approached lightly, Eun Hee's high cheeks rose, almost in a sneer. Or maybe fear? "What?" she gasped.

The man grinned at her. "I'll bet you taste as sweet as this fruit. Would you—"

The pumpkin dropped to the concrete and split. Ko grabbed the young man's shoulder. For a split second he looked surprised, till Ko's knuckle met his forehead. He fell back, his skull striking a man's calves before thumping hollowly on the floor.

* * * *

"He's coming awake," a captain said.

Ko glared down, then snapped back to attention. Damn it. Was he blind? How could he have missed a captain standing in the next booth? He'd tried to explain, but the officer had only held up a hand and said, "Best you don't say anything now, *Sangsa*."

The corporal rolled to his side on the concrete. He blinked hard, two red dots growing on his forehead where Ko's knuckles had crashed down. The captain grasped the corporal's forearm and lifted him, then handed Ko a baton. "Has the corporal been adequately punished, *Sangsa*?"

Ko gripped the hard wooden shaft. He could pummel the man's chest and shoulders without breaking bone. Hindquarters, too. His years as a guard at Hwasong had taught him choice spots for lasting pain without permanent damage. He squared up to the corporal and raised the stick. Eun Hee covered her face and turned away.

Ko dropped his arm. "Yes, sir. I'm done with him."

The captain pointed to the corporal, then an open doorway. "Visit the clinic before you go home."

The corporal rendered a salute and bounded off. The captain looked Ko in the eye, then leaned to his ear and whispered. Ko returned the baton, took a step back, gave a salute, and then grabbed Eun Hee's arm and hurried to the bus.

They didn't speak on the drive out of the city. But once the road turned narrow and bumpy, Eun Hee seemed to find her courage. "Are you in trouble, Abeoji? What did the officer say?"

Ko allowed himself a snicker. A couple with gray hair and wrinkled skin, holding brown bags with greens spilling from their tops, sat across the aisle and stared at him. Several other passengers seemed to be doing the same. Had they all seen what happened?

He brushed Eun Hee's thick, silk-black hair from her ear and leaned in. "He said he didn't know what the corporal had done, but he was disappointed in me. I should have beat him."

# Chapter 9 – Death of a Snake

*February 1964, Suncunzhen, China*

Zhāng Dàwe pedaled his faded baby-blue bike along Fumin Road, the cloudy night sky offering only dim light, barely enough for him to discern rutted earthen trail from drainage ditch. He ignored the ache in his legs as he reviewed his plan of violence, simple though it was. The rusty wire basket hanging from the handlebars squeaked loudly as he smacked through potholes. Another few minutes and he zipped by low wooden houses lining the path, his legs whirling in effort. Though past midnight, a lantern glowed in the window of almost every home. Occasionally laughter sounded around him, as families continued their gatherings, celebrating the New Year.

Twenty minutes ago he'd left his own family party at his eldest brother Tabor's hut. Only four of seven siblings remained, and each year they enjoyed a reunion meal of rice and porridge. One setting had remained empty for ancestors as always, but Zhāng had set a second tonight just for Papa.

The day had been spent mowing the ditch bank with Tabor while his aunts cleaned the house to ensure good luck. The ditch cuttings would be used for goat bedding. His mouth watered at the thought of the garlic-marinated meat from the afternoon's slaughter, set aside for tomorrow's festivities. Now, at nineteen years of age, his body had filled out, but he still craved protein. He'd been surprised how quickly he'd cleared his ditch, while his older brother had to stop every few minutes to catch his breath.

He slowed his pace, then stood on the pedals and coasted between two huts. The acrid stench of pig urine burned his nose as he walked the bike to the rear of the home. A community sty squatted in back, stretching the length of houses. Tabor's pigpen at home gave off the same stink, but the fresh air on the open road to town had cleared his senses. Now the pungent odor accosted them afresh. Leaning the bike against spongy wood siding, he lifted a small sickle from the basket. Sand grated between palm and wooden handle.

He stepped upon a log and placed his hand on the rear doorknob. A celebration of fireworks exploded somewhere down the street as sows in the pen squealed at the sound. He pushed the door inward so the grate of hinges would be masked by the explosions and screeching of swine. The floor sagged beneath his feet. If he stomped, he'd probably break through. He waited for another round of explosions from a few houses down, then shut the door as pigs shrieked.

His uncle, the snake, would be sleeping by now. The old man was seldom sober past six o'clock, Zhāng had been told. He rubbed his thumb against the sickle's worn handle. Would he be able to do this? Was it even right? Papa had admonished his older brother long ago not to seek revenge. But so much had happened since.

The communists had stolen the rest of what little land they had left Zhāng's family. Then they couldn't even grow sufficient food to support themselves. He and his brothers had to hire their bodies out as labor to families who used to be their renters. Abuse was gladly heaped upon this insult. Three years later his father, unable to supply even meager sustenance to the family, dove headfirst from atop their barn. His only remaining contribution was to remove one mouth to feed.

Zhāng smiled and tightened his grip. The old renters had been paid back, though. The communists had, of course, ended up taking everything from them, too. Tears of joy from new landowners who no longer had to pay rent soon turned to tears of fear as the tax rates climbed and payment was demanded by the government. Then they endured their own struggle meetings. In the end, Mao Zedong had enslaved the simple peasant farmers who had carried him to power.

But Zhāng had been shrewd. Too young to be under suspicion of having ties to the old regime, he'd befriended every party leader assigned to their school, using lies for his own gain, pretending to be a loyal communist so convincingly even his own brothers closed their mouths around him. And tomorrow, after the New Year, he would head to Beijing with the party's blessing, to study as an electrician's apprentice. A privilege for which several other boys with better grades had passed over. But none of his peers had been so shrewd.

Zhāng steadied himself against the kitchen wall and slowly leaned out to peer into a dark bedroom, the only other space in the dwelling. Funny, he couldn't hear snoring. The floor seemed to bounce as he stepped in and slid across, hand outstretched and low, feeling for the mattress and the snake that slept upon it.

When his fingertips bumped something that gave way, he froze. A loud clatter and something crashed onto the floor. He must've knocked over an extinguished candle. But still no breathing. Maybe Uncle Snake had heard him come in and was hiding? No, surely he was passed out, sodden with sake. Of all nights to enjoy a drink, tonight would be it.

Zhāng's fingers rustled against bedding hay. He felt farther in, patting a woolen blanket. No uncle.

Suddenly the door burst open and lantern light spilled into the kitchen. "Who's there?" came a gruff voice, but the words ended on a quavering elderly pitch.

Zhāng straightened. "Me, Uncle. Zhāng Dàwe. Your nephew."

"Zhāng?"

He took a step toward the door, holding the sickle behind his leg, out of sight. "Yes."

"What are you doing in my house?"

Another step. "It's the eve of New Year. I came to—"

"To harass an old man."

Another step, this one around the bedroom doorway, into the kitchen. His uncle stood there, paper lantern in one hand, a short walking stick in the other. He'd seen him from across a street hobbling along sometime last year, though they'd never spoken. The old man's black pants were torn at the hem of one leg, but were surprisingly clean. New-looking closed-toe sandals protected his feet. He didn't sway or slur. He was...sober.

"No, to just visit," Zhāng added. "You look well. Have you been celebrating?"

Uncle pointed the club across the kitchen. "Yes, but not at the bar. Neighbors invited me." He lifted the lantern next to his face, lips drawing into a toothless smile. "Your uncle hasn't had a drink for years." His head tilted. He tapped the stick against Zhāng's arm, the one tucked behind him. "You bring me a gift for the new year?"

"Yes, I did." Zhāng relaxed his arm, and the sickle hung to his side.

Uncle's eyes narrowed as he studied the instrument; then his mouth dropped open. He stepped back. His leg shivered. "Why did you come?"

"You know why." Zhāng turned the blade in his hand. "For Papa."

"You...you were so young. You only know one side of the story."

His chest drew tight. "I was there when you beat him. In the crowd."

The snake's voice quivered. "The cadre. The communists made us do it! It was an act. If we didn't, they'd—"

"That's not the way our family works." He slapped the rusty blade against his thigh.

"I was foolish. I drank so much back then. I didn't know what I was doing."

"You never even apologized to Papa."

Confusion spread across Uncle Snake's face. "I did! I tried to speak with him. He wouldn't listen."

Zhāng jerked his head up. "Lies."

Moisture glistened on Uncle Snake's cheek in the lantern's fallow light. He raised the stick above his head, quivering. A pitiful threat. Zhāng rushed forward and plunged the sickle through the man's gut, then jerked it up through his chest. Blood, bile, and water gushed upon the floor. The stench of copper and excrement filled the room. Hot fluids drenched his grip, but the sand on the handle and years of working the tool enabled him to hold fast. His uncle dropped the lantern and club. One hand landed upon Zhāng's shoulder like a claw. He pulled the snake closer, staring into the dying man's eyes.

"I forgive you," the elderly man whispered.

Zhāng muttered through clenched teeth, "Don't expect the same from me." He spat in one yellowed eye, then shoved the limp body out the door. Mud sucked at Zhāng's sandals as he lifted and flung the corpse into a pine pig trough, splashing filthy water over the sides. He waited for a loud crackle of more fireworks, then clapped his cupped hands three times, the call for the swine to dine. Instantly, at least twenty animals trotted over, squealing with delight, grunting in joy as they relished their generous New Year's meal.

Zhāng picked the sickle back up and slipped it into the rusty bike basket. A quick washing in ditch water on the way home and the blood would be gone. A day or two would pass before anyone would notice the snake was missing. By then, if anything was left, there'd be no telling how he'd been killed. And Zhāng would already be in Beijing, starting a new life.

He propped a foot upon a worn bolt shaft where a rubber bike pedal had once been mounted, then glanced back at the pigpen. A new wave of heated bitterness crawled up his back. But why? He'd accomplished a goal thirteen years in the planning. He'd loosed an arrow and pierced a rabbit's hide. What else would he have to do to cleanse himself of this eternal, burning anger?

*You cannot fight evil with hatred, or you will become a demon yourself.*

The nature of a demon is to destroy itself. Just like the communists were doing, slowly. He'd begin plans on how best to strike at them once he arrived in Beijing.

Zhāng swung his leg over the seat, facing a breeze. A surprisingly cold one—it must've been to his back on the way into town. Now it froze his bare shins and blasted through the thin cloth on his chest, making it billow like a sail. But he pedaled all the more feverishly. He'd upheld family law. Justice had been executed. *I did well,* he reassured himself, *and will become no demon.*

The sickle rattled in the basket as he bounced across a rut.

# Chapter 10 – Old-Boy Network

A long-haired brunette escort was halfway down Senator Moses' starched white Brooks Brothers oxford, unbuttoning it with her tongue. His belly stretched the seams of the tailored shirt, making progress slow. He'd have to cut back on the white breads like his physician had been telling him the last few checkups. He tried to keep reasonably fit, but age continued to mock him and the days of six-pack abs when he'd been a linebacker for the Colts was long past. His phone vibrated in his jacket pocket, the suit sprawled on the hotel bed next to him. The ringtone was some female country singer he didn't recognize. Wife? Aide? No, that's right, Lori. His jaw clenched.

He fumbled in the cloth till his fingers brushed the metal device. He winked at the woman. What was her name again? Elaine? Loraine? "I've got to take this one. Only be a minute. Why don't you get yourself ready?" She smiled, and the button popped from her lips, a moist circle of cloth around it. He grabbed for her ass as she slipped off the bed and flipped curly brown hair over bony shoulders. Sure, skinny was the fashion, but someone needed to introduce the woman to a cheeseburger. Maybe she was a drug addict. She stepped inside a frosted glass door to the bathroom and it clicked shut. He sat up on the shiny green duvet, and two cylindrical pillows rolled to the floor.

He punched the green icon on the screen. "Yes, ma'am."

"Since when do you call me *ma'am*?"

He feigned a laugh. "Oh, I thought it was your mother. How's my baby?"

"Good as can be expected."

He waited, but nothing. A glance to the bathroom door. "You just calling to say hello?"

"Uh, yes and no."

*Thought so.* He smiled. "Well, I'm in Stockholm and it's late here, so out with it."

"First, we're on a secured line. I'm calling from work. But nothing is being recorded."

But his cell phone wasn't secure. He straightened. "And..."

"Do you still have contacts with Mossad?"

What the hell? Where'd that come from? "I may. It depends whether I'm talking to my daughter or an employee of the company."

"Your daughter."

Right. That's why she called on a secured line, a work phone. He only got calls when she needed something. When it was convenient to take her politically connected daddy out of the trunk and brush the dust off his bald head. "Anything for you, dear. You need help? Yeah, back when I was in your shoes, I made some friends overseas, with the CIA's blessing, of course. You know, you never really stop working for the company, don't you? I try and keep up with one or two of my friends in Mossad...and a few at CIA for that matter."

"Mossad. Any in particular? What do they do?"

He picked up his watch. "You looking for names? No way." He inhaled a deep breath, and the moistened button popped from its threads. "I suspect one or two are pretty high up by now. I don't know what the hell they do. And if they told me, I wouldn't believe them. What you need to know?"

The line was silent. Then, "I need a favor."

"Use your own contacts."

"I need this one below the radar. Unofficial." That came all too quickly. As if she'd rehearsed it. She knew he'd balk. "For reasons why, I can't say. But trust me. I need you to make a call."

"Trust you? What's the message? Who does it need to get to?"

Her voice became a whisper. He pictured her hiding in a closet somewhere. What was she concealing? "Head of Operations just told me they figured out who was behind the wet team that attacked us. It was Mossad. Said he couldn't give details yet, but the issue was going to be addressed tomorrow morning." Her words came quicker now, as if she were growing anxious. "Look, I don't know who to believe, but I work with Mossad almost every day. I depend on them. If they've got problems, or a leak. Maybe we can head this thing off before it becomes a shit storm."

This was nuts. He cupped the earpiece. "I'm going to pretend this call never happened. I'm hanging up and don't want to hear about this again. The implications are too high. You need to go through your own channels.

I don't want any part of it. If Mossad was behind it, *you* certainly don't want to tell them you know. That's idiotic! Let it go through channels."

"Dad, be discreet. Don't tell them I'm the one that told you."

"Official channels."

A squeak from the bathroom and water splashed in the sink.

"Mossad is an ally. If they're the ones that attacked us, trust me, I want to know. But the head of Operations is a windbag and probably—"

Who was the head of that division now? "That jackoff man? What's his name?"

A grunt. "Jackerman."

An image of a rose-cheeked slouch with a white-haired comb-over clinking champagne glasses with the vice president at the Corduroy restaurant during a recent campaign fund-raiser flashed to mind. "The only mole that guy could catch is in his garden. Can't you guys just euthanize him or something?"

"You see why I've got doubts. Listen, don't mention Jackerman to Mossad. Promise? You do, and it could come back on me."

It'd be nice to help his daughter, but this could come back to bite him. "I'm still not doing it."

"Dad, there's no downside. You've got the relationships. If the accusation is right, they'll probably deny it and things will move on just as if you never brought it up. But if not, they'll at least have a courteous heads-up from an old pal. Either way, Mossad would owe you a favor. Which I'm certain is a chit you could cash in sometime."

She was right. With Mossad, you always needed to have them in your debt to get anything done. Sometimes even that didn't work. His daughter had a quick wit. Got her looks from her mother, but brains came straight from him.

The water stopped running in the bathroom. The door handle squeaked and a long, bare leg slipped out. "Will do. Gotta go." He hit a red button on the screen, then powered the phone down.

# Chapter 11 – The Hit

Red opened the passenger door of his Ford Explorer, frowning at a fresh door ding with a white paint smudge. He ducked his head at a loud *crack-pop*, but it was only a potbellied, middle-aged rider revving the engine of his Harley at the stoplight in front of Mattress Discounters. The new Explorer's door creaked in the cold, as though already old and stiff.

Across the parking lot, Lori shook the restaurant owner Alessandro's hand again, smiling and nodding politely. The man stared entirely too long as she strutted across the parking lot like a runway model, sidestepping a pothole. Her black heels were only an inch long, but she certainly didn't need them. It was the kids' night to be with auntie, which meant good things to come for Red. His foot tapped the pavement with anticipation.

Dinner had gone well. No mention of Lori's father, Senator Moses. Yesterday she said he'd been reluctant but willing to brush the dust off his contacts on the east coast of the Mediterranean.

Lori skipped over a puddle and tossed her hair behind her shoulders. Tires squealed not far away. Red glanced at the stoplight, but it hadn't changed yet. An engine approached fast from the side, Red's view blocked by a blue pickup with a huge camper shell mounted to the bed. Lori glanced in its direction, sprinted a quick-step, then dove straight at him. The windows of the Explorer shattered as she flew, blown inward by small-arms fire. A round slipped through her leg, drawing out a quick stream of blood as it exited, spinning her like a football in midair. Red caught her and fell against the open door, slamming it into the adjacent BMW.

Shots were coming from two P90s, judging by their report and high rate of fire. No time to find other cover. He pushed Lori under the truck and drew his sidearm, aiming down the fat barrel, custom made for the

Det to handle higher-powered propellants. In a few more seconds the shooters would be alongside with a clear line of fire. He ducked below the Explorer. Gas fumes filled the air, but nothing was dripping. Lori had clamped her hands onto her calf.

"I'm going to draw their fire." He had to leave her, but his instincts said no. He jumped atop the BMW, throat tight as if he were abandoning her, but he needed to draw attention away. He'd try for cover behind the blue camper. The shots were coming from a gray Dodge Avenger, visible now, closing fast, shooters at both passenger-side windows. One swung his weapon toward him, then flew forward into an airbag as a white van slammed into the car head-on.

Where did the van come from?

The shooter from the back seat was now sprawled atop the Avenger's crumpled hood, forearm snapped. Red hopped down and ducked as more shots sounded. The driver of the Avenger, camo ball cap turned backward, was out and spraying bursts into the van. The assailant moved quick, controlled, with trained precision. Another shooter in blue jeans and plaid shirt started to crawl on the asphalt toward Lori, dragging a twisted leg, pulling a knife from his belt. His eyes were dazed, or maybe he was high. Red double-tapped him, rounds blowing off an ear. A burst exploded the BMW's windshield, ripped it from the seal, and landed it atop Red's back. A shattered crystal blanket. The shots had come from Camo Cap, the only one left, crouching behind the van. He squatted behind a tire and pointed his weapon toward the Explorer.

Red stood and emptied his magazine as he ran to the camper. Camo Cap retreated behind a green steel Dumpster a few steps away. Red pulled a second mag, the one with blue-tipped ammo. He cracked four shots through the corner of the green box, and boots slumped into view. He put two more rounds through the sole of one, but it didn't flinch. He ran to the Avenger, pistol raised. The one atop the hood looked like he might live, aided by a body cast and traction, but was no longer a threat.

A scream and curses erupted from under the Explorer. Lori was on her side, blood running from her elbow, black tears streaking across a bloody nose. Red scooched on his belly and held out his hands to her. "It'll be OK. Hit anywhere else besides the leg?"

Her eyes bulged as mascara ran like crow's-feet.

"I'm guessing that's a no. I'm going to pull you out. Keep pressure on your calf. Ready?"

The sinews in her bare forearms tensed as she clamped her grip. She growled, "I'm OK. Check the guy in the van."

That vehicle's engine spun high and coolant steam filled the cabin, oozing out from cracks and bullet holes in the windshield. Worton's Commercial Painting and a rainbow scrawled on the side. Had this van meant to help? Or just been an unlucky bystander? A second hit team? He stooped low and jerked open the door. A man rolled out with a groan. He let him hit the pavement, keeping his weapon aimed at his head. The body rolled over and...what the hell?

Red dropped to a knee and slipped his hand beneath the man's skull. "Marksman?" A drop of blood dripped from his ear. Marksman was a contract operator the Det called in when they needed certain language skills. He knew five fluently, ten enough to get by. His hyperaccurate fire had saved Red's ass on at least two ops, which earned him the nickname. But when the mission was over, he'd disappear. What was he doing here?

Marksman coughed with a grimace. "Thanks for catching me, asshole."

"What are you...?"

Lori screamed again from under the Explorer, her voice shrill.

Marksman's eyes wandered in that direction. "She OK?" His tongue was bloody as well. Red ripped open a wool cardigan, buttons flying. He grabbed the neck of Marksman's T-shirt and pulled it apart, then plunged his fingers into the man's abdomen, squeezing to pinch off the artery that was rapidly overflowing the holes with blood. Marksman grabbed his wrist. "Take care of your wife."

"She's hit through the calf. She's pissed, but it'll be OK. You need to relax."

"No, jerkoff." He coughed. "She's in danger. Take care of—" His voice trailed to a whisper. Red felt a gush against his index finger. He pinched it off and Marksman's eyes opened. Sirens sounded in the distance.

"I've only got two hands, buddy. You've got to hold on till they get here."

Marksman's lips moved. Red put his ear close. "Trust her," he said.

"Whatever. Just hold on."

Marksman gripped Red's biceps. Strong, slender fingers wrapped his muscle like a baseball player gripping a bat. He raised his head and his eyes searched, blinded. "You're such an idiot," he whispered. "Give the pistol to my brother. And remember, Lori's not the enemy." His hand slipped off Red's arm, leaving a glistening handprint on his black wool sweater.

# Chapter 12 – Doubt

*Kanggye, North Korea*

River Walk Clothing had no sign outside, but stood on the corner of Twenty-Ninth and Bridge Roads. Like so many other dichotomies in the country, the black market was both loathed and loved. Officially, such private enterprises were illegal. Unofficially, even the highest classes depended upon their wares to keep warm and fed.

Ko Chung Ho's shoulder brushed the store's gray block wall as he stepped from the leeward shelter of a muddy alley, onto the slick sidewalk in front. A bitter wind swept from the Changja River, its icy kiss laced with mud and coffee, maybe from a shop across the green water flow. A slender silver fish leapt from the surface, shaking shimmering droplets, then splashed back in.

Too cold, even for trout. But what else could it have been? His mouth watered at the thought of fresh seared fish on a wood-fired stove. When he was a kid, his mother had always said, "Grandmother loved trout," as she flipped the fillet to cook the other side. "We always know Grandmother is looking out for us when you come home with a nice fat one." Ko had smiled and eaten his dinner, never correcting her. But school had taught him there was no afterlife. No God. Grandmother wasn't looking after anyone.

Now Ko ducked his chin and shrugged the stiff collar of his uniform coat up to his ears, leaving only a narrow band of flesh exposed from eyebrow to nose. Inside, the store was moderately warmer, just no bitter wind. He studied a black peacoat with artificial fur collar, then pushed the hanger along the curved chrome rail and glanced at another. The bare concrete floor scuffed beneath his steps like worn sandpaper. There were two sparse racks of new women's coats from China. He shifted back to the peacoat and flipped its collar to view the tag: eighty thousand won. Maybe if the collar was red fox, or coyote.

He shoved cold hands in pockets—no officer to tell him to take them out, or junior NCO to see his breach of etiquette—and strutted to the back of the store. Three low racks of used coats were propped there. A few long ones dragged the floor. His daughter, Eun Hee, would be happy with a used one, though she had probably stopped growing and this one would fit her for a long time. But she was always grateful for what he provided. They weren't one of the privileged. He was a staff sergeant, no officer, and therefore earned his wage.

The shopkeeper pushed a broom, pretending to clean, eyeing his moves. "Can I help you find anything?" He propped the handle against a table stacked with men's pants and started to shuffle through one of the coatracks.

Ko glanced around the room. "Something for my daughter. I'll... This one looks nice." He slipped out a deep red coat from between two dull and threadbare woolen ones. It was goose down, or maybe poly filled, with a white fur collar. Ko pushed his nose into the pelt, surprised at the soft warmth, and inhaled. Scented of cotton.

"You like? She would be proud of it," the shopkeeper said, stroking his mustache in approval.

Ko turned the coat around, but no tag. Looked about his daughter's size. "How much?"

"For that one? Fifty thousand won."

*Right, old man. You got this hand-me-down from some politician's wife. Probably gave it to you.* "I offer ten thousand."

The storekeeper huffed and threw up his hands. But Ko knew the game too well. "You insult me again! I practically gave you those socks last week. No? Please, be realistic. I have a family to feed, just like you."

Ko scanned the store quickly again. Always empty. How did this guy stay open? "OK. I'll give you twenty thousand."

"Better, but that is what it cost me. For you..." He slapped Ko's shoulder. "I'll take thirty thousand."

Ko hung the coat back onto the rack with a metallic chink. "Twenty-five thousand."

"I can't even buy my corn for that."

"It is not my fault you have no other customers."

The storekeeper bent in a slight bow. "I am sorry, but cannot go less than thirty thousand." Pleading eyes peered up as Ko walked to the front of the store, stretching on leather gloves.

"Twenty-eight thousand!" the man called after him.

Ko kept walking. His hand gripped the door handle and he pushed it open. "Please, please," the man implored. "Twenty-five thousand. I will accept! I will accept."

*Knew you would.* Ko prided himself at the game. His wife had always been embarrassed to listen as he boasted how cheaply he purchased his latest prize. But cancer had taken her three years ago, so it was only Eun Hee who pretended to be shamed now, all the while asking for every detail of the negotiation. Even if it was over a pumpkin at the market. "I want to learn to be as excellent a negotiator as you." At least she didn't call him cheap.

The shopkeeper grinned when Ko turned back. *Maybe I should've pressed for twenty thousand,* Ko thought.

"You always steal from me, you know." The man smiled again, but he must have caught himself because he returned to somber character. He wrote something in a log book, looked behind him, and said, "You are skilled at bartering. A good man."

*This guy is entirely too happy,* Ko thought. *Maybe I really did pay too much for the coat.* But twenty-five thousand won was a fair price.

The shopkeeper tapped his pencil on the counter. "This is how life is. And now I would like you to consider one more thing that could help the both of us."

"I don't need any more clothes. You know I'll be back when the weather warms."

"No, no. Not clothes. Something much more valuable. You see, we all help each other, just like *juche* says. You protect our borders. I provide clothes where the government can't. Like *juche* says, we all are a part of the machine, working for the greater good, for each other. No?"

Where was this going? Ko was hungry for dinner and certainly didn't want to encourage the man, but he hadn't said anything wrong. In fact, Ko had better agree, if *juche* says so. He glanced around the store once more, expecting to see a political officer with one of those loathsome notebooks, waiting to mark down any errant comment. No one in sight, but Ko still kept silent.

"I can help you, if you help me." The man's voice no longer reflected that of the meek shopkeeper. He'd found a backbone somewhere. His smile was contagious. Ko always enjoyed small talk with him, but this conversation...

"Can I go on, my friend?"

The man hadn't said anything wrong, but Ko would have to shut him up if he did. He twisted his wrist, glancing at his watch. No need to hurry, and now he was curious. How did he keep his door open, a light on, and chill off the air? It certainly wasn't by selling coats at twenty-five thousand won. He'd never suspected it before, but this man was shrewd. He had other income. Maybe a whorehouse, or bootleg distillery, or maybe something legitimate. Ko had never been a businessman, but wages for soldiering were no longer consistent. Father had taught him how to catch fish, but Ko never took to it as a living. At Army Ground Force basic training, he'd finally hit his own stride, turning into a salmon in a stream. This shopkeeper...he'd just dropped a hook into the water. But what was he fishing for? "Go on."

The storekeeper bowed twice, then held Ko's gaze. His chest heaved; then he said, "I know where your sister is. I can help her."

Ko's blood rose hot in his neck. He stood straight and balled his hand into a hard fist, but resisted the urge to punch the older man. "You know nothing."

"I'm afraid I do."

"Where?"

"Hwasong."

Ko shuddered. He turned to the door, and back again. Sweat ran down his cheek like a spider on skin. Hwasong had been his second post, a prison guard back then. When he'd arrived it took a week to keep his food down. The first day a prisoner in a tiger cage had baited a mouse with a moldy carrot. He'd snatched it and bit the head off, slurping its bowels like spaghetti. "They aren't people. Weaklings. Societal defects," his commander had said, stern faced, kicking the chest of a prisoner, hands strung behind his back. *Pigeon torture,* he'd called it.

Guards forced confessions—no care for truth. Many prisoners were incarcerated for crimes of family members. Still more claimed they had no idea why they were imprisoned. He was dizzy every time he gave torture, but he gradually numbed. He learned to trust the filth were in Hwasong for reason. They deserved death, but the homeland was merciful for allowing them to live. Then, when he almost started to enjoy it, his assignment was over and he was back to border patrol.

The nightmares came a few months later, memories he didn't know were there, shoved deep and forgotten. He awoke sensing the pounding stench of blood, vomit, and feces filling the air. It was as if their remembrance clamored to get out, and found a weakness during his sleep. In time they subsided, and left completely for five years. The years of his wife's terminal cancer, and his daughter's gangrenous hand. Other dreams took their place.

But now the nightmares were back again. They'd begun one night after he received transfer orders, back to Hwasong. He'd awaken in sweats. Last night even sitting up and dry heaving till Eun Hee came, asking if he was

OK. Apparently they'd never left, the nightmares, sneaking back, like an infection unhealed. The infected flesh needed to be cut out.

Ko turned to the door then back to the man, pacing several times. He stifled a scream of frustration. He wanted to belt the guy till he confessed what he knew, but that wouldn't help his sister if he was telling the truth. "How can I trust you?"

"You will see with your own eyes soon enough, *Sangsa*. You are headed there again, no?" The shopkeeper pointed to Ko's hands. "You are tearing the coat."

Ko looked at the bundle in his grasp. His fingers wouldn't let go. He strained his mind and the grip loosened till the coat thudded to the floor. Wait. The man *had* to be lying. "They would never assign me to a camp where my sister was a prisoner. They wouldn't trust us. Not even me."

The shopkeeper's smile left him. "They don't know who she is. If they did, you would be a prisoner as well just because she's a blood relative."

"You're lying!" He swung an arm, gesturing around the room. "They know everything. And they know who is loyal and who is a tyrant. You, sir, are a tyrant!"

"I have said nothing of the sort. I am loyal to the homeland. My home follows *juche*. I have only said I know where your sister is, and that I can help her. There is nothing tyrannical about that."

Ko grabbed the man's collar and cocked his fist. "Then tell me what you know about her."

The shopkeeper winced, bracing against the counter. "You don't need to beat me to tell you."

Ko took a breath. Then another, and finally he let go.

The man rolled his neck and said, "She is a political prisoner. Christian, I believe."

No. His sister, Soo Jin, was too strong for them. She could never be wooed by such weak political heresy. *There is no God.* He recalled an image of her standing between him and six men, swinging her pocketbook, daring them to take a step closer.

It had been when Shin-Il, a bully from Ko's primary school, had moved back to town the last year of secondary. Ko had thickened in the meantime, his body hard from growing up with two older brothers, rowing Father's boat when the wind didn't blow, and hours on the soccer field. Shin-Il heard about Ko and boasted he was going to beat him up again. Ko had come out of biology class, a black-and-white film on the reproduction system. He squinted in the light, eyes adjusting after a second to see Shin-Il blocking his path and a small crowd around them both. The heat beaded sweat in his hair and sweet cut grass wafted across from the soccer field.

"Remember me, little Ko?" Shin-Il raised his fists. He waved them weakly, and tossed back black hair like a ballet dancer.

Ko stepped toward him. "Shin-Il. I just saw a movie with you in it." His lip curled.

"Yeah, I remember you. I remember you like your father's goats, but I prefer your little sister when no one's around."

Shin-Il screamed something from a karate movie and swung a roundhouse kick, much more quickly than his stance suggested he could. But it was too low and Ko tensed, absorbing the blow to his gut with a grunt. He clamped down on the leg and struck him in the balls with an uppercut that lifted Shin-Il from the ground. He crumpled without a sound, crawling on the earth, dragging his face in the gravel. After what seemed like a minute, a faint wheeze came from his lips, growing louder with each breath.

That's when six of Shin-Il's friends had stepped from the crowd, eyes set on Ko. Soo Jin had jumped in front, swinging a pocketbook. "This is over! No one touches him!"

And no one had.

Yes, she was much too strong to believe in a poisonous foreign religion. He sneered at the shopkeeper. "Not Soo Jin. Plus, they would have known she was my sister and come after my family, too. She was in my house."

"Like I said, they don't know. There is a guard she talks with there. He said she mentioned her religion once. Remember? But you had forbidden her to speak of it ever again."

Ko stroked his cheek, feeling the fuzz close to his ear. She had said something about a man at work who told her about a prophet, but only once. "I haven't seen her for...five years. She moved away. Said she got a government job in Kimchaek."

"But it wasn't government. She knew you were stubborn and would never listen. She went because she thought the government might have been watching. She used a different name. Once caught, she was no longer a Ko. It was for your own protection, what she did."

Ko had looked for her once while on temporary duty near the city, when the letters stopped coming. But by that time her old roommate had moved away. He knocked on every door on the apartment floor, but no one knew her name. At one flat, however, a wife's eyes had broadened when Ko showed her a picture of Soo Jin. Casually ignorant before, she adamantly denied knowing her, backing away behind her husband, who shut the door.

Ko had looked at the picture held between his knuckles, then realized he should have changed from his uniform before asking questions.

Now, Ko picked up the red coat from the floor and brushed it off. A hand-me-down from a privileged wife. Probably wore it once before thinking it unstylish, tossing it aside. Their class was never hungry. Even in the famine, they had enough. Rumors had circulated there wasn't a famine at all, but the government had held back food to subdue an uprising among the people. Ko hadn't allowed himself to believe, until doubt had crept back in, along with the nightmares.

Those prisoners didn't deserve the sewer-hell of Hwasong, no matter what they'd done. It only held prisoners with life sentences. No one was ever released. And no one escaped. If Soo Jin had gotten mixed up with the wrong people, she could be there, in the special block for religious and political prisoners. If so, she was strong. She would last a couple of years, but no more. The fire in the crematorium cooled only for cleaning. He'd be back there within two weeks. The camp had been closed for a year but now was back in full operation.

It would be his turn now, to step out from the crowd, to swing his fists and dare anyone touch her. But how? He couldn't hide her. If caught, he'd be a prisoner in Hwasong himself, and they'd take Eun Hee as well. "If you know so much, tell me one thing. Ask Soo Jin how she broke the heel off her uniform shoes. Till then, this conversation is over. I'll be back next week, same time. Have my answer."

Ko stepped into the bitter wind from the river. The same coffee scent blew past. He stood still for a minute, looking for a fish, but none jumped. If the man's answer was right, he had contact with Soo Jin and could be trusted. Because, if his answer was wrong, he either didn't have contact, or Soo Jin misled him because he wasn't trustworthy. It would be a long week.

# Chapter 13 – Active

*Rappahannock General Hospital, Virginia*

Red lowered himself to a short stainless-steel stool. He tried twisting the seat down but instead the legs spun, scraping the floor. His knees hit tube rails of the hospital bed where Lori lay semi-inclined. The sanitizer dispenser mounted across the hall squeaked as nurses passed, rubbing the germ killer between palms. The alcohol scent reminded him of wiping Nick's hands with the stuff again and again. The kids—thank goodness for Lori's sister. They'd stayed at her house for Red and Lori to have a date night. Because of the relocation, the CIA had advised breaking contact with their regular babysitters, Red's parents, for at least a year. The dispenser squeaked again and he clasped Lori's hand.

*Wish there was as easy a way to clean up this mess,* thought Red.

Lori's eyelids closed and she brushed them with a wet wipe, then handed the black-smeared cloth to him. He wadded it and shot it like a basketball into a shiny corner can. "Same song, second verse."

Lori huffed. "Forgot about that. Just here last week with Penny. The Harmons move to town and we're already adding the ER doc to the Christmas card list."

"You and Penny can hobble around the house together. We'll have mother-daughter clubfoot races."

"I won't be in a cast. Not for this wound." She sighed and put her chin to her chest. "Tony, if we have to move again, I'm going to scream. I can't do this. I feel old."

He pushed his fingers back under her palm, and she squeezed them. Her wedding ring was halfway twisted on a knuckle, green diamond resting next to her pinky.

"A mine-cut di-á-mond," their Egyptian jeweler had said when he mounted the stone. He always pronounced *diamond* in three syllables. "You could recut it and the value go up. But a green stone"—his voice had cracked—"very rare. I would be scared to do it." The stone had been in the family for four generations now. Great-Grandfather had smuggled it back from northern Italy after losing three toes to a Kraut grenade in 1917. He'd said a lovely woman in a yellow lace beret had given it to him, after he'd moved his headquarters from her home without damaging it. He'd fancied the stone a cheap emerald. Only the men of the family knew he'd swiped it. They'd been sworn to secrecy, fearing what the ladies would think if they knew the truth.

The white curtain hanging from an extruded aluminum ceiling track yanked open. A brunette with sagging eyes in blue scrubs carrying a laptop stepped next to Lori's bed. "Mind if I open this up? You've got a private room. Only one we have down this end."

Red pulled the cloth shut again. "Thanks, but she likes it closed."

She put her hand on Lori's. "How you feel, girl?"

Lori lifted her sore leg, gripping the hospital bed side rails. "Like I've been stung by a hornet the size of a Doberman."

"Want something to take down the pain?"

She pulled herself up in the bed. An electric motor spun, and the mattress rose to meet her. "Just some more Advil, please."

"I'll have a nurse bring them...your leg should be OK. The bullet went right through the meaty part of the calf. Not much tearing. It didn't tumble on the way through. It'll look like hell for a while, but the bruising will go away in time." She turned to Red. "You've got to take care of her elbows. Lost most of her skin there. I picked all the gravel out of them I could find. Clean all the wounds twice a day, morning and night, till the skin grows back. Triple antibiotic, plus fresh bandages. We'll give you some samples for home. Enough for a day or two. Don't neglect them. They're more susceptible to an infection than the leg."

"She's in good hands."

The doctor stood and pulled the curtain back again. "You take care of yourself. I don't want to see you down here again. OK? The meatheads outside tell me you're not going to be my patient anymore."

Lori scowled. "They're not making trouble, are they?"

"It was a pissing contest. Same thing happened last year when a different fed got brought in." She tossed her head. "I know how to make them fall in line. They've turned off all the mics on the entire floor. Got some agent hovering at the nurses' station. If I hadn't put my foot down, they'd set a tank outside the door. Said they were taking you somewhere else, probably within a half hour. I told them you should stay put, rest for the night. But if they send you to Johns Hopkins, be sure to drop my name when they ask you who stitched you up. OK?"

She closed the curtain behind her. The door clacked shut.

"They've swept the room. We're OK to talk. You call Carter yet?"

"No."

"Tony, I don't care what it takes. We've got to get this fixed. We might have to go off the grid completely. Permanent. There's a place I know in Ontario where we can disappear for a couple years."

"We've got to see what Carter turns up. Need to give him a chance."

"We may not have time. Shit, this is twice. I thought last time they were after you. But this time they were gunning for me." She put her hands to her sternum. "I mean, what the hell? Why would anyone want to kill *me*? You know how frustrating that is? That pisses me off."

Red smiled. There she was, the Lori he loved. "Eventually you learn to not take it personally."

"I don't want to learn. I'm financial intelligence, for crying out loud. I left fieldwork so I didn't have to deal with this crap." She grabbed his collar. "What could be more boring than fintel?"

Red took her hand and held it between his. "Maybe it's not about your job. Maybe it's something from the past. Maybe about your dad. Or me."

"Dad?"

"Kind of a coincidence that your dad gets involved right before someone takes a shot at you."

"Tony, I know you've never hit it off with my family. But he's not trying to kill me."

"Didn't say that. Maybe just someone he talked to. Someone connected to him. Guess that's for Carter to find out."

"Or maybe it's the Det," she shot back. "Marksman seemed to know something was going to happen."

Red stood and turned to the wall, bracing himself against it. One of those funnel lights they stick in your ear fell from its holder and dangled from its cord like a noose.

Lori's voice was soft. "I'm sorry about Marksman."

Marksman. How the hell had he shown up? Red had always thought he was a spook with the CIA doing business mainly in Europe. He trusted him because that's what you did with your team. But he'd made a connection with Marksman on a different level somehow. An unspoken covenant.

Marksman was unpretentious. As if you could simply trust his words as truth, the few that ever came from his lips.

But how had he shown up at just the right time? Was he trailing Red? Or maybe Lori? What did he mean by *she's not the enemy?*

"He was a good man," Lori offered, rubbing a thumb.

*How would you know?* "But why was he there tonight? You're right. That means the Det could be involved. But I'd know about it, wouldn't I? The Det, we're a small group."

"You're new to the command. You may need to clean house. It only takes one."

"One what?"

She shrugged, her exasperated expression asking, *Do I have to spell this out for you?* "One leak. Mole. Whatever you want to call it. The Det has always been an accident waiting to happen. It's got too many connections, too many agencies involved, and even plays with some foreign governments. *Co-ops,* you call them. Ask me, as soon as more than one person knows a secret, it's only a matter of time till it gets out."

"But we're just a fusion cell...sort of. Only a few of us see the whole picture. Not the co-ops. That's how we control leaks. The co-ops just contribute assets."

"In exchange for what, Tony?" She soft-pounded a fist on the bed rail. "Information. Intelligence. Data. And an occasional service. It may be spoon-fed to them, but there're still connections going on. People connecting with people. And people build relations. And relations can be manipulated. Who'd Marksman belong to?"

Red hooked a stool leg with his foot and pulled it over. He sat forward, elbows on his knees, rocking. "Don't know for certain. I'll do some digging when I get to the office."

"Just be sure to tell Carter...again, I'm sorry. I know you admired Marksman. But we've got no one to trust. Not Dad, not the CIA, not the Det."

And maybe not Lori. Working some financial investigation that few in CIA knew about? Sounded like an excuse for loose accountability. *Now she says they can't trust her side, either. Suspicious. Maybe she's dirty and the hit was the CIA doing housecleaning.* The thought jolted his tired mind.

But not his wife, the mother of their kids. Not in her nature. She'd always put the family first. Even breast-fed all three kids while holding down a job just because a doctor said it was better for their immune system. And she'd never lied to him before.

His eyes darted to her leg. Damn it. There was no way he was getting sex tonight. A wave of guilt filled his stomach.

*Focus.* His mind was getting tired.

No, it definitely couldn't have been a CIA hit. Way too public. Whoever put out the contract was making a statement, or being sloppy. They wanted it in full view, violent, with lots of guns and excitement, enough to win front-page news.

Red sat upright. "We've got Carter. He's a friend, even if a reluctant one. He needs more time. You'd better call your family and let them know you're OK."

She shook her head. "No. They don't know I was shot and they're not going to know anything about this. I'll explain the leg by telling them I got hurt riding. They'll believe it because of what just happened to Penny. No loss without some small gain."

The phone in his pocket vibrated, then rang with three sharp beeps. He flinched. The ringtone he'd assigned the Det.

Lori opened her eyes. Her shoulders drooped with exhaustion. "Go ahead and answer," she mumbled, half-asleep now, squeezing his hand.

Red stepped into the bathroom, and the thick one-hour rated fire door thudded shut. He glanced at the glowing screen, pressed the message icon. It read conference call. His stomach knotted. He'd been activated. The phone beeped again, now an incoming call. It was Grace, his assistant and administrative right hand at the Det. He'd only known her a couple of weeks, but she was so efficient it annoyed him. Her attitude was an eclectic mix of confidence—bordering on cocky—and humility. He never knew which one he'd get. But when he had shown up as squadron commander on the first day, centered on the red mahogany desk was a new eight-by-ten photo of Lori. It seemed Grace had his back.

"We're OK," he told her. "Lori's alive, but took a round through the calf."

"Damn it. Sorry to hear. She enduring it OK?"

"Pissed at first, but now just exhausted."

"Hate to be the one to say it, but you're active. Get your ass to work."

Red sat on the toilet seat. "I was told we'd be dark for at least another week. When did it happen?"

"Just came down. You got the notification, right? I logged in and the activation is command level only, plus the liaisons. You need me to come in, too?"

"So...it may not be an op."

"Not yet, from what little the order said." A baby's cry rang in the background. She whispered, "But it's no coincidence you're active right after all hell breaks loose on you two. You need me?"

"Please."

"I'm already dressed. Be there in half an hour."

Red slipped the phone into his jeans pocket, angry he'd answered it. The Det could manage a few hours without him. He needed to stay here with Lori. He opened the bathroom door, casting light across his wife's body, but she didn't move till he picked her hand back up. She started awake. "The gears are already turning. I'm active."

Lori breathed deep, then closed her eyes again and laid her head to one side. "Might be for the good. If it's about whoever took a crack at me, you've got my blessing. Don't come back till they're dead. Them, and whatever other sonsofbitches..." Her lips moved, but nothing more came out. He bent and pressed his against them, then opened the curtain. He nodded to a bulky tan-suited man and squatty woman, similarly appointed, two pillars standing outside the hospital room door. He pulled the lever below the disinfectant bottle with a squeak and worked the liquid between his knuckles as he stormed down the hall.

# Chapter 14 – Capacitors

*Beijing, China. Present day.*

A cold morning mist wet Zhāng Dàwe's cheek. The Chinese man stepped out of the JAC truck into a shallow puddle. A splash of muddy water flew toward a guard in green fatigues, a subdued red star on each shoulder. It fell short. Damn.

His trick knee locked. Stumbling, he braced the other leg in time to catch himself. The guard lifted a corner of a blue poly tarp stretched across the flatbed, then unhooked a bungee, revealing a pallet of white canisters, each the size of a large can of apples.

The thin, young skin of the guard's forehead wrinkled. "How many of these you need?"

Zhāng looked down. He slid a palm across the edge of the bed rail. "They keep burning up, sir. We figured out it was a design flaw, so the factory gave me all these. Said I was to replace them once a week till they get it right." He counted on his fingers. "The coolers have thirty, so this should last one month. May need more if the factory doesn't get the problem fixed by then." He pointed to a white corrugated-steel warehouse behind a chain-link fence topped with razor wire. "You must run a massive data center with all those coolers. Ever going to let me see inside?"

The guard folded his hands atop the Type 95 assault rifle slung around his neck. "No." He took a step toward Zhāng so they stood toe to toe. His breath smelled of kimchi. "Know your place, old man. No more jokes. Do not ask again."

Zhāng stepped back and bowed. A short man in black suit and glasses climbed into the passenger seat. A new escort, with a chest thick enough to bench-press the truck.

"I can pass?"

The guard lifted another corner of the tarp. "How do I know these are capacitors? Maybe they're something else."

"Pick one up," Zhāng said, smiling, eyes downcast, head bobbing in a mock bow. *Arrogant murderous bastard.*

The guard's hand landed on one of the objects, then reached farther into the pallet and lifted another. He held it before his nose, frowning, as if inspecting grapefruit at the market. "It's light."

Zhāng bobbed his head again. "Yes, yes."

The guard slid a hand under the pallet and lifted the entire side.

"See? Nothing to worry about." *That's right, prick. I'm harmless. Just a senile old man.*

Some years after killing his uncle, Zhāng had begun to have pity for the communists, many of them brainwashed from youth. But at their core they were still the power-lust cadres who'd stolen his family land, humiliated Papa, and destroyed centuries of Chinese progress. Today, most of the population had been lulled into complacency by their overlords loosening their strangle hold of control, but Zhāng was no fool.

Arriving in Beijing at nineteen years of age, he'd worked on an electric components assembly line, clawing his way to supervisor, now even driving a company truck. Surviving through the failure and starvation of the Great Leap Forward taught him to seize *any* opportunity that came. And he had done it yet again, six months ago when approached by an acquaintance with whom he'd often shared a table at lunch. But this man was gregarious, had many friends, and his proposition to Zhāng, somehow, hadn't felt a surprise.

The guard slid the capacitor back into its slot, glanced toward the gatehouse, and lifted a finger. The fence rumbled open. A rock skipped across the pavement, thrown from a tire as Zhāng drove forward.

The escort pointed to a low concrete outbuilding, a brown rust stain streaking down from light boxes mounted on either side of a roll-up door. "Put them out there."

*Careful. Don't show arrogance.* Zhāng cleared his throat. "Sir, the factory says they're burning up from temperature changes. Cracking, and moisture getting in. The temperature in the warehouse is steady. If they aren't kept there, they may be bad by the time I swap them out."

The escort shifted his bulk in the seat. He grumbled.

Zhāng allowed a half smile. "They will fit in the utility area fine. I will make sure of it. There was an empty spot back in the corner, last time I was here." He stopped abreast of heavy double steel doors set in the side of the large warehouse and stepped on the stiff parking brake. "I'll need help carrying the pallet."

The escort held a black radio to one ear, free hand on the warehouse door handle. In a few minutes the heavy slabs swung open, edges notched to overlap. Zhāng carried one side of the pallet, pointing with his jutted chin to a wooden spool as tall as he. Though light, the pallet's sharp edge dug into the calloused skin of his palms. "Let's put it over there, behind that reel of feed cable."

The escort was carrying the other side of the pallet with one hand. "There's already a tray of them there."

"Yes. Those are the faulty ones. They go back to the factory in a few weeks."

They lowered the wooden pallet atop the other. Though the "faulty" ones worked just fine, as anyone with a multimeter could verify. But Zhāng knew no one would bother. He rubbed at the red lines in his palms and stepped over an extension cord on the way to the door.

Outside, he bent his neck in a small bow. "Thank you. It'll take a few hours to replace the ones on the roof. You're welcome to watch."

"Come see me on your way out," the man said. He turned and, crunching gavel beneath heavy steps, strode toward the front gate.

Zhāng pulled keys from his pocket and unlocked a tool crib on the side of the truck. He lifted its lid and ducked below to shield his eyes from the brilliant sun. Every peg held its appropriate hand tool, most with outlines sketched in black onto the white wall. He slipped his fingers into rubber insulated gloves and pulled supple leather sleeves up to his shoulders. The suede rawhide smelled like his childhood donkey, Tiny, after a day's work in the rice fields. Unhooking a tie-down from the toolbox, he lifted it from its bracketed resting place.

Only a few more weeks of putting up with these dogs. They filled their bellies from the efforts of others and lapped at the sweat of their struggle.

He stepped toward a steel ladder scaling the building's side. Fingers wrapped around a steel rung as he started up.

# Chapter 15 – No Body

Carter flashed a sheriff's detective badge to a young, thin-faced officer standing inside yellow barrier tape stretched between a light pole and trash can, blocking one end of the parking lot of Alessandro's Italian Restaurant. Carter flipped the wallet shut and slipped it inside the chest pocket of a brown Theory trench coat. He stepped quickly, trying to look aloof and official. The officer didn't stop him. Carter tugged on the ends of a black-plaid Saks Fifth Avenue cashmere scarf, snugging it around his neck, and tucked them back inside the breast flaps.

As he walked, he lifted his phone and pressed the button his daughter had shown him. In his sleep-induced haze after Red had woken him with a call, he'd left home forgetting to grab his regular camera. He pointed the device at the rear plate of a white van. The flash fired and the picture appeared in the corner of the screen. Looked like he'd done it right.

"Hey!" came a shout near the front of the van. A few seconds later a short, white-haired man with a ponytail down the back of his green jacket stepped around the bumper. He squared up to Carter. "Who you?"

The scratchy voice was distantly familiar. Carter tried to pull up an association but failed. "Detective Carter."

The man grunted. "Who you with?"

*Shit.* "Sheriff's Department. New Kent County."

"What the hell you doing on my scene?" The man glanced at the tall junior officer standing next to the trash can, who'd recently turned his back and now appeared to be instructing civilians outside the police line to step back, though they were already well clear.

Time to see how elastic truth could be. "I'm working an investigation involving the lady who was shot here, and her husband. He called me from the hospital and told me what happened. That's why I'm here."

He pointed with yellowed fingernails. "Already working an investigation? You working with the feds?"

*Damn. How'd he guess that one?* This could go either way. "Yes."

"Some Agent Jackson from FBI told me they were taking over. You can take your needs up with that jackass when he gets here. Until then, this is my scene and you can walk your ass back outside that line."

A memory surfaced of running after hound dogs, the animals yelping and baying in delight. They'd been chasing a scent, bounding through green briars, ignoring the way the tiny daggers tore their ears. Carter snapped his fingers. "The Hastings case."

Ponytail scowled. "What about it?"

"You were there when we ran the dogs. Hastings came through our county's backyard. You guys didn't have dogs. I'm the one that got some for you. We used deer hounds."

"And they flushed fifty bucks before they got to Hastings."

Carter snorted. "But they got him."

"And I got sick as hell from running five hours and wading creeks and getting bit by everything with teeth. I pulled ticks off me for a week."

"But you got Hastings."

Ponytail glanced back at the tall rookie, who was still pretending to perform crowd control. He eyed Carter. Through clenched teeth he said, "What you want?"

"I won't touch a thing. Just some pictures and a few questions."

The man pointed across the dim lot to a stout uniformed woman leaning against a blue RV. "Check in with Cindy. Then only talk with me. Got it? I'll give you three minutes; then you're outside till the feds get here."

Right. He'd be gone by the time any of them arrived.

He walked toward Cindy, but Ponytail turned his back when someone approached him. Carter passed by the officer and pretended to throw something away in the trash can behind her, then returned to the van. Couldn't afford to have any record of his visit.

The vehicle was new, its paint still glossy. Carter snapped a photo of the VIN through the cracked windshield. The vehicle had hit a gray sedan squarely, pushing it down until the front of the van was wedged off the ground by the car's bumper. Blood was smeared on the sedan's hood, and remnants of bandage packaging evidenced EMTs had worked on someone there. A body slumped on the ground behind a green Dumpster and another lay on the pavement next to the car, black-bladed hunting knife still wrapped in its fingers. A bleached-blond boy with acne gripped a camera in one hand and chalked a line around the body with the other.

"Only two?" Carter asked.

Ponytail nodded. "And two still alive. Barely."

"The driver of the van?"

"Yeah. EMTs took him to the hospital."

"But he was dead."

Ponytail regarded him. "Explain."

"I mean, the victim, her husband, he said the driver of the van was dead."

Ponytail flipped open a notepad. "Probably never seen a dead man before. This husband. He is..."

Marksman not dead? Red could have missed it, Lori being shot and everything else going on. But he'd said he had his hands inside Marksman's gut, pinching off an artery. No way he could have survived. Carter considered his response. "He's a fed, a special ops unit."

The man's book snapped shut. "Well then, you guys deserve what you get. Enjoy your little incestuous investigation. Three minutes are up."

"Which hospital did they take him to?"

"Rappahannock. Same as your *victim*."

\* \* \* \*

Carter stepped from darkness onto the lit curb next to Rappahannock General Hospital's emergency room. His watch read 3:00 a.m. He trotted quickly, squinting at a bright light cast from the entry canopy. A red LED above sliding glass doors flashed as they opened. The ER desk attendant glanced his way, then back to a computer screen shining green upon her pink face. Her plump figure suggested she seldom raised herself from the chair. "Can I help you?" she asked, her gaze still on the screen.

Carter put his badge on the counter. "I'm here to see Mar... I mean, I'm here to check on three of tonight's patients."

She swiveled toward him and studied his badge. "The shootout?" she said with bright eyes.

"Yes."

She leaned toward him, then peeked behind her. "One's in surgery. You won't be able to ask him anything tonight. Maybe not never. The lady, they took her down the end of the second floor. I think she's a politician, 'cause they got all kinds of guys with radios and thick chests that way."

Carter grinned, having seen a couple of black Ford vans in the lot that screamed CIA. This lady was being entirely too helpful. "And the other?"

"The other..." She glanced behind again, then whispered. "The other was dead on arrival." She sat back down with a smile and a nod.

Yeah. Probably dead when he was picked up. "Can I speak with the doctor who attended him?"

"Not till he's out of surgery. He's working on the live one. The man's busted up worse than a motorcycle accident."

"I need to see the body."

She leaned back, and air hissed from the cushion. "I can't say no more, 'less my boss say so."

"No problem. You don't need to say anything. Point me to someone who can show it to me."

"This time of night? Ain't nobody."

"Well, the corpse isn't sitting behind your desk. Someone wheeled it to the morgue, right? Let me talk with that guy."

She crossed her arms and glanced at the computer screen. "You doin' an investigation, like on TV?"

"Yeah. Like on TV. Except I'm for real. And I know what the hell I'm doing."

When she laughed, a silver necklace with a small cross bounced atop a round belly. Put a white beard on her and she could be a shopping mall Santa. Her lips pursed. "I like you." She lifted a receiver and punched buttons.

Previously jovial and bright, she dropped her tone as she spoke into the phone. "Rodney, he still here? Yeah. Uh-huh. Tell him get his skinny ass up here. K? Thanks, sweetness." She hung up and glanced at him again, the smile of Mrs. Claus returning to her lips. "He'll be here. I helped you out. You remember that in your report. OK?"

"K."

* * * *

The cargo elevator clattered to an abrupt halt and Rodney led Carter out. The janitor's soles didn't leave the floor as he shuffled down a bright, white-walled hallway. Not even a picture hung from its concrete blocks. Carter had wondered why a custodian would deliver bodies to a morgue, but next to the elevator had been Rodney's picture on a 30 years of service citation. After that long, the man probably had all kinds of additional duties tacked onto his job description. He pushed through swinging doors into a tight room. A single stainless autopsy table stood center.

Carter's first breath brought the heavy scent of bleach. "You guys don't do much volume here, I suppose."

"Don't have nuthin' to compare ta. We's gets busy sometimes, 'round full moons." A sideways glance. "It's tomorrow, you know."

"What is?"

"Da full moon. Dat's why."

"Why what?"

"Why—you know—we got dis guy. Da crazies come out in da full moon." He pushed open a blue metal door and swung his head in a *this way* motion. "He's in here. Dis is jus where dey do da cuttin'."

The morgue was one of the smaller ones Carter had visited. Six chest-high cream-colored coolers lined one wall. The doors on mortuary refrigerators looked like miniature versions of a walk-in freezer for an ice cream shop he'd worked at as a teenager.

Rodney yanked on a handle and rolled out a gurney. A white sheet covered the form of a corpse, shorter than Carter would have expected, smelling of sweaty socks. Rodney flipped the cover back revealing a pale, fat foot with a card tied to a toe.

"Dis da one."

"You sure?"

"Yep. His foot was stickin' out da blanket jus like dat. His little piggy don't got no toenail. I's da one put him in here," he said, patting the face of the cooler, "in ol' number tree."

Carter gently lifted the sheet. The head was crowned with a freckled bald spot surrounded by white stubble. Skin tone looked about midfifties, pale as milk, except for the jaundiced yellow-green hue that comes with death. But Marksman was tall, with a build like a track runner, and midtoned black skin.

"You sure this is the one?"

"Yes, sir. He da man."

"Let's check the others, just to be sure."

Rodney stared at him with suspicion, then slowly pushed the gurney back into the cooler. The others were empty except one that housed a white-haired elderly woman.

"Rodney, I'm going to ask one more time, just to be sure there's not been any mix-up." Carter paused for effect. "If there has been a mix-up, now would be the time to find out." He tapped on cooler three. "Is this the man that came in tonight from the shooting?"

Rodney waved dismissively. "I tellin' da truth. Dat's da man. Came in right after da first poor fella. I's upstairs when dey came."

"He didn't come in *with* the first man?"

"No, sir. Different crew. Few minutes later."

Carter studied the janitor, but couldn't pick up even a hint of elusiveness. No gestures indicating self-consciousness. Steady eye contact. No warning flags. Even if he strapped him to the autopsy table and started tearing off fingernails, he'd probably get the same answers. "The ambulance crew. You mentioned a separate one. You see them?"

"Yeah."

"You know most crews?"

"Don't know none. 'Cept my cousin's. But I know faces good 'nuf."

"You recognize these men, the ones that brought in this body?"

Rodney studied ceiling tiles and scratched his neck. "I was runnin' the Zamboni whens dey came." The janitor held up fists like he was riding a bike. "Dat's what I calls it. It cleans da floor. I walked over to see what da commotion was 'bout. I never seen da crew."

"When did you get called to take the man to the morgue?"

"Not long after. Few minutes. Dey tried zappin' him, but I heard..." He looked as if he were contemplating his next words, then reached for a light switch. "I gotta get back ta work."

"What did you hear?"

Rodney shook his head. "I ain't no snitch."

Carter leaned on the jamb, blocking the exit. "Rodney, several folks died tonight. I haven't seen anything wrong with the way the hospital handled itself. No one's going to get in trouble. Tell me what you heard."

The custodian straightened and, to Carter's surprise, pushed him aside with a firm hand as he scooched feet back through the autopsy room and toward the hall. "Don't need no threats, mister. I tell da truth. I heard a nurse woman say dis man look already been dead awhile. She ask a doc why da crew said he still alive. But dey gone."

Carter stepped quickly to keep up, through swinging doors and out again into the bright hall. Rodney was sliding along at a good pace now. "Can you take me to your security office—where I can look at the video of the entrance?"

The man stopped suddenly and Carter almost ran into his back. Rodney looked over a shoulder. "You better have a warrant you see dat witch." He glided a few more paces, then added, "And a cross and a wooden stake."

# Chapter 16– Higher Approval

A millimeter wave scan complete, Red pushed through a heavy steel door into the Det's marble and mahogany foyer, which was dark as the night outside. A single light glowed dimly from a corner, silhouetting an ever-present Marine guard in battle rattle.

Grace stepped into a hallway between cubes a couple of paces ahead. Tight black skirt, immaculate starched white blouse buttoned halfway. The only evidence she'd been pulled from bed at 3:00 a.m. were a few stray salt-and-pepper wisps jutting from unswept bangs.

She waved Red back. "You're in the command center."

Halfway down the hall, she grabbed Red's elbow and pulled him to a stop. Dusting off his sweater, she said, "Langley was online when I got here a minute ago. Washington is going to join you. So I'll leave you to your vices. Lori still OK?"

Her flowery perfume mixed with the scent of new carpet. "Good as can be expected. We have a new CIA liaison yet?"

"Michele Brooks." She tweezed with fingernails across his chest, picking at something. The lady's concept of personal space was smaller than Red's. "You look like this army captain I used to date, after he'd come back from downrange. Dried mud on your sweater."

He glanced down. "That's not mud."

"Oh." Grace flushed. "Sorry."

"Agent Brooks...is she active?"

"As of last week."

Fantastic. He'd interviewed three replacements for his CIA liaison as first order of business after assuming command. Surprised the CIA had given him a choice. Two candidates had been lifers, but Brooks was even older, close to sixty. She'd been in the field when Gorbachev took down the wall. Cranky, and connected as hell, and a bit overweight. Two husbands had lost out to her devotion to the company. She had been his first choice. "Great. Give her a call and—"

Grace pointed at the open doorway. "You'll be able to talk to her yourself in a few."

Red started for the door, then stopped. "Off the record. When I left the hospital, CIA was going to move Lori somewhere. Forgot to verify before I ran out. Do me a favor. I wanna know for certain where they're taking her."

She turned away, heels already tapping back to her desk. "On it."

Red stepped into the room, or *fusion cell* as everyone referred to it, despite the white Command Center stenciled on its gray door. Inside were three rows of empty desks and screens, enough for thirty techs if needed, with seats around the outside to handle twice that. Seldom were more than a handful ever present, though. The floor echoed hollowly and seemed to bounce underfoot. Two IT guys studying screens on one side turned to look at him. One had the sagging eye pouches of a bloodhound, accentuated by thick-rimmed glasses. The other was all smiles. Evidence of burnt coffee hung in the air from a commercial brewer in a corner.

Captain Richards stood, rustling starched pixilated blue fatigues. An overhead light shone off a bald head mounted to a thick neck. With the Wyoming native's bulging forehead and flat nose, his expression resembled the face of a buffalo. Fitting, since before he joined the military, he'd lived on a farm where they raised the animals. Thus far, the man had proven to be as hearty as the beast.

"As you were. We online?"

The happy technician leaned back in his chair. "Langley only, for now. Even there, we're still looking at an empty room." He picked up a phone and glanced at the screen. "Washington will join at 0330."

Richards sat stiffly upright at a low conference table near the front of the room. "You OK, sir? I mean...your wife?" His brow knitted, deepening the buffalo resemblance.

"She's shaken. And pissed. Considering everything, I'm happy with pissed." Red rubbed at blood in the lifeline of his palm, stirring a scent of raw steak that hand sanitizer wasn't able to cover. Was it Lori's or Marksman's? Thank God she was OK. But shit, Marksman... Why had he been following them? How had he known a hit was planned?

The room darkened with a flicker of movement on one of the large screens. Two blue suits moved in and sat behind coffee mugs, one of the cups steaming profusely.

Red scowled toward the techs and whispered, "We on video? Who called for that?"

The bright-eyed one said, "Nope. We're still dark. But Higher requested this one visual."

"Keep us dark. No video out till my say-so."

The man turned with a grin. "Roger that."

The wall behind the suits on the screen was sterile white. No pictures. No windows. No sounds except a squeaking chair spring as one pulled at his starched collar. A *clean room*, they called it.

The agent behind the steaming mug sat tall with olive skin, slanted almond eyes, and flat features. Korean in the bloodline, no doubt. Voice with a lisp. "Morning gentlemen. Major, sorry to hear about your issue tonight."

Red sat and flipped on a pencil-shaped table mic. "And you are?"

"Agent Mark Young. I know you usually work through your liaison, now Agent Brooks. I'm her boss. Think of me as her handler. We're on the same team, protecting our asset in the Det."

Red had sat on many of these calls with the previous Det commander. At that time, Red hadn't worried much of the politics, power struggles, and pissing contests that arose among the co-ops of a fusion cell. Each one seemed to think they should run the Det. But the building was Langley Air Force Base property, technology systems courtesy of Joint Communications Unit and CIA, weapons systems from all branches, and a few home grown—staff from the four corners. A fusion cell spoken into existence at the unofficial request of the Joint Chiefs, operationally controlled by Joint Special Operations Command, funded by the co-ops, and begrudgingly tolerated by all. Today it was up to Red to hold it together, to be the tight cord running between theory and firing pins, politicians and snake eaters.

And now this shithead of an agent thought the Det was a CIA asset? Was he weaseling for position, sensing a weakness with the recent change in leadership? A man who knew nothing of blood on his hands? Not from an enemy of the state, or a dead comrade. And certainly not his wife.

Across the table, Richards shrugged, buffalo jowls widening in a grin. He didn't seem put off by the agent's presumptiveness. The Det had worked closely with CIA Special Operations Group, Red considered. Maybe Agent Young had made an honest slip, though a Freudian one. "I got no idea who you are. So nothing till I talk with Agent Brooks."

"I'm here, Major," came a raspy female voice from the speakers, as if she'd already been through half a pack of menthols.

The dog-eyed tech pounded a keyboard, nodding his head, indicating voiceprint ID'd positive. Then, a thumbs-up, signifying no measurable sign of duress.

Brooks stepped between the two men on-screen, bending to look into the camera. No makeup, hair scraped back in a ponytail. Pink sweats, though wide hips suggested she didn't do much sweating. With a familiar scowl, she scrunched her nose as she said, "Good morning." A *safe* signal.

"Brooks, I don't like talking to your superiors. Going forward, I want your beautiful face to be the only CIA I ever see." Did he just call Brooks *beautiful*?

Her whiskey laugh ended in a smoker's cough. "Understood. But given the circumstances, this will be expedient. Oh—and I just spoke with Grace. We're taking Lori to Hopkins."

Red lifted his chin. "Get me up to date before Washington's online. Why are we here? The hit?"

"Got a guest with us this morning." She laid a hand on the shorter suit's shoulder. Female, olive complexion, black hair, tight curls, dark eyebrows. Jacket fabric stiff and shiny, like clothes Carter would wear. Sitting at the table, she resembled a news anchor, an attractive one. The yin to Brooks' yang. She removed her designer glasses, slipping them into an inside pocket like a Bollywood actor. She was Mossad, for certain.

"Hopefully she'll enlighten us," Brooks coughed.

"You don't know?" Red asked.

"We're working out the story now."

He shivered as he pushed away from the table. "Gentlemen, I don't want to be in on your internal machinations. My wife's been shot. I'm not intel. That's your department. Figure out what needs broken, then give us a call and we'll propose an op to Higher."

"You've got intel officers on staff," Agent Young's lisp broke in. His Adam's apple bobbed like a soap bubble. "Fifteen, if I remember. Most donated from my organization. You can try to play the *I'm-not-intel* card. But you are, even if only a mutt." He bared his teeth. "Though a devilishly mean one."

Red stared at the screen. Seriously? This guy the best they had?

Brooks quickly rasped, as if to cut off Red's objection. "Major, we'll be receiving a tasking once Higher gets on the other line."

A blurred figure crossed the screen of an adjoining monitor and sat behind a mahogany desk in a similar clean room. Once seated, the image sharpened, revealing Admiral Javlek's narrow gaze and hard jaw. Weathered skin from earlier staff photos was now pale and sallow. As if the last year inside the Beltway had been more taxing than all his duty tours at sea. He neither leaned forward confidently, nor slumped back in apprehension. The perfect political neutral.

A cough. Then Javlek said, "Morning, gentlemen. I was told the Det was also online. I'm only seeing Langley at the moment."

"We're here, sir." Red glanced at the bright-eyed computer geek. "Tech issue. Audio only from our end right now, but we can proceed."

"Right. J2 gave me the thumbnail of the assassination attempt a half hour ago. CIA set this call up. I'm here to provide approval on a proposal. Correct?"

"Yes, sir," Young lisped. "CIA believes we know the source of an internal leak. A mole responsible for providing financial intelligence to China. Specifically key specifications on the new US hundred-dollar bill."

Javlek leaned forward. "These folks also responsible for tonight's hit? Sloppy as hell."

*Let the man talk,* Red thought.

The skin around Young's thumbs wrinkled as he linked his hands tight. "They're connected, sir. I'll give the sixty-thousand-foot view, then fill in the details. China has an unofficial but legal underground banking system called *fie chen.* Undocumented. Deposit in one place, receive a chit. Present the chit elsewhere, usually another country, and withdraw. It has legitimate uses, but most aren't. Money laundering tops the list.

"Sources in-country indicate North Korea has started production of an accurate counterfeit US hundred-dollar bill. Over sixty percent of legit US hundreds are circulated outside our borders. Korea has long been a source of counterfeit currency. But this new one causes greater concern. We've sourced samples. To say the least, they're good."

Javlek brushed a palm across the desk's surface, as if dusting. "Describe good."

"Convincing enough to get past most screenings. It's no small matter to manufacture, especially on a large scale. They've had a head start, help, probably for some time now. The microprint was flawless, the paper indistinguishable. Ink formulations were not completely accurate, which was the only way we determined the counterfeit. We believe China supplied the press, but the technical specs were leaked."

Red rubbed his neck. Surely this guy would get to the point. He checked his watch. He'd left Lori only an hour earlier. *Hope she's getting sleep. Wish she could hear this, too.* She was fintel. Maybe that was how this North Korean counterfeiting operation fitted in. He thought about mentioning the connection, but didn't, remembering her admonition to not speak of her CIA job. But these guys knew who the hell she was. However, very few in the CIA knew about her investigation. Maybe this would help it, move it along, or plug the leak altogether.

He straightened in his chair, careful to listen.

Young continued. "In the past, North Korea printed counterfeit money and deposited it into *fie chen*. *Fie chen* loaned the money to Chinese businesses. These paid back the loans with interest. Proceeds were split among the three parties. China has access to cheap cash without having to dirty their hands."

"But China is an economic ally," Javlek interrupted. "Hell, they own half the US. Why hurt their investment?"

Young jerked his chin at Bollywood Mossad. She pushed her mug to the side. "If I may..." she said. "At first we thought this the act of a few smaller parties, unconcerned with the greater good of China. But then our sources in-country discovered a more coordinated effort. Their Ministry of Intelligence is performing a balancing act, ensuring the counterfeit flow is steady, enough to provide benefit, but not so much it would harm Chinese interests. We have no indication the conspiracy stretches into the People's Bank of China. They would never approve. And since China is the largest holder of US debt, it's like they're buying the US, slowly, for free. Since it's orchestrated by the Ministry of Intelligence, I don't consider it economic terrorism, but economic warfare. The US versus your largest economic ally."

Javlek stared at the camera and yawned. "So why am I here?"

"We're proposing a solution," Young murmured. "One that includes US military assets."

# Chapter 17 – Turning

*Kanggye, North Korea*

Ko followed the shopkeeper toward what looked to be a closet in a wall of the small North Korean black market coat store. A worn push broom leaned beside it. The man closed a plywood door behind them with layers of thick brown corrugated cardboard stapled to its back. Was he keeping heat in, or preventing sound from bleeding out? Inside was a small room that smelled of kerosene soot. The tiny yellowed heater stood in one corner opposite blue and green plastic tubs with sleeves and socks overflowing.

The man had lost his meekness. Stern eyes studied Ko. "You followed?"

"Followed?" Ko had walked his regular route, but hadn't thought to worry about that. "No...not that I know of."

The man huffed, and his voice deepened. "You need to watch now. Check behind. Remember faces. But give the political police no reason for suspicion. When do you start at Hwasong?"

The mention of his next assignment shook Ko from self-condemnation. "Next week. We're leaving the day after tomorrow."

"This is the last time we meet. You'll be contacted at Hwasong."

"By who?"

"You won't know."

He frowned. "Why not?"

"That's the way it's done. Better for you, too."

Maybe no one was actually going to contact him. Maybe Soo Jin got a government job in Kimchaek after all. She'd always done well in school. Maybe she'd been recruited by the secret police and they were testing him to see if he'd betray his country. "You never told me how she broke the heel off her uniform shoes."

"She didn't. You did." The shopkeeper made a hammering motion with his arm. "She said you used her shoe to drive a nail in your front steps. The next day, the heel fell off at morning muster."

Ko's neck eased. Soo Jin had given the right answer. As long as he trusted her, he could trust this man as well. She'd protected him so many times growing up. She'd still do it now, wouldn't she? He grabbed a wooden folding chair leaning against the wall, thinking he'd like to sit, but the seat fell to the floor. "How will I be contacted?"

"I don't know. Just go to Hwasong. Give them no reason to doubt your loyalty. Be ready for the contact. Follow instructions perfectly. You'll get your sister out of the camp, and they'll bring you out of the country."

"What? But...where?"

"Not your concern. But it'll be a better place than here."

The scarf around Ko's neck was so tight it itched. He pressed his fingertips against a rickety card table, top torn and sunken in the middle. "There is nowhere better than here. We can stay in-country. Anywhere with a harbor. I know how to fish. I have money saved. They won't find us."

His sister had spoken of other places with plenty of food. And medicine for many sicknesses. Again, he'd always forbidden her to mention it. Lies from enemies.

"Too much to explain now. You've decided to help your sister. This is how it's done. Both of you will be better off in the end." He stuck his head out the door, then shut the door again. "But they will require something for getting the two of you to safety."

Ko's fingers balled into fists. "I'm not going to prostitute my sister!"

The man's lip curled into a sneer. "No. Not that."

"Nor my daughter!"

The man waved toward the ground, a warning. "Quiet! Or we'll both be at Hwasong, inside the fence. Listen, you're going to drive a truck. With some men in it."

Ko's pacing foot hit a long black tire iron propped against a plastic tub. He flinched as it clattered to the floor. "Where? What kind of men?"

"*Sangsa*, you don't ask questions. You'll be driving a truck with men in back. Go where they tell you. Whoever contacts you will explain what you need to know. It isn't risky...if you follow instructions. If you don't, you'll join your sister on the inside. If you do, you'll save her from a wasting death and be able to nurse her back to health."

"And my daughter. These men, they'll take my daughter along, too. My parents and wife are dead. They take all three of us, or none."

The shopkeeper's lips drew tight. "So be it."

\* \* \* \*

Agent Young's shoulders had started to droop a half hour earlier, Red observed, as someone offscreen passed the man yet another refill in a maroon Virginia Tech Hokie mug. He took a swallow and continued. "The FBI has been surveilling the fed for two years, trying to determine where the leak originates. They recently intercepted communications indicating the mole is meeting with North Korea's Ministry of State Security, at their insistence, at the counterfeit printing facility. We're requesting approval on a covert military action to eliminate the mole, destroy the production facility and the Ministry of State Security's data center. They're colocated in Chŏngjin, North Korea."

Javlek glanced off camera. "Still haven't told me why I should care. Or why I want to take out their data center."

"During surveillance of the fed, the FBI initially got nothing. But we now know the mole is not in the fed, but within the borders of the CIA, stealing info from the fed and leaking it to North Korea. At the same time, Mossad has been investigating a separate, related leak. Stay with us a couple minutes, sir, and it'll be clear how your interests are involved."

Bollywood Mossad remained stone faced. "Our leak was resolved a couple hours ago. Both Mossad and the Det utilized a freelance agent, Jordan Leman. At one time he was Russian FSB, even KGB decades ago, though not born within their borders. He retired and posed as an international businessman, fifty-six years old, black. We used him sparingly, buying humint only, but I understand the Det used him to a greater extent." One eye opened wide. "As an operator, for language skills, I believe."

Red pressed his elbows onto the hard table. His calves started to jitter as he listened to this crap. "You talking about Marksman?"

Young nodded. "I believe that's what you called him."

*Yeah. Whatever.* "You think he was a leak? The reason someone took a shot at my wife tonight? That's bullshit."

Young's hands slid a paper to the side. "We have surveillance confirmation."

"Don't care what you've got." Red pushed away from the table and stood. "He was a solid operator. Several of my team, myself included, owe our lives to the man."

Young held his palms toward the camera. "He was only doing what was in his own interest. He played you, for years. Then betrayed you."

Red clenched fists, pacing behind his chair. "No. Marksman would never—"

Javlek slapped the table. "Major, *quiet!* Agent Young, stop wasting my time. Get to the purpose of this damn call."

As an operator, Red had never been concerned with Marksman's true identity. He'd been cleared as an asset, so that was someone else's job. Sure, he was probably a spook of some flavor, but he'd saved Red's life on their first op in Brazil, and he'd trusted him implicitly ever since. Now he'd saved his life again, at the cost of his own.

Young continued. "The CIA utilized Marksman just like Mossad. He provided humint only. He had no access to anything deeper. But he sold the intel gathered from his experiences with the Det to China, then to North Korea not long ago after the Det blew up their newest ballistic missile, the KN-08, on the test pad. Thus the Det is compromised with both China and North Korea."

Javlek leaned in. "So you're proposing..."

"A joint op. To erase any records leaked, and destroy North Korea's counterfeit capabilities at the same time. The CIA will take care of China. The Det can handle North Korea. We will execute simultaneous strikes on three Chinese data centers. All fintel leaked was electronic. Each center backs up to the other two. Hit all three, they'll have nothing left. It'll take five or six years to fully recover."

Javlek furrowed his brow. "You're asking me to authorize an op to blow up the entire data system of China's Ministry of Intelligence?"

"No, sir." Young tapped his chest. "CIA takes those. All three will be hit by electromagnetic pulse—an EMP—erasing the data. We already had a solution in place for this eventuality."

Javlek snorted. "Sounds like a convenient excuse. The CIA's been waiting for this opportunity?"

Young allowed a small, tight smile. "We're only seeking your approval on the Det striking North Korea's Ministry of State Security facility in Chŏngjin. Where the mole is scheduled to make the final transaction. The MSS keeps things centralized. They don't have funds, like China's Ministry of Intelligence, to run three data centers. Just one in Chŏngjin. The printing facility is in the same complex. So, we'll erase any leaked records of the Det, and take out their counterfeit abilities at the same time."

"And why kill the mole? Why not grab him?"

"I never said it was a *he*, sir."

"Don't deflect the question."

"US Code allows the death penalty for treason, sir."

"But with a trial. Innocent until proven guilty, Agent Young."

He shrugged. "The mole being on-site, treason is certain. It's the act of a single party. Eliminating them would be...much less painful than the alternative. The CIA's action in China will go forward regardless of your decision. We're simply requesting your approval for a discreet Det op. If a CIA mole is killed in the process, that would be most delightful. The Det has previously proven their ability to operate within those borders. With this action, the effects of the leaks, through CIA and through Marksman, will be alleviated."

# Chapter 18 – Locker

Carter laid Marksman's black battle dress uniform on the polished gray concrete floor of the Det's cavernous hangar on the far side of Langley Air Force Base. He ran thick fingers across the fabric, smoothing out wrinkles. The knees were threadbare, faded. He glanced up at Red standing a few feet away, eyes swollen and pink. He appeared worn as thin as Marksman's pants. "You look like hell."

Red rubbed the bottom of his nose with a knuckle. "Maybe. But I can get a shower and some sleep. At least I'm not plain ugly."

Carter snorted. "You're a dick."

"And you're a Wop with a subscription to *GQ*."

Touché. At least the man still had a sense of humor, considering his wife was just shot and he'd lost a close friend, a comrade in arms.

The hangar's ceiling towered a hundred feet up. This visit, two Bell V-22 Ospreys and a single MH-60 Pave Hawk sat at one end, raptors at rest. The old girl Sikorsky MH-53 Pave Low still sat in its corner. The building was so vast it still seemed empty. The locker he'd rifled through was bolted to the hangar's concrete block wall.

Red glanced around, as if to make sure they were alone. Apparently satisfied, he said, "Just got out of a meeting with Higher, FBI, and Mossad. Long night." He relayed Mossad's accusations that Marksman had been a mole, then pointed to the uniform. "What are *you* looking for?"

Carter sat back on his haunches. "I'm looking for...well, I don't know. Anything. A clue. I'm starting with the basics. You knew Marksman best, so tell me if you see anything here that says who he was. You pull his file yet?"

Red jerked a thumb over one shoulder. "Grace is working on it. So his body never made it to the hospital?"

Red turned away from the monitor and folded his arms. "Why don't you know who the mole is?"

"Short answer: well trained. A skilled field asset based on how they've covered their tracks."

The allegations against Marksman were crap. Except...Young had said they had surveillance confirmation. But why would he give his life to save Lori and himself just a few hours earlier? A change of heart? What had Marksman meant by saying, *Lori's not the enemy*? His head throbbed and he rubbed temples. Marksman was an operator, and you always trust your team.

Still, if the Det could pull off the op, it could mean no more threat to his family. "Sir, we can be discreet. If you approve, we'll get this done without any trace left behind. Agent Young is right. If they take care of China, the Det can take care of North Korea." Red hoped Javlek would accept such an arrogant statement, considering he hadn't even looked at a map to see where Chŏngjin was.

Javlek massaged between his eyebrows with a thumb, pinching and yanking, as if pulling a hair from the root. He swept his hands across the desk. "Fine. But I want final approval on your mission plan." He leaned into the camera. "Major, your predecessor and I had a unique relationship. I loved the man, but also fantasized about killing the prima donna. His saving grace was he confided everything about the Det to me. *Everything.* If you're to enjoy the same free-range discretion, I expect that transparency to continue." He slammed a fist on the crimson surface, not as hard this time. "The geezer was past his prime. Got himself killed. Had a nasty habit of leading his own ops, and I hear you're cut from the same cloth. This is one op you're not attending. Stay home. Take care of your family."

Javlek stood and walked out of the camera's view. A door latch opened and the screen went black.

Red's *predecessor*, as Javlek had called him, had been a close friend, Colonel Jim Mayard. To be certain, titling him a prima donna wasn't far from the truth. He had been a sonofabitch, but he also got things done. He'd use any tactic at his disposal to accomplish a mission, even blackmail. Stay home? Yeah, right. Red had learned from Jim taking care of family often meant getting dirty.

"No. The corpse I saw belonged to some midfifties lawyer. Died of a heart attack. I even made sure the patients didn't get switched around at the hospital by accident. The live one in the operating room was a young guy. Looked kinda Mexican. Not Marksman, for sure. Won't be able to talk with him for at least a week, if he lives. I also reviewed the hospital's security camera footage."

His neck twitched in an involuntary shiver. The janitor had warned him about the night security manager, but seeing her had introduced him to a whole new realm of creepy. Face pale as milk, crew-cut jet-black hair. In her dim office in a video monitor's glow, at least a dozen studs had shimmered from her lips and eyebrows and ears. Still, all had gone well till she'd caught his gaze and straightened, arching her back, exposing the clear outline of nipple rings beneath a tight black shirt. "Need anything else?" she'd asked, tongue flicking out to lick the corner of her mouth.

Carter had snatched the stack of DVDs off her desk and was halfway down the hall when he'd run into the janitor again. His expression must've told the story. The man had leaned on his mop and grinned. "Guess you forgot yo wooden stake."

Carter brushed out the last wrinkle on the dead man's BDUs. "The officer in charge at the parking lot said Marksman wasn't dead. He claimed EMTs took him to the hospital. We've got witnesses who corroborate the ambulance, but after that his body somehow...vanished."

Carter had even stepped into the fusion cell to track Marksman's tag, a passive, nonelectronic tracking device half the size of a postage stamp. Each operator in the Det had one surgically implanted into the left buttock. The Det could track tags anywhere in the world, with a few exceptions, but now no one could locate Marksman's. "You sure he was dead?" Carter asked.

Red chewed his lower lip. "No pulse. Blew an artery. Amazing the man lasted long enough to say anything. You see all the blood on the ground?"

Carter closed his eyes, imagining the scene again. "I had to step around some that had pooled there, but it wasn't much." He rose, raised his phone, and thumbed the camera icon. The flash fired and he flinched.

Red smiled. "What you trying to do?"

"Look at the photos I took last night."

Red snatched it from his hands. "Gimme that thing." He pressed the screen a few times and the flash burst again. "Shit." His lips pressed thin as he fiddled some more. "OK—there. One shot of a license plate, and a bunch of dark ones of the vehicles."

Carter pointed to the one where he'd photographed the VIN. The close-up of the vehicle only took up half the shot. "Look at the asphalt next to the van. That's the bloodstain I was talking about."

Red zoomed in on a dark red puddle. "That's not right. Would the EMTs have cleaned it up?"

"No. If he was alive, they'd be more worried about working to keep him that way."

"The police?"

"It's a crime scene. No one would've touched it."

Red shrugged. "I don't know. It was coming in gushes. It stopped when he died. Maybe his clothes absorbed the rest. Either way, the man was dead as any corpse I've seen."

Red's voice was steady, but his shoulders, always upright and square, drooped. His head was bowed. Never a tall man, but he looked somehow...diminished.

"I've got a lot to follow up on," Carter said. "Review 911 calls. CIA's records. I need a staff. Start with two. I'll take the offices at the end of the hall."

Red held up a hand. "Hold on. Your investigation is under the radar."

Carter pointed to the hangar's towering ceiling. "The Det is on Langley. And Quantico is just around the corner. Get me a special agent from Air Force Office of Special Investigations with a good investigative background. Experienced, but not old school. Someone hardheaded, with an attitude problem. The second can be junior grade. A yes-man."

"How're you gonna keep a lid on this?"

"You're a fusion cell. There aren't two people in the entire building that walk alike. No one will notice." Carter stooped again, straightening the BDUs on the floor. "Lori? She OK?"

Red blinked at him as if coming back from a trance. The man really did need some decent sleep. "I'm a bad husband. My wife gets shot in the calf and I spent the night drafting a mission plan."

Carter stretched a nitrile-gloved hand into the BDU chest pockets. Nothing. Then he checked a cargo pocket and felt the crackle of stiff paper. He pulled out a small scrap of white, a corner torn from a larger piece. On it was printed in black letters: *Pick up the leaf on your way home. Mount one over the headboard. Burn the rest.*

He held it in front of Red's face. "Know what this means?"

A glimmer of recognition flashed across his face. "No. But I've got the same note. It was in my own locker in the armory. Found it not long ago."

"And?"

"Didn't know what it meant, so I threw it away. Thought maybe I'd remember later. Funny, though. My note was in Lori's handwriting. This one isn't."

Carter folded the paper and slipped it into a plastic bag. Lori was wrapped up in Marksman's death deeper than either of them knew, but Red always dismissed the idea. To him, she was faithful, infallible. But she'd only answered just enough of Carter's questions to get by. Typical with agents who had worked in the field. But something had never settled in Carter's gut about her. So that's the way he'd left her, an open file in his mind, set aside till he could find the folder she fit into.

Carter set the boots back in the locker. His back to Red, he closed his eyes. "What did Lori say about the note?"

"What? Oh, I never asked."

Carter whirled about and shoved Red in the chest. "What the hell is your problem? You find a cryptic note in your locker, in her handwriting, then the same note in a dead man's BDUs—a man who died saving *her* just as much as you—and you're not even a little suspicious? Whose side are you on?" He shoved Red again, but this time it felt like pushing against a concrete block wall.

"She's my wife, Carter."

"Yeah. Well, if she was mine, I'd be pruning her fingers with garden shears till she came clean."

"You gotta trust your team."

"Open your eyes, is all I'm saying. Be objective."

Red took a step back, his gaze on the floor, words flat. "I trust her. Why can't you understand that?"

"I swear, you'd make the world's worst detective! How can an operator be such an idiot?" Carter balled up fists, though he had no intention of swinging at the man. "Are you covering for her?"

"What?" Red sneered. "No."

Carter gripped his shirt front. "So help me, if you've got me running this investigation as some diversion, you *will* regret it."

He locked hard into Red's eyes. Still, nothing in the man's manner raised a flag. But no one could be this blind, could they? The fact that Red didn't appear evasive was infuriating. It didn't match the circumstances.

Sergeant Jimmy Crawler stepped from the weight room into the hangar. Shit. This single-digit-IQ, poor excuse for an operator was the last man Carter wanted to tolerate now. In his single prior experience with the Det, the cheap-beer-guzzling lowbrow had been a constant irritant. His belly appeared less expansive now, but it still managed to stretch a large T-shirt that read keep calm and carry guns. His barrel chest seemed to jut a bit farther. Red must've been pressing him to slim down. Carter ignored him, but the stocky New Yorker stepped closer.

"Hey, Major?"

"Piss off, Crawler!" Carter shouted.

"I ain't talkin' to you, G-man."

Red gripped Carter's wrists. "We're fine. Just a chat between friends."

Crawler stepped even closer. His breath was garlic, tomatoes, and stale tobacco. "Youse sure, now? G-man's wrinklin' your shirt, Major."

The grip on Carter's forearms tightened, and pain shot like an ice pick through his funny bone. He let go. His eyes were hot. He turned to Crawler. "I said piss off!"

The man cocked a fist, but Red stepped between them. "Sergeant. Not your fight."

Crawler chewed his unlit stub of a cigar so hard it jerked. At last he stepped away. "Yes, sir." He strolled back toward the weight room, banging a shoulder into Carter, making him stumble. The sergeant lumbered off, the thick flesh of his legs pushing against the other in turn.

Carter massaged his forearms. "I don't even work for the feds anymore and the ignorant bastard still calls me G-man."

Red stooped and swept the BDUs from the floor, hanging them back in the locker. He shut it with a slam. But when he glanced back, he was smiling. He turned toward the front of the building, where the offices were. "If you're done shaking me down, I've got something that might help your investigation."

\* \* \* \*

Red walked through the maze of sterile cubes. Conference tables were surrounded by analysts and operators alike, many still with bed heads firmly in place. Damn good team. The buzz of the area felt comfortable, fitting. Above it all hovered the welcome burnt-molasses scent of Mr. Frank's coffee. He'd be brewing pot after pot of that oily black concoction for the team in chain-smoker succession.

Why was Carter so suspicious, especially of Lori? He seemed convinced she hadn't come completely clean. She was just a CIA analyst working fintel. But he had to concede one point. This time, the wet team had gone for *her*, not Red. And a big part of this op was fintel driven.

He needed to call, let her know what he'd learned in last night's planning session. How Mossad thought Marksman was a leak. Ask her about the note Carter had just found. But he couldn't talk about that stuff by phone, probably not even a secured line.

"Just a sec," he said, holding a finger up to Carter, trailing behind. Red stopped in an empty cube, lifted a receiver, and pressed Lori's mobile number. He could at least ask how her leg felt. The call went straight to voice mail, though. It never did that. *Why'd she turn her phone off now?* They continued toward his office. Grace's voice shook him from his thoughts as they passed her desk.

"Detective. Nice to see you again," she purred. Red glanced back. She was standing, shaking hands with Carter. She must've slipped home last night for a shower because she wore a black blouse now, unbuttoned further than most women in the office wore. Thick salt-and-pepper hair fell to her back, not even a lock in disarray. Rolled sleeves exposed muscular forearms, ligaments stretched tight to the wrists. He loved how the combination of her mature beauty, tight body, and audacious smile left most men ill at ease. Except Carter.

The detective smiled warmly. "Hello, Grace."

She stared after the man as he passed. Red closed the double mahogany doors behind them. "That woman's going to seduce you one day."

"Worse things could happen," Carter shrugged. "Best to keep up the foreplay. When I need a favor here in the Det, she's always helpful."

Red stared at the man. So Carter was flirting with Grace just so he could get stuff done?

"Don't worry," Carter said. "I'm not sleeping with her. Because if I ever did, I wouldn't have to sweat a divorce. Wife says she'd just slit my throat." His nose twitched, as if from an unpleasant odor. "And she would. She's got the most beautiful blue doe eyes, but I swear I've seen daggers drawn in their reflection.... This office, OK to talk in here?"

Red glanced about. He'd never thought about his room being under surveillance. Maybe he should have someone sweep it.

"How's it going, clearing my file on Marble Hill Madmen?"

What a cluster. The question seemed to drain what little energy Red had held in reserve. "It's in process." He'd pulled every string he had hanging to get at the data. Went directly to one of the Det's own moles in the CIA, a techie hacker somewhere below the chief information officer. The man had complained about how it was impossible to delete the thing. "It's not like the old days where you break in and steal paper. Electronic files are versioned, backed up, archived, and in some cases chiseled—undeletable. There could be hundreds of copies of it in multiple locations."

In the end, he'd promised the job could be done, though now Red owed him several favors. *But that's the only way shit gets done,* Jim would have said.

Red lifted a beige metal lockbox from a desk drawer. He smiled as he slid an orange sticky note with a phone number scribbled on it from beneath a stack of old IDs. He passed it to Carter. "Marksman gave me this after his last op, before he left. It was how I was supposed to get in touch with him, if I ever needed to."

Carter slid it into the same plastic bag as the scrap of paper. "You ever call it?"

"Hold on." Red punched some buttons on his phone. A young, groggy, male voice picked up. "Jamison."

"You track that number yet?"

"Oh, yes, sir! It was—"

"In my office." He hung up and glanced at Carter's pressed blue suit and black wingtips. He was going to love Jamison.

A minute later Grace opened the door, smiled at Carter, and let Jamison step in. Lime-green Chuck Taylors stuck out below wrinkled yellow jeans. The skinny kid had graduated from James Madison University with a degree in modern Middle Eastern studies, minoring in computer science. His paycheck said FBI, though he wasn't a special agent. His psychological screening had indicated too high on self-preservation. So they'd put him to work hacking and listening in on the Arab royal family till he'd been assigned to the Det.

"It was a burner phone," he said, his voice nasally. "An old one, too. No GPS."

Carter slouched in his chair. "So, you ping it?"

*What the hell's a ping?* Red thought. *Like, from a ship's sonar?*

The kid's eyes brightened. "Oh, yeah. Got it pretty good. I'd say we're a hundred percent. The signal was within range of four cell towers, three pretty strong. The azimuths intersect at an apartment complex near Mount Vernon. But there're fifty apartments. Get close, we can call the phone again. I've got a tool I made that'll point us right where it is."

Red thanked the kid, who blushed and let himself out, hanging jeans scrubbing the floor as he walked.

Red pointed toward the far wall, outside of which lay Grace's station. "She'll get started on your request for staff. Take whatever unoccupied offices you want. If anyone asks, you're on a short-term assignment, reporting to me. I'll pass the word, so you should get cooperation."

Suspicions would be manageable for a month or so. Hopefully this private investigation wouldn't take that long.

"That can wait." Carter pointed to the lockbox. "Get your FBI creds. You're coming with me to this apartment."

"I've got an op to plan." Right. A plan that now seemed a thick mist he was swimming through, dragged by tides, driven by winds, always groping for a beach he could crawl onto. Everyone wanted to make things so damn complicated, but at its core this op would be just like so many others. Get to point A, destroy something, get out, don't let anyone see you. This time collateral damage wasn't a concern. In fact, standing orders were to kill *anyone* present. A mission pitched clean as they come.

The detective walked toward the door, curling his fingers in a *follow me* gesture. "You've got a capable exec. He'll fill in. You knew Marksman as good as any. I need you along while I look at his place. Just like the locker, never know what you might see."

"I'll come with you, but later." What he'd give to be a plain operator again. Now that he was squadron commander, everyone vied for his time. And the Det sucked him dry...a fusion cell, a mist of an organization. Officially, he wasn't even in charge. Javlek said his position was de facto only. But in practice, he needed to be the chemical bond that held the amalgam together.

"It can't wait, Red. We don't even have the man's body, so we aren't the only ones interested in him. Someone else may have zeroed in on this apartment, too. If Mossad thinks he was dirty, they're not going to leave it alone. I need your eyes, and your gun."

# Chapter 19 – Lock Pick

Red steered a blue Ford Taurus northeast on Richmond Highway. The scent of Givenchy cologne reminded him the car had been Jim's not long ago. Red hadn't yet returned it to the motor pool, and his predecessor's silver eagle on a small blue plate still hung from the front bumper. Carter rode shotgun, staring out the passenger window. Wearing a shiny double-breasted black coat, the detective looked more like he was taking a date to a high-end nightclub than working an investigation. Red scratched his neck where the collar of his green woolen L.L.Bean sweater had irritated his skin.

They crossed over Pohick Road, one of Fort Belvoir's main gates, then skipped over Mount Vernon Memorial Highway, and made a turn between two strip malls. In an out lot, Vinto's Boxing Club shone in neon blue and red in the window of a weathered cedar-clad office building. A couple more blocks, and he spotted Mesa Square Apartments, beige three-story buildings more like town houses squeezed along a circular drive.

"He'll be on the second story," Carter said as they rolled in. "So he wouldn't break a leg if he had to escape from a window, but it'd be more difficult to access than from the ground."

Red slowed and pulled halfway onto a sidewalk. A thirty-something woman in pink sweats the same shade as Lori's crossed in front of their bumper, scowling, walking a white dog the size of a house cat. He thumped the steering wheel with a fist. "We've got to figure this out. I can't have my family scared our entire lives."

His father, Tom, had been a piece of work—brash at times, but at least they'd lived a relatively stable upbringing, despite the frequent moves. Mom had seen to that. So Red had always tried to be a better father, involved, even to the point of feigning interest as Penny droned on about stuff like horses and dressage. But he *was* interested, not because of the sport, but because she loved it. Same with Nick and Jackson, though both were still too young to know anything more than Legos and trains. What kind of father would he be if his children lived in constant fear, always on the move? They'd have been better having Tom as a dad, with all his flaws.

Red pointed to a metal box the size of a cigar case Jamison had given Carter. "Got that thing on?" Its face held a dial with a black needle.

It reminded him of an old analog voltmeter Tom had taught Red to use as a kid. Most times, Red had been scared to be near the man. That contraption had been the subject of one of the few father-son moments they'd shared. "See how the needle sweeps up with the blinker on?" Tom had asked, crouching behind the family station wagon, pointing to the oscillating appendage. "That means the turn switch is working. We just got a bad bulb." He'd held the faulty marble-sized glass orb between two fingers, then squeezed till it had popped, making Red flinch. "Even though it *was* new, it's broke." He'd laughed then, an uncommon occurrence.

Now, Carter had Jamison back at the Det on speakerphone. "We're ready."

"Dialing," droned the tech's nasal voice.

Jamison had said that once Marksman's phone started to ring, he'd transmit a code to the box in Carter's grasp. After that, the needle should simply point the way.

An orange light flickered on the gadget's white face. "Transmitting. You should see it now."

As Carter swept the box in an arc, the needle steadied toward one of the buildings across the street. Red dropped the transmission into drive, tires squealing as he pulled from the curb. The muzzle of the white cat-dog, now a hundred meters away, flashed as it fired silent barks, the noise drowned out by the racing engine.

The meter had pointed to one of the buildings in the center of the circle, but others stood behind it. They had to run the whole loop to be sure which one it was pointing toward.

Carter clutched the seat with his free hand. "Why you driving so fast?"

"How you know that phone we're calling is plugged in?"

"I don't. Why does it matter?"

"Burners are cheap. Just picking up a signal eats battery. We don't know if it's got five seconds or five days left on it." He glanced at his reluctant partner. "So I gotta think of everything?"

Carter snorted and braced an elbow against the door. "Get bent."

Halfway through the loop the needle steadied at a building on the outside of the circle, backing up to a ditch with cottonwood trees shading the roof. Beyond the barrier lay a parking lot for a grocery store.

"I'll bet if we looked, we'd find a trail across that trench," Carter said. "He probably left his car in that big lot and came in the back way to keep a low profile."

Red jumped out and gravel crunched beneath his foot. For a second, the scent of pine filled the air, but a cold breeze replaced it with diesel as a dump truck clattered down the main road. He followed Carter and jogged toward the apartment building. This one looked like three duplexes stacked atop each other, with an open stairwell between. The detective stopped and cursed, slapping the device. After another call to Jamison, it lit back up.

Red eyed the dial, pointing to the right side of the building. "That narrows it down to one of those apartments. Any way of determining altitude?"

Carter turned the device sideways. It seemed to point toward the second floor. He grinned smugly.

Red took the stairs three at a time. The door was a cheap flat slab, though it held a fat dead bolt. The one on the first floor he'd just passed didn't have that. The paint was fresh and unchipped. No signs of forcible entry. He drew his pistol and stood to one side. Carter took the other. Both froze in silence for a couple of minutes. No movement sounded from the interior.

The knob didn't budge. Red stretched an arm and knocked, quickly stepping back. Warm, damp exhaust from the dryer vent of the facing apartment floated by his cheek, smelling of lilac. He pressed an ear to the wall, then the door, cupping a hand to listen. Still nothing.

Carter reached in a pocket and pulled out what looked to be a fat pen. Red raised an eyebrow. "You know how to pick locks?"

A flat needle poked from one end of the tool. "Some better than others."

"That's a Schlage, commercial grade. Won't be easy."

Carter glanced back, doubt on his face.

"I've got a past you don't even know about. I picked up some special skills."

"Like how to pick a Schlage?"

"Yeah." He snatched the device from Carter's hand, pushed a red button, and another pin popped from the opposite end—this one thicker. This thing was useless. Needed a breaching ram. But mostly they needed to keep moving. "Whatever." He flung the instrument at the door, and it stuck just below the peephole like a knife in dirt. He stepped back and launched, planting a flying kick squarely above the handle. The jamb splintered with a sharp *crack* as the dead bolt ripped through it. The door flung open, slamming against an inside wall, punching the handle through gypsum board. Not the proper way to clear an opening, but it would do.

Red landed low, weapon drawn. Carter followed, wide eyes searching. Red lifted a long brown suede couch and peered beneath. Nothing. He turned a corner into a hall and they cleared the kitchen and two bedrooms. Evidently no one was home. He slipped the sidearm underneath his sweater and holstered it.

Carter went back and yanked the lock pick from the front door it had impaled. Then, gripping the outside handle, he jerked it free from the hold of the drywall. He slowly ran his fingers into the crater where only half the jamb stud remained. He picked out a few shards, allowing the door to close completely, with a little coercion from his shoulder. "Special skills?"

"Works on most locks. Kinda universal." Red glanced around a taupe-walled living room. Over the couch hung a watercolor painting of ducks with wings set, landing among decoys. He frowned. Was this even the right house? "Get Jamison to call the number again."

The dial lit up, but no phones rang. Red walked back down the red-oak-floored hallway, stopping between bedrooms. A low buzzing came from the one with an unkempt bed. He lifted a pillow and a black phone with tiny silver keypad glowed yellow, vibrating. "I found it." He stretched fingers toward the device.

"Don't touch!" Carter yelled.

He jerked back his hand.

"I swear, you're worse than a kid." Carter reached inside to his breast pocket. The coat hugged his V-shaped frame nicely. It looked expensive, like the one Bollywood Mossad had sported. Red glanced in a mirror with a wide silver frame. Green sweater, scruffy red beard, and dark half-moons sagging below his eyes. The whole effect, he decided, suggested a hungover Irishman. Maybe he should pick up some fashion tips from the man.

Carter pulled out two pairs of blue nitrile gloves, handing one set to Red. "I'll get this." He slipped the phone into a plastic bag. "Have a look around, but don't touch anything. The forensics team will appreciate it later."

Forensics? Sure, they could get a team, even the best in the country, but what would Red tell them to look for? And the more people who knew of their search, the higher the chances any link between Marksman and Lori might lead to another attempt on her life.

"We can't do that. The only thing we've got going for us is keeping a lid on this investigation."

Carter squared up to him, looking even taller and broader in the mirror's reflection. His complexion was sallow. "You're doing it again. You can't give me a job, then cut my legs off."

*Secrecy is our only ally,* Lori had told him. "I'm not saying that. But we don't know where the leak is. Let's see what we can get while we're here. Maybe we don't need to treat this like a crime scene."

Carter, expression still morbid but somewhat appeased, walked out of the room. Red stepped around a queen-sized bed. Only one side had covers thrown back. The rest of the room was neat, sparsely furnished. Orange walls with small framed prints of red and blue flowers hung in groups of three. Slowly, he opened bifold closet doors. Two black Pelican rifle hard cases leaned in one corner. Another sized for a large pistol sat on the tan carpet. Atop it, a tidy wooden box.

He leaned to pick up the smaller cases, then straightened. Would Marksman have booby-trapped his closet? Maybe. He knelt and studied the carpet at the threshold, then the wood trim up the sides of the opening and across the top. No trip wires or optical sensors he could discern. Carefully, he reached in and slid the boxes out.

Starting with the plastic case, he slowly pinched two releases. It was an SKB military spec container. He lifted the lid and whistled a catcall. "Hey. Come here."

Carter stuck his head back in. He was putting clumps of black hair into a plastic bag, using tweezers. "I said *don't touch.* What'd you find?"

Red lifted a matte black six-inch Korth PRS. Like a balled fist, a short silencer was affixed to the end. A laser pointer was clamped to a Picatinny rail beneath the slide.

"What is it?"

"About a year's mortgage. A Korth, the Mercedes of handguns. What'd you find?"

"Got some hair from the shower. For DNA. Also found some baby powder under the sink and used it to lift three prints from the vanity. There's a laptop on the desk and..." He trailed off, pointing to the wooden case. He stepped next to Red. "What's in that? Looks like a silver chest."

Red flipped a brass catch and lifted the lid. The container held a box of Nosler Match Grade 9mm ammunition, an oil rag, but no weapon. Still, the blank cavity in the foam traced a pistol's distinctive outline, but with a fifty-five-degree grip angle. The Luger. So Marksman *was* outside their house that night three weeks earlier when a wet team had attacked his family. Even then, he must've been protecting them. "Before he died, he said, 'Give the pistol to my brother.' He knew we'd find this."

A black uniform flashed into the doorframe. "Police. Hands up!" Carter's arms rose. Red's eyes flashed to the Korth. It was Marksman's, so there'd be a full clip and one in the chamber. He could get to it faster than his own pistol beneath his sweater.

"I'm a detective," Carter said, stepping sideways. "We're here on official business."

The officer curled his lip. "Yeah. Detectives always bust doors and trample a scene like a pack of monkeys."

Carter pursed his lips and squinted at Red. He slowly pulled out the lapel of his coat. "Let me get my ID, and—"

The officer pointed the weapon toward Red. "I said *hands up!*"

Red hesitated. He could drop and snatch the Korth. The officer might get a shot or two off, but the bed's mattress would provide some cover while he squeezed a double tap himself. Marksman's rounds probably had tungsten steel cores. Go right through the man's Kevlar.

"At me! Point your gun at *me*," Carter said. "You don't want to aim anything at him."

"Quit talking and put your hands up! Both of you!" The pistol wove like a cobra's head, moving between the two of them. "We'll find out who you are in a minute."

Was Carter wanting Red to make a move? Drawing the man's attention away on purpose? All Red's instincts told him to neutralize the threat. He was no peacekeeper. No policeman, either. His nature was to make war, sanitize the area, neutralize the risk, stop it breathing. But this man was an innocent civilian. Then again, how'd he get to the apartment so quickly? And why was he so plainly nervous? It was as if he'd known they would be there.

Carter took a step toward the man, hands still up, and said calmly. "I'm on your side. We'll wait till your backup arrives. For your own sake, don't point that toward—"

The officer was unstable. He radiated the aggressive musk of fear. Carter must've sensed it too, or he wouldn't be advancing. The weapon swung once more toward Red. Bending at the knees, throwing himself back, he dropped toward the floor, grabbing the Korth on the way down. One shot from the officer's gun zipped by his chest. Red squeezed the trigger twice before his back hit the carpet, out of sight behind the mattress. A heavy thud sounded across the room.

"Son of a bitch!" came Carter's voice, then the scuffling noises of a struggle.

Red peered over the bed, but neither man was in sight. He scrambled around the end. Carter lay atop the officer's back, holding one uniformed arm racked painfully high. He threw the police revolver upon sheets, then slipped the cop's own cuffs onto his wrists.

"Don't shoot me! Please. I've got a family," the officer pleaded through blood-smeared lips.

"I'm not going to shoot you, idiot! I just saved your damn life." Carter stood, a foot still pinning the man to the floor. He shoved Red in the chest with a free hand. "What the hell was that? You almost shot *me*."

"He was unstable."

Carter snarled, "*You're* the unstable one."

"The guy was going to pull the trigger, even if he didn't know it."

Carter pressed a finger to his lips. Pointing toward a pillow, putting on a low, guttural tone, he growled, "Get me the cover."

Red yanked off the pillow case and Carter tied it over the cop's head. Groping across his chest, Carter yanked off a body-worn camera and slipped it into his pocket. He leaned close to the man's ear and whispered, "I saved your life. So we're the good guys. I suggest you tell your sergeant that while checking the apartment you engaged a suspect and were struck from behind. Now, I'm going to give you a knot on the head. It'll hurt, but it'll be convincing. Understand?"

The hooded head nodded.

Carter grabbed a baton from the man's belt and struck him a glancing blow across the back of the skull. Muffled curses pressed through the gag. Red grabbed the wooden box and the Korth while Carter snatched the laptop and a notepad resting near it. Thirty seconds later, they were driving out a rear entrance as sirens sounded from the front.

Carter flipped through the notepad. "Hmph."

"What?"

"Jamison, he's a computer geek. Right?"

"He's a geek on many levels."

"This laptop will be encrypted. You've got the resources to crack that, though it'll take time. The notes on this paper are pretty obscure, but here's one that talks about a leaf."

Red, pulling back onto Richmond Highway, narrowly dodged a blue RV. The note from his locker had read: *Pick up the leaf on your way home.* He shot Carter a glance. "We've gotta get that thing decrypted before I pull the trigger on this op."

# Chapter 20 – Reload

Red leaned over Jamison's shoulder, squinting at a laptop screen. His shoes tapped, thumping the floor like a dog scratching a persistent itch. His desk was shoved in one corner of a square cubicle cluster, with a workstation in each corner. Three oil-soaked pizza boxes were stacked on the edge of a printer. The other cubes were separated by a steel work counter spread with computer intestines like a coroner's table, autopsy in progress.

Red waved a hand as if he were shooing a fly. "Just skip to the point." The kid had called him back only an hour after Carter had dropped Marksman's computer off to him.

Jamison's eyes widened. The geek pushed narrow black cat-eye glasses higher on the bridge of his nose with a pinky. "The hard drive wasn't encrypted. I just used a password reset USB dongle and got in. All the data is here."

"OK. But you said you'd found something." Ask this kid what time it was, and he'd tell you how to build a Swiss watch. Short on sleep now, Red had no patience. Carter stood several steps behind him, keeping his distance.

Jamison wrinkled his nose and shoved his spectacles with his pinky again. "I started going through his e-mail, but thought that'd be too obvious. I checked his browsing history. He'd searched for lots of random stuff, but there were several IP addresses he'd visited regularly. I dialed one and came to a user ID and password screen; both were already input. He'd never cleared his cache."

Carter leaned onto a desk. "This is too easy."

Jamison pushed his glasses back up. "How old was this guy?"

Grace hadn't delivered their file on him yet, so Red guessed. "Midfifties, I'd say."

"Not uncommon. Elderly folks just don't know how to cover their tracks."

Red's neck tensed, and anger started to rise in his belly. "The 'old' guy could speak seven languages and split your skull at three hundred meters."

Jamison wrinkled his nose, pushing the spectacles back up. "Well, data can be just as deadly."

Red took a few steps, closing the distance between them. "Only when someone like Marksman decides to act on it."

Carter's hand fell on his shoulder, pulling him back. "Let it go," he said.

Red closed burning eyes. "OK, fine—so what did this IP thing have to say?"

"It was a file server. I've only gone through one directory, but called you when I found this memo." Jamison clicked a mouse and a document filled the screen. The writing looked like blocky hieroglyphs. "I ran it through optical character recognition, then a translator. There isn't any mention of Mossad, but it's written in Hebrew." He glanced up.

"And what made you find this one?" Red asked.

"Ran through files with the most recent updates. The first few were benign. Requisitions. Bank transfer confirmations of small amounts, a couple thousand US dollars at the most. This one..." He paused. "But this one isn't pretty."

Red glanced at Carter, now leaning against a partition with a huge black toner stain blossoming in the middle, the picture of disinterest. "Please, help me with this kid."

Jamison pointed to the document, as if finally getting the hint. "Someone was ordering your man Marksman to shadow the *asset*, ensuring protection. This guy Marksman was an undercover bodyguard, best I can tell."

Carter walked to the far side of the examination table. "That would explain why he was at your house, Red, the night the wet team hit."

Jamison shook his head. "Nope. Can't be. One, the asset is referred to with a female pronoun. A *her*."

Lori? It was becoming difficult to deny a tie between her and Marksman. He pointed to Carter, then an empty office. The two stepped inside and closed its heavy door. Red kept his voice low. "If he was assigned by Mossad to protect Lori, what the hell does that mean? And why'd he carry an antique Luger when he could've brought any weapon he wanted?"

"Could be lots of reasons, but who cares? Don't get sidetracked. You've got the note talking about a leaf. That's one link. You've got Marksman's Luger you found at your house, that's another. Then he died protecting her. Now you've got this *protect their asset* memo. The data point here is that Lori and Marksman are definitely linked. And with CIA and Mossad saying he was dirty, this doesn't look good."

Red drew a breath and held it. But the idea of Marksman being a mole was crap, too. Still, Carter wasn't accusing anyone. Yet. "Maybe. But how?"

Carter spoke through gritted teeth. "Ask your *wife*."

Red lifted his hands in surrender. "I would if I could find her! She was under CIA's thumb yesterday at the hospital. Now I can't even get her on the phone. I'm about to go into the ops center and have someone track her tag." He would, but couldn't think of a good excuse to put with the request. He paced the room. The more he learned, the more questions he had.

"Don't worry about tracking her. It's only been a day. Hear Jamison out. Information never hurts."

Unless it comes from Jamison.

The two stepped back into his cubicle cluster. Red pushed a small shiny box out of the way on the workbench to clear a space, breaking a wire affixed to it. Jamison winced but didn't say anything. Red leaned on the newly tidy surface.

Jamison's pinky pressed his sliding glasses. "I'll print you a full translation of the memo, but the CliffsNotes reference a mole within the CIA who leaked a list of names of the Det's cooperating agencies and foreign governments. Even names of operators, analysts, and agency liaisons. The memo says it's to North Korea's Ministry of State Security."

Red closed his eyes. He had to be misunderstanding. "Say again."

"A mole, sir. We've been burned, it claims. The memo is somewhat vague, but clearly states the intel was uploaded to a North Korean server two months ago."

Carter leaned on the table now as well, across from Red. "Don't believe this shit. It's too convenient. You don't just find a laptop, unencrypted, with server passwords not cleared from the cache. I don't know much about computers, but this evidence was planted."

The information, though painful, was consistent with what he'd heard from Mossad back in the command center. Maybe they had planted the computer, knowing it'd be discovered. Maybe they were trying to frame Marksman for some other leak. Needling pain shot through Red's temples. If Marksman had been dirty, what about Lori? He massaged the bridge of his nose. Marksman's reputation was taking hits from all sides, but it could end up sinking Lori's as well.

"This is how it works," said Carter. "Everything is a lie until verified. After that, it still may be a lie. We don't have the whole picture, and from my experience, never will."

Carter was right. No telling which side Mossad was on. Red pushed off from the counter and started toward the hall. "Thanks, Jamison. Keep digging. Let me know what else you find." Red's boots thumped down the marble-tiled corridor toward his office. He needed a nap soon or he'd be no use to anyone. Carter's heavy footfalls sounded behind him. The man couldn't sneak up on hippos humping in a river. "You still with me?"

"Of course. But by your look, your mind is set. My advice, don't pull the trigger on this op till you have more definition around the players. Who knows what you'll be walking into."

Red jerked to a stop and turned. Carter was following so close they bumped chests. Red glared into his friend's deep-set eyes. "A wise man once told me, *Lead based on what's in front of your nose. When in doubt, reload.*"

Carter snorted. "Could you be a little more cryptic?"

"It means proceed based on what you know. Intel has been leaked to North Korea. Now we hear this intel could affect every member in this building. It's not just my family's safety at stake, but my team's. I'm going to turn that North Korean data facility into a bubbling, molten crater." He smiled. "Just in case."

He started toward his office again then stopped once more, turned, and pressed two fingers into Carter's chest. "And if Higher thinks I'm sitting this op out, they're mistaken. I'm not delegating this one to anybody."

# Chapter 21 – Cuttlefish

Spray frosted Red's cheek as the Zodiac bounced across the Sea of Japan. In the bow he stretched against the ballooned black gunwale and gripped a lifeline, taut against the neoprene inflatable's surface. A lightweight dry suit fit tight around his wrists and neck, sealing out the cold. The outfit's black Cordura matched the boat, as if born of the same mother. No scuba gear, but a woolen black watch cap itched his forehead.

His tongue ran over his lip and bitter salt lit its buds. The craft lifted, scaling the crest of each swell, and dropped gracefully into a meter-deep trough, nudging his stomach toward his esophagus as if he were driving a rolling mountain road.

Sergeant Lanyard gripped the outboard motor's tiller and steered them westward. The son of a devout Quaker minister, he still professed belief in the faith of his father, but with an MP5 strapped across his back he obviously took a more liberal view. "My family thinks I'm a cook," he'd told Red once. He'd come to the Det from First Reconnaissance Battalion at Camp Pendleton, California, and often complained of the poor surfing conditions around Virginia Beach. Now he grinned tightly each time the Zodiac descended a swell, white teeth lit faintly by starlight.

At 0220, the only evidence of a horizon was a dark line beneath white-hot dots suspended from a cold sky. Red searched the distant absence where the submarine had dropped them ten minutes earlier. Seeing only a wavering road of green bioluminescence churned by the engine's prop, he turned away.

Once more freely breathing the icy sting of salt spray, he hoped he'd made the right decision, ignoring Higher's orders to sit the op out. His spirit reveled in the open sea's cold. Thirty-six hours in the cramped belly of an Ohio-class submarine had it gulping for fresh air.

"She's huge," the executive officer had said, pointing to the ship's elevator.

Even so, the craft had seemed tight to Red as his head rested in a bunk. Fluids had hissed and murmured from her belly, digesting him. He'd placed his hand upon a wall wet with condensation, sensing the spirit of the beast.

*Death,* she'd whispered.

Red had jerked his hand away, then had extended it again as if probing a stove for heat. *What do you mean?*

*Shhhhh,* it had said. *Death. I am she.*

Maybe it'd been a sleeping pill–induced dream, or maybe the stress had gotten to him, but it had seemed real enough. Either way, how had the submariners fifty or eighty years ago maintained a will to live in much tighter, darker spaces? Surely he'd wither as well, weak and useless, watching an op from the constraints of the Det's command center.

The club of the great huntsman Orion swung from the constellation's belt low toward the west, where Lanyard steered them. But in the open his team was most vulnerable, though the Det was watching by satellite and, tomorrow, an MQ-9 Reaper unmanned aerial vehicle out of Yokota Air Base.

The club pointed only toward the twin blackness of horizon and sea. Red peeled the cover from his watch. The Zodiac started to drop and a dim light flashed from one o'clock, like a camera from a mile's distance. He pressed the comm in his ear. "Thirty degrees starboard."

At the crest of the following swell, nothing. After that it flickered again. As they neared, the glint became a steady burn, growing in strength until, even at five hundred meters, the ship's floodlights seemed as if nothing could hide from them.

"Not where she's supposed to be. We're at least ten klicks too far north," Lanyard commed.

"Matches the description. I don't see any others. Probably doesn't have GPS." He peeled the cover again. "We'll know in a few minutes."

They held at five hundred meters distance, idling slowly after the swaying ship. Looked to be sixty feet long, white, with large orange patches running down the sides. The light beams lumbered to one side, then the other, as swells rocked the trawler. At least thirty of the glowing half spheres topped the ship's cabin, pointing down toward the water, a siren call to squid and cuttlefish.

*Ironic,* Red thought.

Four crewmen manned skewer lines, reeling up their catch onto the deck.

Maybe this wasn't the right ship. The lights should have gone out five minutes ago. He glimpsed another flash on the horizon, dim, about nine o'clock. Damn. Maybe that was their contact. It could be ten klicks. But they couldn't make it there before—

The floodlights suddenly dimmed. A welcome night sky once again covered the sea. Red smiled at the darkness beneath the cooling orbs. A red flash from the cabin window. "That's it." The Zodiac lurched forward and the vibrations of the motor stepped up, though the muffled noise didn't increase, as if propelled by an electric motor.

Lanyard steered toward the churning whiteness at the ship's stern. Ten minutes to get aboard and stowed, before the captain "fixed" the generator that ran the lights. Right now he'd have the crew forward, toward the bow warming themselves in a cabin during the brief reprieve.

Brooks had given background. The captain ran a cuttlefish boat from the city of Rason, out of Songpyong harbor, North Korea. Illegal, of course. But in the northern city, many were improving livelihoods through such activities. Black markets were ignored by officials since they, too, depended upon them for basic necessities such as food and clothing. And greasing the appropriate palms ensured the captain was not only a free agent, but encouraged in his pursuits. He went to sea often just to keep officials adequately bribed.

"You won't see the captain. Don't make contact," Brooks had said. "He always tells us where the boat will be, controls his fishermen, and it's up to us to get on board and in position." She'd put a picture of the man on-screen. "If you see him, let him alone. He'll only bring a skeleton crew, knowing you're coming aboard. The workers are *sakbeoli*—hirelings, they call them. Sometimes even military labor among them to make ends meet. Most captains are abusive. Some *sakbeoli* just don't come back with the ship. No one says anything because they want to keep a job."

Red had raised an eyebrow at that. "You trust this guy?"

Brooks had not met his gaze. "Of course not. But everything is consistent, as we like it. And he's having trouble keeping bribes flowing. We're a source of repeat business. He needs the money, so he needs us. Here, that's better than trust."

Such assurances felt thin as he spotted a climbing rope lashed to a white guardrail of the ship just meters ahead. He reached for it, inhaling diesel fumes. He gripped it and jumped, planting wet soles against the trawler's rusted sides. Lanyard had slowed the Zodiac, trailing ten meters behind. Captain Richards and Sgt. Zin Gae raised MP5s toward the deck.

Red had selected Gae after a quick review of candidates with Korean language skills had revealed several possibilities, but none could be sourced fast enough. Red had spoken to his Delta liaison who came back suggesting he try South Korea's 707th Special Mission Battalion. "Instead of looking for one of our guys who can speak it, get a real Korean who speaks a little English. I had ice-dive training with the 707th. You won't be disappointed.

Dr. Cooley rounded out the small team. Only the whites of his eyes seemed to hover in the darkness amidships. His frame stood narrow and his dark Pakistani complexion dulled to invisibility with the application of camo paint. "Only five," Brooks had said. "I know you want more, but that's the most the captain says he can do."

"Clear port," came from Richards.

"Clear su-tar-board," from Gae.

Red's hand slipped on the wet nylon rope as he pulled himself up. He gripped a rail bracket, slick and sharp with rust, peering over the gunwale. Four skewer reels lined each side of the ship. Yellow and green plastic buckets slid over the deck with passing swells. A lone squid on the brown surface raised a tentacle and snagged one of the containers as it passed. The center cockpit was fully enclosed with less than a meter's passage on either side. Its door was shut. The steel deck reeked of a summer beach where he'd vacationed as a kid, near Duck, North Carolina, filled with rotting jellyfish after a strong nor'easter. He gripped the middle rung and pulled. The weight of equipment and food stores warmed his lats as he hoisted himself upward. He vaulted over, but the boat sank passing a wave and his feet slipped, jamming a metal canteen into one kidney as he hit. A second later he was up again, MP5 trained toward the cabin. A gust of salt spray misted his target. Faint laughter floated after it from the bow. A few seconds with no movement, then he stuck a hand over the rail and gave a thumbs-up.

Dr. Cooley was next. Then he covered while the rest of the team boarded. Lanyard was last, stabbing his KA-BAR into the Zodiac's rails, slicing down their entire length, then the floor. He had only planted his feet upon the deck when the little craft sank and dropped out of sight, bow slapping a swell like a lobtailing humpback.

The hatch to the holding tank was smaller than Red anticipated, barely a half meter square. The crusted steel door hinges squeaked as it opened to blackness. Dr. Cooley aimed a light into its mouth and flashed a red beam down its throat. A gelid surface undulated a couple of feet below, full of thrashing cuttlefish. He shrugged, then lowered himself, feet kicking as if feeling for the bottom. "Water's only chest deep," he commed.

On his back Lanyard carried the Laser Guided Sniper System, or "LEGS," as they called it. The anchor plate hit the steel deck as he lowered himself. Red pushed a foot against the disc and Lanyard exhaled, slipping past the protrusion. His gaze caught Red's and he pointed toward the cabin. A gaunt crewman in yellow slicker and brown pants leaned against a skewer reel there, back to them, peeing into the ocean. Red slipped his KA-BAR from its sheath. The man shook, zipped, then staggered backward and headed toward the bow. Red was returning his knife to its scabbard when a swell crashed against the starboard side. The man stumbled, reached for the handrail, then missed, spun, and grabbed the cabin wall.

His gaze rose toward the open hatch.

*Shit. Why'd you have to look this way?* Red strode quickly, slapped a hand on the seaman's mouth and slashed his throat, then tossed the limp body over the guardrail. He peered around the side of the cabin, but no one emerged. Another swell crashed and mixed crimson with hull rust, then sluiced it from the deck. The body trailed in their wake, then quickly dropped out of sight at the same point where the Zodiac had sunk. In one second, an innocent life was obliterated.

"It just wasn't her day," Red's father, Tom, had said ten years earlier, after a Vietnam veterans' peer support group meeting. His coffee mug had shaken brown drops onto their blue-checked vintage kitchen table. "Gun bunnies could never get a spotting round within a half klick. One second she was on her bike, narrow hips, beautiful brown skin under one of those paddy hats. Next, the earth beneath her exploded. All that was left was a wheel limping along like a kid trundling one of those hoop toys. Just unlucky, I guess."

Red was *not* going to become his self-loathing father. This hireling he'd just killed, he'd died for a reason. He'd make sure of it. Nothing could impede the mission. Even if it meant making widows. His arms were heavy and he suddenly felt fatigued. No, killing an innocent wasn't right. The man had just been unlucky.

"Clear," came Lanyard's voice through the comm, yanking Red's attention back. Lanyard's shoulders were out the hatch, weapon aimed portside.

Red glanced at the cabin. A ghost-pale face hovered in one porthole, the captain in the photo that Brooks had shown. The man scowled and Red reached for his pistol. But the captain only pointed at him, then to the hatch, in angry jabs. Red ran to it, squeezed in, and closed the squeaking door above him.

Cooley's red beam lit the tank, barely large enough to hold the five. As Red eased himself into the water, overflow gurgled out a drainpipe. A jet of cold liquid hit his ankle as he pushed flat against a wall. Even with a circulation system running, the water was thick with putrid black ink as the fish bumped and fought and mated. Something hit his belly and he grabbed for it instinctively. He lifted a squirming cuttlefish and it blew a water jet across the tank in an effort to escape. The seaweed stench of the air tightened his throat. This was worse than the submarine. Now he really was being digested. He longed for the open sea again.

Would the team be able to trust the captain, now that he'd seen his cargo? Now that they'd killed one of his crew? But he couldn't turn them in. How would he explain their presence aboard to the officials, to the state? In deep, they were beyond bribes now. Red could track their progress by GPS and get the team overboard before they docked. But that was a risk, too. They could kill the captain and crew now, and take the boat. Or follow the plan and trust it. There were too many variables to consider.

But just as he tried to focus his thoughts, Lori came to mind. He hadn't even been home since leaving her at the hospital. The CIA had scheduled the drop three days out, and every hour had been dedicated to op planning. He hadn't even been able to talk to her. The kids were OK, Lori's sister having taken them in the meantime. But now he'd gone from the belly of a submarine to the belly of a dilapidated trawler, and he'd screwed up by killing one of the crew.

He met each team member's gaze, except Lanyard's. He pointed to the far wall. "You three against that side. Lanyard, with me on this one. When they lift that hatch to dump more buckets, we go under. This one looks full, so we might be OK till they head home. One of the crew saw me. He went overboard."

The captain would likely circle back, feigning a search to satisfy the remaining crew. One would probably stick his head into the tank as well. Depending upon how good or bad the catch, they could be another twenty-four hours in the steel coffin. *Never thought a damn submarine would look so good,* he thought.

Gae's lip curled. He touched his ear. "You guy-j do this op-ten?"

Lanyard shook his head.

"Next, give us more than a day-j war-ning. We get you north. Through China. On dry tu-rucks." He raised hands above the water, as if clenching a steering wheel. Ink splashed his face and he spit it back out. "This cwap." After a second, his eyes widened at Red, shining despite the dim light. "At least you keel one. Peel good, ha?"

\* \* \* \*

A beam stronger than daylight wedged its light around the hatch and cast a U shape upon the writhing black surface. It had arrived hours earlier along with the low hum of a second motor bow-ward, probably the generator. The glow continued till daybreak, when the hum ceased, the tank darkened, and the ship seemed to heel to port. No one had emptied any more buckets through the hatch, but it had opened a few times, presumably for inspection to ensure the circulation pumps were still working. Each time the team had held their breath and submerged. Beaks had nipped ears and lips as the cuttlefish writhed in the jelly. Each time they surfaced, they blew out the microphone orifice on their comm sets.

Red held his locator up toward the hatch slit but couldn't get a clear GPS signal. Judging by his watch and the angle of the beam of daylight creeping in, they'd been headed southwest for eight hours. The ship was real garbage tow.

Prebrief had said they were headed to Songpyong harbor, in the far northeast of the country. A truck would be waiting there to take them south along the coast to Chŏngjin, though the driver didn't know that yet. Gae was to inform him. If the driver didn't agree, they'd eliminate him, take the truck, and rely on satellite surveillance to avoid checkpoints.

Red glanced at Gae. The smallish commando had cut out the oval bone from a cuttlefish and was slicing the body like a tomato, holding a portion out to Cooley. The Pakistani's eyes narrowed and he shook his head. Gae shrugged and slipped it into his own mouth, chewing the raw meat like bubble gum.

The diesel chugging slowed. The rudder grated out an objection at being angled too far. Within an hour the ship fell silent, except for the steel bulkhead squeaking against something and the thud of feet above. Red felt the floor of the tank with a boot. It funneled toward the center, with a ten-inch pipe at the bottom.

"They're going to pump the fish out, right?" Cooley asked.

"North Korea?" Gae flicked his fingers, miming an explosion. "If the harbor has a pish pump, it no work."

Just then the hatch on another tank further astern crashed to the deck. A muffled cry came through the bulkhead. "Hirelings get in tanks and scoop the pish in baskets." He drew his knife and held it next to his face. "This is where we pind out if captain sold you."

The thumbhole in the hatch above went dark; then it swung up.

None of the team submerged this time, but crouched with eyes above the waterline from the dark corners of the tank. Red squinted to veil whites as cold salt air filled the space, a siren song calling him out of the ship's cramped, squelching belly.

The captain's face appeared in the opening as he knelt over it. Just as quickly, the door shut and the heavy grating of a full fish crate slid overhead, covering any slice of light left from the dull, hazy afternoon.

Gae pulled himself up to the hatch at the sound of voices. He slowly pushed the steel flap up an inch, eye to the slit, but it hit the bottom of the crate. "One say he arrange tank be pumped out. He's sending hirelings away."

Cooley's beam again lit the tank to blood red. Richards peeled a cuttlefish off his watch cap. "Good sign."

Gae lowered himself back into the liquid swarm. "Or bad. One grenade and we dead."

# Chapter 22 – Chaoyang Park

*Beijing, China*

Mist hung in the air as mud swirls in water. It clung to Zhāng Dàwe's mustache, freezing it stiff on the tips. He'd walked a half kilometer since the subway exit, but his knees had started to ache back at the stairs. Despite being in the middle of Beijing, Chaoyang Park rested this late at night, her slumber stirred only by an occasional jogger.

He wandered past a green triangle and musty spruce drew him back to his boyhood farm. What was it? Seventy years ago now? He rubbed his forehead, as if the scabs were still unhealed. "Eyes up!" Papa had cried. Ignorant of the saying, young Zhāng had turned to watch for something but got a whip of spruce raked across his forehead as a tree fell. It had been a family joke for his entire youth.

Beyond a long reflecting pool, a shadow walked slowly into a low clump of leafless trees. Hunched over, it was probably another homeless person, as best Zhāng could perceive through thin fog. Two runners exhaled cottony puffs, chugging along a sidewalk across the shallow pond, its fountain silent for the winter. Their frozen vapors floated behind at each heavy breath, like a steam engine chugging along a track. The clouds dissipated, their individuality swallowed by an unyielding city.

Zhāng reached the bench opposite the fountains, the one where he'd been instructed to wait. He winced at his knees as he lowered himself. The bench curved comfortably beneath his bony legs. Warm from the walk, he welcomed the cold seat's embrace. He leaned back and pushed his cap forward over his eyes to indicate no one had followed. He always did like he'd been told. Bike. Then taxi. Then subway. He never saw a face more than once.

\* \* \* \*

"You OK, sir?" someone asked. Zhāng lifted his head. The back of his neck ached. Must've dozed off. A man in a gray suit and blue tie sat next to him now, the one who always met him, wearing that same outfit. If he could afford one suit, shouldn't he have more? If they always changed meeting locations, shouldn't he change what he wore?

The man with the blue tie had never given a name. Or who he worked for. None of the employees of state-owned businesses could be trusted. Could be one of them. They were as bad as the communists. Greedy, ignorant, backstabbing, thieving whores.

"Yes." Zhāng's mustache stretched stiffly as he smiled. "I must have fallen asleep."

Blue Tie slid down the bench and put his arm around him, rubbing his shoulders. "Not something you want to do in the cold. Might not wake up. There, we look like friends now."

Zhāng gazed down the pond to where the homeless man had been. A thin crust of ice floated atop the water, cracks wrinkling its surface. Sidewalk lights shone upon it in an algae green hue.

"Status?"

Status of what? Zhāng tried not to smile when the memory came to him. Must be tired, or the cold. "The wire harness is almost complete. I've got both pallets of capacitors in place now."

"Already? They'll be suspicious."

"I've been swapping them off the building coolers. They think they're faulty, impregnated with moisture."

"I don't like used equipment."

"I test each one before I bring it in, and again after I pull it off the coolers. All still good up to 450 volts, one full farad."

"And the coil?"

Zhāng straightened. His buttocks ached. "Still there. A full spool of feed cable, left over from the new electrical drop. I told them to leave it, that I'll need it to run a failover circuit."

"And the core?"

"Rebar. Or iron pipe. I think...yes, there's rebar in a stack against the wall. But judging by the bank of capacitors, we won't need it." Zhāng rubbed a box beneath his skin, next to his collarbone, his pacemaker, the size of a pack of cigarettes. Come to think of it, he could use a cigarette about now. Warm these cold lungs. He felt in his jacket pocket.

"You OK?" Blue Tie asked.

Zhāng nodded. How late was it? Having a hard time keeping hold of his thoughts. "You know this will kill, don't you? Anyone with a pacemaker, like me. Probably within a couple hundred meters."

"The greater good, sir. It will save the lives of many. Plus, I am told the pulse will not go out of the building."

Right. Dual 380-volt direct feeds, firing both banks of capacitors. "It will. Even though the building is shielded."

Blue Tie slid back down to the far end of the bench. "Maybe. But the electromagnetic pulse will fry any microchip inside. Right?"

"But they've got other sites. Each backs up the others."

"Don't worry. Your efforts won't be in vain. There won't be any backups to be found."

"When do I get the controller?"

"Still next week I'm told. It will be dropped as agreed."

"I need to test it. Nothing ever works right the first time."

"It has been tested. The same controller, using capacitors from the same factory, same batch. As long as your harness is hooked up correctly and the controller has a full, unmetered feed, it will fire. Time and again, once every second, till every piece of data is wiped. It will take years to recover." Blue Tie's heavy eyelids curled up with his smile.

"I want the controller now. To make sure I know how to get it installed. That the timer on it works. I don't want to be close. I may be old, but I'm not ready to die."

A runner across the fountain in an orange exercise suit with reflective stripes slipped and fell flat. *Ughhh* echoed off several buildings, but no hard smack of a head hitting concrete. Blue Tie stood, but the runner was back up as well, looking behind, then around, as if embarrassed. He continued his jog in a lighter gait, much less graceful, a fawn placing each leg carefully onto a frozen lake top.

Blue Tie's voice was a low rumble. "We can't. It doesn't get here before next week. And it needs an antenna."

What? The Americans couldn't be that inept. Maybe Blue Tie was an agent for the Ministry of Intelligence after all, trying to root out subversives. Maybe that's why he never worried to wear something different each meeting. But if he was, the Ministry of Intelligence would have arrested Zhāng already, wouldn't they? Or maybe the Americans *were* behind the plan and Blue Tie was just leading everyone along, trying to learn as much as he could before he slit Zhāng's throat and buried him in the foundation of a state-owned factory.

This meant he would have to test the controller. Make sure it would fire. If not, he'd still hit the data center. All he needed was a mechanical circuit controller and a timer. He'd fry their damn computers no matter what. Even if he had to flip the switch himself. Even if it killed him. All this shot through his mind in a nanosecond, now awakened from his slumber.

Blue Tie pulled his hands from his pockets and sat back down. A polished stainless card case smacked the concrete next to his feet. One of those fancy cases with a spring-loaded lid. It snapped open and business cards fanned out like playing a hand of Pusoy. A green triangle of the Yanje Group logo displayed on each one. Blue Tie swiped them quickly. His hands shook as he shoved them back in their case.

Zhāng worked for Yanje Group as well. Never anyone else. Why had he never seen Blue Tie? But the company had over ten thousand employees. Or had he dropped the cards on purpose, trying to win Zhāng's favor? "Ten years ago one of our engineers died outside Baodi. How?"

Blue Tie sighed, frozen steam enshrouding the card holder in his hands. He slipped it into his pocket. "Lim Chang. His apprentice said he didn't follow protocol before swapping out a breaker." He shook his head. "I never believed him. Lim formed our safety team. If anyone followed protocol, it was he. His wife was crazy, with family ties to Triad. Rumor says he found out something Triad didn't like and his wife paid the apprentice to fry her husband."

Good answer. "This antenna—you know the building is shielded. An antenna will be impotent. A limp dick."

"It's only a three-meter wire. Needs to be outside. Hung vertically."

Zhāng shrugged. "And how am I supposed to do that?"

"You're an excellent engineer. You've wired a hundred of these buildings."

Zhāng warmed at the compliment. Blue Tie was the only person who had ever expressed appreciation for his work.

"You can figure it out. They've got you running a failover circuit, right? Install the antenna then, where the wire comes into the building. This thing needs to fire. The antenna needs to work. They'll pay you, in addition to moving you out of the country."

Zhāng spat on the sidewalk. The edges of the spittle froze instantly. "Tell them they can keep their money. I'd do it for free. I'll have their damn antenna hung, from the west wall." He caught Blue Tie's gaze. "Tell them that—*from the west wall*. If it's not the way they want it, they can figure it out themselves." His shoulder ached. The pacemaker drew in a chill. Had to get moving. He stood and rolled his shoulders. "You never told me when it's going to go off."

Blue Tie's face was unreadable. "You don't need to know. The less you know, the safer you are. The controller will be programmed already. I suspect the antenna has something to do with that. When it does, you'll be on a container ship headed east."

Blue Tie stood and bowed. "*Shī péi le.*" He turned and walked away, next to the long, silent fountain, passing where the homeless man had slumped off the path. A grim figure rose from the black ground among the trees, hands extended toward Blue Tie, begging. He walked past without lifting his head, then disappeared into the mass of fog.

# Chapter 23 – Return to Hwasong

*Hwasong, North Korea*

A single-engine spotter plane buzzed overhead as the troop transport ambled down Myŏnggan Highway. Ko Chung Ho stooped his neck and leaned toward the windshield of the truck to gain a better vantage point. *Must be near Kuktong Airfield, so only a few kilometers until the town of Hwasong.*

A wheel slammed into a pothole and fine yellow dust floated up through a crack in the floorboard, settling on the cuff of Ko's woolen green uniform pants. The jolt racked his neck, which was already sore. *Worry,* he reasoned, rubbing his nape.

An enormous pile of white tailings from a fluorite mine, active at his last station, had grown a week-old beard of brown scrub brush. Fields, formerly lush with rice, now lay littered with dead brown leaves, unkempt after the fall potato harvest. Farmers across the homeland had been angered by an empty promise from the government, that they could keep thirty percent of their harvest. The government had obviously hoped the incentive would increase production, but the infrastructure of the Public Distribution System hadn't changed and their entire harvest had been demanded as usual. Surely next year the fields of those despondent farmers would yield poorly, no matter what quotas were levied. Having hungered through the last famine, Ko would start stockpiling food now.

On his last drive to Hwasong prison camp, he'd ridden in the back of a transport, huddled with other guards and families. Now a *sangsa*, he rode up front and would be the third-ranking enlisted in the area, in charge of all guards at the camp.

"Your exemplary performance has gained you this high honor," his commander had said.

But behind his smile of pride he'd hidden bitter memories of shame. Prison camp was no honor. Would he lose himself again? All too quickly he had forgotten his father's instruction: "All creatures deserve respect," he had said, sticky silver scales from a trout clinging to his bloody hands. "Even this one." And then he'd chopped off its head.

Ko could start fresh, lay down new expectations of conduct upon his guards. Punish those who raped prisoners, passing around a girl all night, burying her battered body before morning. But the shopkeeper had warned him to give no reason to doubt his loyalty. Would pressure to overlook cruelty come from above? He'd still be required to torture.

He pulled off a glove and pressed that hand against the frozen windshield, thawing a patch of frost to peer through. The driver did the same, leaning so close to the glass his chin rested on the steering wheel. The dirty town cowered ahead below a gray-brown sky. Stalks of smoke curled from several chimneys, vanishing in the low clouds. It would snow again soon.

The truck turned north on Gulag 16 Road, past the soccer field where they'd exercise each morning. The same one where he'd given his senior NCO a concussion when they'd both tried to head the same ball. A shiver shot through his neck as he rolled down the window at the guard shack.

The thin man studied his papers, then straightened and passed them back to Ko with a smile, pointing up the valley. "Please proceed, *Sangsa*." As the truck rolled forward he glanced up a ridge, trying to spy the next guard tower, but it was hidden behind thick evergreens. There were twenty towers around the perimeter, with a three-meter electrified fence topped with concertina wire running between them.

He'd been told Hwasong camp was the largest in the homeland, over five hundred square kilometers. Though it held only twenty thousand prisoners, the facilities had never been designed to support even half that many. The far northwest corner was where the nuclear warheads had been tested. He had spent an entire year there directing labor, digging tunnels for equipment, though only a few small yellow metal boxes connected with cables were all he'd seen put inside.

After several miles of potholed road they stopped outside headquarters. The yellow block building with a sagging brown tile roof squatted in front of six rows of houses in a similar state of decomposition. Those housed teachers, factory supervisors, and higher-ranking military with family. Conditions looked even worse than last time. Most of the wooden fences separating backyards were missing or lying deep beneath snow. He'd have to erect one again, to keep deer from eating the vegetables. Anyone with a home filled every centimeter of backyard with whatever produce they could raise. Chwinamul, bok choy, and tatsoi grew best in the poor, stony soil and cold weather. Guards in dorms were allowed to tend gardens in common areas set aside just for them.

Ko jumped down from the cab and glanced across from headquarters to the security fence surrounding the detention block. That was where he'd spent most of his time last station. Problem prisoners were kept there in solitary confinement till their sins had been adequately cleansed, though the Great Leader had said it took three generations to cleanse family blood. Was Ko condemning future grandchildren to be tortured just because he wanted to help his sister? Was he being too reckless?

Burrowed into a rising hill was a concrete entrance to an underground facility where they'd torture anyone caught plotting an escape, stealing, or breaking any of the more serious camp rules. Once he'd hung a child by the ankles and wrists over a fire after he'd ratted out his mother who was planning an escape. Ko had been told to ensure the kid didn't know of any other conspirators. The child had lived, though it took four months for his wounds to heal.

Eun Hee's legs dangled from the truck's tailgate. He held out his arms, but she shook her head and jumped down with a *thump* onto the packed snow. Only her eyes were visible between a black scarf and hood. She turned around once; then the bridge of her nose wrinkled. "Abeoji, does it always smell like this?" Small white clouds puffed through the scarf.

A *chŏnsa* passed down a wooden crate, then another. All their clothes and worldly possessions in two chests.

"Yes," he told her. "It gets worse in summer." But would they be here till then? How long till he was contacted—tomorrow? Next month, next year? Could he locate his sister before that without raising suspicion? Twenty thousand prisoners spread over five main compounds and dozens of villages. It would not be easy.

"Give them no reason to doubt your loyalty," the shopkeeper had said. He intended not to.

* * * *

Ko paused in the lee of an icy wooden snow fence to warm his face in the bright sun after inspecting a guardhouse outside the prison camp's garment factory.

"Don't turn around. To save your sister, bend down and tie your boot," growled a guttural voice from behind the barrier.

He twisted to see who it was, but the fence blocked his view.

The voice snapped, "Idiot! Tie your damn boot!"

He dropped to a knee and fumbled with perfectly tied laces. The voice was raspy, as if spoken through gloved hands. It sounded almost...female.

"Detention block, cage confinement, number thirteen. You know this area?"

Of course. He'd spent two years around Detention block. He started to turn his head, then thought better of it. "Yes."

"Cage thirteen. Remember it. One guard will leave to use the bathroom. The other will be sick, sleeping on the floor. You'll have four minutes to get her out."

"Where to then?"

"In a troop transport. Take the ZIL-130. The same blue one you came in on."

"When?"

"Tonight. 0130."

"Tonight? But, I haven't even been here a day."

"Shut up!" came through the snow-encrusted wood. "Drive to Songpyong harbor."

Ko frowned. "That's almost a five-hour drive."

"Be there by 0600. The harbor is small. There's a new warehouse there, bright red roof, shaped like an L. Park in the closest spot facing east. Stick a piece of white paper in your window, no more than ten centimeters square."

Ko shifted his weight, pretending to tighten strings on the other boot. A prisoner—a foreman—trotted by carrying a sewing machine. Once the man was past, the voice continued hoarsely, "Your truck will be full of fuel, enough to drive there. Men will get into the back. One will sit next to you. Do what they say. Ask no questions. Present no resistance."

"Can we wait a day or two?"

"If you wait, you will disappear. You and your daughter. I'll make sure of it."

Many prisoners disappeared from Hwasong. Years ago, Ko had helped dig a grave one night on the far side of the western hill for a prisoner seamstress who became pregnant with a fellow guard's baby. They'd had to dig an additional grave when another prisoner stumbled upon them. Before Ko could say anything, his friend had raised a shovel and slammed it across the prisoner's head. He could never clean the dirt of that grave from his boots. The same could happen to guards. "Anything else?"

"Yes. I'll be watching."

# Chapter 24 – From Darkness into Night

*Hwasong, North Korea*

"Can you not sleep, Abeoji?" Eun Hee's voice came from the dark. "You are restless."

Ko sat on his cot in the black concrete bedroom and pulled his woolen cap over cold, tingly ears. The platform abutted Eun Hee's, right above the coal furnace flue that ran beneath the floor. Coal was one commodity of which Hwasong was not short, though you would never know it by their frozen cell of a new home. The vinyl window glowed faintly. Low moonlight would provide excellent concealment.

"I'm going to use the bathroom," he lied. A good excuse since all were ordered to use central latrines so the sewage could be collected for fertilizer. "You get dressed, too. Do not ask why. Wear your warmest things, like when we camped near the river a few years back. Make no noise. Do not light a lamp. I'll return in fifteen minutes; then you'll come with me for a walk."

Ko waited till he heard the wooden chest open, then slipped out the door. Frost bit his lips. A light glowed in a window from headquarters, but no guards were in sight. He closed his eyes and heard only a low hiss, like static in a speaker, in the direction of the iron works. No stars shone through the low December sky. He started toward headquarters, intending to pass in the shadows to the south. An icy drift's crust cracked beneath his feet, but he didn't fall through.

He paused to lay a hand on the yellow concrete building and listened again.

Only the same hiss, though it seemed to resonate from the air. Must be the frost dropping.

As he scurried across an open court, he tripped on an icy rut and fell, smacking his lip on a chunk of frozen brown sludge fallen from a truck's mudguard. His hands had punched through the drift and ice seeped cold around his wrists. He stood, spat, then resumed his trot, careful to lift his knees to avoid another fall. *It would've been better to bring Eun Hee with me and get her to the truck ahead of time.* And if she was caught, she could at least claim she didn't know about an escape. That would do nothing to satisfy her torturers, of course. The only mercy she could hope for would be death by firing squad.

He reached the tunnel entrance and paused in front of the door. Why was his heart pounding so? He hadn't done anything wrong...yet. Just out on a surprise inspection, if anyone asked. He felt for the reassuring outline of the holstered Makarov 9mm pistol on his belt. He gripped a metal entry handle with the other, the cotton glove sticking to it. The door shrieked on its hinges as he pulled it open a crack. Inside, he walked past the cargo elevator, stepped lightly upon the stairs, and headed down. Four flights later, the air was heavy and warm—fifteen and a half degrees Centigrade all year long, due to its underground location. The door to the cage block room was wedged open.

Rank sewage burned his nostrils, so he breathed through his mouth. Even so, he could taste the noxious mixture of oozing infection, ammonia, and fecal matter. The prisoners had pots and cans for eliminating, but sanitation was not cage detention's concern. *Nothing a fire hose once a week can't wash away,* they'd always said.

He slipped inside and pressed close to one wall. A mouse scurried along its base, then shot across the walkway toward the center of the room. Half the size of a hockey rink, the expanse seemed less crowded than he remembered. Waist-high cages were no longer stacked one atop another. Each one a little over a meter long, they cramped their unlucky occupants for months at a time.

Moans, coughs, and sobs ebbed as he stepped along slowly. A figure in one metal crate shifted, eyes downcast.

Ko straightened, reminding himself he wasn't doing anything wrong. Prisoners were conditioned to snitch on one another, but never on a guard. He rested a hand on the butt of his pistol and scowled in feigned belligerence.

Green numbers on the far wall evidenced the order of the cages had changed. They ran backward of what he expected, putting cage thirteen near the guard post. When he peered around a corner, dim light shone through an office window, silhouetting a single soldier in its frame. His head was down as he turned pages of some government magazine. The only other light glowed from a lone bulb hung from a wire in the center of the cage room. No clocks, so prisoners lost track of the days. The guards would often change shift timing, to further confuse them.

Ko stretched his forearm and twisted his wrist to reveal a flat-faced, yellowed dial. 0120. Ten minutes before the guard would get up to relieve himself. Ko leaned against the wall again and his heel sank into something that squelched like mud. Across the aisle, an arm extended from one of the cages, fingers slack. A door slammed and the fingers shuddered.

Ko peered around the corner again. The guard was gone. He stepped out into the aisle and walked toward the glowing room. His watch now said 0122. He hoped the guard's timepiece was fast, and that he wasn't just stepping out for a cup of water. Ko reached the first aisle and counted to cage thirteen. Prisoners withdrew from the sides of their pens as he strode by. He stooped and gazed through thin steel bars at what he'd been told would be his sister. A figure lay inside in a fetal position, facing away.

He stepped around the crate, covered all but a narrow slice of a flashlight lens with his palm, and switched it on. The body didn't move, but the stomach expanded slowly, in short jerks. He stooped to study the face more closely. Surely this couldn't be Soo Jin. The hair was cut so short, the cheeks hollow. A mole the size of a mouse track below her earlobe. He gasped. It *was* her. Purple shadowed her eyes near the nose. The tip of an ear was missing.

He snapped open the latch and lowered the side. Her left knee twitched, dirty skin protruding through holes in filthy cotton pants. Her eyes opened and she screamed. Ko slapped a palm over her mouth and raised his head to look around. No movement from the guard post or the side door where the soldier had left. Only a hoarse cough from across the room, followed by the clank of a pan as it hit the sides of a crate.

He bent to her ear. Lice crawled between his fingers. Her abdomen squeezed tight as she tried to scream again. He nearly smiled. Still a fighter, even in hell. "Quiet, sister. It's me, Chung Ho. Do you understand?"

Sweat washed through the dirt across her nose. Her eyes were filled with fright.

"I am taking you out. Not for torture, but somewhere safe. Do you understand?"

She nodded in short shudders.

Ko removed the hand and lifted her over his shoulder in a fireman's carry. She groaned as her abdomen sank around the back of his neck. The seat of her trousers were worn through in two small holes. He stepped toward the stairwell, turned back and closed the cage, then ran up the stairs. She weighed almost nothing. *Probably less than thirty-five kilograms,* he thought.

At the top, he paused by the stairwell door he'd left cracked. He pressed one ear to the opening. All was silent, but the faint scent of cigarette smoke implied someone was close. A throat cleared. Someone spat. Ko gripped his pistol and retreated inside the stairway, beside the entry, ready to club whoever might step through.

A shadow flickered across the dim wedge of light cast upon the floor. The freight-elevator motor hummed. He holstered the pistol and peered out into the cold night. Only marginally brighter now, but there was no sign of activity in the courtyard.

He stepped out into the snow. Each boot sank through the crust with a loud *crunch.* Trucks were parked outside the motor pool, a quarter mile down the main drive. *It'd be shorter to get Eun Hee now,* he reasoned. But too risky, carrying his sister at the same time.

Soo Jin began to shiver. The sooner he got her stowed, the less the risk for all.

"You see this finger?" his father had once asked, holding up the middle one with its missing tip. Of course he had. He'd seen it often, each time his father chided him to take his time scaling fish. "That was me pulling in a gill net, trying to beat a thunderstorm. Do the job right. The storm got me anyway."

\* \* \* \*

Rust pocked the faded baby-blue tailgate of the ZIL-130. Though he lowered it with glacial speed, the tailgate hinge gave a grating cry that echoed off the motor pool yard. Limit chains pulled tight, and Ko laid Soo Jin on the metal surface. He hopped up, carried her underneath the tented canvas, and placed her gently upon a bench. He turned around, but finding nothing to cover her, unbuttoned his jacket and stretched it over her torso up to her shoulders, tucking the collar edges under her neck. She glanced at him, then up to the canvas as she shivered.

His hand stroked her cropped, bristly scalp. "I'll be back in a few minutes. Going to get Eun Hee, then we're leaving. Don't make any noise."

"She's...she's..." Soo Jin shivered.

"Don't talk. Stay here, sister. I'm not leaving you." He jumped down and stood silent on frozen ground for a few seconds. An owl cried from the west, high up the slope, but no human sounds. It wasn't time for a shift change, and no posts were near the motor pool. He raised the gate, neck tensing at the hinge's vocal resistance.

A cough from inside the repair building. Damn it! The yard was well trampled, so there was no clear evidence of his passage to point to Soo Jin lying in the back. The farther he got from the truck, the better.

He trotted out the yard and back up the hill. The night was cold, quiet, and most importantly, empty. No guards in sight, even near headquarters. Sweat beaded on his cheeks by the time he slipped through his own front door into damp, stale air. Eun Hee was in the bedroom, sitting on her cot, thin knees together with hands pressed between.

Ko dragged a small trunk from beneath his bed. It was stuffed with a couple of blankets, a two-kilo bag of rice, and a photo of Un Jong, his wife. The state had failed her, too. She'd lain on a mattress, struggling for breath as the ulcerated breast cancer ate her from within. A doctor had given pills for pain, but they did little to quiet the terrible nights.

"Come."

Eun Hee stood and, without a word, followed him to the front door. Placing his hand on the knob, he considered his daughter's fate if caught. He glanced down at the trunk under his arm. How would he explain that? Without it, he could just say they couldn't sleep and were out for a walk. He set it on the cot, removed the photo from its frame, and slid it into the inside pocket of a frayed work jacket. He slipped his arms into its too-short sleeves and zipped up.

"We're taking a walk. That's all. Hold my arm. If anyone asks, I couldn't sleep and insisted on a night stroll." He placed her hand upon his elbow but she pulled away. He slapped her across the cheek. "You may see some things you don't understand. But keep quiet. Do as I say. It is for our family."

Her woolen cap bobbed. "Yes, Abeoji."

The walk behind headquarters was again uneventful. Down the hill, they passed the holes where, a few minutes earlier, he'd punched through the snow crust, even as light as his sister had been upon his back. Around a corner of spruce, the motor pool fence was the last barricade between them and Soo Jin. Ko's pace quickened.

A figure stepped from the far side of the gate into the opening and unslung a rifle from his back to port arms. "Halt! Who is there?"

Ko stopped and forced a smile, though the guard wouldn't be able to see it in such dark. "*Sangsa* Ko."

"Approach one."

Ko huffed quietly. *Why'd we have to get the one guard who obeyed as trained? And why is he even at motor pool? Is this a setup?*

He glanced toward the truck just forty meters away that held Soo Jin shivering in its bed. He pulled Eun Hee's hand from his elbow and stepped toward the guard. He was very young. A full trench-style coat drooped on thin shoulders, dragging in the snow.

He glanced at Ko's collar, obviously looking for insignia, but his uniform jacket was in the back of the truck. "Papers," he demanded.

Ko reached into the inner pocket, pulled out frayed tan pages along with his wife's photo. He held the papers out to the guard and slipped the photo back into his pocket. A flashlight lit the documents. Ko squinted when the guard shone it up into his face, then Eun Hee's. Again, to his dazzled eyes, the night was black as death.

"Why are you out, *Sangsa*?"

Ko swung his head toward Eun Hee, several meters back. "Just on a walk with my daughter."

"After curfew?"

"Curfew? There's never been a curfew."

The guard raised an eyebrow. "How long have you been in camp?"

Ko's neck itched. "You realize I'm the new camp guard, don't you?"

Without a change in his dull expression, the guard handed back his papers. "Which is why I'm following protocol. But I was told you aren't filling that position till next week."

"Right, but—"

"There's been a curfew for a couple months, *Sangsa*. Camp commander made it after a guard froze to death. Near the foundry, of all places. He slipped and hit his head."

"Since when do we post a guard at motor pool?"

"About the same time. A captain found some truck headlights on the black market, stolen from one of ours."

Ko chuckled. "So now we're tending pigs *and* keeping an eye on the farmer." He slipped his right hand into his belt near the small of his back, next to a knife sheath, feigning a relaxed pose.

"I may have seen someone tonight," the guard continued, flashlight beam on Ko's chest. "I heard some noises in the yard and came out to see what it was. Someone was running up the hill." He flashed the beam toward the motor pool. "I just finished looking around and was about to go inside and report it. Please come with me."

Ko glanced to Eun Hee. Almost any other guard would just let them go now. Why'd they have to run into this idiot? "I'll take my daughter back to our house. You've done a good job. I'll remember that. Thank you for telling me about curfew." He stepped away.

The guard smiled widely and wagged an admonitory finger. "Ah! You're trying to test me. I am sorry, *Sangsa*, but I must report both of you to the relief commander. Once he says you can go, then you can." He swung an arm toward the building. "I've got hot tea inside. Have some while I call."

Ko frowned. "Your radio?"

The guard pulled a black plastic brick from his belt. "Dead. Batteries quit charging right. Only last a couple hours, so they're gone by now."

Once again, Ko turned to Eun Hee. He inhaled the resinous scent of crisp spruce from the near woods. All was silent and dark, except for a low glow up the hill from headquarters. His eyes locked with hers and he mouthed *Shhhh*. He wished there was some way to avoid what he was about to do. If the guard spoke with the relief commander, they'd have to return home. Soo Jin might freeze before they could sneak back out. Even so, how would they deal with this nosy guard? If he gagged and tied him, shift changed in an hour. His replacement would find him. Not enough of a head start for their escape. So, one life for another. Was that fair? Would he turn on a fellow soldier in arms to save his sister? The guard had started away, his weapon slung over one shoulder.

*Yes,* Ko reasoned. *For my sister, my wife, and my daughter's maimed hand. The state failed us all, and it will fail us again. Famine will return because of poor management. Family must be protected.* His father hadn't been well off or politically connected, so the family hadn't enjoyed the privileges of upper class. But the fisherman's family had never gone hungry for long.

Inside the gate, once in the shadow of a large transport, Ko slipped his combat knife from its sheath with a quivering hand.

He lunged and gripped the guard across the mouth from behind. The man turned instantly, surprising him. Ko's knife caught his throat, but the young guard had jerked back, so the gash didn't penetrate deep enough. He dropped his rifle and held his neck, then turned to run. A scream bubbled from his lips in muted gurgles. Ko launched himself again and landed at the man's feet, tripping him. Like a mountain climber setting an ice pick to scale a glacier, Ko drove his knife into the man's leg. Stab, pull, stab, pull. He worked his way up the torso, across the chest. More gurgles, now hissing from holes around the ribs. He plunged it into the guard's neck a second time. The man's legs shuddered then went limp.

Eun Hee stood three meters away, one hand braced to steady herself against the bumper of a huge green cargo truck. The other clutching at her own neck.

What would she think of him now?

"Help me cover the blood." He stomped on the snow where it was darkened, not knowing if the stains were blood or dirt or oil, then scooped fresh snow upon them. If he left no trace, maybe they would have more time to escape. The replacement shift guard would report the absence of his predecessor and a search would commence, but not in haste. Headquarters was not well organized. In a camp as large as Hwasong, orders got crossed, guard schedules mixed up. Ko didn't have official duties for two days. So maybe they'd never even connect the guard's disappearance to Ko until then...if there was no evidence of foul play.

Eun Hee looked away, then slowly shoveled a handful of snow and dropped it on one of the dark spots. Her hands shook. She was sobbing.

Ko pointed to the blue ZIL-130. "Help me carry him to that truck."

They laid the guard's body in the back, under the bench opposite his sister. He stripped off the long coat, perforated with blood-soaked slits, and wrapped it as a blanket around Soo Jin. He jumped down from the truck and ran inside the motor pool building, returning with a cup of hot tea and a stale slice of bread.

He stretched Soo Jin out on the floor, propping her back against one wall of the truck bed, then turned to Eun Hee. "Feed her these. It's all I could find. Stay back here, quiet. Once we're outside the camp, tap the back of the cab if anything goes wrong. It's going to be a long night."

"Yes, Abeoji."

# Chapter 25 – Songpyong Harbor

Hours dragged until even the dim light visible from the overhead hatch disappeared when evening passed. Red started to shiver and removed his assault pack. He lifted the black bag above the waterline, unzipped a sealed pouch, and felt for a peanut butter protein bar. Tearing it open, the dry paste was sweet as ripe berries and gone in seconds.

"Hunger makes the best seasoning," Lanyard murmured.

Red thought about another, but stowed the wrapper and zipped the bag back up. If he had to crap, the dry suit would complicate matters.

He held the locator up to the hatch again, but still couldn't get a signal. He unzipped another pouch and gripped the sat phone. But beneath the thick steel deck, nothing made it through.

"Crate can't be that heavy," Richards said. "I could pry up the door with the butt of my weapon."

Red started to jog in place, legs slapping now-placid cuttlefish. "It just turned dark. We'll give it another hour." The circulation system was still running, shooting a water jet past his thigh. He pumped a few more minutes then sank to his neck and moved his cramped back against it. The pulsing water relaxed his muscles, and the claustrophobic grip of the tank eased. The putrid fish odor had waned, his nose numbed to it.

The image of the startled crewman's face flashed to mind, the slick yellow of his vinyl rain suit, his confused expression, eyes still open as the sea covered them. But Red had done the right thing. Eliminating the threat had been reaction, and even now he could think of no better option. If he'd gagged him and tied him in the tank, he could still be a threat. The life of an innocent crewman for the lives of men in his charge. And the success of the mission, at the end of which lay the safety of his family.

Lori could finish recovering at Hopkins. And the kids, they didn't need to know what had really happened to her, or what Dad had done halfway across the world to protect them.

He glanced at the hatch. All this waiting. Three days of hell getting this op planned on lockdown, and he hadn't even had time to call the kids for bedtime prayers.

A sandpaper-grating screeched above. Red cracked his eyes, then checked the time. Must have fallen asleep. Everyone backed into corners. The hatch opened a wedge and the outside loomed as dark as the tank. "Sibbun." The captain's voice. Then the hatch slammed down.

All looked to Gae. He touched the comm in his ear and whispered, "Ten minutes."

Red stood and lifted the MP5 from the water, which was now less viscous than the gel-like fluid when they first had dropped in. He released the clip, shook out any remaining drops, uncorked the barrel, and did the same. Water alone wouldn't jam it, but cuttlefish tentacles might. He'd thought about slicing one of the creatures up just as Gae had, but for spite. He hated sushi. The rest of the team followed suit, holding their weapons above their heads, then checking each other's gear.

Red pushed open the hatch. Crisp air blew against his eyes. Vision well adjusted to the dark, he spotted several fishing vessels with salt-sea-rusted patina lashed side by side to a near bulkhead. He flipped down a monocular and the vessels turned to green-scale in the night vision scope. Hot exhaust plumed yellow from the idling engine at the stern of one. Thermal overlay was working. A deckhand glowed yellow as well, stepping from one bow to another, making his way to shore. There seemed to be a second line of boats beyond the first, but a mist obscured them and the rangefinder provided random reads.

Their own ship was one of the largest in sight, moored to a wooden pier piled with green and yellow crates. It lifted and sank, rubbing gently against thick black tractor tires. No lights on the pier or near buildings, and only an occasional dim bulb on a boat.

"The red-roofed warehouse is directly off stern. No movement on our pier, but some workers on a line of boats fifty meters starboard. We've got good cover—no lights. Low-crawl to the stern and enter the water. We'll move under the pier to the warehouse. We'll recon the rest at closer range."

Beneath the wharf, Red welcomed fresh salt water, though tainted with oil, washing away a coat of slime from the holding tank. No stars gleamed above, and a fine mist hovered over the water, too thin to call a fog. He removed his watch cap, dipped and wrung it out several times, then returned it to his head. They moved silently, except for one of the team bashing a knee on a submerged wooden cross member.

They reached the start of the pier and Red steadied himself against a bulkhead. The blackened beams, though thick and sturdy, bowed against the strain of holding back the earth behind them. Roots grew between boards where gaps had widened. The wood, worn as it was, exuded the acidic scent of creosote. It looked to be made from a recycled railroad bed. Shells and rocks, washed out through the cracks, stirred below him by wave action. A smaller vessel that listed to one side was moored to the pier and provided cover.

Red pointed to Lanyard, then the bulkhead. Lanyard swam a distance down, stopping halfway to the line of fishing boats. Red scoped the closest vessels, waited for a fisherman to make his way below deck, then commed, "Clear."

Lanyard gripped the bulkhead's whaler above his head and pulled up, then the next, like Jack climbing the giant's beanstalk. He peered over the top, paused, then slipped out of sight. A minute later, "I'm at the corner of the warehouse," he said. "Good cover here. Little movement, but someone's walking the street twenty meters away. Two trucks in the lot. One looks like an old Ford. A farm truck. But it's got a canvas back and it's where it should be, easternmost part of the lot. One warm body in the driver's seat. Low heat signature from the back. Engine's cold, too. The other truck is a ten-wheeler, like a troop transport. No heat from it at all."

"Which one has the square paper in the window?"

"The farm truck."

"That's the one."

Red sent Gae up next, Lanyard providing cover. Within three minutes, the rest of the team had dry feet, concealed by rusted conveyors and derelict processing equipment next to the warehouse.

Gae moved to the truck, approaching from the passenger side. He yanked open the door and the driver's hands went up. Red broke cover and moved to the tailgate. If Gae's introduction didn't go as planned, he'd dispose of the driver and the team would still need to be under cover in the bed.

The truck had no bumper, so he pulled himself up on the tailgate until his nose broke the plane. The wood-plank floor held a single bench down either side. Beneath one was a bundle huddled in a trench coat, presumably the driver's sister, her freedom in exchange for the driver's services. He swung himself onto the floor, his sudden appearance startling the passenger. She let out a short scream, but as he moved to cover her mouth, another hand slipped from beneath the jacket and silenced it. The girl's eyes were wide, but the unknown hand gripped her mouth tightly. The fingers were thin, knuckles raw.

He pushed up his monocular to reduce his otherworldly appearance. He held up a hand in an attempt to look nonthreatening. The other clicked the safety off on his weapon. He moved a finger to his lips, all the while eyeing the coat, ready to roll away at any movement. Whispers came from beneath the fabric, the girl nodded, and slowly the bony fingers loosened their grasp and slipped back beneath the covering.

He inched to her side. The visible one's skin was smooth, her nose small and rounded like a marble on the tip. Only a few years older than Penny. The coat was bloodied with jagged slits. He gently pulled down the collar, and his gut knotted. The corpse-like body of the other lay thin and shivering. Skin stretched over bone. The sunken cheeks were deep as the dog he'd found with Lori alongside a wet road.

"I told you it was still alive," Lori had said, stroking matted fur. The animal's tail had twitched as it tried to lift its head. "We can't just leave it," she'd pleaded. They'd passed the creature, circling back at Lori's insistence. Red had been certain the mess alongside the road had long been dead. They'd stopped, and his fingers had rubbed ribs as pronounced as black keys on a piano, ends pointed as if they'd puncture the skin—almost like this woman's jawline. Her eyes were deep set and dark.

"Cooley, need you ASAP."

The doctor boarded with a too-clumsy *thump*, followed by the rest of the team. He hovered over the woman, moving the young one away to examine the older. Without the extra warmth, she shivered even more. He pressed her stomach and she grimaced. He gave her some pills, a drink from his canteen, then motioned for the girl to lie beside her again, tucking them both beneath the trench coat. He handed a Muscle Milk protein bar to the young one and, with points and gestures, instructed her to feed it to the woman.

Cooley slipped next to Red on the bench. His eyes were slits, and his lips barely moved as he growled, "Broken cheek. At least one rib. Severe malnutrition. Whoever does this shit needs to die. I gave her something for dysentery—you can smell it. Put a chem-pack between them to last a couple hours. Not much more I can do now. Get her warm, food, clean water. If we can get some calories in her, maybe she won't go hypothermic."

"Keep her alive. She's our leverage with the driver."

Cooley tucked the coat around her legs.

# Chapter 26 – EMP Prep

*Beijing, China*

"Why you mounting that there?" asked a rotund technician in white lab coat breathing hoarsely, surgical mask over his mouth and nose. The covering had a wet circle in the middle. Flu had been more than a bother this year in China, state news reporting a ten percent illness rate in Beijing just last week.

Zhāng Dàwe leaned against the electric service room's wall and huffed, but forced a smile while trying not to condescend. "It's for failover. We've brought in a second line." He pointed at the silver conduit which housed a black cable thick as a man's wrist. Then patted the control box Blue Tie had dropped into the trash receptacle behind his apartment. "This one, from farther down the grid. If the primary power fails, this box will switch it over. Another layer of redundancy before the generators kick in." Those generators had been exercised frequently this winter. They'd burned through five thousand liters of diesel already.

The man shoved half a fried dough ring into his mouth, then turned on black rubber heels with a *screech* and walked back into the data center, metal security door clicking shut behind him.

Zhāng squeezed the trigger of a hammer drill. Fine smoke puffed from the shallow hole as the tool sank into the concrete wall. He pounded in lead anchors, then finished fastening the control box. From the conduit he slipped out a narrow black wire he'd discreetly fed next to the main cable and snapped its connector in place. Outside, the antenna wire lay hidden against folds in the metal siding. If the Americans couldn't get a signal now, then *gǔn dàn*.

"Timeline's been stepped up," Blue Tie had told him that morning, blank faced.

"When?"

"Tonight. It needs to be operable by midnight."

Zhāng slid a crated water pump in front of the door to the data center. If another tech tried to come in, it would give him time to cover his work. Three pallets of capacitors were stacked in the utility room's far corner behind an entire reel of feed cable. The spool was well over a meter high and twice that in diameter, wound tight with electrical wire thick as his thumb.

He lifted the top pallets of capacitors and stacked them to one side. With a practiced precision, he connected each capacitor to a wiring harness. He'd performed the exercise for an hour each evening, eventually without lights. He'd affixed slip-on fittings for speed and aligned each capacitor on the pallet prior to delivery. Sixty seconds and all hundred were hooked up.

He stacked the next pallet on top and repeated. The last pallet was for cover, so he left it alone.

Each wire ran as a vein, hidden toward the inside of the pallet, with only a single artery exiting from the back of the crate. Casual observation would reveal only a strand of feed cable from the spool lying against the wall, running behind the pallets.

Zhāng lifted lengths of rebar from a neat stack of rusting iron and stood them within the spool's core till it could hold no more, being careful that none protruded noticeably. This would act as the weapon's core, doubling its potency.

The last connection would be the most obvious. He'd already run conduit from the control box to the floor. He fed the wire harness up through it, slid the thick cable into the control box's connector and screwed it down tight, leaning random-sized remnant sheet-metal siding against the wall to conceal his work.

He looked around the small room. He'd made a practice of moving the contents each time he worked in it, just so any change would appear normal. On his fingers he counted back from the spool. Yes, it was connected to the wiring harness. The wiring harness to the capacitors. The capacitors to the control box, the control box to both power feeds. The LED on the box showed only that the main power was hot. Secondary hadn't been switched on yet, but that would be activated after a phone call on his way out. The main power feed would be plenty by itself, but both would mean a devastatingly powerful output.

Not even the thick shielding of the building's metal skin would contain the electromagnetic pulse, better known as the EMP. Every piece of data stored inside the center, even on hardened devices, would be wiped clean. With such a powerful pulse from zero range, it would be a job well done. Though there could never be payback enough for the theft of his family's land, destroying all for which his back had labored as an adolescent. He savored the approaching consummation of revenge.

Helping the Americans meant the wound would be infected. He wasn't an idiot, no matter what Blue Tie thought. In the aftermath of such a disaster the Ministry of Intelligence would cut corners to quickly rebuild the centers. Certain components, no doubt, would be of misleading origin, a Trojan horse, maybe even assembled in Silicon Valley, with extra chips inside for listening silently to data traffic. Such an infection, though not lethal, would be more painful to the communists than a neat, clean slice easily stitched.

He smiled at the thought.

# Chapter 27 – Welcome

*Songpyong harbor, North Korea*

Ko leaned his head against the truck window, breath frosting it. He'd checked on Eun Hee and Soo Jin an hour earlier, both tucked under the bench in the back. It'd be warmer in the cab, but he couldn't risk them being seen.

The road had been icy, wide and empty. Guards at all the checkpoints had accepted his papers and story with little hesitation. He'd said he was headed to pick up a new corporal for duty whose orders had been misprocessed. A few of the lads at checkpoints he'd recognized from prior assignments. They'd merely waved him on.

He'd stripped and buried the body of the dead guard deep under a sand dune near the oceanfront of Ijin-Dong. Incoming tide and wind would cover any trace. An hour later, the man's papers and clothing had been doused with diesel and set ablaze a klick down a mountain trail. If the body was ever discovered, it'd be too late to identify. The only delay in their trip had come during a visit to a fuel depot just off the main road. The tanks had not been filled as he'd been told. But two packs of cigarettes ensured the attendant didn't check for authorization or log the job in his records. He'd parked the truck at Songpyong harbor at 0612, slightly after he was supposed to arrive.

All day long he'd waited, glad to catch up on sleep. But now where was his contact? He'd not been given any instructions on who it would be or how he'd get in touch. Just that he'd be driving some men. And he'd not even been told to where.

He'd almost missed the turn for the harbor but spotted it at the last minute, and now was parked at the new warehouse with the red roof. In the easternmost spot facing the water, with a small square of white paper stuck to his window, just like he'd been told.

So, where were they? What kind of men would they be? Had they moved on even though he'd merely been a few minutes late? Had he missed the chance to save his sister's life? If the men never showed up, he'd have to drive north and escape to China. But he had nothing to barter with. Nothing to exchange for food or a hidden bed. No wonder so many men who escaped ended up as slave farm labor, and women as sex workers.

But he couldn't borrow worries from tomorrow. He'd watched the sun rise over the water, the bright orange orb warming his face, melting frost from the window. But now it had set and his breath froze to the glass again. The men might still show.

Every hour he'd tapped the first three notes of "Old Mr. Turtle" on the back window. Every hour they'd been answered by taps of the next three on the wood deck. Eun Hee had never known his mother. She'd sung the song each time she lit the stove fire, so the replies had to be coming from Soo Jin.

He peered over the hood. Judging outside was dark enough to safely step out and check on them, he gripped the door handle.

Just then, the passenger door flew open and the muzzle of an assault rifle was thrust into the cabin. The weapon was short, like a Russian submachine gun, with a blunt silencer mounted to the tip. A commando with a black-painted face and small scope strapped to his head trained the weapon rock-steady at his chest. "*Sangsa* Ko Chung Ho?" he barked.

Was that a question or a statement? Ko's hands instinctively rose while his eyes flashed to the pistol on his hip.

The commando shook his head and held out a hand.

Ko unsnapped the security flap on the holster, but apparently he moved too quickly. The commando's grip on the submachine gun tightened. Ko slowly pulled the weapon with two fingers, wrapped the barrel in his fist, and held it out.

"*Sangsa* Ko Chung Ho?" the man repeated.

So, it *was* a question. Ko nodded slowly. The state had found them. Eun Hee would be tortured, eventually killed. They'd make him watch, along with the rest of the prisoners. Perhaps it had been a setup all along. Had his sister been in on it?

His shoulders drooped. "Yes. I am Sergeant Ko."

The commando's cold smile was haunting. He sat in the passenger's seat, stinking of rotting jellyfish, just like the shoreline where Ko had buried the guard. "You're going to drive us. I'll tell you where once the rest are in the back. You will do exactly as I say. One bad move, and I kill you. You, and your sister."

Damn it! Ko had finally placed the man's accent. He'd thought it was because the guy had been shivering with cold, but he'd actually spoken a different dialect. No commando, but an assassin—from the south!

The jellyfish commando lowered his weapon. "Do what I say, and you and your sister will be safe. We have a doctor with us. You're not going to give any trouble. Right?"

Ko wrenched the door open and rolled to the ground. He jerked a knife from his belt and jumped to his feet, clutching it. A *thump* on the back of his head. The night fell darker still.

* * * *

Ko's skull felt as if it rested on a pillow of broken glass. He forced his eyes open with much effort. The silencer of the same submachine gun was resting on his upper lip. Jellyfish's knee was pressing his gut. Ko was stretched out on the dirt parking lot.

"I thought we weren't going to have any trouble."

"Damn you! Damn your country and your whoring mother! You can kill me, blind traitor. But I'll not help you assassinate the dear leader!"

A wicked smile. This time, with a chuckle. "A bit late for remorse." Jellyfish stood and said something to another man next to him, no taller, with a tight, curly beard the color of a pumpkin. Why was his hair that color? Birth defect? More words were exchanged. Pumpkin Beard gestured for the commando to point his weapon away from Ko.

"We don't have time to explain, *bbalgaengi*." Jellyfish sneered. "We're not going to kill your fat leader. You agreed to drive us. Then we will free you and your sister. Either you do that, and we nurse her back to health, or you don't, and you both die. Understood?"

"And my daughter," Ko gritted out, wincing at the pain in his head.

"What?"

"My daughter. She's back there, too. You take all three of us, and I'll do as you wish."

He'd spent fifteen years in the Korean People's Army Ground Force. Seventeen before that, with *juche* teachings every numbing day beginning in elementary school. Those years seemed an east wind he strained against, rowing his father's fishing boat away from shore, into deeper water. But one wave after another had splashed over the bow, till now it seemed the hull wasn't long to stay afloat.

He'd killed a fellow guard, a comrade in arms, and justified it as protecting family. Hadn't the dead man been a kind of family? Helping these commandos would mean even more death to someone.

But he had no alternative. Twisted in the storm, the beach no longer in sight, all he could do to keep afloat was row into the wind. There was no way he could stay in the homeland now. The government knew everything. The thought of leaving pained him. Maybe he could get a job in China on a fishing boat.

Jellyfish spoke to Pumpkin Beard, who nodded, then stretched a hand down to Ko. He grasped it and was pulled to his feet. Pumpkin Beard pointed him to the truck cabin. Ko held a finger at them and walked toward the tailgate to check on his daughter and sister, steadying himself against the bed rails as the ringing in his ears subsided. Someone must have coldcocked him from behind. When he wiped his nose, blood smeared his cuff.

He peered over the tailgate, arms shaking. "Eun Hee, you OK?"

Her voice quivered. "Father! Are you all right? What are—"

Soo Jin's hand slipped over Eun Hee's mouth. "Shh," she whispered. Her muffled voice came from beneath the dead guard's coat. "We're OK, brother. Do what the men say."

He filled his lungs with cold salt air. Jellyfish poked him in the ribs with the muzzle of his weapon, then waved it toward the cab. Gravel and ice crunched beneath Ko's boots as he trudged toward it.

The engine turned over slowly, but finally fired. A *pop* loud as a gunshot came from the carburetor. Ko flinched, then sighed, relieved not to have to steal another truck's battery or lie about his cargo as he asked for a jump start.

He shifted toward reverse and the gearbox grated. "Shit," he muttered. He hadn't depressed the clutch. Arthritic pain stabbed beneath his kneecap when he pushed the pedal. A short growling objection from the engine, and they were backing away from the harbor. Gas still registered three-quarters of a tank. "Where we going?" he asked.

Jellyfish pointed south and pressed two fingers to his ear, then said something in...must've been English. Sounded feeble, like a love-struck girl talking to a suitor. South Korea was nothing more than the United States' bitch. So, the other commandos must've been American. But Americans didn't have pumpkin-colored hair, did they? At least none he'd seen on bootleg Chinese CDs of *Charlie's Angels*.

Jellyfish gazed through the windshield and said, "Chŏngjin."

\* \* \* \*

Red peered beneath the flapping canvas tailgate cover as the truck jostled out the parking lot and accelerated down a wide, icy road. Tall marsh grass stretched two hundred meters east across a mud-flat, their tufted tops clumped with snow like a field of white cattails. Silver crystals stirred by the tires floated and spun, sparkling in the beam of the vehicle's single working taillight. Red pulled the flap down, but snaps to secure it had long since vacated their post. He pulled his KA-BAR, cut a few thin strips from the edge, and used them to fasten down the blowing fabric.

Dr. Cooley tucked the trench coat collar back around the young girl's neck, but left a breathing hole for the emaciated woman. He sat on a green wooden bench above the pair, stretched his legs out, and leaned against a metal pole that supported the rubberized tarp above. His deep sigh sent a swirl of frozen vapor to the top of the covering where it ballooned and twisted, then flew like an escaping spirit out an open seam. Red envisioned it swirling and mixing with the frozen exhaust, lost forever in the dark prison of North Korea.

"I could use a cigarette," said the slender Pakistani doctor, rubbing his mouth.

"I thought doctors didn't smoke."

His eyes were closed, but one side of his lip curled. "Sure. And a dentist never eats sweets."

Red jutted his chin at the bundle below his legs. "Still OK?"

"Maybe. Need to keep her warm. The chem-pack should help a little till her system can convert the protein bar to body heat. If the weather drops cooler, we can take turns huddling with her." He lifted his head and scowled. "She looks like death warmed over. I've seen bad shit, like that refugee camp in Girdi Jungle. But something's eating me about this one. Maybe because the communists are so damn pompous, denying these camps even exist." He clasped his hands in front of him, as if resolved. "If we get the chance, I'm not going to kill any of the commie bastards. Just slice with a dirty blade." Cooley had always possessed a vindictive streak.

"Just keep her alive."

The doctor stood, steadying himself against the vertical metal pipe. "I'll do that. I'm not the one you need to worry about. Better keep Gae from killing her brother. See the way he looks at him? He'd just as soon slit the man's throat as shake his hand."

Red silently cursed the CIA for their insistence on such a tight timeline. Two more days and he could have had his own Korean-speaking asset.

Instead he was stuck with a half-cocked South Korean operator. He pressed the comm in his ear. "Gae, how long?"

"One and hap hour. Driver say two checkpoint on way. I say two hour."

"We've got no real cover back here. Need something to hide us better before the first checkpoint."

"Cigareettes and chocolate."

"What do you mean? Crates? Boxes of them?"

"No. Driver say no check truck bed on big road. Only going on camp. He give guards cigareettes and chocolate with papers. Say, 'In hurry.' Then wave him through."

Red leaned back against the cab. No window in it to spy on Gae riding shotgun. Richards was kneeling near the tailgate, peering between the canvas flaps, just like their last op in Iran. But then they'd had crates stacked in the bed, concealing them from any casual inspection.

He straightened his back. Fatigued as hell, but he couldn't risk relaxing. Jim had always said, "Ops go to hell when you feel too comfortable." The team would have to strap themselves to the bottom of the truck before they got to the MSS site. Unpleasant, but he'd done it twice before. And the girls? Leave them somewhere and pick them up on the way out. But he doubted the driver would agree.

Just then a shot rang out from inside the cab. The truck lurched sideways as if it would tip over, sending the huddled women sprawling against the bed's steel side.

# Chapter 28 – Not Broken

*Langfang, China*

Zhāng Dàwe rolled whiskey across his tongue, then down his throat, warming his esophagus. He inhaled deeply, hoping the fermented beverage would clear his clogged sinuses.

Four other apartments, stacked like concrete shoe boxes, abutted his own narrow space on the building's eighth floor in Langfang, just outside Beijing. A packed brown suitcase leaned against his rumpled bed. He wriggled his toes, feet resting upon an upturned wooden box with circuit breakers, 450V stenciled on the side.

The thin man had worked his entire life for Yanje Group, tolerating meager cost-of-living increases each year, and only slight pay raises as his responsibilities grew. Only after his fingers went numb from decades of handwork could he afford his own apartment, without a roommate, in a part of town with new concrete streets etched in a bricklayer pattern. With electronics outlets on the first floor of every building, he enjoyed watching the younger generation attracted there.

He glanced at the suitcase with a tinge of regret. China sheltered such a beautiful, diverse society. His homeland. But even with the reforms of recent decades, the communists, at their core, were still the murderous henchmen of Mao Zedong, who'd driven his family from the fields they'd planted. In the swat of a fly, they'd reallocated lands, destroying generations of labor with empty lies. *They* were the reason he would strike. Yes, now this feeble old man—a single transformer in their massive electric system—would send a jolt they'd not forget. Zhāng was patient.

Another sip. Someone rapped on his door. He scowled. Too early for Ms. Yang, the slightly younger widow three doors down. They'd spent an evening together just last week. Her aged libido typically ran on an every-other-week cycle. Though he'd only had two fingers of the beverage, when he stood the room seemed to tilt, but righted itself as he strode to the door, smiling. No one there. As he stepped into the hallway, the stairwell door clicked shut. He shrugged and sucked the last bit of whiskey from the cup. Stepping back into the apartment, his bare feet crinkled over paper. Stooping, he pinched the edge of a sheet and lifted it: *Tonight. One hour. Contingent location.*

Zhāng glanced down both ends of the hallway once more, then shut his door, twisting the dead bolt and securing the chain. His last scheduled meeting with Blue Tie was tomorrow, after the EMP ran during early morning hours. Then he'd be on his way out of the country.

They'd never had an emergency meeting before. Why now? Blue Tie had always been so careful, following strict protocol, always communicating something like this through drops. Why had he risked such a public contact? Maybe it wasn't Blue Tie at all. Maybe the Ministry of Intelligence had discovered him and now they were going to follow Zhāng to find out...what?

He strained his whiskey-dulled mind to make sense of it.

No, if MI had made Blue Tie, they would've just arrested him. But something had gone wrong. Maybe with the EMP. Maybe it was the Americans.

\* \* \* \*

An hour later, Zhāng paced a narrow alley behind a woman's handbag outlet facing Xinhua Road. An occasional car zipped past the open end, tires slapping over a seam in the pavement, echoing coldly off metal dumpsters. Footsteps came up from behind. He turned to see a silhouetted figure in a suit swaggering down the alley toward him. Zhāng sighed in relief. By the thick build and slight limp, it was Blue Tie.

Zhāng backed into shadows between two trash boxes. "I'm here," he said in a low voice when the man came into view. Blue Tie stood next to him, shoulders almost touching.

Zhāng tightened his grip on a length of rebar behind his back. He'd ground the tip to a point just a half hour earlier.

"It's not working," Blue Tie muttered.

"What isn't?"

"The controller. They can't get a signal."

Zhāng held up a palm. "All is installed correctly. Exactly like the one we tested last year. Both power feeds are live. All LEDs on the controller are green."

"But they can't contact it. Did you install the antenna?"

"Just like the test. I even ran a continuity check and checked resistance. A hundred ohm, just like the specs say."

The cold night air had sobered Zhāng, but Blue Tie still seemed to lean in. "Then you need to check it again. Make sure nothing changed. Troubleshoot it, just like in the instructions. Maybe someone was in the utility room and flipped a switch."

"It's not a place where anyone would be so careless."

Blue Tie straightened his neck. "Check it. It's got to be operable tonight." He pushed his thick fingers into Zhāng's chest, making him stumble against a dumpster. "If not, you don't get out of the country. Ministry of Intelligence is going to know very soon the data center is a target. They'll be on you when they find the device."

Zhāng retightened his grip on the rebar as if it were the handle of a sickle. "If MI is onto me, they'll be on you, too."

Blue Tie spun, jerked Zhāng's shoulder, and pinned his neck against a block wall.

Zhāng jabbed the rebar toward the other man's stomach, but something gripped his wrist and wrenched the weapon away. Before he could blink, it was hovering over his own eye.

Blue Tie's lips pressed thin as a knife cut. White breath streamed from his nose. "There is but one way this works, old man...."

Zhāng gasped for air, but managed only a thin wheeze.

Blue Tie weaved from side to side. "And that is, you get into the electrical utility room. Tonight. And fix that damn controller. I don't care what it takes. If it doesn't work, I'll kill you before you have a chance to talk. We're watching. Understand?"

His grasp loosened enough for Zhāng's chest to heave a breath. He spat upon the concrete. "Yes," he panted.

* * * *

"Of course you didn't know about it," Zhāng explained a half hour later to a guard wrapped in a tight black uniform jacket, rubbing gloved hands outside a phone booth–sized shack. Thankfully, it was the short one. Zhāng was always able to make him smile with a joke. But tonight, he could think of none. "We've got it wired to call me if something happens," he added. "One of the power lines went down. Everything's still working fine off the primary. It's just that we're no longer redundant. And with this snowstorm coming tomorrow, we need everything running perfect. Please, I probably messed something up here earlier today. Let me fix it, or it's going to be my ass."

The guard rubbed his hands some more. Was the man looking for a bribe?

"Listen, it's almost midnight. Wouldn't be here unless I had to. I left your fat wife in bed calling for me." With that, the man finally smiled and, shaking his head, opened the gate.

Zhāng stopped the truck next to the data center. A tech in a white lab coat peered from the utility room door as soon as he shut off the engine. *Guard must've made a call.*

"You again?"

Zhāng hung his shoulders in mock disgust. "Yes. Just closed my eyes when the phone rang, telling me the new power feed failed. Thanks for letting me in. Going to be a long night."

The tech turned, skirted a cardboard box of light switches on the floor, then pushed open the data center door and disappeared. Zhāng waited for it to close, then quickly slid another crate in front like last time. Slowly, quietly, he pulled a remnant of metal siding from where it leaned against the wall, setting it gently onto the floor.

*Wait—why am I trying to be so quiet? Wouldn't I normally be making noise? Yeah, I'd be pissed for being dragged out of bed.*

Banging and clanking as he moved the rest of the siding, he still couldn't lose his paranoia. The last piece revealed the control box and conduit that hid the wiring harness to the capacitor banks. He'd eyed the antenna on the walk inside and all looked in order, still tucked neatly in a seam. Maybe that was the problem. Could the siding be interfering with the antenna? Maybe he should hang it elsewhere.

He squinted at the control box. LEDs indicated both power feeds were hot. However, the antenna LED wasn't on. A close inspection revealed it was still plugged into the socket. But when he pushed on the connector, it slipped down, illuminating the LED. Had someone loosened it? He studied the light for a minute; then it switched off. Pushed it down again. The stretch on the antenna had drawn the connector out. He pulled slack in the wire then pushed the connector once more, wrapping it with electrical tape. This time, the LED stayed on.

He walked outside to his truck, placing a rock between the door and jamb to keep it from closing, then called the new number Blue Tie had given him. The ringing was answered with silence. Only a low hum in the background.

"It's fixed," he said. "Antenna came unhooked. Can you connect?" As he said the words, he remembered his pacemaker and laid a hand over it. But such a feeble shield would do no good. He reached inside his pocket for truck keys.

A young female voice spoke, her accent local, close to Beijing. "Still can't see it. Are all LEDs lit?"

"Yes," he said, glancing back at the door, wishing he'd straightened up the mess before he made the call. "You're not going to activate it now, are you?"

"We're not going to activate it at all if you don't fix it."

"I've done everything right! This is your equipment. It's hooked up just like the test. Would the metal siding interfere with the antenna?"

A pause. "No. We're...close. We tested for that eventuality."

"What, then?"

"Hold."

Zhāng pressed the phone to his ear and walked toward the warehouse, then turned back, remembering the phone would lose reception the second he stepped under cover.

A muffled yell came from within the data center. Then another, an answer, in a different tone. After a minute, the voice on the phone returned. "Recheck all your connections. Are all the LEDs lit?"

"Yes! I've checked them. All four are lit. We've got full power on both leads to the device. Continuity and resistance checks all the way through the system. If it's not working, the device is at fault."

A sigh from the earpiece. "You have very little time. Check again."

"The other sites. They go down?" Stupid question. Blue Tie had been so anxious. Of course they'd gone down.

"The controller is not flawed. Get it working, or you don't get out of the country. MI is on the way."

Zhāng hit end, then threw the phone onto the gravel and stomped it under his boot. Damn Americans were just as incompetent as the communists. No matter what, he'd strike a blow, despite their bumbling. Thieving, murderous, socialists weren't going to win this game of Xiangqi.

He ripped open a toolbox drawer from the bed of the truck, grabbed jumper cables, high-voltage insulated gloves, and a small quarter-inch steel plate he sometimes used as a makeshift anvil. He inhaled acidic molten-plastic fumes, spewing from an injection-molding factory's chimney across the parking lot, the stench held low to the ground by frigid night air. He turned and ran toward the warehouse.

The short guard a hundred meters away was talking into the window of a white Toyota pickup. Damn, hadn't he seen a similar vehicle parked across the street from his apartment the last few nights? Must be MI. No getting out now.

Zhāng yanked on the gloves and clamped one end of the jumper cables to the primary power feed, carefully holding the other end in the air. He faced the large cable spool from which the EMP would flash. He slipped safety goggles over his eyes and held the steel plate over his pacemaker. Probably a futile attempt to keep its circuitry alive, but worth a try. The machine only paced out ventricular tachycardia. His heart would still work without it, wouldn't it? Maybe like a truck with flat tires. But he'd had one for almost twenty years, replaced every five.

He jammed the other end of the jumper cables onto the bare end of the wiring harness, bypassing the controller. Sparks flew from the connection, burning his cheek. A droning as from bagpipes filled the room. The EMP would fire when he broke the circuit, pulsing the capacitors. Warm heat from the jumper cables crept through his glove. He jerked them away and a drop of liquid copper hit the floor. The rebar packed into the middle of the spool clanked loudly as the magnetic impulse collapsed through it.

Zhāng's heart stopped for a beat, maybe two, then seemed to strain hard on the next contraction. The loud beeping of an alarm rang from inside the data center. But not even that should be working, if the EMP was potent. He shoved the jumper cables onto the wiring harness again, sparks lighting the air. The room filled with the stink of ozone and burning hair. Molten metal scorched his shirt cuffs above where the gloves stopped.

He smiled—still had power.

He pulled back the jumper cables and another alarm sounded, this one closer. A new babble of voices rose from the direction of the data center. Instructions had said the controller would repeat the sequence a thousand times a second, so he batted the cable's jaw against the wiring harness like a snare drummer on a roll. Sparks showered till the clamps were eaten through. His left arm began to ache. His breath came hard. One of the outside generators started and raced.

After a minute of more smoke and sparks, all alarms fell silent.

The door to the data center slapped against the crate. It grated across the floor as someone leaned a shoulder against it. "What did you do?" a tall tech asked, surgical mask crinkling under a long nose.

"Me? Nothing." He staggered behind the pile of metal siding and pretended to inspect the control box. "Sparks just started flying in here.

Must've been a surge. Look—burned my gloves almost clear through. I'm lucky to be alive."

The room tilted, though he'd stopped drinking a while ago.

The outside door opened and the new, thick-chested guard he'd seen last week pressed in, squatting menacingly, gripping a black pistol.

Zhāng steadied himself against the wall, trying to stay upright. But his fingernails scratched weakly across the metal, and he fell upon concrete.

He lay there, barely conscious. He'd done it! He'd struck a wound with a filthy blade to weep putrid infection for years. The whoring communists would rebuild the data center, but with CIA-compromised components.

The guard knelt next to him, placing the muzzle of his pistol to his forehead, finger probing for his jugular. Now Zhāng couldn't even open his mouth to curse the bastard child. He longed for death, for one last trick, to cheat the government of the satisfaction of inflicting it themselves.

As he descended into darkness, he realized he was already there.

# Chapter 29 – New Wheels

*Songpyong harbor, North Korea*

The steering wheel shimmied under Ko's grip as a tire hit a bump. A light tap on the brakes seemed to correct the vibrations for the moment. *Worn steering knuckles,* the motor pool would say. But he only needed this truck to last through the night. When he released the clutch it grabbed hard, the same way it had yesterday. Wheels spun on ice as they left the parking lot.

Jellyfish rested his weapon in the crook of an elbow, muzzle still pointed toward Ko's chest. Before leaving, the man had pulled a crisp green corporal's uniform from a bag and pulled it over his black rubber suit. His eyes were like crinkled wax paper. Ko's nephew's eyes had looked the same when he'd sniffed too much ice. Ko sensed this commando enjoyed death—or at least inflicting it—like the sergeant of the guard at Hwasong who'd taught Ko so much. How to make it slow, elusive even. To know the exact amount of food a minder should give to keep the end close, but the Netherworld Emissary still hungry.

"The face is the best way to tell," he'd said. "The body will eat itself alive, the brain last of all." He'd pointed at a young boy in a cage, leg splint shattered, tongue protruding halfway from the mouth as if he lacked strength to draw it in. "That pig. See his eyes, how deep? We'll feed him a little today, and keep him alive for a few more." That sergeant's own eyes had been detached, vacant, less alive than even that boy's.

Just like Jellyfish.

*Bang!*

The shot rang from ahead and the truck lurched sideways. Next came a scream, hissing under the hood. The engine continued to run, though it clanked and rattled now, worse than when his father's strapped-together outboard motor had blown a bearing. Ko strained against the slipping wheel and pulled the vehicle straight again. Not daring to brake too fast with a blown steering tire, they coasted to a stop in fifty meters.

He looked over at Jellyfish. The man waved his rifle's muzzle, motioning outside.

Ko tapped lightly the first three notes of "Old Mr. Turtle" once more on the back of the cab. Silence. Then after a few seconds the next three notes returned.

He jumped onto packed ice. The passenger-side front tire was shredded, half the tread lying below the step rails. But what had the scream been? He knelt near the front bumper, ducking his head to look below. He inhaled the sweetness of hot coolant as it dripped from the radiator, melting through ten centimeters of ice to the pavement below.

A jagged square of fur dropped into the new pool. As coolant filled the hole, dim moonlight illuminated it...pink. Ko stood and climbed onto the front bumper. Jellyfish jumped out, pressed his ear, and spoke again as if to no one. Must have a radio, maybe talking to the men in the back, though at first he'd thought the devices in the man's ears were swimming plugs.

The metal hood crashed like a cymbal as he lifted it. He shoved it hard, up till it rested against the windshield. A puff of vapor wafted past his cheek, again carrying the deceitful sweetness of antifreeze. He squinted into the truck's open mouth, shielding his eyes from the headlight glare. They quickly adjusted, and plug wires, rocker covers, and steering gear appeared along with the rest of the machine's vital organs. A half-moon glimmered on the radiator, newly cut aluminum glinting, sliced by the fan blade. He reached in and pulled out a piece of shredded belt, sighed, and jumped down.

Jellyfish stood looking down at the tire, still talking in a tone as if to a lover. What a weak language. He straightened his back. "What'd you find?"

Ko tossed a mangled, furry leg onto the snowbank. "What's left of a cat. Rest of it's on the road behind us. Must've crawled near the engine to stay warm when I was waiting for you. Best I can tell, the tire blew and it shook him loose, into the engine fan. It bent the blades and slashed the radiator."

"You have a spare tire?"

"No. We could take one of the back ones. But the radiator's dead. We'd be lucky to get a half kilometer before it seizes."

\* \* \* \*

The shot had come from the front of the truck, near the cab. Red flicked the safety off his MP5 and knelt on the truck bed, stooping low. He lifted the canvas and saw the truck was sliding sideways, but then straightened. The side-view mirror reflected the driver's face, eyes large with fear, but the man was still alive. So he hadn't been hit.

They coasted to a stop. "Report!"

"Clear," called Lanyard, weapon and head angling out the back to scan one side, then the other, optics over one eye. "No heat."

Dr. Cooley had his weapon slung across his back, checking the girls for bullet holes or fresh blood. Lanyard jumped over him, pulled up the canvas, and cleared the other side.

"Bad tire," Gae transmitted.

"Someone could've shot it out. Let the driver check it."

A forest of tall evergreens with snow-stooped branches stood on either side of a road wide enough for three vehicles to drive. Red listened, ear pressed atop the bed rails, but heard only the crunch of ice beneath the driver's boots. He turned the gain on the enhanced auditory all the way up till it buzzed like an elderly woman's hearing aids in church, but the night was silent. He squeezed out below the tailgate flap, dropping onto an icy crust. Small drops of blood trailed in the snow between the truck's tracks, like the time he'd shot a buck in the rump and Tom had helped track it for six hours. But then the crimson-dotted trail and hoofprints had stopped, as if the animal had just vanished.

The frigid air immediately frosted his nostrils. Gae pointed to a front tire, rubber strip peeling off like a busted tank tread. A bloody cat's leg lay next to the wheel.

"Shit. Can we fix it?"

"No. Cooler beroken. Need new truck."

Red pulled the cover from his watch. Six hours till showtime, a two-hour drive, and they needed at least an hour to get set and in position. That left three hours to secure a new ride. He turned to face the direction of the harbor. A sharp trench cut into the snowpack where the truck had slid sideways back there.

"We're five klicks from the harbor. Maybe seven. There was another truck parked there. Looked to be a troop transport. You and the driver, run back and get it."

Gae turned to the man and spoke in angry tones, or maybe that was just the way Korean sounded. The driver's eyes searched the ground, then pointed a finger to the truck. "He say that same truck at harbor yesterday. No think it work."

"Too bad. We've got no choice."

"He say you kill girls now."

"Tell him that's not part of the deal. We'll keep them breathing—as long as he comes back."

*An ironic twist of fate,* Red thought. Three data centers in China were probably already destroyed, but his portion of the op in North Korea depended upon keeping an adolescent girl and her frail, disfigured aunt alive in zero-degree temps while their brother stole a truck, all because of a bad tire and a stray cat.

He could send Lanyard and Richards, but if they ran into natives they had no language skills and no disguise. The team could hijack another vehicle, but that could end badly if a local got a quick radio call out before they gained control of the situation. Pulling a trigger usually means you've already failed, Jim had taught him. He'd already killed one innocent civilian. Red owed it to the dead man to get the driver and two girls out.

He gripped Gae's shoulder. The man's finger rested on the trigger guard. The safety was off. "We need him back alive. Your life for his. Understand?"

Gae's narrow eyes tightened. He pulled his shoulder free.

The only leverage he had on the guy was that a US Navy submarine was their egress. If Gae killed the driver now, chances of making it through checkpoints were slim. The Det would have to scan the road ahead with the UAV and come up with go-arounds, adding hours to their timeline. Red walked over to the tailgate as the driver and Gae jogged off down the frozen stream of a road, carefully planting their feet inside icy tread tracks, masking their own.

He pointed after them. "Lanyard, dig us a burrow inside the tree line two hundred meters that direction. Richards, go with him. Be our eyes around the curb. I'm taking position a hundred meters ahead. Cooley, get the girls ready to move. Keep 'em warm in Lanyard's dugout." That would be the coziest place for them in such an icy prison. He spat. It hit the ground without a crackle. Based on that, it was around ten degrees below zero.

Red jogged ahead, beyond the truck, also keeping his steps in fresh dual-wheeled tracks. The waffle-patterned tread crunched at each footfall. At a hundred strides, he jumped over the shoulder, landing just beyond a dirty snowplowed bank. One more pace, then he squatted on the lee side of a spruce behind a low drift. This vantage point provided a clear view of the next quarter mile before the road curved away again. He looked back to inspect his trail, satisfied his tracks were relatively inconspicuous. He leaned a shoulder against the tree's trunk. Wind blew stinging ice up his nose. *Too cold to even snow,* he thought, as tree limbs crackled in a breeze of frozen rain. What a hellhole this county was.

* * * *

Pumpkin Beard gripped Jellyfish's elbow, capturing the man's gaze. He spoke in authoritative tones, but Ko could tell Jellyfish resented it. He shook his shoulder free, then came over and snarled, "We need to go back and get the other truck."

"Who? All of us? My sister...she's too weak."

"No. You and I. We're going to run back, stay out of sight, and steal one."

Ko pulled himself up till he could see over the tailgate. The small commando—a doctor, they'd claimed—was kneeling beside Eun Hee and Soo Jin. "It's OK, brother," Soo Jin said. "Go get the other truck. We'll be here when you return."

Jellyfish passed his machine gun to the short one who knelt next to his sister, then held Ko's pistol out to him. He accepted, holstering the weapon.

"You can't go like that," said Ko.

"Like what?"

"Your uniform. It's too new. I saw an old jacket stuffed beneath the driver's seat. Use that."

The man disappeared around the side of the truck, then returned wearing a thin, oil-stained brown cotton coat, buttoned halfway.

"This isn't proper uniform."

"Of course it's not. We're not on parade. This way you won't draw attention."

The commando slipped his own pistol into a pocket and started down the road from which they'd come, quick time. Ko caught up. As they jogged away he heard Pumpkin Beard barking more orders. He turned to look and stumbled on an ice chunk.

"Stay in the tracks!" Jellyfish hissed.

A half kilometer later, Ko's legs began to burn.

* * * *

A vise squeezed Ko's stomach, sharp pain twisted beneath his belly button. He hadn't run so far even at soccer practice. After a half hour he'd stopped to dry heave. Yet Jellyfish was barely breathing. His mouth was closed, but vapor streamed from his nostrils like a Chinese dragon.

The man glanced over one shoulder at the wide road behind them. "Almost there. Quit making so much noise."

"Dying isn't quiet," Ko managed between breaths.

The commando sneered. "Oh. That what you're doing? Sounds more like you're slaughtering a sow."

Ice crackled from somewhere and Ko straightened, head tilted toward the salt marsh, listening. The rising and falling of tides frequently sent sharp echoes across the grasses, but this one had sounded different. They jumped to another track in the road, then over a snowbank and into trees. After a few minutes a green dump truck approached slowly, plow rumbling as it scraped on ice, a plume of twisting snow trailing behind. The wind, having picked up over the last hour, blew the shifted white powder back across the road.

Jellyfish leaned to Ko's ear. "Follow me."

The truck passed. The plume of plowed snow blanketed the pair where they squatted behind the bank. Jellyfish jumped out and ran after the vehicle through a swirling fog of sparkling crystals thrown skyward. Ko scrambled out too, straining to keep up, the knife jabbing his side resurrected as his breath came harder. Every drawl was accompanied by suffocating ice-mist, just like in primary school when the older boys had used to tackle him and rub his face in a drift. He could no longer see the commando, but strained after the truck.

A sudden gust pushed the snow fog away, and he spied the man already clinging to the tailgate. Ko put out one more burst and managed to grab a chain, climbing up a rusty step. He pushed chin to chest and covered his mouth with the coat collar, shielding lungs from breathing the frozen plow mist.

Ten minutes later, they passed the first dark house of Songpyong. The commando shook Ko's arm, then dropped off the back of the truck. Ko followed, staggering and sliding on ice. His lungs no longer hurt, but his hand was frozen, cramped from gripping the chain. The truck clattered on ahead, its white plume now shrinking as the houses blocked and slowed the wind.

Ko pointed down a side road. "I know a shorter way."

After a heavy run they stopped to peer around a tall holly bush. A motor clattered somewhere beyond a thin fog covering the harbor. A gust of wind suggested diesel exhaust. Loud squeals sounded as tire boat fenders rubbed against steel and wood. A sigh of relief. The troop transport was still parked in the harbor lot. "Can you see anything with your scope?"

Jellyfish stepped next to him. "I didn't bring any of that gear."

"Why not?"

"In case we get caught, you idiot."

"Fine." Ko shrugged and walked toward the truck. "I don't see anyone."

One of the rear tires was half-flat, but the others looked OK. The drift piled on the driver's side suggested the vehicle had been there awhile. Ko peered into the back. Empty. The door opened after several yanks, cracking a thin, transparent sheet of ice around its seam. The driver's seat was a wooden crate. A Ural model truck, but an old one.

*There's a reason this thing is still sitting here.* He got in and depressed the clutch, moved the gear lever into neutral, and pressed the start button. A single click came from the engine compartment.

He got out and lifted the heavy hood, propping it up with a driftwood branch he'd grabbed from behind the sea bulkhead. Jellyfish pressed the button several times. More clicks came from the starter. "Could be the battery. But no one would abandon a truck for that. Too easy to get a jump. Probably the starter."

Jellyfish kicked the wheel hub, then marched in a circle, limping. A loud grating came from across the parking lot. The green dump truck had pushed a pile of snow away from the boat ramp and was now backing up.

"Get him to give us a jump, then!" Jellyfish ordered.

Ko hopped down and ran across the lot, waving. The driver tried to roll down his window, but it, too, appeared frozen. At last he cracked the door and peered out. "Huh?"

Ko stared into a deeply furrowed face with gray eyebrows and earflaps pulled down tight. "I need a jump."

"Why you out so late?" The man's eyes drifted to the three gold bands across the point of Ko's collar. The driver only had two. Reserves—or just incompetent, considering his age.

"Ordered to get this truck back to post," Ko said, jerking a thumb casually over one shoulder.

The man lifted his head, gazing across the parking lot. "That piece of crap's been there a week. Just a dead battery, huh?"

"Don't know. But you'll help us find out."

The driver frowned. "It's colder than a witch's tit. Where's your tool truck?"

Ko looked at his boots, thinking. A little truth couldn't hurt. "It broke down."

The man wheezed a laugh. "Motor pool got its hands full, all right. OK. Let's see if she'll crank."

He pulled up beside the troop transport and dropped the plow. The old driver insisted on attaching the battery cables himself, muttering like an old woman. Sparks arced with a loud crack when he clipped one side to the transport's battery. He switched the clamps around, looking not at all embarrassed of his mistake. Jellyfish stood near the plow, just behind the old man.

Ko pressed the starter button, but it still only clicked. He stepped down next to the plow driver. "Maybe we gotta let it charge awhile."

The driver brushed ice crystals from a short, thin mustache. "Nope. She sparked hard when I crossed the cables. Battery's not your problem. See, you need a—"

*Crack!*

The man's eyes rolled up. His body crumpled against Ko.

Behind him stood the commando, holding his pistol outstretched, muzzle pointed at Ko's head, that wax paper gaze as if seeing beyond him. A boat fender squealed loudly, followed by grating of metal.

Ko braced for a second shot, this one for him.

# Chapter 30 – Only If I Have To

The driver slumped into Ko's arms. He stumbled backward at the weight as the man's dirty brown hat fell onto ice. "Why'd you do that? You didn't need to kill him."

Jellyfish Commando's eyes seemed opaque as opals now. "I didn't. He won't be out long. Help me get him into the back of the dump truck." His pistol was still trained at Ko's chin. He decocked the hammer with his thumb, then slipped it back into his pocket. Ko lifted the old man's shoulders and the two hefted him atop a truck bed half-full of sand covered by a black mesh tarp.

"Then, why *didn't* you kill him?"

The commando ripped an earflap from the driver's cap and shoved the makeshift gag into the man's limp mouth. "Why did you? Why didn't you?" he mimicked. "Make up your mind. Kill only if you have to." He knelt on the unconscious man's chest and pressed the pistol against a temple.

The driver moaned, opening an eye, then wriggled his jaw, tongue exploring the inside of his cheeks and the gag.

"Don't move. We won't kill you, unless you make noise."

The prisoner's eyes darted around, full of confusion and fear. He jerked his shoulders, as if trying to sit up but then remembering being told to stay still. Finally, he nodded.

Jellyfish pointed to Ko. "You drive. Do anything foolish, I kill this man then have the others execute your sister and daughter. Understood?"

What had Ko gotten his family into? Only trying to save his sister, and now all their lives were threatened by the men doing it.

He lowered both trucks' hoods and climbed into the cab. The seat was warm against his legs and a heater blew hot from beneath the dash. The driver must've been doing his job a long time to merit working heat.

He gripped one of three small levers mounted near the shifter and pushed. The plow sank into the earth and the truck's front wheels rose from the ice. Ko pulled it out and the plow lifted, dropping the front of the truck back down. But now the blade was so high he couldn't see the road. He fiddled with the control till it held somewhere between, then tested the other levers, angling the device side to side.

Knuckles rapped at the window. It was Jellyfish, leaning down from the bed. Ko lowered the glass. "What?"

"Go! Who cares about the plow?"

"Give them no reason to suspect," Ko said.

The answer seemed to please Jellyfish, who slipped back under the tarp, telling him, "Keep that window cracked." No one would want to stop a simple snowplow. This would be better cover than their previous truck. Ko shifted into first and released the clutch, surprised at how well the tires gripped. Must be the weight of all that sand in the back.

Why hadn't Jellyfish killed the driver? It would've been easier. They still had his sister and daughter to ensure Ko's cooperation. What good would an old man be?

*Only if I have to.*

Had Ko really had to kill his fellow guard at Hwasong? Could he have just knocked him out and tied him up? Eun Hee had screamed when he'd thrust his blade into the young man. Perhaps this commando wasn't as evil as he'd seemed. As dire their situation had become, he'd held a presence of mind, a small respect for life. It was Ko who'd been sloppy.

Back on the main road, he shifted into third and dropped the plow, blowing crystal whiteness atop the already high drifts. The more it looked like he was working, the more convincing the cover.

Passing the marsh for the third time tonight, he caught a whiff of a muddy, fishy stench that blew through the crack of the open window. "It's all kinds of rotting stuff," his father had said. "A marsh is in a constant state of decay. But crabs live on it. Small fish breed there. Life, from death." Then their motor had sputtered and cut off, its gas tank empty. His father had lifted a wet oar and passed it to him with a grin. "We didn't run out of fuel. Got a full tank right here."

Thinking of this now, Ko glanced at the dump truck's gas gauge. *Damn. Probably only ten liters left.*

\* \* \* \*

To keep warm, Red jogged in place behind a dirty snowbank and some sort of pine tree with short needles. Its branches drooped beneath the frozen burden.

He unzipped a pouch of his assault pack and pulled out another protein bar, fingers grazing the black rubber Iridium sat phone. Stretching his neck over the drift, he glanced both directions down the icy road. All quiet, he punched secure, then the Det's speed dial.

"Base Supply."

"Grace, this is Red. Can you—"

She dropped her voice to a hushed whisper. "Red? Why the hell you calling this number? I'll patch you to the fusion cell."

"No, I need you to—"

Her voice quieted even more. "Yes, I will. All hell's broken loose. Mr. Steele's here."

*What?* "Repeat."

"You heard me. Director of National Clandestine Service."

"Why?"

A huff. "How should I know? Well...I couldn't help overhearing he said Javlek's pissed you're on the op."

That was coming. But Red was willing to take the ass chewing. Relieve him of command, for all he cared. He had to protect his family, and the Det. No one else had been moving fast enough. "Grace..."

"OK, OK! Mr. Frank told me something about a leak. Not able to watch from CIA's command center. Red, I think the CIA is completely dark on this op. I swear, I don't think anyone knows about it. Even Steele didn't till a little while ago, after your feet were wet."

"Who else is there?"

"No one. Steele tried to get a few others in, but the first shirt took care of it."

*The first shirt...* Red smiled. The stubby Inuit had a skull thick as a pit bull. He'd reviewed old performance reports his first week in command, and one from the sergeant's prior assignment had said he should be locked in a crate labeled open only in case of war. Well, the man did his job.

"I'm not talking to anyone. I just want an update on Lori." Red leaned back across the snowbank. The frozen highway still lay silent. "Make it fast."

"I called to Hopkins again first thing this morning. Still no luck. A nice fem in patient relations said they had no record of her. Doesn't surprise me—the CIA covering their tracks. They must have discharged her. I tried her cell again, but no answer. That's three days since I've spoken with her."

Red wriggled cold toes in tight boots, staring at a streak of frozen moss on bark. It looked like a tiny green waterfall bursting from the tree. He wasn't concerned that Hopkins had no record of her. But why hadn't she answered her cell? Three days.

Just as he hit end, Gae's voice crackled in the comm. "Eenbound. Dum-p tu-ruck. With plow."

Red closed his eyes and pinched his nose, pondering the sounds coming through the comm. *Speak English, damn it.* What the hell did he just say?

"Maybe like that plow truck that passed a while ago," Richards commed.

*OK, we can work with this.* Not quite an hour delay. Still enough time to get in place, as long as nothing else went wrong. A three-hour reserve, less than optimal for the distance, but doable.

The crunching of tires on ice came faintly from afar. Red leaned over the snow dune to look. One corner of the road glowed with headlights, the opposite direction from which Gae would be driving.

Red punched his comm. "Vehicle coming our way. Half a klick." He glanced back at the blue farm truck, listing on the side with a blown tire. Fifteen minutes earlier an old green Volvo had stopped next to it. A woman in a felted black wool coat like his mother's had rummaged through the empty cab. Stepping down with a half-full plastic bag, she'd slammed the door and driven off.

"Gae, how far you out?"

"Not know. Under sheet. A five minutes?"

Red pulled the locator from his belt and leaned over the black screen, then pushed the brightness up till the four tags of his team were just visible. He cursed silently, remembering Gae wasn't a tag. *What a cluster. Could this have been any more of a thrown-together mess?* "We've got something coming down the road opposite you. Slow down. I want them clear of the area before you get here."

The distant glow turned into the hot eyes of two headlights. The vehicle rolled around a curve, a white box truck streaked dirty charcoal down the side. Blocks of splash-ice in the wheel wells had grown so large they rubbed the rear drive tires, hanging like stalactites from mud flaps. It slowed and stopped beside the broken vehicle, just like the Volvo. A crackle as the icy driver-side glass rolled down. A young voice spoke inside the cab, then a man's head stuck out the window and peered around.

Red crouched lower.

The driver shouted. He seemed to stare at the ground next to the tire, then turned and glanced up the road, almost directly at the spot where

Red had jumped over the plow drift. The window rolled up and tires spun as the truck gained speed.

"Richards. White truck, headed your way. Think he noticed my tracks. You see Gae yet?"

"Affirmative, but over four hundred meters away. Plow's shootin' a rooster tail of snow."

"Cooley, Lanyard, get ready to move the ladies." He flipped down his monocular. "Forward is clear. Once you verify it's Gae, everyone load up. I'll come to you."

* * * *

Lanyard clung to the top edge of the dump bed, holding a black-gloved hand down to Red. The two locked wrists and Lanyard hoisted him up. Red slipped under the tarp and dropped to a mound of sand. A small man with weathered, deeply creased skin sat in the far corner, wrists and ankles tied, shivering, Gae's pistol trained at his belly.

Red tossed Gae his tactical pack. "The plow driver?"

He made a clicking noise with his cheek.

"He'll get in our way."

As soon as the words left Red's mouth, Gae smiled and slipped a serrated blade from its scabbard. Red grabbed his wrist. "That's not what I meant."

The commando wrenched his hand free, but slid his knife back into its sheath.

"Lanyard, cover the old man. Gae, get the driver moving."

Red slipped off his watch cap and ran fingers through tangled curls. *Holy shit. We're supposed to be bringing out two assets, the driver and his sister. Now we've added his daughter* and *an old man. Looking more like a gypsy band than a spec ops team.* Epic fail on his first op command. How were they supposed to eliminate a mole and blow up a semisized printing press while making sure none of the locals ran off? The ladies were leverage against the driver, and vice versa. But now this old man... He had no dog in the fight. He was unexploded ordnance.

Maybe he should let Gae kill him. At least then he could blame the bloodshed on South Korea.

No. One innocent fisherman was already dead, and by the looks of the bloodied trench coat wrapped around the ladies, its prior owner hadn't faired so well, either. The next person to die should be an actual target.

The truck lurched forward. Red peered over the tailgate. The white crystal rooster tail from the plow buried the blue farm truck as they passed.

A hand gripped his shoulder. He jerked his head around and peered into Gae's yellow eyes.

"Driver say no gas."

"How far can we go?"

"Depot close. Say ten minutes."

\* \* \* \*

Ko turned a corner and tall white fuel tanks came into view by starlight a half kilometer ahead, one with what looked like brown molasses trailing down the side. They stood in two rows, like the fuses in the electric box his father had once shown him at the old fish processing plant. They'd hired his dad as a handyman at times, till once he'd accidentally shut down the entire heading and gutting line when swapping out one of the ancient fuses.

The dump truck's gas gauge read below empty now. He braked and the needle rose a mark. Good. Must be just enough fuel remaining in the tank to slosh around and bump the needle up. Not completely dry, but close to it.

He turned toward the depot, bouncing across railroad tracks. Only then did he remember to raise the plow. He gripped the lever, but hesitated, not remembering which way to manipulate it. Making a guess, he punched it forward. The truck pitched to a halt as the plow dug deeper, like setting an anchor in sand.

The rear of the truck still spanned the tracks. He pulled the plow up, but too far. Now he had to stretch his neck to see over it. He shifted into first and released the clutch, bouncing through the slit trench in the snow he'd just created.

Hopefully the depot manager he'd bribed earlier that night was no longer on duty.

He stopped in front of the gate, a white board across the road, but the guard waved him on, moving the barrier without even checking papers. Ko leaned behind the frosted window, obscuring his face. He parked in front of a cluster of pipes and tubes and motors—a gas pump. From the top of each tank a pipe ran down its side like a vine, gathered at points into larger trunks, separating again like strings of a spiderweb tangled in the struggles of a wasp to free itself. Some lines ran close to the railroad, others disappeared underground, and several smaller branches terminated at the green pump.

Ko stepped down from the truck and peered into the attendant's plywood shed. No one.

Across the railroad tracks on the opposite side of the road was Najin Bay, which opened directly to the East Sea. So close he could hear waves lapping onto rocks. His father's small boat could never venture out into the open sea, though Ko had always dreamed of working upon deep water. Maybe these men he carried now would let him do that. But to what country would they take him—America? China? South Korea, maybe?

Satisfied the attendant wasn't around, he pulled the black pump hose and started to fill the truck's tank. A couple of minutes into pumping, a breeze carried the scent of cigarette smoke to him, even over diesel fumes.

*Who the hell would be smoking here?*

The shed's door slammed. He turned off the pump and stepped around the vehicle. Maybe the attendant had just gone off to the bathroom. Better get his forms filled out now, before topping off the tank. His wrinkled brown papers were in one hand and the shack's doorknob the other when he heard something thud to the ground from the dump bed.

* * * *

Red scowled at Gae. They'd just bounced hard over railroad tracks. The driver seemed only to know how to stomp the gas or brake, ignorant of the existence of any transition between the two. He'd been steering like a drunken Sergio Perez, the Mexican Formula 1 driver. The vehicle had wandered all over the road, clearing a wavering path through the snow. Gae pushed up the tarp a crack at the front, just behind the driver's window, and spoke to him.

*Hope he's telling him to slow the hell down.*

Red peered out his corner opposite Gae. Lanyard and Richards covered the rear. Their position was well protected, kneeling behind chest-high steel sides, eighth of an inch thick. They'd be shielded from small-arms fire. Even Sergio would be afforded some limited protection by the plow. He'd raised it high, as if in anticipation of a firefight.

The truck rolled toward a few dozen tanks thrust upward in three rows, like a belt of Striker 40 grenades. All safeties clicked off as they slid to a stop at the entry gate, merely a white-painted board with red stripes spanning the road. A cigarette glowed orange in the guard's mouth as he casually waved them on. After another minute they parked between a sagging plywood shack and what must be a fuel pump. The bottoms of several tanks were stained brown where they'd bled diesel. No containment wall surrounded the tank farm.

Sergio stepped out of the cab and yelled. Gae, still peering beneath the bed's cover, reached behind his back and made an OK sign. "He look por gas officer," he whispered into his comm.

Metal clattered below, almost directly under Red's feet, then the slosh of fluid and whir of a pump starting. Red had shifted to the other knee and was quietly brushing sand from his leg when the driver's emaciated sister moaned. He shot a glance at Cooley, whom he'd tasked to cover the old man. The doctor holstered his weapon and knelt next to her. She opened her eyes and glanced around, as if waking from a bad dream.

Sergio turned off the pump and stepped around the truck out of Red's view. He eyed Gae. "Going to gas officer house," he commed.

His house? Must mean that decrepit shack.

The old man, quick as a bufflehead duck diving beneath the surface after the blast of a shotgun, sprang over the tailgate.

Red dove for him, but missed his boot by inches. Footfalls crunched upon gravel. He rolled and knelt next to Gae, peering through the tarp crack.

The man hopped toward the guard shack like a rabbit chased by hounds. He stopped, apparently seeing Sergio next to the door. He yanked wadding from his mouth and yelled, raising bound arms toward the fuel depot operator who was studying something on a desk.

"Takedown?" from Lanyard.

Red drew a bead on the depot operator, only partially visible now through a small front window, who still seemed oblivious to the old man's commotion. He was about to order takedown when Sergio dropped some papers, stepped toward the old man and gripped his arm, obscuring a safe shot.

Sergio shoved him toward the truck. The old man hollered, but the driver clamped a palm over his mouth and lifted him from the ground, carrying him. If Sergio got him to the tailgate, they could pull him back in, out of the depot operator's sight. The road guard was a couple hundred meters away and out of earshot—this might be recoverable.

Lanyard and Richards reached over the steel side as the driver stomped closer. "Shit," swore Richards.

The scuffle of gravel came from beneath the truck bed, moving toward the cab. "Driver dropped him. They're both under the truck," said Richards, swinging a leg over the bed to jump down.

Gae's weapon rested on the side rail, aimed toward the guard shack. He shifted and the bolt slapped twice. Two hot, spent 9mm brass shells smacked Red's cheek, Gae's silenced shots sounding only a muffled *pop pop.*

"Enough this shit," muttered Gae.

Red pinned him to the steel rail. "I didn't give the order."

"Initiative. I just save your ass. Officer on pone."

Red nodded to Richards. He and Lanyard dropped outside. "Old man's shot, through the skull. Guy in the shack's dead too, one in the chest. Gae's right. Phone's lying on the desk, off the base."

"Put the bodies back here with us. Clean up the shack. Maybe they'll think the operator stepped out for a crap." It might only delay him from being reported missing for a few minutes, but any break would be in their favor. He lifted the tarp a crack. The old man's corpse sprawled in the path, crimson fluid steaming as it melted through snow. "Shovel any bloody crap into the back with us." He pushed Gae toward the tailgate. "Tell the driver to get this damn thing filled and back on the road."

Four minutes later they drove out, past the gate guard who lifted a desultory hand to wave. As large as the dump bed was, it was getting crowded with five of his team, the two girls, and two corpses stacked next to the tailgate. They'd have to bury them under the sand to get them out of the way.

A cough, then a wheeze. A puff of vapor floated next to Richards' thigh. He rolled the old man's limp body aside.

Cooley bent an ear over the depot operator's mouth, fingers probing the skin of his neck. "This one's still alive."

Red knelt next to him. "For how long?"

Cooley rolled the man to his shoulder. "Bullet didn't go all the way through." He unzipped a satchel. "Depending on what's hit, he could live."

Red glanced around the truck bed. His eyes burned hot. They met Gae's gaze. If the mission was going to have a snowball's chance in hell, there couldn't be another loose end. He had to block off the unmarked trail this old man was leading them down. The team needed certainty, and this variable had to be eliminated.

Cooley gripped the guard's shirt to tear it off. Red pushed him aside and plunged his KA-BAR into the guard's throat, eyes still locked with Gae. The South Korean's breath stunk of fish. The guard's chest sank, and a flap of throat skin wheezed next to the blade like a reed whistle.

"What the..." said Cooley.

Red pulled off his watch cap and itched his scalp. "Everyone, back to your post!" He sheathed the blade and took up his position in the corner opposite Gae. The South Korean slipped next to him.

*Great. Last thing I need now is grief from this rampaging psycho.* Red had done what was needed, not what he wanted. *Always double tap, moron.* Or maybe they didn't teach that in the 707th. Why was he constantly having to clean up someone else's crap?

Gae's lips puffed smugly. He whispered, "You do good. You got it here." He patted his own chest, then crawled back to his corner.

Red gritted his teeth. Four dead North Koreans. Two military. Two civilian. Instead of treading lightly, they were wallowing like a tractor bogged down in a potato field, tires spinning, treads throwing muddy chunks, leaving deep trenches.

But they had to keep moving. Momentum, though slight, was the only law on his side. The next person to die—the next one would be a real target.

Clouds had thinned and now a few stars shone dimly. The smooth road ahead was already well plowed down to a hard surface. Good, because Sergio seemed to need all of it, wandering over its entire width. Wind from the sea must have blown the snow off before tires could pack it to ice. Dunes and a narrow slice of marsh separated it from Najin Bay. The scene reminded him of driving the highway south to Kitty Hawk, North Carolina, the summer he'd turned fifteen and met a cute brunette. He hadn't thought of that girl for decades. They'd made out on the beach till her parents came looking. Strange how memories could be buried so deep under sand, drawn out by a similar landscape a world away.

He shook his head, forcing his mind back to destroying a printing press and data center, then getting his team back out to sea. But he struggled to keep it there. Why hadn't Grace been able to get in touch with Lori?

# Chapter 31 – Echoes

Red's ears popped as the dump truck strained up an ice-slick cutback, the way the VW van had done when his older brother drove them into the Poconos for a ski weekend. He peered through a slit between the screen-woven tarp and the truck's bed. Unlike everything else in dim light or the green glow of his monocular, the road was smooth. No potholes or ruts. Houses and apartments, all block or concrete with dark tile roofs, glowed only faint yellow with warmth. Their walls cracked and sagged in modest disrepair.

The truck rounded a curve and the road pitched down. *The approach to Chŏngjin,* he recalled, having memorized the briefing maps during the cramped submarine ride. Anything to keep his mind from the suffocating space he'd been jammed into.

The street was empty this time of night. Or maybe cars were really as scarce here as they'd been briefed. Occasionally the truck passed a figure hunched over handlebars, slowly peddling. Most bikes had a large plastic box, an egg crate, strapped over the rear wheel.

The engine raced, Sergio keeping to low gear on the descent. Rounding another curve, lights glowed dimly in a valley three klicks ahead. Had this been South Korea or China, they would have seen the blaze from a city the size of Chŏngjin ten minutes earlier, even over the trees. But much of North Korea's electric grid dropped off at night. The way downhill followed steep-sided slopes that opened to the city's low plain. A streambed ran along one side, flanked by piled-rock levees. As they continued, the levees turned to concrete walls, though only a thin watercourse stood frozen among their meanderings. The truck crossed over on a riveted steel bridge that could've been yanked from Philadelphia's dead industrial sector.

They turned onto a four-lane road next to which drifted a harbor at least five times the size of Songpyong's. Over a hundred rusty hulks were lashed together near the mouth like a log-jammed river. Opposite the bottleneck in the city square prominently stood twin golden statues of Kim Il Sung and Kim Jong Il. Bouquets of red flowers marched in rows at their feet—platoons passing in review before the dead leaders.

The engine sputtered and backfired as Sergio shifted, passing the spires of Kimchaek Steel Works. A massive rail yard with loaded coal cars stretched before six brown brick chimneys, four small, two large, the landmark signaling they were almost through the city and about to turn north.

Red had moved Gae back into the cab to direct Sergio once they'd cleared the last checkpoint. But Gae kept his comm on all the time, even when yakking with the driver. With the man's poor English, Red had trouble knowing who he was addressing.

"Driver no want go north."

"Deal with it. That's why you're here."

"Prison camp up there. He want talk to sister."

Red yanked one speaker from an ear, followed the wire behind his neck, and pulled out the other. He stretched his jaw and a *pop* sounded in an eardrum. Pulling the trench coat collar down past the sister's hollow cheeks, his gut spasmed at the putrid scent of tooth decay. He held the comm to her. She blinked, as if waking, then mumbled something. Her hand pressed the speaker close, listening. More talk, then after a minute she pushed it away.

Red inspected the gadget and blew it off before he fitted it back in place. The conversation must have gone well, because they turned north. This road paralleled another stream up a slow rise, but it was full of holes. The truck bounced as they ground slowly up the icy path.

"She real punny. Told bu-ro-ter do what say or she cut off balj."

"Balj?" Red glanced at Richards.

He mouthed *balls* and gripped his crotch.

*Must be an older sister.*

After three klicks Red moved to the tailgate with Richards. His knee sank into soft sand where they'd buried the two bodies. At the base of a cutback, the truck slowed.

"Clear," from Gae.

Red peeked out. No vehicles were behind, either. The road was rough and icy, so bikes shouldn't be a problem.

Red swung to the ground. Pain shot through his knee, still sore after a long jump and hard landing on the last op a few weeks ago. The truck crawled forward, wheels spinning as it accelerated. Richards dropped out next.

Red ran toward a steep hill dotted with shrubs like overgrown tumbleweeds with pale, peeling bark. He knelt behind a clump and hinged down his monocular. Nothing warm in either direction, except for the dump truck jostling ahead. He swept the scope up the hill, where all glowed drab green except a spot of yellow behind one of the shrubs. Too obscured by foliage to recognize what species of varmint it might be. He closed his eyes and listened, turning the gain on the enhanced auditory all the way up for a few seconds. Snow crunched beneath his knee as he settled and wind flapped peeling bark. A bell clanged, sounding of a buoy lifted on passing waves, ringing from the city below.

He stood and pointed to Richards, then to the top of the hill. Moving behind more brush, he started the ascent, feet punching through ice-crusted powder to his knees. The hill was steep and at every other step his soles slid a bit, legs trying to cut through snow as a plow furrows earth.

Richards followed, forging his own trail to keep from slipping himself. His buffalo-stanced frame weighed at least thirty pounds more than Red. With the added burden of LEGS strapped to his back, plus fifty rounds of ammo, his legs pumped, knees high to clear the crusted blanket.

"Like elk hunting back home," Richards said. Comms were set at lowest level for now, so no worries anything past fifty feet picked up the chatter. He spoke in a whisper lower than his breathing.

"You do this for fun?" Red had done his share of deer hunting, but didn't possess the call of the chase as much as many of the operators in the Det. He was a predator to be certain. But not the hard-core chase-down-an-elk-and-kill-it-with-a-ballpoint-pen kind like Richards.

"I like trackin' 'em and scoring with a bow. Best way to do it, like the Native Americans. Followed a blood trail fifteen miles once after a bad shot. Six hundred pounds gutted and fully dressed. Buddy with a snowmobile had to pull her out." He stopped for a second and glanced over at him. Plumes of vapor shot from his mouth in rhythm. "Have any idea how long it takes to eat six hundred pounds of meat?"

Red grabbed a branch, pulling himself up. He contemplated moving down the ridge and coming up at a more shallow angle. A faint memory surfaced of his first summer at the Air Force Academy, when he and other doolies had snuck out one night to climb a hill of loose shale and stretch their squadron number with bedsheets across the Flatiron. Each step had given way, as if hiking in skis.

Now, near the crest, his quads were numb. The knee pain had become agonizing. Probably a torn meniscus. Have to get it checked out when he got back.

One last pull on an overhanging bush, then he low-crawled to the base of a sharp Buick-sized rock and peered over. Snow melting from body heat wept into the cuff of his glove, and he shivered. Richards lay down on his belly next to him, panting hard, producing clouds of frozen breath that floated over the rock.

Red pointed at it, then to the powder beneath his head. "Breathe into the snow till you quit wheezing," he whispered. "Cuts down on the vapor."

He lifted his head and flipped down the monocular. The ridge they now lay upon stretched for a half klick, descending gradually until cut off by another iced river. The stream meandered back down the pass toward Chŏngjin. A white-meadowed valley stretched two hundred meters below them. Rangefinder showed a little over two klicks across. A low breeze came from the mountains, pushing down into his face. Cold, but it seemed to have pushed back the fog and moved the sleet out to the ocean. A waning half-moon rose behind him from the sea, providing excellent visibility, but lousy cover.

The compact MSS campus appeared surreal in the middle of the ice-bleached meadow, like a mock-up set on a bare briefing table. Peering through the monocular, he felt he could reach down and grab it, swat the damn thing off the table, and be done. An imposing concrete four-story square office building rose from the middle with a brown steel warehouse, the printing shop, tacked onto the rear. Moonlight glinted in ribbons from the seams of its galvanized roof. The contrast between the two portions of the structure, new against old, displayed more clearly than in the satellite photos the team had studied. Another gold statue, this one two meters high, welcomed all the brainwashed lemmings to the building.

The panorama reminded Red of the time he'd opened Jackson's door to collect him for church and he'd found the child sprawled on the floor in front of an extensive multicolored Lego landscape of buildings. "Bang!" his son had shouted, pointing a blue-and-red tracked machine at what appeared to be an action figure of Luke Skywalker.

"Did you get him?" he'd asked.

"Blew his brains out!" Jackson had crowed.

Lego carnage. Always a great prequel to Sunday mass. Now he couldn't stop his mind from slipping a bit further. Back to the family. And where was Lori? He groped for the sat phone, then decided against it. Had to stay focused. If Grace wasn't able to get ahold of her, neither could he.

And Lori's sister had said the kids could stay as long as needed, so no reason for worry there. Plus, the whole gaggle was being watched by a CIA minder again, too.

Still, he shivered, feeling as if he'd abandoned them, though they were really why he was on top of this frozen ridge, an hour from blowing up the intelligence repository of the world's most unstable nuclear power. But this op could only be a temporary fix. Marksman couldn't have been Mossad's leak. That mole was still out there. Maybe Carter would have a lead when he got back. More loose ends he had to clean up. All that would go on the same to-do list as getting his knee checked out.

Something moved suddenly on the roof of the office building, drawing him back. He zoomed the scope to it. A narrow fall of snow slid from the tiles and buried a bike rack. Two and a half seconds later, a faint *whump* reached his ears.

Red considered the dead fuel depot guard. He had to assume that once the North Koreans discovered the man was missing, a call would go out to the local authorities to be on the watch for a stolen dump truck. Someone could eventually link that to an overdue plow driver. Sure, the theft had only been a few hours ago, but luck was not on their side tonight. They'd kept watch, but no other trucks during the drive had seemed a good target for a quick swap.

Red pointed to a tree an arm's length away. Richards crawled to it on balled fists like the bulldog on old *Tom and Jerry* reruns. The guy did push-ups the same way. He could PT the entire team till they passed out. Sharp, confident, Richards for certain had his zero set on taking over command when Red moved on. But like Jim, Red planned to resist the military's planned obsolescence of personnel. He'd hold on to this command as far as he could aim his rifle. This was the job every kid with a toy assault rifle envisioned as they crawled through backyards with friends in mock battle. Leading a small team of highly skilled professionals in the art of combat. They were doing good. Helping people. And making a difference. Without all the bureaucratic red tape that came with other stations. No, he wouldn't be shoved behind a desk unless his body gave out. However, the weight of this new responsibility was still heavier than he'd expected.

Richards released the straps that held the .50 cal on his back. Low-hanging branches and a thick clump of the tumbleweed shrubs should hide the muzzle flash. LEGS was nothing more than a Barrett XM500 with an electronic black box clipped to the side and laser-guided ammo. It could also be used as a regular sniper rifle.

Richards flipped the bipod down and pointed the weapon toward the parking lot. Red's rangefinder flashed green numbers: distance to the building was just over a thousand meters. A minimum of two hundred were needed for the projectile to stop spinning and stabilize. Then it would seek a target. Red scoped the rest of the campus and did some mental math. At this distance, they could kill anyone from the front gate to the back of the printing shop without having to reposition the weapon.

Richards reached to the small of his back and slipped a twelve-inch round baseplate from a strap. He clipped the stock of the weapon to it, careful to muffle the high-pitched *clink*, cupping gloved hands around it. He swept aside snow from beneath the rifle, digging to bare brown earth, stirring the scent of spruce needles. He eased the plate's teeth into soft dirt below the freeze line.

Beside it he laid five clips of laser-guided ammo. He was to be the weapon's care and feeding, slapping in a new magazine when needed. Then he snapped the electronic module, a black box the size of a mobile phone, to the trigger assembly.

The barrel with the arrow-shaped muzzle break resembled a cobra with spread hood. Its vent pointed back toward Red. His face would be smacked with unspent powder and stinging snow when it fired, so he low-crawled to the far side of the rock as Richards silently edged the bolt forward.

"She's hot," Richards commed.

Red pulled a fat canister the shape of a thermos from his pack and snapped it onto the Picatinny rail of his MP5. A *blazer*, they called it. The twenty-four power scope allowed him to lase a target and see in low light, though that wouldn't be a problem with the clearing sky.

Each team member had one. They would lase a target, push a button, and send a round. The black box imprinted each with the firing laser's frequency, giving the whole team better than sniper-accurate fire, regardless of windage or elevation, all from the same single weapon. Red had never seen it till a couple of weeks ago, the system only being two years old.

The CIA had given assurances their targets always walked from the parking lot, past the gold statue, and into the office building. No way to drive directly up to the structure, except for around back at the printing press warehouse. This gave the team fifteen clear meters to bring down what they suspected would be no more than eight men.

And humint had reported none wore body armor. Important, because LEGS didn't do well against it.

"The ammo can't penetrate," the first shirt had said, spitting Copenhagen juice onto brown grass of the outdoor range floor. His tongue seemed to click with his Inuit accent. "Bullets made of too much electronic crap. But slap someone in the head with an iPod at three thousand feet per second, they'll still come down. They got some geeks working on armor piercing now."

Two faint white dots flared around the ridgeline a klick to the east, close to the river. A couple of seconds later came the sound of crunching ice and a straining engine. They turned toward the MSS valley and disappeared among powder-sugared trees. If all went well, in another minute they would break into the open and motor to the front gate.

He checked his watch and smiled. An hour till showtime. If CIA's communications intercept was correct, the mole would be arriving alongside the MSS deputy director.

Red flipped down his monocular as the truck broke into the clearing. Good. Only one warm body in the cab. No one had commed anything to the contrary, so the team must be suspended beneath the vehicle now. But he could still see a faint yellow heat signature coming from the truck bed where the women were concealed. He'd told Cooley to get them buried under the sand in case a guard looked in the back. His med kit had some tubes they could use to breathe. But it looked like that hadn't happened.

He heaved a sigh as the truck approached the small tile-roofed shed in the middle of the clearing, wire fence stretching from either side of it all the way across the meadow. Red followed the divider to its termination at the base of the ridgeline where he lay. The satellite photos in prebrief had been obscured by shadow there, but the fence just stopped at a boulder. Why would that be? Anyone could climb up and around it in a few seconds.

The dump truck slowed as it approached the glowing white circle cast by the guard shack's floodlight upon snow, a cuttlefish entranced by a siren song. The twin beams cast by the plow were swallowed and lost in the searching brightness. The truck stopped, and a guard shod with what looked to be platform heels stepped to the driver's door.

Red swept back across the parking lot, office building, then the printing warehouse. He scoped the forest edge as well, around the surrounding meadow. Cold. Still. No movement or heat signatures out of place. With everything that had gone wrong over the last day, it was as if he'd feel better noticing something amiss. The team had made it to the valley on time. They weren't in position yet, but close. His worst anxiety was not having anything to occupy worry.

He sensed something big was waiting just beyond sight, outside the cast of light. What was it about this op that didn't lay flat? The printing press, he could care less about. Sure, it was a minor threat to the nation's economy, but currency dilution and exchange rates and all that other crap was for someone else to worry about. It was the data center that had to be destroyed to erase sensitive information leaked regarding the Det, and more importantly, Red and his family. Eliminating that would provide safety.

But it was all too convenient. Two targets, one location, and a mole to boot, all lying in neat order like bait corn in a field for Canada geese. The CIA and Mossad, it had been too tempting for them to refuse. Or were those organizations doing the taunting? And Lori, working CIA fintel, investigating a leak on her own. That couldn't be a coincidence. And no one had heard from her for three days.

The dump truck still sat in bright light next to the guardhouse. Red turned his comm power up and broke radio protocol: "All's clear, but eyes open." A goose blind was hidden in the field somewhere, he could sense it.

# Chapter 32 – In the Valley

Ko rolled the plow truck's window down a crack. Beads of sweat formed on his forehead, despite the heater being off. He glanced into side-view mirrors, peering back along the flanks of the dirty green truck bed. None of the three men tied to its undercarriage were visible. He'd never seen gate guards check under vehicles, unless a high officer was visiting.

But where were they were going? This road was unfamiliar. Chŏngjin prison camp was somewhere in these hills, but Jellyfish had ordered him to turn down a side road.

Half a klick back, they'd pulled off the drive, between a frozen earthen berm and a dilapidated yellow barn. Jellyfish and the small doctor had tried to bury Eun Hee and Soo Jin in case a guard looked into the back of the truck. Soo Jin had helped, digging down with her bare hands, the same way he'd seen prisoners—caught trying to escape—forced to dig their own graves. Eun Hee had refused, eyes wide with fear.

He'd told her, "Do it. Obey the men." What kind of father was he becoming? Even after he'd slapped her cheek and started to dig himself, she'd stood firm. He allowed himself a smile now. She had her mother's strength after all. But with her still lying atop the sand, Jellyfish would have to kill any guard who tried to peek in the back.

He huffed. No guard would bother to do that to a plow truck. Well, maybe near Pyongyang, or an MSS facility. Not out here.

He cranked down the window another turn, his skin starting to itch.

There was the turnoff. On the side away from the river, a road between birch trees, wide and—damn it—already plowed. What excuse could he give the gate guard now? He turned onto it, gravel crunching beneath tires. A single stone skipped ahead and shot off the road, as if trying to flee.

Within fifty meters, the stand of birch gave way to young, thick spruce. In a half klick, those dwindled to open meadow blanketing a narrow valley. The road split the field down the middle, flanked by tall grasses. Directly ahead a single golden statue stood before a tall gray concrete office building. Snow still frosted the roof in spots. A sedan and flatbed truck sat in the parking lot in front of the statue. Light glowed from a couple of windows. *Electricity? Up here, at this hour?* Had to be MSS.

Ko slowed the truck as he approached a brown stone guardhouse. Wire fencing, its zinc coating still shiny in the moonlight, stretched from either side. Nothing as elaborate as in the prison camps, but sparkles of razor wire coiled across the top nonetheless. He'd always guarded fences to keep prisoners in. This one's purpose was to keep others out. He imagined the wire reaching out and coiling around him as he eased the vehicle forward. A floodlight illuminated a small area before the gate. The rest of the valley beyond its cast seemed to disappear as he pulled into its beam.

A female guard in dress greens and a cold-weather cap stepped from an open doorway. Two chevrons on her collar. Frozen breath puffing from full lips. A faint scent of flowery perfume. He felt for the photo of his wife, Un Jong, in his coat pocket, and his fingertips stroked the soft, worn edges. The guard was tall, accentuated by military issue midpumps, with a round nose and fair skin. She'd almost be attractive if it weren't for her unibrowed scowl.

"Haven't seen you before," she grunted, rubbing her hands together to keep them warm, glancing too curiously at the truck bed.

Ko kept silent, his mind racing. The parking lot, a hundred meters ahead, was clear, down to packed gravel. Someone had already plowed it. Maybe she'd still let him in if he kept silent.

"Why you here?"

He pointed ahead. "Plow the lot. Let me get at it."

Her unibrow furrowed once more. Ko had an urge to pinch the short black hairs across the bridge and yank.

"The lot's clear. We don't need you." She pointed behind him. "Main road's still a mess. I have to walk my bike the last mile. Clean that crap up."

Not good. "Sorry. Just following orders. I was told to get my ass out here and—" He squinted toward the office. The rear tires of a few bicycles poked out from a pile of snow fallen from the roof, as if their handlebars were suffocating beneath. Her gaze followed his. "Clear the walks. My guess is, some important people are coming."

Her eyes widened. "They told you who it was?"

"No. Just a guess." He glanced at the guard's belt, her black radio brick clipped clumsily to it. One call from her and his family would never get outside the country's border. He'd be shot, if the state had mercy on him. Soo Jin and Eun Hee would receive the same fate, but only after gang rape in prison camp.

"Oh." Her cheeks drooped. "I was supposed to be off tonight."

"Looks like your bike may be buried. I'll clean that up, too. Get you home a little earlier." He pointed at the lot before him. "This is meaningless. It's always meaningless. There's probably no one coming. You know how they treat us. Always ordering us to do something that never makes sense. Like they just want to keep us busy... I just remembered I lent my shovel. Can I borrow yours?"

Her eyes studied his collar. "*Sangsa*? What'd you do to be plowing snow?"

*Good question. A long story that includes a little high treason. Damn it, just let me through or this guy who smells like rotting fish will spray your brains across the snow and make me pretend to be the gate guard.*

He put on what he hoped to be an inquisitive expression and gave her the only answer he could think of. The same reason his best friend, Gyeong, had been demoted. "Caught messing around with my supervisor's wife."

She pressed fingers to her lips and giggled. Only a second, then the foreboding scowl returned.

"It's complicated. For now, I'm shoveling snow and chipping frozen crap out of latrines and whatever other shitty duty they can assign."

*Twang!* The snap of a metal spring from under the truck bed. She glanced toward it and took a step back. He reached into a pocket for his papers, hoping to distract her. The front one only held the picture. He patted the others, probing down to the seams. Nothing.

She took another cautious step toward the tailgate.

He needed a different diversion. "So, can I borrow your shovel?" he said quickly, maybe with a bit too much force. "I'll get your bike out. Then plow that main road, best I can now that it's pack ice. Say, got some nice whiskey at my house. Not that bootleg stuff. Want me to drive you home after your shift?"

Standing next to the rear tire now, she met his gaze in the broken side-view mirror and glared. Then stormed past the cab into the guardhouse. Was that a scowl or a flirtatious smirk? She returned gripping a shovel at port arms, handle broken halfway. A smile for him as she passed it through the window. "Have fun with yourself."

"Guess that's a no on the drink?"

"Sounds like you could use a night off."

Ko raised two fingers to his temple in a mock salute, revved the engine, and pulled away. He crept forward slowly, now outside the floodlight, till his eyes adjusted and the valley came back into view.

He turned in front of the golden statue of the Great Leader, pointing a finger down toward Chŏngjin. Bitterness filled his belly. It reminded him of the state's failure to provide even basic medicine for his wife and daughter, despite his fifteen years of excellent service in the military. Yet it was as if the hand were pointing to him. *Look, here he is! The traitor.*

A dried brown floral arrangement with bright red bow lay on its side, presumably blown down by a crisp gust. Driving at a crawl, he steered the truck to a corner of the lot near a stand of silver fir. Backing up, he parked just like Jellyfish had told him, with the truck bed nearest the trees.

The door hinges squealed and he jumped down. He marched toward the building's front entry, only a short distance. Glancing back, he thought he caught a shadow of movement slipping into the woods.

The building's gray exterior was well kept, as if it'd been recently washed. The path from it to the statue would be an hour's work, but he'd been told to move back to the truck quickly once he saw other vehicles approaching the gate. Jellyfish had said if he tried to leave, he'd be shot. The commando had also warned, "Some men are going to die. Then the buildings will burn." Somehow, all of this would only take a few minutes. Ko had asked how they were getting away, but Jellyfish had only sneered. *It has to be on a boat,* he thought, if they meant to keep him alive at all.

Anger and fear swelled his gut. These men, they could kill Ko, his daughter and sister, and could still escape. How helpless he was, a sailboat in seas without a rudder. Would he be any better off with these commandos? *No,* he reassured himself. He'd made his decision and would not relent. He couldn't change his mind now even if he wanted. Ever since he left his cold house with Eun Hee in tow, he'd given up choice. He was still a slave, but to a different master.

As he bent his back and tried to force the shovel beneath packed ice, it struck a rock and sparked. The flash recalled a boy with scraps of fabric tied to his feet. Ko had given him an implement with a broken handle just like this one, to clear a path between a sawmill and the debarker. There'd been at least twenty of his classmates there, working with hoes and shovels and hands. But for no reason he knew, the image of this one boy had always remained clear in his mind. *Cleanse your sins through work,* the guards had always told them. But the boy had died from exposure, still a teenager. Even if Ko labored his entire life, it could never wash his sins of torture and treason.

\* \* \* \*

Red's cold, numb calves started to shiver. He planked on his elbows and toes, rocking forward and back to keep warm. The less the contact with frozen earth, the slower heat was drawn from his body. With every sway, he resisted the urge to launch toward the office building, down the ridge, and across the open meadow. The data center needed to be completely destroyed if Lori and the kids would ever enjoy a day without worrying about someone wanting to harm them. He'd tried to work other forms of ingress that would have allowed them to carry enough C4 to take down the entire building and reduce it to a smoldering heap. But at each turn, the team was limited to a small, light unit. Could five men accomplish such a mission? Would sufficient flammable accelerant be stored in the printing warehouse? Taking down buildings was not an easy task, let alone two of them.

On the locator screen, Lanyard's tag had just moved out of the printing warehouse back to a position opposite the parking lot. Red rolled to one elbow and pressed his comm. "Report."

Lanyard's voice was raspy, pausing every few seconds for breath, "Press looks unguarded. I cracked a door. An entire corner is filled with ink barrels."

The CIA said the ink was combustible, like diesel. Counterfeit samples confirmed it. The team had humped in heat charges, just enough boom to diffuse the stuff across the warehouse, and enough heat to ignite it. The result should be a complete meltdown of the structure.

The office building was another story. Solid block. No intel on the inside, so they couldn't say how much would burn. The data center was on the second floor, around the middle. That was what Gae had just checked out.

"Computer room, two guards. No get close. After kill parking lot, we no problem. Puel truck this side."

What the hell? He got the part about the computer room having two guards posted but was still trying to make sense of the rest. Why had he assigned the data center, the most important target, to a psycho South Korean commando? Of course, at the time of mission planning, he had no idea of Gae's impulsiveness. The man's mastery of the language and a stolen uniform was supposed to allow him to get close enough to the data center guards to take them out without a firefight. But other members were ready to move in the event he failed.

Lanyard commed, "Fuel truck looks about a thousand gallons. I tapped on the tank. Sounds half-full. There's a big generator this side, behind the office building. Got a tank next to it as well. We could use the fuel truck to get the office building fired up."

The original plan had been for the team to get two of the fifty-five-gallon drums of ink from the warehouse into the office building, using them as fire accelerant. Gae would place his charges in the floors above the data center, blowing a chimney all the way through to the roof. They'd open lower windows and the entire building would act as huge furnace. The fuel truck would make it faster. Maybe their luck was finally starting to turn.

Headlights appeared around the ridgeline, moving slowly. Another set followed, till three in all ambled along the roadway. Red zoomed in with the blazer, but could only make out what appeared to be a Mercedes sedan, a van, and a jeep-like vehicle. They turned off toward the valley.

"They're here. Four minutes to showtime."

\* \* \* \*

Lights flashed onto the high walls of the office building. Ko straightened and turned toward the guard shack. Several vehicles approached it, one low and dark, the other a high van. Unibrow stepped from her stall.

Ko rubbed his back, trying to look casual, then strode toward the dump truck. His heart, already pounding from chipping ice, throbbed in anticipation of when the shooting might start. He ducked behind the bed and pulled himself over the gate, pushing his head below the tarp.

"You still OK?" he whispered.

He could barely make the seal-shaped form of both women huddled toward the front. "Yes, Father." The coat shook as the pair shivered.

"There's going to be some rifles firing soon. Don't be frightened. Then they'll burn the building, but we're staying here till it's over. I'll be up front, in the cab."

He dropped down and pretended to fiddle with a cracked brake light, sneaking a glance at the visitors. From his angle, three pair of lights shone now. The last one must've been hidden behind the large van earlier. The dark sedan crept forward. He moved around to the plow truck's passenger side, opened the door, and ducked low as he slid across the bench seat. The windows were frosted now, the moonlight glinting off crystals spread upon the glass like poplar leaves pressed in a book. He put two fingers against it near the bottom seal, melting peepholes, then put his face to it.

The vehicles parked one next to each other, like in a practiced parade, directly in front of the Great Leader's outstretched hand. The statue had seemed a distance away when Ko had first arrived, but now he realized he was close enough to recognize the black sedan's three-pointed star. A Mercedes.

Doors opened and one, two...seven men in all stepped from the vehicles. Not good odds for the Americans. And at least two looked to be MSS bodyguards, judging from their size and the intent way they glared around the parking lot. He'd seen their kind before when MSS high officers inspected Hwasong.

*Damn it.* He hadn't considered what would happen if the Americans didn't know what they were doing. *Arrogant whoremongers.* How could five of them, one only a doctor, capture seven MSS, several of them trained bodyguards? MSS knew everything. They might even know the Americans were waiting to ambush them.

A woman stepped from the passenger side of the black sedan. Tall, with long blond hair hanging below a fur cap, just like James Bond's Russian girlfriend in his illegal video of *Dr. No.* A tight, dark skirt stopped above her knees. Long, smooth, flawless calves glowed the milky white of birch bark. No way to dress in this cold. An angular blue shape, the edge of a neck tattoo, rose past her collar. She gripped a briefcase in one hand. No one steadied her elbow as she stepped gingerly onto the icy walk that Ko's shovel hadn't yet reached. One of the men stomped ahead toward the building. Another smiled at the lady and pointed after him. She followed, the whole group picking up speed once they hit the shoveled path.

Where were the Americans? Where was Jellyfish?

The group was almost to the portico when the lead guard's head exploded silently, as if there were a bomb inside it. Remnants sprayed the lady's face and she stopped, watching the body fall before her. Erupting quick as a string of firecrackers, chunks of other heads burst across dirty snow, one sprinkling the golden statue. A small chunk of skull clinked onto the hood of the dump truck. Only after a few bodies dropped did a rapid booming, as if by distant artillery, echo through the valley.

An arm flew off at the shoulder. With his remaining hand, the MSS guard grabbed a pistol from his belt. But that shoulder ruptured crimson as well, though it remained attached. The man dropped to his knees, and his neck spewed open. The body fell facedown into snow.

Ko stared in shock. How had they all been killed so quickly? Where were the Americans? It was as if shots had come from the sky. No rush of men. No hand-to-hand combat.

A blur ran toward the office building. The woman—she hadn't been hit. She disappeared inside and the door closed behind.

Ko glanced toward the distant entry guard shack. The sentinel stood next to the door, apparently still unaware of what was happening. Ko rolled down the window and lifted cupped hands to his mouth like a bullhorn. He drew a deep breath, about to yell a warning, when she fell backward upon the road, followed by a distant *crack*.

They didn't need to kill her. Were they going to shoot everyone? What about Eun Hee and Soo Jin?

A dark figure sprinted past the dump truck. Startled, Ko drew his pistol and aimed it after a man running toward the office building's front door. Peering over the frost line in the windshield, it looked like one of the commandos. Probably Jellyfish.

*No,* he thought. If they were going to kill them, they would have already done it. He glanced at the pistol in his hand and wondered if they could see him holding it. He quickly slid the gun back into its holster and raised his fingers toward his face. They shook, but not from the cold. He reached behind the seat and tapped the first three notes of "Old Mr. Turtle."

The next three notes echoed back.

# Chapter 33 – Mule Neck

Red's jugular thumped against his throat as he lay prone, stretching his neck to eye the approaching vehicles through a blazer. Sergio had hurried back to the dump truck when the three autos arrived. The Mercedes stopped in front of the guard shack and Red zoomed in. Tinted windows obscured everyone except a black-coated driver who lowered a window to pass papers to the guard.

Red flipped down the monocular and zoomed in as far as it could go. Hard to tell, but two blurred forms suggested warm bodies in the rear seat. Only the driver was visible in the van, plus two others in the jeep. "I count six targets. Unknown how many in the van. Lanyard, you've got the driver of the Mercedes. Gae, van. Cooley, jeep. I'll take whoever comes out next. Call the rest in turn as you terminate your target. On my count."

The Mercedes parked directly in front of the gold statue, the others next to it. Red switched his eye back to the blazer. The barrel of his MP5 was propped upon a rock. He'd never shoot his weapon this way, but the crude rest served well enough to steady the high-powered optics. He took a breath and held it, crosshairs oscillating a few inches with each heartbeat. He exhaled slowly and the bead steadied.

A short man with a wide face stepped from the rear of the Mercedes, pulling a blue parka down around his waist. The passenger-side door opened and a woman stepped from the vehicle. Tall, high waisted with long, delicate arms. Definitely not Korean. Had to be the mole. Stupid bitch wore a pencil skirt in the frigid temps. She closed the door, then turned slowly, as if searching the valley perimeter for something. Red zoomed in further. When she turned his direction his breath froze in his throat. *Lori?* It looked just like her, even at such distance.

The bell from the distant buoy clanged faintly.

*What the hell?* The mission was clear. Destroy the press, the data center, and kill everyone present. The CIA had emphasized the requirement to eliminate the mole. But Lori was no more a mole than Marksman. His friend's dying words haunted him: *She's not the enemy.* Maybe the CIA had just mistaken her for the mole. Grace had said not even Mr. Steele had known about the mission till after it'd begun. And Lori's unit...investigations could use bait. A good decoy could look like the real thing.

He stared but she stepped without a limp. She strode quickly, calves flashing too fast to make out any residual bruising. Even with a healthy dose of pain meds it'd be difficult for the wound to not affect her gait...but Lori was tough as nails. Maybe she *was* the mole. Maybe this was why Higher had been so adamant Red not be on this mission.

This all stank like shit. Too much of a coincidence. It had to be her. The Det had been played.

"I've got the girl," said Cooley.

The team was already calling secondary targets. "Negative. I've got the girl," Red commed. That would make her his own primary. But what now? Training and duty necessitated the plan be followed. Execute it. Others already had done the background research. Don't second-guess. But this was his wife!

The group was halfway to the portico. He had to decide quickly.

"Why'd you keep on flying, Grandpa?" a ten-year-old Red had asked the old man one Christmas. He'd been holding the black-and-white picture, yellowed with age, of a tired-eyed younger grandpa in front of a B-17 with his crew, Mae West slung over one shoulder. "The Germans had so many fighters. Why'd you keep going?"

His grandpa had smiled, eyes looking puffy then, too, though not with fatigue. "No choice, son. Duty, I suppose. It's in the training. No matter what it takes, you complete the mission."

Red's finger rested upon the blazer's trigger. *Complete the mission. She's not the enemy.*

*She's my wife, for crying out loud.*

"Sir?" said Richards.

*To hell with it.* "Fire!"

The .50 cal boomed in rapid succession. Lori froze in place when the guard in front of her went down.

*Go, damn it! Run!*

But she just stood there, unlike the night of the hit. Back then, she'd taken off like a dog after a squirrel.

Red pointed the blazer at a column on the portico just ahead of her and bumped the trigger three times. The projectiles struck, chipping deep into concrete. She glanced at the pockmarks, then sprinted into the building.

"Reloading," Richards commed. The bolt slapped shut and the weapon boomed again.

Red jumped to his feet and ran down the ridge toward the office building. "Cooley, get the gate guard. Mole's on foot. I'm pursuing inside. Everything else, go as planned."

The valley floor rose rapidly as Red jumped from rock to rock, snow cushioning landings. What he would do right now for a pair of skis. Reaching out to steady himself, his hand fell upon a palm-sized stone beneath the snow. He scooped it up and slammed it against the casing of the blazer. That should throw off the calibration enough to excuse him missing his primary target.

A few more shots boomed overhead. Cooley taking out the electrical and telephone wires. Lanyard would've already activated the communications suppression system, muffling any radio chatter from the valley. But a facility like this had hard lines below ground. Some communication would get out for certain. They just had to be away from the area before any response team arrived.

He hit the meadow and sprinted across, gulping air in deep draws. The snow in the open was only a few inches deep, so he kept up a full gallop. Rangefinder had said it was a thousand meters to the office. He'd done that distance in three minutes once upon a time. But running down the ridge had slowed him, so Lori would have a good head start. Gae and Lanyard would be detonating charges in ten minutes. How could he find her quickly enough? Throat numbing with cold, he tried to send out a sixth sense, to feel her presence. He'd done it before but now came up empty. No time to concentrate.

One boot sank deep into a hole and he sprawled, hitting the ground in a full belly flop, skidding to a halt. He pushed himself back up and glanced at the locator on his belt. That could find her. Lori had an implant. She was a tag. But his locator was only programmed for the Det, for his team. Previously he'd been given a security key to view CIA tags. He resumed his sprint, straining his mind to remember it. How it looked after he punched the characters in. That was the only way he could pass basic anatomy class back at USAFA, envisioning entire pages from his book.

With two hundred meters to go, Red's knee stabbed pain up the inside of his groin.

"In buil-jing. Go-jing up su-tairs."

So little time. Gae would be setting charges before Red was even through the front door. He pushed harder. His vision started to close in like a tunnel. He ran through the portico, past the concrete column pocked two inches deep where his bullets had struck. All the targets lay fallen to one side of the path, as if directed by a murderous choreographer, snow inked in red splashes.

The heavy wood entry doors had recessed panels. He raised his weapon, lowered a shoulder, and bounded through, into a dark corner hallway. One passage led down the front of the building, the other to the side. A single florescent dimly lit each. Ten meters away one branched off and a pair of black boots stuck out past the corner, as if their owner were lying down in the adjoining corridor, asleep.

Red ducked behind a table with a bouquet of yellow daisies and purple chrysanthemums bound by an orange string in a china vase. He fingered Uniform, Mike, Niner, Foxtrot, Yankee into his locator. The screen flashed and five tags lit the display. He'd remembered it! One tag glowed green, unvalidated. That one had to be Lori. The image was moving now toward the printing warehouse, down the hallway with the boots.

Red raised his weapon and glanced in both directions. No movement. He sprinted toward the boots, stopped short of the corner, held his breath, and listened. Only the tidal pull and shush of blood in his veins. He angled his weapon around the corner. Two spent casings lay on polished concrete across from a fallen guard in green uniform. Red took a step closer, one boot stamping crimson prints onto the flat tan surface. He rolled the body facedown. An elbow bent unnaturally beneath it. The head flopped too lazily. The neck was broken. Maybe Gae had—but no, the Korean wouldn't have come this way.

The guard's holster was empty. If Lori had done this, now she was armed. Wouldn't she know the team was American? Should he contact the Det? Maybe the CIA had a way of communicating with her. But if she *was* the mole, or she knew enough not to trust the CIA...or was it Mossad? Maybe the Israelis fed them dirty intel so the Det would clean up their crap?

He shook his head. *Always trust your team,* Jim had said. And Lori was a part of his, though the struggle to defy orders soured his gut. Was he endangering the rest of his men in an attempt to protect Lori? He held duty to both...but family came first.

He glanced at the locator. She was inside the warehouse now. Gae's elevation looked as if he was on the second floor. Muffled automatic-weapons fire came from somewhere above. Gae was moving in on the data center.

A green blur burst into the hallway ten meters down. Two shots cracked loud in Red's ear. One hit above the trigger guard, wrenching the MP5 from his grip. The side of the weapon blew open as several shells in the magazine exploded. He dove back around the corner for cover, but managed a glance down the corridor. The blur had been two men, green uniforms, sidearms drawn.

His hand stung. Blood oozed through slices in the Cordura glove, though a quick glance revealed all his fingers were still attached.

Footfalls pounded his way. They were rushing him.

Red tore a fire extinguisher from the wall and, backing away, filled the hall with thick, powdery fog. He yanked his sidearm from its holster and jerked his head down, swinging the monocular over an eye. A second later, two fuzzy people-shaped forms glowed warm yellow in the haze. Red fired twice into one, who fell with a heavy thud upon the ground. The other rushed on, shaping into the figure of a man as it closed in. He aimed for the torso and emptied his clip into it. At each shot, the sidearm kicked hard as a .44 Magnum, powered by the Det ammo.

But the man still charged on. He broke through the fog screen at a full sprint. *Damn.* This guard was huge, with a neck thick as a mule's.

North Koreans were supposed to be starving. Where'd they grow this guy?

The guard's legs pumped, quickly closing the gap between them. A fat ballistic vest stretched across his chest and a green helmet snugly crowned an oversize cranium. Mule Neck raised his weapon and Red tucked a shoulder, rolling toward the man, aiming to sweep his legs out from under.

But the guard dove over, then stretched out thick arms and caught himself. He hopped quickly to his feet, firing as Red dove through the nearest door. Brooms and a mop scattered like pick-up sticks as he landed hard.

No time to reload. Red's fingers grasped the handle of his KA-BAR, thankful for the sharp pain in his hand, indicating it still worked. Mule Neck kicked in the door and fired twice, both shots hitting Red squarely below the chest. Since there was no SAPI plate in his own lightweight ballistic vest, the shots needled like fingers digging deep into his sternum. Knowing they hadn't penetrated the Kevlar was no consolation to him or his locked diaphragm. He stepped close and jabbed the knife into Mule Neck's forearm. The guard screamed and dropped the pistol, but still managed to clamp onto Red's good hand and head-butt him away. His helmet smashed the monocular to the floor. The KA-BAR fell, clattering into the hallway, out of reach.

Red rushed him again. Mule Neck lifted him from the ground and pinned him against the doorjamb. He clenched his hairy knuckles in a fist, but

Red jabbed at his Adam's apple. The fist still flew, telegraphed, and Red tilted his neck. Knuckles smashed the wooden molding next to his ear.

He tried a head-butt, and the jagged aluminum mount where his monocular had broken off caught Mule Neck across the nose, crushing it flat. The blow stunned the man for a second, long enough for Red to twist free and grab a broom. He broke the handle over one knee and thrust the splintered end under Mule Neck's groin flap. It sank deep and came out the back of the big man's thigh. He bent, and Red thrust the other half under his chin so hard it drove through his brain and lifted his helmet.

The guard collapsed, broom sticking out his leg.

Red snatched the Korean's sidearm and pointed it toward the open door, holding his breath, listening. The buzz of a florescent light. The rush of fluid through bare pipes in the utility closet, but no footfalls. He was suddenly aware of the intense pain in his hand. He shook it a few times, then held it to the dim light spilling through the doorway. The middle finger canted unnaturally to one side at the knuckle. Maybe broken. He took a chance, pinched the end, and gave it a solid yank. It popped back in place and he flexed, happy all the fingers responded, though the dislocated one still stuck out stiffly from the pistol grip, as if a vulgar gesture to his assailants.

"Fitting," he mumbled.

The extinguisher fog had dissipated to a hazy mist. Thick white dust covered a sprawl of bodies and equipment, like snow over rocks. Red scooped up the smashed monocular, then slipped it into his assault pack. He lifted the locator and brushed off the screen to find it a spiderweb of cracks. Wires stuck out the back. A boot must've nailed it. He cinched the MP5's shoulder strap tight, fastening the ruined weapon across his back. Leave behind as little as possible—standard operating procedure.

He rolled Mule Neck over and retrieved his own sidearm from beneath him. Starting down the hallway, he slipped on extinguisher dust but caught himself with a hand on the wall, leaving behind a red streak upon whitewash.

At the end stood a tan steel entrance. Why didn't Koreans ever put windows in the doors? He pressed through into an identical hall twenty meters long, sprinted its length, and pushed open another, brown rust around sagging hinges. He stepped into darkness.

He reached to flip down the monocular but remembered it wasn't there as his fingers grasped at air. The shuffle of his feet seemed to echo, as if in a larger room. The air stank of sulfured grease and machine oil. A dim light grew in the distance as his eyes adjusted.

Five meters ahead, across yellow lines on a floor, stretched a machine that looked like the guts of a several stainless-steel combines stacked to the ceiling. Threshing drums and sieves and straw walkers, connected by belts and conveyors. Steel ladders formed an exoskeleton, running two stories up to catwalks that stretched the contraption's length.

*Ah, the printing press.*

Dim light shone from the other side. It flashed once upon a near wall. Someone had walked in front of the bulb.

Red pressed his comm and whispered, "Lanyard, report."

"Charges set on the ink barrels. I'm back with Cooley in the tree line. Two minutes, fifteen seconds to go."

So the movement wasn't Lanyard. "Can you delay?"

"Negative. Just timed charges, like the plan."

Red ran to a ladder at the end of the press. Peering around one corner, he discovered an identical printer, forklift parked in the middle of the aisle separating them. The light he'd seen came from a single bulb above a doorway at the far end of the warehouse. Two dozen barrels were stacked on pallets in a corner, fifteen feet high.

He stuck a finger to his ear and turned the gain on his enhanced auditory all the way up. A crackle of static, then faint breathless exhalations. He turned his head, trying to get a fix on the direction, but it seemed to be coming from everywhere.

He glanced at his watch. A minute thirty seconds. No luxury of waiting them out. He cocked his head at the grit of sand under a heel; then he heard a muffled "Shit." A click. One of the barrels seemed to darken. It had been illuminated from beneath. Someone was crouching behind a pallet of rolled paper ten meters away. They'd just closed a phone or some other light source.

"Lori!" he whispered.

Silence.

"It's me. Tony."

An eternity passed. Then, "Tony?"

Her voice was hoarse, maybe from running, or distorted by the enhanced auditory.

"Come on. Let's go."

A sigh. "I'm so glad it's you guys."

She stood and strode toward him. The light behind silhouetted her form, shading her features. Like a phantom emerging from fog. Or Mule Neck from the haze.

He broke the cover of the press and waved a *hurry up.* "Move, damn it. We don't have—"

She raised a pistol and fired four times into his gut. He went over backward, flailing like a drowning man. He reached for the ladder as he fell, but missed. Why'd his wife just shoot him? His team had been sent to kill her. But certainly she'd trust *him*, her husband. She must be so deep in whatever investigation she was a part of, she didn't know who to believe.

She turned and fled toward the door. He tried to yell after her, but his spasming lungs managed only a wheeze. Maybe he'd been hit beneath the vest.

If she got outside... Richards would be covering the area by now. That man would drop her before she got ten meters. Red raised his pistol. Periphery vision was fading from lack of oxygen, his aim as if sighting through a scope. This heaving for air was worse than drowning, as his chest locked tight. He sighted his weapon on her hip, the front blade quivering. A swallow to ease the oxygen craving, then he exhaled what little breath was left in his lungs. The blade steadied and he squeezed the trigger as she passed the roll of paper. He felt no recoil.

Her leg buckled. She fell on her side, but sprang back up and hopped on the other toward the door, reaching for the handle.

A *hiss-pop* from the corner and everything turned salmon pink. *Boom!* A rush of air ripped a seam in the building's siding, spraying the far end of the warehouse in burning, boiling liquid. Splashes landed thick near Red, but he was shielded from a direct blast by the large press. Smoke rose from the top, hissing like a steam locomotive. Across tongues of flame and wavering heat, Lori lay on the concrete, clothing smoking, skin melting. Heat pressed Red's face as he gasped for air that wouldn't come, wouldn't come.... The fire darkened to black.

# Chapter 34 – Heat

Fists pressed into Red's gut, like a medic performing chest compressions on his belly. A cold breeze licked his eyelids, and he cracked them open. Boots flashed before his face, kicking up snow. One arm hung limp, fingers almost touching the heels that whirled below them. Lanyard had him over a shoulder, running. Red lifted his head as a side door of the warehouse slammed closed behind them.

Snow crunched under Lanyard's soles. His breathing was gravelly. A few seconds later came a loud *boom-whoosh*, and the warehouse door flung open. Blue fire billowed from it like a demon threatening to grab Red's wilted arms and drag him down. The concussion blew them forward, and he landed on his back, sliding away on the icy crust of snow.

A shallow breath pierced his diaphragm like a knife. He tried another, body clamoring for air, more air. Short gasps were all he could manage. A blink, and Cooley was kneeling next to him. The doctor unzipped his dry suit and frigid air locked his lungs again.

Icy fingers thrust under his ballistic vest, probing. Finally, Red managed a full inhalation. "Son of a bitch," he moaned.

Cooley yanked his hand out and glanced at Lanyard. "No bullets went through." He gripped the shoulder of Red's vest. "Help me get him to the truck."

They lifted Red to his feet and he started toward the warehouse door in a stagger. Lanyard spun him back around and, with Cooley, propped him between their shoulders, running toward the parking lot. "Don't wanna go back there. Your bell's been rung."

"She's...she's..." Red tried.

"Fried like scrapple." Lanyard laughed. "We toasted that bitch!"

Red turned to look back toward the warehouse. Black smoke billowed from its shattered roof. Charred blackness grew above the doorway. "What?"

"Saw you on my locator. I was almost there when my first charge blew. Lucky you didn't get burned, close as you were."

They thought he'd killed the mole. His legs pumped in air as the team lifted and carried him. At last, they sat him on the gravel lot and he leaned against a truck tire. Each breath still brought sharp pain, though less intense now. But the agony in his mind was still exploding. How could he explain to the kids what had just happened? Three children, no mother, and *he'd* done it. He gripped his calf in both hands and lifted, bending his knees to lever himself upright again.

"Stay put," Cooley snapped. "Let me see that hand."

Red lifted his arm, heavy as a wet log. He didn't give a damn about his hand, or the op, or the Det for that matter.

Cooley pinched his fingers, one by one, running down each, squeezing the bones and joints.

"Lori's dead," Red whispered.

Cooley smirked and tapped one temple. "Not supposed to name the targets. Bad for your head."

"Doc. That was my wife."

Lanyard shot a glance at Cooley. The doctor let go of his hand. "You're in shock. The mole's dead. Your wife's fine. Catch your breath. We need your head here, with us. We're three minutes from exit."

They just didn't understand.

A dark figure sprinted from the office building a hundred meters away, toward a white flatbed with a silver cylindrical tank strapped to it.

Gae's voice crackled in Red's ear. "Thirty seconds till boom."

Half a minute later, a small blast like a couple of grenades cracked from the roof. No smoke. A few seconds after that, another explosion, then a third, both from inside the building. A single window blew outward on the snow. The fuel truck's engine started and Lanyard ran toward the building.

Red still had the team to get out safely. And the Koreans. He owed it to them, too. He pressed his comm. "Richards, report."

"Pair of headlights coming down the main road from the direction of the prison camp. Nothing else in sight."

"How long till they get here?"

"On that crappy road? Five minutes."

Red hopped to his feet. Cooley tried to lean on his shoulder to keep him down, but Red pushed him away. He ran toward the golden statue and, for a second, the sweetness of honeysuckle blew past on a frigid gust. He stopped on the walkway, reached into the black nylon assault pack, and snaked out a black box the size of a cell phone. Then he stepped toward the first target, fingertips numbed by cold. Removing a lens cover, he pressed record and held the device over each target.

The effectiveness of the .50 cal was astoundingly gruesome. There wasn't enough left of most of their faces for the CIA to identify. None were in uniform. Only two had pistols on belt holsters. He stepped over a man whose arm lay three meters away, the other only partially attached. His face was intact, the fatal shot having ripped through his neck. This had been the driver of the jeep—Cooley's target. Red clenched his jaw and glanced toward the plow truck. The man was vindictive. No way could this butchery have been an accident.

He video recorded all six and slipped the device back into his pack. Running toward the plow truck, his stomach churned to vinegar, the only relief being having not recorded Lori's body lying there.

He'd have time to think about that later. Right now, he had to keep flying. Keep pace. Get the team out safe, along with Sergio and his family.

"None of us wanted to be there," his grandfather had said to him, twenty-something years ago. "We all hated it. Each mission, fewer and fewer made it back. But..." He sighed, the exhalation ending in a higher-pitched wheeze. A breath risen on sorrow, it seemed, his heart still off somewhere in 1944. "But your crew's depending on you. And the infantry on the ground, too. Something had to break down the Nazi war machine."

Only now did Red remember what his grandfather had said next, tousling his hair. "Someday, you'll understand, though I pray you never have reason to."

* * * *

Ko hunched below the dashboard, peering through a shrinking slice of defrosted glass above where the heater, now cold, had been running. He tapped on the back of the cab the first three notes and waited. No answer came back. He tapped again, this time so hard his knuckle stung. Still nothing. Jellyfish had just run from the office building and was driving a fuel truck toward it. If something was wrong with his sister, now'd be the time to check. The doctor was speaking with Pumpkin Beard on the other side of the truck, so he lifted the driver-side door handle. His boots landed upon hardpack. He stepped gingerly toward the back. Would his head suddenly explode, too?

He glanced around the tailgate. Flames cast shadows of trees to dance upon the snow and rocks, stretching and flapping, outlined in orange, pale yellow, and blue. He stepped up to the bumper and gripped a chain, the same one around which his fingers had cramped a few hours earlier. He pushed his head beneath the tarp and strained eyes to see in darkness. Shortly, Eun Hee came into focus. Her arms were wrapped around Soo Jin, rocking her.

"She keeps falling asleep, Abeoji. One of the men told me to not let her doze off. But it's been so long. She's cold as ice."

Ko dropped down again and ran to the cab. He shifted the truck into neutral and hit the starter button, cranking the engine to life. They had plenty of gas and didn't need to be quiet any longer. He flipped on the heater.

The passenger door flew open. A pistol gripped in a bloody, sliced glove pointed at his head. Pumpkin Beard brandished the weapon.

Ko's hands rose instinctively. He thumbed toward the bed. "My sister, she's too cold. Not moving."

Pumpkin Beard's eyes narrowed. They were rimmed with pale red and too shiny, as if possessed by an evil spirit.

Hands still raised, Ko slowly lifted the clutch, showing the man he wasn't trying to run away. He started to slide out the door; then a muzzle jabbed his back. He turned his head. The doctor was behind him.

"My sister." He pointed to the bed again. "She's freezing." He wrapped his hands around his shoulders and pretended to shiver. The doctor nodded, but didn't lower the weapon. Did that mean Ko could move now?

*Whatever.* They'd just have to figure it out. Soo Jin needed to get warm or she wouldn't wake up, ever. He lifted his hands again to show he wasn't going to run or fight, then walked to the tailgate. The doctor followed, weapon raised.

When Ko stepped around the back, Pumpkin Beard was already there, pistol again aimed at Ko's head. He pointed to the bed, then mimed a shiver once more. He climbed onto the tailgate and pointed inside. Pumpkin Beard spoke sharply. The doctor holstered his weapon, then scrambled beneath the tarp. He shouted as he shined a flashlight into Soo Jin's eyes, prying apart her eyelids.

Her gaze seemed fixed on the distant sky. But then, suddenly, her mouth curled up when her eyes met Ko's.

Her speech was slow and soft. "I'm OK, brother. It's much warmer, now."

Like hell. It had dropped at least ten degrees with the increase in altitude. A medic had once told Ko you always felt warmer before cold death came.

*David McCaleb*

Each year border guards had to sit through an hour's training on how to recognize the signs.

The doctor lifted and heaved her over the tailgate to Ko. He pressed his cheek against hers, cold as a frozen potato, and ran to the cab. He climbed up and swung her in, then slid next to her.

Her head flopped loosely on her neck. She leaned away, to lie upon the seat. "So...tired. Let me rest."

He gripped an arm and pulled her back up, raising the collar of the stiff woolen trench coat to warm her neck. "Not now, sister." He slapped her cheeks gently. "Stay awake for a little bit. I need you to..." The medic had also said to give the patient something to think about. Some task or job to keep the mind awake. He glanced around the cab. What could it be?

Pumpkin Beard opened the passenger door and slid in. His weapon was still gripped in one bloody hand, but no longer trained at Ko. Eyes were still swollen and red. He carried the scent of burnt wool. Several holes were punched in the chest and belly of his rubber suit. He unsnapped a catch across his stomach and slipped a backpack from his shoulders, letting it thud onto the floor. From a pouch he pulled out what looked like an ammo clip wrapped in brown plastic. When he tore open the covering the air smelled sweet, like dried plums. He held up a tan bar and passed it to Ko, pointing to Soo Jin's mouth.

Ko sniffed the block. Chocolate and something meaty he couldn't place, but the scent reminded him of dinners at his mother's table. His mouth watered. He broke off a piece and held it to her lips.

She turned her head away. "Let me sleep, brother."

Pumpkin Beard slid closer, sandwiching Soo Jin upright between them. He lifted an arm and wrapped it around her shoulder, just as Ko was doing on the other side. His weapon lay on the seat next to him, now. Sweat beaded on his face as the engine warmed and the heater blew hot. He unzipped his rubber suit. Several shiny metal pieces stuck out of a black vest beneath. He pinched one and plucked it out. A bullet. Ko had seen many mushroomed flat like it, digging into a sand berm behind targets at the firing range. Its jagged edges snagged on the vest's fiber. Pumpkin Beard held it up to the dim light spilling through the windshield, then placed it in Soo Jin's palm. As he spoke gently her fingers wrapped tightly around it. A drop of sweat ran down his nose.

The red-bearded man squeezed her tightly, moving his legs closer to hers. It wasn't sexual, Ko knew. He'd seen the hateful pangs of lust in the eyes of guards. This man was just trying to provide the aid of any body heat he had. For a minute, his face even softened. More sweat, or perhaps a tear, ran down his cheek. It was then Ko knew Pumpkin Beard understood the bond of family. A tie that anchors us to our parents, our ancestors, back through the ages, to men and women we never knew, but to whom we were indebted nonetheless. This American spoke a foreign language and grew a beard the strange color of a vegetable. Yet he, too, was tied to his family, and must understand why Ko had betrayed his country. The two of them might not be so very different.

The man smiled, but it vanished as he pressed his ear with his free hand and spoke to someone calling on his miniature radio.

Ko patted his sister's cheeks again. She was starting to shiver. A good sign. "You've got to stay awake and tell us when it's OK to go. When you see all the men run to the back of the truck."

She spoke slowly. Her voice, a whisper. "Yes."

He lifted a piece of the sweet bar to her lips again. "This man says you must eat this." She sighed, then opened her mouth like a child and accepted it. She sucked on the bite for a minute, like a piece of candy, then began to chew.

Windows from the office building shattered as one of the soldiers broke them from the inside. Another stood atop the fuel truck's tank and lifted a hose to a second-story opening. He shouted down to the one at the pump who waved an arm and yelled back. That one fiddled with valves, but he'd forgotten to engage the gear case. Pumpkin Beard frowned and pressed his ear again. He spoke in rapid bursts, looking toward the commotion.

Ko pointed to a lever below their seat. "Got to engage the gear case."

Pumpkin Beard scowled, sliding his hand across the seat and gripping his weapon.

Ko pointed toward the tank truck again, then beneath their own seat, near Soo Jin's ankles. "The gear case. It will not work unless he engages it." If these men couldn't even figure out how to work a fuel truck, how were they going to get his family out of the country?

The man pointed his weapon at Ko, then waved it toward the fuel truck in a *get moving* motion.

Ko cupped Soo Jin's cheeks, turning her face to face him. Her body quivered, but he caught her gaze. "Stay awake. Let me know when we can go, remember?"

He backed out and the door closed with a solid *click*. Vapor rose from the hood of the dump truck. He ran toward the tanker, the incompetent soldier still looking puzzled and twisting valves, glancing back at Ko, as if he'd been anticipating his arrival.

# Chapter 35 – Fatal Fall

Ko stopped near the cab, feet sliding on ice. He pointed to the gear case. "You ready for me to turn it on?"

The man pressed his ear radio and spoke gibberish.

A second later, Jellyfish stuck his head out of a broken window, scowling down. "What now?"

"The gear case isn't engaged. You've got to do that to run the pump. You ready for the fuel to start coming?"

The man actually smiled. "Yeah, dog meat. Screw it up!" He waved the nozzle out the window and ran inside, the squeak of the winding hose reel echoing from otherwise silent darkness.

Ko stepped up into the cab, reached beneath the seat, and pulled on a black knob. It slid out several inches, the last few only after the grind and pop of gears engaging. Immediately from the broken window above came muted singing, but only a line or two. Ko tried to make out the words and caught something about the "East Sea's waters." Heresy! It was South Korea's national anthem.

Jellyfish ran from the door toward the dump truck. "Let's go!"

Everyone sprinted faster than Ko could keep up. This time, when he opened the dump truck's door, Soo Jin's lips were no longer blue.

"They're all back, brother. We can go."

Pumpkin Beard was gone. Jellyfish slipped into the cab in his place. Soo Jin leaned over and puked on his boots. The man didn't seem to notice. The cab smelled of sticky sweetness and stomach acid, like lemon water.

Curling his lip, Jellyfish pushed her away. "Drive! The same way we came."

Ko let out the clutch and pulled his sister close before shifting again. He drove straight for the guard shack, slamming over a parking curb, past six silent bodies sprawled on ice mounds he'd shoveled not long before. The truck passed the golden statue, its hand still outstretched, but the accusing index finger had somehow been broken off.

Yellow light from fire flooded the valley now, illuminating the guard shack, stretching its silhouette across the meadow all the way to the forest toward which he drove. The shadow of the truck cut across the shed as they passed the steps where Unibrow lay facedown, halfway in the road.

Ko squinted into the side-view. Hot blue-and-yellow flame reached like arms from the roof of the office building. The fuel truck ignited and the top of the tank flew skyward, spinning off like the flying saucer in the black-and-white movie his mother had once allowed them to watch as a child. He steered clear of the dead guard, smacking the side mirror on a fence post. Concertina wire sounded a metallic *ching-ching-ching* vibrating from the strike. He pushed the side-view out again, its mirror shattered, but he could still study the dancing flames in the cracked glass, the statue silhouetted black by golden fire.

*You failed, dear leader. Family is stronger than* juche.

Jellyfish wrinkled his nose and edged back in the seat, then cracked the vent near the windshield. "We need to put her in the bed with the others."

Ko shook his head. "No. She's coming out of cold death. It'd kill her."

"Having her in front might get her killed. Us, too. Our lookout says headlights are coming down from the next valley."

White-and-brown birch trunks flashed past the window behind Jellyfish. His eyes no longer seemed the odd texture of crinkled wax paper. They were large and round now, like a drum fish, as if he were scared.

"The doctor put her up here," Ko added firmly.

Approaching headlights blazed around the turnoff onto the main road. Jellyfish pushed Soo Jin down to the floorboard, trying to tuck her beneath the seat. Thin as she was, however, several lengths of chain stored down there made it a tight fit. She grunted in effort.

"Shut up!" Jellyfish hissed.

The lights swerved into the middle of the road, blocking their way. Ko pulled the truck forward till the raised plow shielded his dazzled eyes.

"Don't ram them. Go, see what they want," Jellyfish whispered. "Just get us past. Lookout says others are coming a few minutes behind."

Ko raised an eyebrow. "Can't you just blow up their heads?"

"No. Trees in the way."

"Shoot them?"

"It just takes one call; then they lock down the port."

A figured stepped from a Kozlik jeep. Headlights obscured a clear view. Ko shifted to neutral, set the parking brake, and stepped from the cab. He ambled to the plow and leaned against it, holding a hand up to shield his eyes. "I need to get past. I'm supposed to—"

"Stay where you are!" a voice shouted. Ko could make out the form of a rifle now, slung around his neck, pointed toward him.

He smiled. "I'm not moving. Get your jeep out of the way."

"Walk forward. Arms up!"

Ko scowled. "Why? Who are you?"

The figure marched toward him. Once in front of headlights, Ko saw he was a guard in full winter coat, field belt, and PPS-43 submachine gun held to his hip. Glare shone from polished black boots. Ko straightened and held his arms out, parallel to the ground.

"Get away from the truck."

"Why? What's going on?" Damn it. Other vehicles were only a few minutes away. Was this guy alone? Maybe he could knock him out.

Black Boots swung his weapon to point at the jeep. "Get in the back."

"I'm a *sangsa*. I demand to be allowed to pass."

"I don't care who you are. Get in the back." The guard raised his weapon in front of him.

"OK. No need to be ugly. But I demand to speak with your captain of the guard." Ko stepped slowly toward the jeep.

Passing the vehicle's front tire, he noticed another soldier in the front seat, a radio to his mouth. "We'll hold till you arrive," he was saying.

How could Ko take out two of them? The headlights must be blinding the commandos in the back of the dump bed from shooting. Black Boots, the one prodding his back with the rifle, was following too close. Might be able to wrestle the weapon free, but then the other would—

"*Sangsa*, what's going on?" Jellyfish shouted. He stepped from the cab and walked toward them, hands raised.

"Stay where you are!" the soldier with the radio yelled.

Jellyfish cupped a hand to one ear and leaned forward. "Eh, what's that?"

*The ruse may work,* Ko thought, *since both vehicles' engines are still running.* He glanced at Black Boots, whose attention had been diverted to the new scene.

"Where you taking my *sangsa*?" Jellyfish grumbled. "We supposed to plow this road or—"

"Stay where you are!" the radio guard shouted again, louder.

Still Jellyfish kept the hand to his ear as if he couldn't hear. The soldier put down the mic, chambered a round in an identical PPS-43, and marched toward him. The commando stood still, both arms raised now, hands steady. Radio Guard stopped in front of him and shouted, "I *said*—"

Jellyfish whipped a hand down and across, gripping the weapon. Quick as a trout striking a line, the machine gun was upside down in Jellyfish's hand. He squeezed, and blood sprayed from Radio Guard's back onto the jeep, the muzzle buried deep in the man's belly, muffling the shots. "I heard you the first time," he sneered.

Black Boots' eyes widened. He swung his own weapon toward Jellyfish. Ko slammed the jeep's open door against his side, shoving him against the vehicle, but the man managed to keep his footing. Ko pinned the weapon to the window, clenched his fist, and pounded the man's face, envisioning his punches hard enough to sink deep into his skull, just as his unarmed-combat instructor had once taught. Black Boots slumped onto the road, and Ko heaved a sigh. His side hurt like hell. Maybe he'd pulled a muscle. But then he looked down and noticed the blade in Black Boots' hand, its tip dipped in red.

Ignoring the pain, he snatched up the bloody knife and thrust it into Black Boots' neck. No one was going stop him from getting his girls out. He heaved the dead man and threw him onto the cracked black vinyl of the jeep's rear seat. Pointing to Jellyfish, he said, "Dump yours in the back, too." Ko slid behind the steering wheel. He grabbed the mic, still warm, and pressed the black transmit button: "This truck checks out. Saw other lights coming from the valley. Driving in to investigate." Before whoever was on the other end could respond in protest, he ripped the mic cable from the radio.

Jellyfish leaned over his shoulder. Ko met his gaze. "They'll think we drove toward the office building." He gripped the steering wheel. "I'll take this jeep to the base of the ridge. Tell the last commando to meet us there. I'll hide this jeep, then get back in the plow truck." He gripped Jellyfish's collar. "You watch my sister and daughter." Then he shoved him away, shifted into reverse, backed up slowly, and started onto the main road, turning off headlights. The vehicle bumped onto the icy hardpack, bobbing like his father's boat in soft chop.

The dump truck's lights dimmed as well, its gears crunching with the unsettling sound of a tooth snapping off. Above the valley a low cloud floated eastward, reflecting flashes of gold and yellow against a starry sky. It seemed to follow them. *A good omen,* his mother would have said. But then she had seen good omens in everything. Still, maybe she was sending one to Ko, now.

It seemed an hour passed, though it must've only been ten minutes before they made it over the potholed road to the bend where they'd first dropped off Pumpkin Beard and the last commando. Ko's side ached, right above his belt. He'd pressed one forearm against it but was scared to look down again. Maybe the doctor could stitch it up, though he'd probably do more damage than good on this hellish road. He kept the accelerator pressed, setting a good pace. The passengers in the back of the dump truck had to feel like tossed salad.

Pulling to the road's shoulder, he opened the door and swung his legs out. Standing, lightness whirled about his head. He hadn't eaten for over a day. Maybe he was hurt more badly than he'd thought. His pants felt cold, stuck to his leg. Glancing down, he saw they were halfway soaked in blood. He pressed his side harder with both hands.

The last commando appeared next to him, as if from nowhere.

"Think I need the doctor."

The man said nothing, just got into the jeep's driver's seat.

"Hey! You can't—"

The man held up a hand, put a heavy rock on the accelerator, and jammed the gearshift into first. He turned the wheels toward the edge of the road, stood with one foot outside on ice and popped the clutch with the other. The vehicle lurched forward, spun, and went over the edge, down toward the river. The engine growled like a grinding wheel until it clattered to a halt.

The dump truck stopped and the last commando ran to the tailgate. As Ko opened the passenger door, heat burst from the cab. Soo Jin no longer had her coat wrapped tight. More sweat rolled down Jellyfish's cheeks now.

Ko tried to step up, but his leg wouldn't cooperate. He frowned as his grip on the door handle slipped. He was falling backward, so he sat down with a crunch, then toppled onto hard ice. Soo Jin jumped from the cab. She grabbed her coat and covered his body with it, pinching his cheeks like she used to at the kitchen table. Her mouth moved, shaping words. *I think she's crying,* he marveled. But why?

Jellyfish pushed her away and jerked off the jacket, then ripped open Ko's uniform top.

*Funny,* he thought, *it's warming out here. Maybe I've got cold death.*

He managed to grip the commando's collar. "My girls. Keep them...safe."

Jellyfish nodded, eyes once again the sheen of wax paper, as if killing a hundred would never be enough to warm them.

Ko smiled. *Soo Jin isn't sad,* he thought. *Those are tears of pain. She's just chipped a knuckle beating that mean boy in primary school, the one who always took my rice.* She had sucked on it and a little pink oozed slowly from scraped skin.

And neither that boy, nor his gang, had ever threatened Ko again.

# Chapter 36 – Karen

Red's eyes cracked open. He lay upon a thin, black, rock-hard mattress, still in his boots and Cordura suit. As he tried to sit up, his stomach burned in objection. An antique ship's clock perched on a narrow shelf across the cramped, pale gray room.

*Shit. Stuck in this beast's bowels again. Must've fallen asleep.*

A white blanket covered his legs and torso. Someone had covered him. Where was the rest of his team? He'd accompanied the sister to sick bay, nothing more than a closet even on this nuclear submarine. He recalled lying in a rack across from hers, but that was the last memory.

Retracting a hand to lift the covering and inspect his belly, his arm was clamped in place. Had they strapped him down? Submarines didn't pitch like boats.

A gurney had been pulled next to his bed, abutting it. The pale complexion of the sister contained a deathly green hue. Dead? Horror cinched his chest as he remembered Lori. Had he lost Sergio's sister, too?

An almond eye cracked open. The iris black as onyx. Her cheek twitched and seemed to warm to a more healthy pink. *Thank goodness!* Not a corpse. A sheet cascaded over her frail body like a blanket of hoar frost. Thin black hair stuck out at awkward angles and a white powder like confectioners' sugar topped it. Must be a delousing agent.

He tried to withdraw his hand again, but both eyes shot open. Fingers squeezed his wrist. It was she who held his arm. He smiled, but her eyes remained wide, pleading. Finally, her lips drew back in a grin, revealing three chipped teeth.

With much effort he managed to sit up, knives in his gut. A corpsman in blue pixilated fatigues burst into the compartment. Dark skinned, shaved head. Features similar to Marksman, except for some extra weight around the middle.

He gazed at Red. "Stay down, Major. You've got a cracked rib and multiple deep contusions. I gotta get you wrapped up." One of his cheek nubs was a patch of pink shaped like a clover. He pointed a blue nitrile-gloved finger at the sister. "Think you can get this lady to eat something?"

The skin on the sister's forehead furrowed as she peered suspiciously at the man. Maybe she'd never seen dark skin before. "Eat? That her first priority?" Red asked.

He pulled a Nature Valley protein bar from his pocket and held it to him. From a miniature side table bolted to the wall the corpsman lifted a plastic cup filled with amber liquid. "Just need to get calories in her. Best thing right now. I couldn't find a vein. Too dehydrated. She fights me like a cat. If you can't get something in her, I'm going to sedate her to find an artery. I'd rather not, in her condition. Need to get at least four of these glasses in her."

What about her brother? "Sergio. He OK?" The sister's eyes widened. He knew she couldn't understand English, but his words must have come out frantic.

"Who?"

"The other one. The Korean soldier."

The medic pushed the glass into his hands. "Oh. He should be OK. Just came from him. Lacerated kidney. He's patched up for now. I put a couple quarts of plasma and blood back in him and he was purring like an angry commie. Got him sedated, strapped down, and guarded. Should be stable till we get you guys off-loaded in a few hours."

But Lori... He hunched over till elbows rested upon knees. His eyes burned and the glass shook in his hand, rippling the surface. A single bubble floated atop the fluid, glistening a rainbow's purple like an oily swell, then popped.

Bony fingers wrapped around his hand, steadying the tremor. The sister was sitting up, white powder floating down upon bare shoulders. She took the cup and lifted it to his lips.

\* \* \* \*

Red stepped down from a concrete curb, away from the Det's matching cold exterior. Frigid, humid night air stung his windpipe, though it was a welcome difference from the numbing heat inside the building. The team was there, catching some much-needed sleep prior to debrief, but he had an unpleasant task to complete before he allowed himself rest. The kids would be excited to see him, but there was no way to soften the news he was bringing.

He opened the door to his black Ford Explorer and shut himself in. Closing his eyes, he heaved a sigh. They burned with the lids shut, so he lifted the center console and fumbled through pink hair bows, a *Fireman Small* CD, and DVDs of green elephants playing a piano. Spying the eye drops, he squeezed a few in each one till the salty fluid ran down his chin.

The port at Chŏngjin hadn't been closed, though two MQ-9 Reapers had been prepped with four Hellfires each, circling twenty miles offshore just in case. The exit hadn't necessitated being squeezed into a cuttlefish holding tank, but the cramped Ohio-class submarine had been almost as bad. He didn't care how big the captain thought it was. The ship hadn't spoken to him on the return voyage, so he'd figured he must've dreamt it on the way out. Though as Red placed a hand on its steel bulkhead again, the beast seemed sated with its new cargo.

The sister had screamed hysterically any time Red tried to leave, so he'd slept next to her. She was a reminder he'd been able to help someone, and a short-term excuse to keep from talking with others.

Red replaced the small bottle in the console, dropping it onto a pair of Lori's sunglasses, black with silver along the arms. His questions still had no answers. Had she been the mole? Or had she just been doing her job like she claimed and another division of the CIA had mistaken *her* for the traitor? The organization was so compartmentalized, it was possible one hand didn't know what the other was doing.

A whisper came from the back seat. He turned, but it was empty. The space inside the truck seemed to shrink, to press upon him. He was pulled back to the confined interior of the submarine, as if asleep, and the leviathan was speaking to him again. It drew him into its steely consciousness, water slipping past its smooth, acoustic-tiled hull. Above and around, frigid liquid pressed on his lungs. He couldn't breathe. If he opened a hatch, the reality of Lori's death would come spilling in and drown him.

A horn sounded and Red flinched. He glanced to the road beyond the parking lot and a hand stretched from the window of a white sedan, waving at a passing vehicle. Had he fallen asleep? He checked his watch. If so, it hadn't been for more than a minute.

Maybe Carter would have some answers by now. He considered giving him a call, then decided to wait till after the sun broke the horizon. He pulled out of the parking lot and accelerated toward the interstate.

\* \* \* \*

Past Gloucester on Route 17 a single blue pickup flashed past going the opposite direction. Red watched the vehicle in the rearview until its taillights disappeared around a corner. On either side of the road grew tall pines straight as fence posts. Another mile and the trees gave way to deep green fields, a rolling sea of winter wheat. A breeze stirred it like the marsh grass back near Songpyong harbor. The flowing emerald blanket appeared as vigorous as in spring, but its life was frozen, lying dormant in the hard soil until a warm sky could infuse it with vigor once again.

To the east, a narrow slice of sun pierced the horizon, blazing the underside of high clouds in purple. Early morning rays spilled through the window and warmed his cheek.

He eased off the accelerator and pulled onto a shoulder of dry grass. For a moment, he studied the deep hues. They lightened to pink, then washed to white as the sun continued its course. Sergio's emaciated sister burst to mind, lying atop a crisp-sheeted hospital bed, face now bright and alive. Her adjustment to freedom would take years, even a lifetime, but Red had made a difference in *her* life.

He accelerated onto the road and the tires thumped in rhythm over pavement seams until he reached a sign in brilliant red and yellow, a Spanish flag with *Colina de Arroyo* across the middle. Creek Bluff, the development where Julie, Lori's sister, lived. He drove past an empty gatehouse and after a couple of blocks pulled gently to the shallow curb in front of 6924 Candleflower Lane. The Cape Cod was painted a cheery yellow, not the screaming hue of the Spanish flag, but the subtle shade of a beach bungalow. The grass in the front yard stood as bright as the wheat field, despite both neighbors' lawns lying flat and brown.

As Red stepped from the truck, Nick's blond head bounced behind the front window as he jumped, wide eyes barely above the sill, fingers pointing outside. A second later the boy had opened the front door and all three kids spilled onto the lawn, pajama pants flapping with the flash of legs. Penny pushed her younger brothers aside as she trotted with a limp, her fractured shin still splinted. Her hair was neatly woven in a single braid like a horse's tail, so tight her eyes were pulled back as if in surprise. Just like Lori had used to tie it. She wrapped her arms around his neck and jumped, swinging on it like a maypole, lighting on his back, giggling. Nick and Jackson collided against his legs so hard he nearly stumbled. His throat burned as he considered how, and when, he'd break the news of Lori's death. Better wait.

He eased Penny down and hugged the three of them. Nick's hair smelled of baby shampoo. Jackson patted his beard with sticky citrus fingers. "Julie give you an orange?" The kid consumed at least two every day. "I'll have to teach you how to peel them without making orange juice."

Jackson stuck a finger in his mouth and yanked it out with a *pop*. "Mommy peeled it for me."

Lori had always prepared a bag of the fruit before dropping the kids off for an extended stay. Red stood and grasped his son's hand. He'd pushed this moment out of his thoughts the entire return trip. They'd only been in the submarine six hours, then a C-17 from Yokota Air Base to Langley, nonstop with two aerial refuelings. But now that the moment was here, he still couldn't think of a gentle way to break the news. He'd want to have—

"Thank goodness you're here," Julie called from the front door. Red glanced up, and two women stood on the front porch. Julie *and* Lori. He stared; then the deep bruises in his abdomen where she'd shot him seared in pain. He hunched over, not believing the image. How could it be? Had it not been Lori in the warehouse?

She stepped down low stairs onto plush grass and limped his direction. "Kids, inside!" she called. "Don't want you guys catching cold."

Julie waved toward the door. "Come on. Finish your breakfast." All three children released Red's hands and legs and trotted away.

Lori stepped close. "So glad you're here. Work called and there's some sort of emergency. They're sending a car to pick me up. Julie's about worn out."

Red straightened, but his gut burned all the more. His ears filled with the roaring of a conch shell. He leaned against the hood of the Explorer and studied Lori's face. Same tiny beauty mark below the corner of her mouth. Even so, how?

"You're pale. You not sleep much?" She wrapped her arms around him and drew him into a hug. Her breasts pressed against him. "I don't like an empty bed."

Her hand stroked his thigh.

*It is her.*

"You OK?" she asked. "Not saying much."

His throat burned. The image of a charred corpse covered in liquid fire flashed to mind. The stench of seared hair and flesh filled his nostrils. "I just...I wasn't..."

The cold bit his eyes. They were tearing.

She smiled. "You're sweet. I'm glad to see you, too. But you smell like a sewer. Don't they have showers at the Det?" A white Chevy Suburban slid to a halt behind them. "Gotta go. We'll get caught up later." She pressed her lips against his and slapped his chest directly atop a swollen lump. It burned all the way to his spine. "Tag—you're it. Take care of the kids. I'll be back this afternoon. I want dinner and a clean husband. I'll bring dessert." She squeezed his elbow and stepped toward the vehicle.

"What's going on? Why do you have to leave?" His mind was a muddy sponge. It was all he could think to ask.

Her smile dropped and even the cold nubs of her cheeks washed to pale. She glanced at the vehicle, then bent to his ear. "Stacy called early this morning. Something went wrong. I was supposed to go on a drop two days ago, but with my leg being shot she sent another agent. Karen. Remember her? The one whose ass you grabbed last month at the Christmas party thinking it was me." Lori wiped fingers beneath her eyes. "She's missed the last four check-ins. We're assuming the worst."

# Chapter 37 – Never Forget

The SUV's tires hummed as Red accelerated down the washboard gravel drive toward the stables. Lori sat in the passenger seat and lifted a yellow travel mug with a smiley face to her lips. Steam poured from the vent. Behind her, Penny unfastened her seat belt and stood. She hopped, blond curls bouncing.

Lori turned. "I know you're excited, Penny, but sit back down. Stay buckled till we stop. And don't jump on your hurt leg."

Penny stretched her neck toward the window as she clicked her belt. Early morning rays lit the tops of trees across the field like torches. First light seemed to cast a golden hue on everything.

Red scanned the edges of the field, but all the deer must have sought the shelter of the forest by now. "You sure Penny's up to riding already?"

Lori's calf jittered. Her voice, usually groggy with sleep so early, was crisp and bright. "We're not riding. Not till Penny's out of that boot. We'll just lunge the horse to give her some exercise. Let her know we haven't forgotten her."

She lifted the cup to her lips again and the happy face tipped up. Her own smile returned as she wrapped her hands around the warm mug. It had been three days since his return, but relief still flooded his chest every time he gazed at her. Marksman had been right. She *wasn't* the enemy. Red was home. Lori was alive. And except for an occasional wince and limp, her attitude had proven brighter than ever. Even more, her libido was about to wear him out. Many more nights like the last few and he'd have to get a prescription to keep up.

He'd allowed himself to distrust her earlier, his own wife. No longer. *Doubt is always crouching at your door, waiting to pounce the minute you open it. Trust is a decision. And you always trust your team.*

Red glanced at Lori's jiggling leg. *I'll not forget again.*

"I want ice cream!" shouted Jackson, sitting high in his booster seat. "You promised last time but Penny fell off the horse."

At least kids never forgot a promise. And ice cream was made from milk. And milk went on cereal, which was good for breakfast. So ice cream wasn't far off. "We'll get some while the ladies do their horse duty."

The Explorer slid to a halt next to a maroon four-wheel-drive pickup with wheels the size of a Stryker troop transport. The tires were rimmed in knobby lugs like a balled fist, and damp mud was arced across the side of the vehicle and splashed against a black horse trailer hitched behind it. Lori and Penny hopped out.

Nick pointed toward the pasture. "I wanna feed the horsey again. *Then* ice cream."

Red followed the boys as they trotted toward the fence. The scent of water and manure greeted him. A thin fog hung over the mud and sparse grass of the corral. It glowed like a cloud of gold dust as the rising sun's rays struck it. It'd be burned off in minutes. Two brown horses walked toward them with necks bobbing. One lifted its head and nipped the hindquarters of the other. Red's phone vibrated. He glanced at the screen. Carter was calling. He lifted the device to his ear. Two beeps indicated the connection had been secured. "It's Saturday morning. You always this needy?"

The detective's tone was gravelly. "Where are you?"

Red leaned on a wood railing. The boys yanked grass stalks from a muddy ditch bank. "At the stables. What's going on?"

"You tell Lori yet?"

*Give it a rest.* "No. And I'm not going to. CIA requested the op. It went through proper channels. We got the green light and pulled it off like clockwork. It's a shame Karen was killed, but it's obvious one part of the CIA didn't know what the other was doing. I'm just glad Lori wasn't the one caught in the middle."

"So you still don't trust her?"

*Carter can be such an irritating, cynical prick.* "I trust her. But I'm not ready for the sorry-but-we-killed-your-friend conversation. Let CIA figure things out themselves. It's their own bad news. Let them deliver it. Lori doesn't need to know it was my team. Plus, we don't know the whole story. Maybe Karen was the mole after all." Jackson lifted a handful of grass on a flat palm. A gray horse with brown splotches ambled over and lowered its neck over the fence. Its lips opened and vacuumed up the snack. "I need to go. Why'd you call?"

"Jamison did some more digging on Marksman's laptop. Like we suspected, Mossad was doing their own investigation on an intelligence leak. Looks like it also involved misuse of funds. Lots of inferences their leak is linked to one in the CIA. Pretty high up, all things considered."

"That's not anything new. Lori told us her team was looking into a fintel leak themselves. Probably the same mole."

Carter grunted. "Or, maybe Lori's the leak. She may be off your list of suspects, but not mine."

*How'd I pick this guy as a friend?* "Does it cause physical pain to be as skeptical as you? Remember what Jamison showed us first? That document called Lori the *asset*. She's who Marksman was protecting. If she was leaking info on Mossad, he'd have taken her out instead."

"Which got me thinking. Other than Lori, who else do we know has ties with Mossad?"

Red pushed off the fence post and walked toward the boys. Where was this conversation going? "I'm sure CIA has lots of ties with them."

"But who, in our circle, do we *know*?"

*Slap, slop, slop.* Footfalls sounded inside the pasture, beyond the mist. A dark shadow distilled into a human form emerging from the fog with thick, broad shoulders, helmet, and rifle at port arms. Like Mule Neck driving through the extinguisher's screen. But Red had killed that man.

He slipped his hand beneath his sweater and gripped the Sig hanging in its holster. Two more steps and a horse followed Mule Neck. The forms sharpened to a man in blue jeans and cowboy boots guiding a pony, wearing a riding helmet. No rifle, but in its place a thick lead line stretched straight back to the bridle.

Red breathed a sigh and released his grip on his weapon.

"You still there?" Carter asked.

"Yeah. What was your question again?"

"Other than Lori, who has ties to Mossad?"

The man walked past Red and lifted his chin. "Mornin'," he greeted with a slow Georgian drawl. His thick arms and lumbering gait reminded Red of Lori's father, Senator Moses.

"Moses! He's got those connections."

"Kind of a big coincidence, wouldn't you say, how Lori asks for her dad's help to use his old-boy network with Mossad and the next day she gets shot."

Lori and her father's relationship was strained. But surely the man wouldn't try to kill his own daughter. "It's a possibility. The man's a conceited blowhard. But smart as hell. You've got my permission to look into him, if that's what you're calling for. But watch your step." He stuck a finger into the air, as if Carter could see him. "Lori's off my list. You need to drop her as well."

"I don't make that decision, Red. An investigation goes where the evidence leads. I just follow the trail."

Red pressed end and slipped the phone into his pocket.

Nick held up another handful of grass, giggling as the animal snatched it from him. "His lips are soft," he said, patting a tiny hand against the horse's muzzle.

The screech of rusty bearings echoed as a board-and-batten barn door rolled open. It thudded against its stops. Lori stepped out with Penny behind, leading the black Friesian. Its mane hung down like a shiny cashmere blanket. The animal towered over his daughter, yet followed her as if a child. Stopping the animal next to the fence, Red scratched behind its ears. The creature's shiny black eyes closed.

Penny pulled on the line. "Don't let her go to sleep, Daddy. She's getting fat. We need to make her run it off."

*The daughter of her mother, for certain.*

Jackson trotted toward the Explorer, dropping a clump of green grass blades onto the drive. "Ice cream!"

Lori reached over the fence and grabbed his collar. She drew him into a kiss. Her lips were warm, soft, and tasted of cherry. "Get ready for tonight," she whispered.

The woman was going to kill him. He got more sleep on an op than in his own bed.

She squeezed his arm and followed after Penny. "Enjoy your ice cream breakfast. Kids never forget a promise."

Red grinned as she walked across the pasture, graceful hips swaying. *No,* he thought. *They never forget.* And neither would he.

Don't miss the next exciting Red Ops thriller by David McCaleb

RECON

Coming soon from Lyrical Underground, an imprint of Kensington Publishing Corp.

Turn the page to enjoy a preview excerpt....

# Chapter 1– Betrayal

Frederick Johnson squinted through the scope mounted atop a Remington 783. The crosshairs wavered over his target, a red-bearded man throttling a black Ford Explorer down a country dirt driveway wild as a cat escaping a bath. A quarter mile of lush soybean field stretched between them. A mist hovered a few feet above the leafy green carpet, the fog uncommon in June. The low angle of the early morning sun blazed it in golden brilliance.

He shrugged off a cold shiver that crept up his neck.

The vehicle sped toward the end of the long driveway. "Brake...brake," Frederick whispered as the Explorer jerked to either side of the path, dodging potholes. A dust trail rose behind it and melded with the fog. The way this guy drove, the only chance he'd have of a clear shot would be when Red Man stopped at the end of the drive.

"Five hundred meters," his spotter murmured. "This guy drives like a maniac." Wendy was crouched beside him in the abandoned hunting hide, shrouding her eyes behind rangefinder binoculars. Shiny, jet-black black hair hung in a ponytail. Her bare arms were skinny as hell. Not the anorexic, lingerie-model brand of skinny. More like the steel cable, personal trainer, women-can-do-anything-a-man-can-do-but-better kind. Yet she'd proven to be a quick study. And didn't ask questions. Just watched and learned. "Three hundred fifty," she said.

Frederick kept the crosshairs over Red Man, then reached long fingers and twisted the elevation knob two clicks. The Remington was chambered in .243, a hyperfast, flat-firing round. He'd chosen ammo with heavier 115 grain bullets since the projectile would pass through windshield glass. The weightier shot would decrease deflection.

A wisp of haze, a specter's arm, reached from the foggy floor and floated across the scope's field of view. Red Man twisted the wheel and the vehicle veered almost completely off the drive. Frederick chased him with the X. The Explorer wasn't slowing. "Brake, damn it!" At the end of the drive the SUV slid and accelerated onto the main road with a chirp of rubber. The speeding engine sang over the field and a flock of crows exploded into the air from beneath the fog blanket.

"Shit!" he huffed, raising his head from the rifle as the vehicle raced away. "Why didn't you take the shot?"

He lifted the bolt handle and yanked it back. The ejected round flew toward Wendy's head, and she snatched it from the air like a cobra striking prey. "No clear chance. I'm good, but no sniper. Even the best would have a hard time hitting a moving target like that. Plus, his wife wasn't with him."

She dropped the rangefinder so that it hung from her neck, resting between undersized breasts. "Worth the risk, though."

How much should he tell her? Working in a team, the rule of thumb was disclose as little as possible. And this was only her second job with him. Still, inform her too little and it could bite him in the ass later if she made a stupid move. "Red Man, and even his wife, isn't a target you take a risk on. They've been contracted before. Didn't turn out so well for those guys."

Wendy crossed her arms and shoved the overturned five-gallon bucket she sat on against the plywood wall.

*OK. Should have told her.* He gripped the rifle barrel and lowered the stock to the floor. "Yeah, we're getting a huge payout for this one. But I got no idea from who. Never do. Never want to. But big payout means big risk. Every kill needs to be a sure thing. Double so on this guy. We wound him, and all the sudden we're the ones with a target on our backs. I don't know the whole story, but we ain't the first team that's tried to take him. And we only get paid if both are dead." He pressed the magazine latch and it dropped into his gloved hand. "And watching him these last few days... The bulge under the shoulder of whatever he wears. The way he drives five different routes to work. The way he cuts his eyes. Hell, just the way he carries himself. This guy's a predator. He ain't prey."

Wendy crossed her legs. Her tan calves were knotted rope. "Typical alpha male. I've taken his type before."

"Maybe. But if you want to stay alive, never take potshots."

"What're our options, then?"

Heat radiated from the wall behind her. Six o'clock in the morning and the rising sun was already warming the cramped space. The humid fragrance of decomposing timber filled the hut. They needed to get out of the field before anyone spied them. Deer season was long past, but no one raised an eyebrow at a man with a bolt action in rural Virginia, no matter what time of year it was. Likely just a farmer with a kill permit protecting his crop. And when they'd spy Wendy next to him, all suspicions would vanish. Only a guy teaching his girlfriend how to shoot. That's why he'd chosen her. Couples were invisible.

"We can't get to them at home. Too risky." They'd driven by Red Man's long driveway several times. Vehicle sensors flanked it, which just meant more security up the way. A $250 frequency identifier showed surveillance system emissions from the house at 433MHz all the way up to 5GHz, plus some lower-frequency stuff on military bands. "And we can't get him at work. It's Langley. Plus, he drives as if he knows someone's after him. She's almost as bad."

Wendy squeezed her elbows and rolled her neck. "So? Options?"

He stood and ducked his head to keep from smacking bare pine branches stretched across the close box as a ceiling. His tall frame towering over the tiny woman. He pulled a worn Baltimore Ravens ball cap over thin brown hair. Lifting an olive drab cloth covering a narrow opening, he stepped down atop a wooden ladder rung and stopped. "We wait till he's out of his routine. Away from here."

"How long's that going to take?"

How much to tell her? *Two can keep a secret only if one of them is dead.* Nah. She knew enough at this point. He managed a smile. "I've got a way to speed the process."

\* \* \* \*

"So, you shot your wife?" the therapist asked, as if still confused who had actually been killed.

Tony "Red" Harmon leaned back in a low, hard black vinyl chair. He'd explained it to the woman three times already. It wasn't that difficult to understand. How many degrees did she have? He scratched his tight, curly copper beard. "I didn't shoot my wife. I only thought it was her." Which was the truth. And he'd done it trying to save the woman's life. "So, that's not the problem. Let's get past your maybe-he's-an-ax-murderer theory and get on with the session." There. Easy to understand.

The psychiatrist, Dr. Christian Sato, settled atop a high-backed wooden stool behind a vintage green enameled steel desk. The shrink needed the tall chair just to see over it. Red was short by most men's standards, but this woman of Japanese descent made him feel like a basketball player.

Old government was the motif of her office. Red would go nuts if he had to work at a desk. Tan metal file cabinets covered one wall. The kind that would tear off fingers if slammed in the door, or crush small animals if tipped over. The corners of manila envelopes stuck out from the front of several in an effort to escape. Ancient, nicotine-stained vertical blinds hung in a window like prison bars.

As a military operator assigned to the Det, a fusion cell of three-letter government agencies and the Department of Defense, Red was required to undergo periodic psychological evaluations. The Det was short for Detachment 5, of Joint Special Operations Command. At most of these sessions he handled it a bit like an interrogation. Quick replies, not offering any additional information. But Sato was one of the good shrinks, meaning she never asked how long he wet his bed or whether his mother breast-fed him. He'd been endeared by her sick, sarcastic humor and direct, no-frills approach.

As commander of the Det, he'd requested she limit her inquiries to the task of ensuring his group of professional killers didn't have too many loose screws. A good operator was never entirely sane, and Sato seemed to recognize that. But today's session was on Red's dime and at his request. He'd woken up last week with a distinct understanding that, despite his best efforts, something was broken in his head that he couldn't fix. Sato being the only shrink he knew, he'd made the call.

His wife, Lori, sat up in an identical seat next to him. "It took a while, but we've gotten past that issue. A big mix-up. He thought he'd seen me die, and he'd contributed. But it's behind us. Tony's a good man. A great father."

At least Lori acknowledged he was trying. A half foot taller than Red, she somehow made sitting in a child-sized chair appear natural. She reached behind her head and pulled long, dirty-blond hair to one side. He leaned closer and the scent of Extatic captured his attention. Her eyes were bright but rimmed in pink. Taking time away from work for this session, her office attire was a black skirt that hiked up to midthigh when she sat. She crossed long, slender legs that just last night had been wrapped around him for over an hour. On her calf, a round dot the size of a nickel marked where a 5.7 millimeter bullet from an assassin's P90 had passed through. An awesome wife, mother, and an absolute rock.

She lifted a finger. "But he's never present, mentally. At least not with me. He's great with the kids. I'm jealous of them. Other than sex, there's zero connection anymore. I'm an island."

All truth, though not for lack of effort. He'd date her, take her to dinner, even spend all Saturday with her at antique stores staring at furniture in various states of disrepair. *Yes dear, that chair is a great-looking piece of crap. It's a lot like the ten other pieces of partially dismantled crap we've got in the garage from our last visit. Let's bring this one home so we can shatter its dreams as well.* But those musings were unfair. They'd actually refinished one piece of furniture. He'd taken it completely apart and sanded everything down. She'd stained it and brushed on a polyurethane topcoat.

"It's not the chair," she'd told him. "It's taking something broken and making it better."

Why couldn't he do the same with this problem?

Like the numbness of his thumb past a three-inch scar courtesy of an Ethiopian hunting knife, he no longer sensed a deep connection with her. His closest friends anymore were other operators.

A vacuum hummed outside the office door. Window glass rattled as the janitor smacked the machine against the wall. Sato placed her pen atop the desk and leaned forward on her elbows. "How long have we known each other, Red?"

Maybe he shouldn't have called this woman. This was going nowhere. "About a year, I suppose."

"And in that time, you've progressed from being an operator to commander of your organization."

Red grunted at her labeling the Det an *organization*. A fusion cell was moderately controlled chaos at best, a football field where three-letter offices and the military huddled together and cooperated for each one's gain, sharing intelligence, expertise, and most importantly, assets.

"How many operations have you executed during that time?"

A *whack* from the hallway, followed by tinkling of broken glass. "Fifteen major ones probably. Then there's training."

Sato scribbled something on a yellow-sheeted pad. At a hundred fifty dollars an hour, she probably had to have something to show for it. "And how long does it take," she continued, "from planning to execution to debrief?"

Lori leaned forward. "Two weeks at best. When he's planning an op, I never see the man. Then he's off to a place where the locals are trying to kill him. He comes home and we get the scraps. By then, he's an empty hulk."

Sato waved. "Red needs to answer the questions." Her eyes studied him now. Mascara was caked into her crow's-feet like black veins. She hopped down from the stool and waddled around the edge of the desk. He didn't have to look up to her, even though he was sitting. She stood with her nose almost touching his. Her family must have had a much-smaller concept of personal space. Her voice was grave. Breath of garlic. "You don't need me to diagnose your problem. Don't be an idiot. You thought you witnessed the death of your wife, just to discover it wasn't her. On top of that, you make your living in the profession of arms. You're the walking wounded. All your men sing your praises. But you're not invincible. Your symptoms are classic post-traumatic stress disorder. PTSD."

He leaned away from her breath. "But I don't drink too much."

Sato's cheeks rose and she cackled a laugh. "Not everyone with PTSD is an alcoholic."

*Fine. Whatever.* "So how do I fix it?"

A black cat jumped upon the windowsill outside. The angle of the sun cast its shadow as large as a mountain lion upon the carpet. Sato stepped behind the desk again. She stood on the stool's footrest and leaned onto the desk, arms braced as if doing a push-up. "You're not a machine. There isn't a quick fix. No magic solution. It's different for everyone. But for you the first step is time off. A vacation. And I don't mean Disneyland. You need time to be bored. To watch the sun go down. Time for your head to process what's transpired, instead of being constantly distracted."

Red raised a hand. "Now's not a good time. We've got—"

"For me, either," Lori jumped in. "We've lost ground at work. Maybe in a few months we could do it."

The shadow of the cat's tail swished like a whip crack across Sato's desk; then it leapt from the frame, as if to an adjoining office's balcony. The psych's eyes were slits. "Major, here's the sitrep. You've started to exhibit signs of PTSD. The path to recovery can be long, but if you don't start on it now, it just gets longer. Most operators, unless they take action, are in divorce court in six months. Within a year I have to declare many unfit for duty."

Wow. Maybe he didn't like her direct approach after all.

She flexed a pencil between thumbs. It snapped. "Funny, don't you think, how soldiers can be so dogmatically decisive when bullets are flying, but can't bring themselves to make basic life changes like the one before you now?" She pointed the splintered instrument at him as if it were a pistol. "Get away together. Don't take your work phone. Don't check e-mail. Don't even tell anyone where you're going." She patted her chest. "Doctor's orders."

Just then, rap music blared from Lori's black Coach purse. *Ho ya baby! You drive me crazy!* "What the—" she snapped, then yanked the bag off the floor, pulled out a phone, and lifted it to her ear. She plugged the other with a finger. "We'll be right there. Thank you," she said, then tapped the red button on the screen. Her mouth hung open. "Penny just slapped Jenny at school."

That made no sense. Penny was as gentle and tolerant as a kitten. And Jenny her best friend.

"Teacher said she'd pulled out a chunk of Jenny's hair by the time they were separated."

Sato scribbled a note with the short pencil. "Has Penny done this before?"

Lori frowned, then stood and slung the bag over a shoulder. She grabbed Red's wrist. "Let's go. We'll finish this later."

Sato knelt on her stool, as if trying to appear taller. "You need time off. Both of you. Then we can talk about what's next. Make a decision. *Now.*"

Red stood. Lori stepped past him toward the door, but he pulled her to a halt. "School's out in two weeks."

The edges of her eyes glowed red. "No time right now."

"No shit. Me either. But, if this is step one, let's do it."

Lori gripped the doorknob. Her fingers trembled. "OK. In two weeks, once school is out, we'll get away. Now, come on!"

* * * *

Martina Banderas wheeled a gray plastic trash cart down a narrow hall of Westwood Psychiatry. The carpet had recently been replaced. The Play-Doh scent of vinyl adhesive still hung heavy in the air. She'd vacuumed earlier and the pile still looked new as—*Oh, Saint Zita!* Dark coffee had stained the rug outside an office. She bent and rubbed at the spot with bare fingers. Still moist. Good. She could spray it with cold water and dab the blemish up.

She straightened, then did a double take when she spotted the name etched into the door's glass. DR. CHRISTIAN SATO. A chill shivered her neck, just like the ones she used to get whenever she heard the voice of her manipulative aunt Florencia. Each time the janitor saw Sato's name, she heard it as if spoken in the annoying high-pitched voice of her dead aunt. The doctor spoke praises like honeysuckle to clients but flashed scorn to the help.

A dim light shone from behind the pane. Better knock to let the doctor know Martina needed to run the carpet cleaner. A tirade came any time Sato was working late and Martina made too much noise. She always had to bite her cheek to keep from laughing out loud at the Japanese lady.

She rapped on the glass timidly. No answer. She tried again, this time harder, the pane rattling in the frame. Still nothing. She cracked the door. "Doctor Sato?" The light on the baby-puke-colored metal desk cast a warm glow over a broken pencil and pad of paper.

Her heart quickened. This would mean an extra hundred dollars!

"It's just a way to get a message to a good friend without his wife knowing," Sato had told her three years earlier, blinking both eyes, as if attempting to wink but unsure how it was done.

Martina stalked inside, fearing Sato might actually not yet be gone. Another peek around, then to the desk. On the pad was written a number 3. Nice! Two months had passed since Sato had last requested a delivery, but location number three was Martina's favorite. She was to get a French manicure from the Vietnamese nail place next to Kroger supermarket, then "pay" with only the pink note.

She snatched up the trash can and lifted out a crisply folded colored square and slipped it into her cleaning apron's chest pocket. She stepped over the coffee stain and dumped the rest of the trash into the cart.

Martina had tried to figure out which of the nail stylists Sato was seeing. But all the men there seemed so young.... She'd always been careful not to pry, but—really? That old lady and one of those Asian hunks? Her fingers drummed against the empty can. She reached in her pocket, pulled out the note, and unfolded it.

*Package headed out in two weeks. Pick up. Discard both.*

# About the Author

**David McCaleb** launched his Red Ops thriller series with *Recall*. He was raised on a farm on the Eastern Shore of Virginia. He attended Valley Forge Military College, graduated from the United States Air Force Academy, and served his country as a finance officer. He also founded a bullet manufacturing operation, patented his own invention, and established several businesses. He returned to the Eastern Shore, where he currently resides with his wife and two children. Though he enjoys drawing, painting, and any project involving the work of hands, his chosen tool is the pen.

*Reload* is the second novel in the Red Ops series. Many more are planned. Please visit David McCaleb on Facebook or at www.davidmccaleb.com.

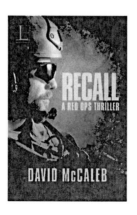